I CAN'T HEAR YOU

*Silence
is the
Loudest
Terror
of All*

VIKKI KESTELL

*Faith-Filled
Fiction*™

www.faith-filledfiction.com | www.vikkikestell.com

I CAN'T HEAR YOU

Silence is the Loudest Terror of All
Vikki Kestell
Also Available in eBook Format

BOOKS BY VIKKI KESTELL

THE TAHOE MYSTERIES
Book 1: *Number 1 with a Bullet*
Book 2: *Be Quick or be Dead*
Book 3: *Death on the Big Blue*, 2026
Murder by Accident, A Miss Finch Prequel

A PRAIRIE HERITAGE
Book 1: *A Rose Blooms Twice*
Book 2: *Wild Heart on the Prairie*
Book 3: Joy on This Mountain
Book 4: *The Captive Within*
Book 5: *Stolen*
Book 6: *Lost Are Found*
Book 7: *All God's Promises*
Book 8: *The Heart of Joy*
Book 9: *Rose of RiverBend*

NANOSTEALTH
Book 1: *Stealthy Steps*
Book 2: *Stealth Power*
Book 3: *Stealth Retribution*
Book 4: *Deep State Stealth*
Book 5: *Stealth Insurgence*
Book 6: *Stealth Triumph*
Book 7: *Stealth Genesis*,
  A Nanostealth Prequel

GIRLS FROM THE MOUNTAIN
Book 1: *Tabitha*
Book 2: *Tory*
Book 3: *Sarah Redeemed*

STAND-ALONE BOOKS
I Can't Hear You
The Christian and the Vampire

LAYNIE PORTLAND
Book 1: *Laynie Portland, Spy Rising*
Book 2: *Laynie Portland, Retired Spy*
Book 3: *Laynie Portland, Renegade Spy*
Book 4: *Laynie Portland, Spy Resurrected*
Book 5: *Vyper, A Laynie Portland Sequel*

I CAN'T HEAR YOU

Silence is the Loudest Terror of All
Vikki Kestell
Also Available in eBook Format

TWO SCENES, TWO WOMEN, two separate deaths, yet neither death suspicious *in and of itself.* What confounds Detective Richard Hawke and his partner Dov Mayer is the blood left at both scenes . . . blood that does not belong to either of the deceased.

The mystery surrounding the two deaths and the inexplicable "blood ritual" found with both bodies grows when Grace Warner, a local physician and psychiatrist specializing in hearing disorders, receives a scrawled note and brings it to the homicide detectives:

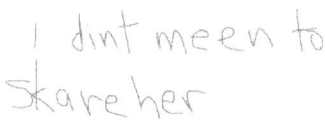

Was the note written by a juvenile or by an adult with a patchy education?

Hawke and Mayer's working theories fall apart when the city experiences a third death, a definite homicide this time, complete with the same strange blood ritual found with the first two bodies. Worse, the grisly murder is followed by another . . . and another and another.

As panic takes hold of the city, pressure on Hawke and Mayer to find the killer and end his killing spree intensifies. At the same time, the commonalities between the first two deaths and the ongoing string of murders cannot be ignored.

Hawke begins to realize that something much deeper is in play, something hidden yet intensely sinister. Can Hawke and Mayer outthink the killer and capture him before they or those close to them become the hunted?

ACKNOWLEDGEMENTS

THANK YOU
to my awesome proofreader,
Cheryl Adkins,
who held her nose and jumped in
to help me remake this awful old story
into a book that glorifies God.

And HUGE THANKS
to my beta readers
for their willingness to help
and their wonderful feedback,
Col. Bill Best (Retired)
Jeanne Huch Diehl
Donna Krecklow
Bryan Varney

SCRIPTURE QUOTATIONS

COVER DESIGN

Vikki Kestell

FOREWORD

A Blast from the Past:
"Dusting Off" an Old Story

My Dear Readers,

A while back I penned a note on Facebook called "Did You Know . . . A Little History Behind my Series, A Prairie Heritage." In the second paragraph of this note, I wrote,

> "Actually, for 25 years *A Rose Blooms Twice* was my only book. Wait, I take that back. Did you know . . . that I also wrote a clean murder mystery right after I finished *Rose*, just to see if this 'writing books' thing was a fluke or not? Someday I should dust that murder mystery off, rewrite it, and publish it. *What do you think?*"

One comment on that paragraph was, "I would definitely read a rewritten murder mystery."

My thought was, *Like I have time for that!*

Then, just before I began my much-anticipated six-month sabbatical in June 2020, guess what was also happening? You got it—the COVID pandemic—the closures and enforced quarantines nixing many of our plans. So, I decided to pull out that old murder mystery and take a look at it.

Let's start with the facts of what I found.

I Can't Hear You was written longhand, then typed on a Commodore 128 computer and saved to a stack of five-and-a-quarter-inch floppy disks. I no longer had those disks (or any means to read them if I did have them), but fortunately, I had a couple of printouts. I asked my daughter-in-love, Brandi, if she'd like to type up the manuscript for me.

And that was the start of quite the drama.

At the time, my son and his family lived across the river from Albuquerque, a distance of about fifteen miles through congested areas that take a good thirty to forty minutes to drive. Mailing it was easier than making the drive—or so I thought—so I sent the only bound copy I had to her.

When the manuscript hadn't arrived after several days, I tracked the package. I found that the post office, in its infinite wisdom, had routed the package from Albuquerque to Denver to be "sorted," then sent it on its way to Rio Rancho.

You know. Just across the river.

Fifteen miles from its starting point.

Go figure!

Finally, the manila envelope I'd mailed the manuscript in—now an *empty* manila envelope—arrived with a note from the post office apologizing for the package's "condition." (What "condition"? You delivered an empty envelope!)

Not to worry. I pulled another copy from my files, and because neither of us now trusted the post office, Brandi came by to fetch it. She typed diligently away—only to discover that the copy was not a complete version.

And I started getting nervous.

I dove again into my files and found to my chagrin that my two remaining copies were mere samples. Finally, after a thorough search, I found that I had *one source* of this book left—a thick, double-spaced, single-sided stack of dot matrix fanfold paper sliding around all these years in the *lid* of an old box inside *another* box.

Whew!

Brandi went to work, finished her typing, handed me a flash drive—no one was trusting the USPS to deliver it at this point—and I began to read a story I had only vague recollections of.

Terrible.

Oh, yeah: It was awful, horrible, no good, *really bad*, and I had to laugh. The writing was wordy, overly dramatic, and rife with error. But it was a halfway decent story, and I could work with that. Too bad it took me *four more years* to actually do the rewrite!

All that aside, may I offer three points to ponder before you dive in?

First, this was not originally a Christian book. It was a "clean," albeit quite bloody murder mystery/psychological thriller. It's now a Christian mystery/suspense/thriller with the blood and gore tamed *but also given purpose*. (You'll find out!)

Second, since the story was written and set in in 1989, I decided to keep it there.

Third, since the original setting for this book was an unidentified city, I also left the location to the reader's imagination.

My dear friends, I hope you enjoy *I Can't Hear You*—and I Can't Wait to Hear How You like it!

Big hugs,

—Vikki Kestell, author of Faith-Filled Fiction™

CHAPTER 1

"SQUAD A! PREPARE to move on my command. Squad B! Hold position. Snipers! Hold position."

"Roger that. Squad A waiting command to move."

"Squad B holding position."

"Snipers holding position."

Barnard, the FBI commander overseeing the impending takedown, whispered to the figure squatting beside him.

"Detective Mayer, you and Detective Hawke are to reposition yourself farther east of here. You will find cover and remain well clear of the action. You are to observe only. You are not to close on the target or engage. Got it?"

"Uh—"

"Tut! Not negotiable and not your call. Observe only. Special Agent in Charge Cuttiford's orders."

"Yes sir."

Mayer glided away; in the pre-dawn shadows he was scarcely a flicker. Moments later, he joined his partner crouched by his departmental vehicle parked far down the dark alley a hundred feet east of the target.

"Barnard says we have to move *farther* east. We are to, and I quote, 'find cover and remain clear of the action.' We are not to close on the target or engage. In other words, he ordered us to sit on our hands."

Hawke sighed. "Tell me, Dov. Did we or did we not break this case?"

"You mean did *you* break this case, Rick? Why, yes you did. Me, on the other hand, your lousy partner, didn't help a whit. And for the record? I didn't say I liked Barnard's orders. I'm just delivering them."

"Fine. Let's move."

Hawke and Mayer backed away from Hawke's ride and retreated south down the alley until they reached the intersection behind the op's designated perimeter. They jogged to the next alley east of the target, moved up to its mouth, and took cover behind the rusted hulk of a late model Chevy out on the street.

The Chevy wasn't the only stripped and burned derelict vehicle on the street, which in the moment, tugged Hawke's interest. His curiosity petered out, however, as they settled behind the rusted car and scoped out the scene from their new perspective.

The target was now half a block distant, up the street and on their right. The command post was directly ahead on the left but a safe distance beyond the target. Hawke's car was tucked, unseen, down the alley closest to the command post.

Dov lifted his two-way. "Hawke and Mayer repositioned as ordered." Two clicks acknowledged his update.

HAWKE TURNED INWARD. He had expended four months of brutal legwork to arrive at this moment, yet here he sat, spending his Sunday morning sidelined. Cut out of the action.

"Coulda been getting up slow and easy today. Off to church midmorning, lunch with the guys, and football in the afternoon, but nooo. Gotta be up at the crack of dawn to watch the feds steal *my case*."

Not that he'd been in any way convinced of the outcome when he'd begun his investigation. He'd followed his gut regardless—"gut" being the place deep inside where instinct—or the Holy Spirit—sometimes prompted and other times warned him.

Today's op owed a debt to a confidential informant's whispered warning in late May, a tip so certain and intense that it had lodged in Hawke's heart like a hammered spike.

Is that you, Lord? he'd wondered. *And if you're speaking to me, what do you want me to do with this intel?*

Unable to scratch the itch triggered by his CI's intelligence, Hawke had spent an evening at the city's main library searching newspaper and news outlet accounts on microfiche. A week of similar diligence left him sleep deprived with dreadful possibilities running through his head. It also left him alone in his disquiet.

When he'd attempted to outline his concerns to his colleagues, they listened, laughed, cited their own pressing caseloads, and tuned him out. Before that, when he shared his findings with his partner, his response had been more emphatic.

"Rick, do you have any idea what people would say if I, a Jew—although a nonobservant one—brought up the possibility of Islamic terrorism on American soil? I'd be labeled a racist. Why, even the Anti-Defamation League, in their quest for 'tolerance,' would sooner mount my head on a wall than be associated with such an 'intolerant' accusation. No thanks. I have enough bias to navigate without adding 'Muslim hater' to my rep."

A bit desperate, Hawke had approached his boss, Chief McCormick. His pithy retort was, "If I catch you spending department time or resources chasing conspiracy theories, I'll have your badge, Hawke—and I don't care how many commendations you've earned."

Not one individual in Homicide Division placed any credence in his CI's intel or Hawke's follow-up research. They poo-pooed his worry, smug in their certainty that Islamic radicals posed no threat. Nope. Not here. Not in the US.

The responses of his boss and coworkers hadn't entirely deterred Hawke. He was on friendly terms with a pair of local FBI agents, so he took his concerns to their field office and briefed them and Cuttiford, the city's FBI Special Agent in Charge.

Cuttiford's response had been, "This is America, Detective Hawke. They wouldn't dare."

Hawke had walked away, tight-lipped and fuming, convinced the fed's premier law enforcement agency was fooling itself and, in turn, fooling the American people. In Hawke's estimation, it was not *if* an attack would occur, but rather *when*—only a matter of time before some militant jihadist cell blindsided an apathetic and unprepared US.

Hadn't other nations believed themselves immune only to find out the hard way they were wrong?

The '72 Lod Airport massacre in Tel Aviv or the attack on the Israeli athletes during the Munich Olympics, same year, were considered further examples of the ongoing enmity between Israel and Islam, nothing more. But then came the 1979 storming of the US embassy in Tehran, resulting in the hostage crisis—which was blamed on regime change, not Islamic malintent toward America. But the hostage crisis had been followed by the bombings of multiple US embassies in 1983, not to mention the 1985 Rome and Vienna airport attacks.

And, dear God! What about the bomb planted on Pan Am Flight 103 just this past December? The plane had exploded midair and rained down fiery death on unsuspecting Lockerbie, Scotland, killing all passengers and crew aboard as well as eleven victims on the ground.

Hadn't those incidents and others done anything to prove that Islamic terrorism *in western nations* was on the rise?

These terrorists are inching closer and closer to our homeland. Just a hop, skip, and a jump across the ocean and they're on our doorstep, Hawke told himself. *Unless they're already here, honing some audacious and evil plan. Perfecting its delivery.*

Not until Islamic fanaticism struck at the heart of America would its citizens realize that the US was *not* immune.

Hawke had been forced to reevaluate his options. He was loathe to "track" a *supposed* cell of Islamic radicals through the city's ghettos and slums when he scarcely knew what to look for. So, he educated himself, read up on known terrorist groups and their leaders, learned their ideologies and objectives, and studied their attack models. He moved on from there to view suspect profiles on microfiche newspaper accounts. He did his best to memorize faces and names. Then he identified every mosque and Islamic center within a fifty-mile radius of the city.

Armed with little more than his CI's thin intel, Hawke started his reconnaissance by watching nearby mosques and other gathering places to get a feel for the men, women, and families he saw and following whatever wraithlike leads struck his fancy.

Pick a card; any card, he told himself.

He sat hours of surveillance on hunches and whims, always alone, always after his shift ended or on weekends, and always using his personal credit card to gas his departmental ride. And wherever he went, he took along a decent camera and photographed whatever sparked his interest, taking the money spent on film and development from his own pocket.

By dint of repeated review and comparison, he began to recognize individuals and to take note of who they interacted with frequently, particularly those men who arrived and left together. He followed individuals and groups until he knew where they lived, where they worked, and who they hung out with.

And after months of frustrating, unproductive drudgery, he had nothing to show for his efforts.

*Lord? I gotta have a sign. Something—*anything—*to encourage me and let me know that I'm not a total fool, chasing shadows.*

No, what I must have is a breakthrough, Lord. Please.

A week ago, Hawke had picked up yet another packet of developed photos during his lunch hour. He riffled through the photos, plucked three of the prints from the stack, and stared at them, his mouth opening and closing like a fish out of water . . . broke the speed limit getting to the library, pulled up the images he needed on microfiche, and compared them to the photos in his hand. Used a flatbed scanner to print the microfiche screens. Raced back to his department and pounded on his boss's door.

What ensued between Hawke and Chief McCormick was a shouting match loud enough to wake the dead lying in the morgue down in the base-ment. Abruptly the shouting stopped and a deadly hush fell on McCormick's office. The division detectives out on the floor stopped pretending to work and gathered in small knots across the room to toss around conjectures.

Five minutes later, when Hawke emerged from the chief's office and returned to his desk, every eye in the department followed him. He ignored the stares.

The other detectives gestured to Mayer, their unspoken message, *Get the skinny. Get it now.*

"Hey, Rick?"

"Busy, Dov."

"Busy, as in cleaning out your desk busy?"

Hawke plastered him with a withering sneer. "Your vote of no confidence is noted."

"Sorry, that's not . . . I mean, did you catch a break?"

"A break on what? You're as up-to-date as I am on our joint cases."

"So not one of *our* cases." Dov glanced up and ran into the impatient glares of the other detectives. He tried again.

"Rick, we both know you've been burning the candle at both ends to verify your informant's intel. Have you uncovered anything actionable?"

Hawke wasn't able to contain all of his elation; a smile leaked out—a hard, gritty, inflexible smile. "Guess you'll find out soon enough."

He lifted his voice to address those huddled across the division, staring expectantly in his direction. "Yeah. All you losers will find out soon enough."

He'd left it to his boss to wrangle a meeting with Cuttiford in McCormick's conference room the next morning. A skeptical and barely civil Cuttiford arrived with Hawke's two FBI friends in tow—although the look of loathing those "friends" bent on him likely signaled the end of any affable relationship.

Hawke spread blowups of the three photos on the table in front of their guest. The SAC barely glanced at them. One of the two agents bent closer. He frowned as if something had snagged his attention but he hadn't yet puzzled out what it was.

"That's it?" Cuttiford sneered. "You've burned a lot of good will between our agencies, Chief McCormick, dragging us in here to view Detective Hawke's family's photo album."

Hawke ignored the insult. Standing over the photos across from Cuttiford, he singled out one picture and slid it under the SAC's nose. His agents leaned in to study three young males in working men's garb walking together. Hawke tapped the middle face and said softly, "It's just that we're wondering, Special Agent in Charge Cuttiford, *sir*, what Ibrahim Azize is doing in the US."

"What the—" The SAC and his agents knew the name, as well they should. The man was wanted by Interpol as the mastermind for several European bombings.

"Just in case you aren't all that familiar with Azize's face, here's a microfiche printout to confirm his ID." Hawke dropped the printout next to the photo.

Hawke watched recognition and alarm bloom on Cuttiford's face. The man stood. His agents jumped up with him.

Cuttiford studied Hawke for a moment. "Thank you. We'll take it from here." At a jerk of his head, one of the feds gathered up the photos and the microfiche printout before they walked out.

"A week later, here we are," Hawke muttered, "the scarcely tolerated, ugly, red-headed stepchild at what should have been *my* Cinderella ball."

"Yeah, I was especially looking forward to a new gown," Dov snickered, "and do you prefer pink or blue?"

"Shut up, Mayer."

As he and Dov waited, Hawke never took his eyes off the falling down, two-story dwelling in a line of condemned houses. The target was shaded by overgrown bushes and appeared uninhabited. It was not.

The six FBI agents comprising Squad A were stacked across the house's rear, waiting to breach the back entrance. Squad B lurked behind the command post van. When the op commenced, they would move to the front corner of the house, across and up the road from the van. Squad A's task at the rear of the house was to flush the quarry out the front into Squad B's waiting arms.

Four sharpshooters crouched on the rooftops of four buildings providing overwatch. One of those snipers was poised atop the building closest to the detectives' position. The snipers had the front and both sides of the house in their crosshairs. Additional FBI personnel manned spotlights in upstairs windows directly across from the house.

While Mayer monitored the radio, Hawke waited, his eyes returning to another junker on the street. This one, two of its wheels missing, leaned against the building beneath the sniper closest to them. Curiosity pinged him again, but he pushed it down and yawned. Night was waning, and no one had as yet reported movement in the dark house.

Mayer listened to the radio and looked up. "Go time, Rick."

A blaze of floodlights lit up the target. The lights revealed the six members of Squad B stacked and ready to handle anyone fleeing through the front door. Hawke's eyes jerked up, his attention caught by the unexpected red glows that appeared in both second-floor windows.

A moment later, a tremendous *whoosh* and a trail of smoke shot from the window nearer Hawke and Mayer. Dismayed, Hawke's eyes followed the path of the rocket propelled grenade as it flew across the street, certain the grenade was intended for the command post.

Just as he'd given up hope for Barnard, his support staff, and the van they occupied, the RPG jinked left and shot into the nearby alley. Hawke's jaw dropped as the RPG flew far down the alley, struck his departmental ride, and lifted it straight into the air. The *boom* echoed up and down the street— but before the fiery debris even hit the ground, a second grenade launched.

Its target was the abandoned car beneath the sniper nearest them.

The terrorists had planted the rusted car there for a reason. A reason? Maybe an explosive-filled reason?

Hawke screamed, "Dov!" and threw himself to the ground just as a concussive roar filled his ears. He covered his head as bits of debris rained down. The air was thick with choking smoke, making it difficult to breathe and nearly impossible to see what was happening.

"Dov! Dov, you okay?"

"Singed, but I'll live. You?"

"Same."

Hawke figured the sharpshooters perched above the roiling smokescreen were fuming. Their job was to eliminate threats to Squad B and ensure no one escaped the FBI's net. With this dense smoke cover, they could do neither.

Hawke bellycrawled across broken asphalt, every breath tasting of oily, sickening fumes. He was determined to put eyes on the target, snatch a look at the terrorists' movements through the smoke.

Hawke squinted. He thought he'd seen the front door open . . . *and he had*. A man's lithe figure leapt from the porch and ran into the smoke, using it as cover while he ran down the street in Hawke and Dov's direction. The hand-held machine pistol he gripped delivered a spread of shells to clear whatever might be in his path ahead. At the same time, the peculiar *ack-ack-ack* of assault rifles reached Hawke's ears, automatic gunfire erupting from four points in the house.

"RPGs, smoke screen, and covering fire," Hawke murmured. "They've known about the takedown all along."

The man racing through the smoke jinked toward them.

"Dov! We've got us a runner. Get ready."

"I see him, Rick."

The runner, legs pounding furiously, came abreast of the rusted ruin where Hawke and Dov were lying in wait. Hawke and Dov, crouched side by side, sprang on the man, Hawke high, Dov low, executing a perfect quarterback sack. With a muffled grunt, the man lost all his air. Unfortunately, he'd hung on to the machine pistol and managed to swing it around toward Dov.

Hawke yanked his sidearm and clocked the guy just above his ear. The man crumpled and lay twitching between them.

Dov pulled out his cuffs. "*Whew*. Thanks, Rick. I'll hook him up."

Through the smoke eddying hypnotically within the spotlights' dual glares, Hawke slowly stood and took in the scene around the house. The two FBI squads were herding prisoners into the street. Barnard was moving among the prisoners, a tense expression on his face.

"Looks like the action's over, Dov. Let's get our guy up and moving."

Dov yanked their prisoner to his feet. "Hey, Rick?"

"Yeah?"

"This guy look familiar to you?"

Hawke turned and studied their prisoner. "Well, well, well! Ibrahim Azize, I presume?" He grinned at his partner. "We just bagged the *big* prize, Dov. Let's go see Barnard."

"Dude, you or I handing off Azize to Barnard is not going to endear us to him or Cuttiford. Maybe we should deliver him to someone else on his team. Let them take the credit."

Hawke snort-laughed. "Are you kidding? The chief's gonna love us for this. He'll probably buy us dinner for tweaking the SAC's nose."

"Way to push your luck, man."

"I don't do luck, Mayer." He thought of something else and smiled wider. "Hey, I'd love to get a photo of us handing Azize off to the feds. Bet you ten bucks, the chief frames it and hangs it in his office."

"All in the spirit of interagency cooperation, right?"

"Precisely."

They walked a wobbly Azize down the street, straight to Barnard. "Here you go. One Ibrahim Azize."

He reddened. "I gave you specific orders—"

"Guy ran right into our arms, Barnard. I figured you'd prefer that we catch him as opposed to standing aside and watching him stroll away—am I right or am I wrong?"

Barnard exhaled, somewhat mollified. "You're right. I suppose thanks are in order."

He extended his hand and Hawke took it. They glanced up as a flash went off. Dov stood next to the agent photographing the scene; he gave Hawke a thumbs up. "Great shot!"

"I'd appreciate a copy of that photo, Barnard," Hawke said evenly.

Barnard offered him a sheepish smile. "In return for the assist, I'll send you a copy. The *only* copy."

"The only copy?"

"You don't think I'm stupid enough to print one for Cuttiford, do you?"

Hawke chuckled. "No, I do not. Come on, Mayer, let's go."

"Go? Go in what?"

Hawke stared down the alley. "Well crud. They blew up my car."

"Gee, tough break, Hawke."

"Shut up, Mayer."

AN HOUR LATER, one of the feds dropped off Hawke and Mayer at the downtown station. They wanted to get a jump on their after-action reports, but first Hawke had the distasteful task of reporting bad news to the transport Officer of the Day. Dov went along for moral support.

After Hawke finished explaining why his ride existed mainly as tiny toasted bits floating around a crumbling neighborhood, he filled out the necessary paperwork and put in a request for a departmental loaner. In the meantime, Dov checked in with his wife. By the time he and Dov got off the elevator on the fourth floor, it was close to 9:30 a.m.

Hawke yawned. *If we crank out our reports quick enough, I can make the 11:00 a.m. service,* he thought as they walked onto the floor.

They were both surprised to see lights on in the chief's office. "That can't be good," Dov said under his breath, "and I have plans with Lisa."

Chief McCormick poked his head out of his office doorway. "Hawke? Mayer? Everything shake out?"

"Yup. We got him, Chief," Hawke said with a smile. "The beauty of it? Azize ran straight into our arms. We tied a ribbon around him, stuck a bow on top, and presented him *personally* to Barnard."

McCormick smiled with satisfaction. "Way to go, you two. I'm headed home myself."

Relieved, Hawke turned to his partner. "Hey, let's crank out our reports quick as we can and head out. I want to catch the eleven o'clock service."

"Oh? And just how do you plan to get there?"

Hawke put his hands on his hips. "Well, since I can't pick up a loaner until tomorrow, I *was* counting on my partner to drop me off."

"Wait. You need me to drive you clear across town in my personal vehicle, and it's what? Thirty minutes one way—*to church* no less?"

"Don't worry; I'll sit in the backseat. Wouldn't be seemly for me to ride in the front with my driver."

"Haha. Very funny. Sorry to disappoint you, but I'm meeting Lisa at The Savoy in less than an hour. You can call a cab or join us for brunch. We'll drop you home after."

Hawke scowled. "You know good and well that big comic book convention is in town, making a huge fuss over that Tim Burton *Batman* remake." He shook his head. "Why can't they leave a good thing alone, I ask you? Anyway, every taxi in the city will be shuttling convention goers to and from restaurants or to the airport. I'll be lucky to snag a cab by one or two o'clock."

"Brunch, then?"

"Brunch it is."

So much for church.

Drat.

CHAPTER 2

TERRY PULLED THE HOOD of his jacket far forward and clasped the jacket's thin material around his middle to ward off the damp and cold. Eyes cast down, he shuffled along cracked pavement, slowly bypassing boarded-up strip malls and faded piles of trash, his unsteady steps miming the gait of an aged and life-wearied man . . . although Terry was not old by any means.

Not twenty years ago, Terry's defunct neighborhood had been home to a lively, thriving community. And although many of his childhood memories were cloudy, recollections attached to *scent* hung on, rich and vibrant. When he closed his eyes, he could recall the fragrance of spring flowers, the heady aroma of fresh-baked bread wafting from nearby kitchen windows, and the bliss of a young woman's perfume as she passed by.

But that was before the government built the expressway.

The monstrosity that towered over them had overwritten the fragrances that delighted Terry's young heart. Morning or evening—it didn't matter which—dirt and grime from passing vehicles silted down on them. Now the air reeked of exhaust fumes and musky urban rot. The concrete behemoth had even devoured the peaceful hush of evening and dawn. Day in and day out, the reverberating clang, clatter, growl, and roar of speeding trucks and cars never abated.

Oppressed by the overhead expressway, the community's cohesion had shuddered, fractured, and died. A protracted exodus followed, leaving behind defeat and decay. The residents who remained, including Terry, were those who could not afford to relocate.

Terry blinked as a rumble shuddered through his bones, a rolling, expanding *boom* much stronger than the elevated traffic. Dark, hostile clouds overhead carried with them an early dusk. He sniffed the foul air and caught a trace of the scent particular to lightning.

Rain was coming, but he walked on.

To the police who patrolled the ruins of his neighborhood, Terry was harmless and unremarkable, just one of the many homeless individuals who huddled against the massive pylons supporting the expressway, clinging to their tattered tents or wilted cardboard boxes . . . the very impression he sought to convey.

Except Terry was neither homeless nor steeped in drugs or alcohol. He had his struggles, yes, yet in his own way he was resourceful. Clever even.

He had to be. He was alone in the world now.

His mother had passed away in her sleep a few years ago. She'd been housebound for months before her death, sick but refusing to see a doctor. Visited by no one due to the neighborhood's mass migration.

When she died, Terry chipped and chiseled through their basement wall and dug into the hardpacked dirt. With gentle care, he wrapped her body in her pretty bedspread, placed her in the deep niche he'd carved, repacked the hole, and cemented the wall closed.

No one can ever hurt you again, he thought as he mourned her loss.

And since no one remarked upon her absence, Terry continued to deposit her monthly social security checks in their joint account and live in her small home as if she were still alive.

With one caveat: After carefully watching her lips as she whispered her final instructions, he'd moved himself and whatever he needed on a daily basis to the basement. He would never spend the night upstairs again.

"*I cannot watch over you forever, Terry, so please trust me on this: Live as if you are in danger, because one day you will be. Be very careful, my son, always careful. Board up the house. Make it look empty like the others. Hide yourself, your real self, and remain on your guard at all times.*"

Most of the old cookie-cutter tract houses around them were abandoned, veering toward ruin. A few scattered neighbors remained, but none of them were near enough to notice Terry's comings and goings. Nevertheless, whenever he left the house, he did so from his back door, after adopting his artfully crafted "other" persona. His guise and uncertain gait supported the impression of aimlessness, which allowed him to come and go without attracting interest.

In other words, he was careful. Always careful. *Careful* had been his mother's longstanding maxim, not just her last advice to him.

And yet today, under darkening skies and despite the paranoia woven deeply into the fabric of his psyche, Terry pushed on. This day, *Need* dictated a dangerous departure from the safety of *Careful*.

Terry reached an intersection and paused. With a flick of his eyes, he checked right and left. He turned himself as if uncertain of his whereabouts. Employed the motion to scan behind him.

No one. He was alone, his objective close at hand, the early twilight a bonus.

He wandered across the street and down another half block. He turned the corner, then slowed even further as he approached a chest-high iron fence bordering the sidewalk.

The shoots of an untrimmed hedge poked through the fence's bars, their thorns seeking to snare unwary pedestrians. Terry had been snagged by those greedy, thorny hands last time and kept a wary distance from their grasp.

Partway along the fence line, a wide breach appeared on his right. Within the breach was a flight of worn steps and a fractured walkway. And at the end of the walkway, sooty stone walls reared upward, their heads jutting into the burgeoning clouds.

Set in those stone walls, two double-door entrances glowered at him like a pair of slitted, disapproving eyes. Terry detected no threats between himself and the church entrance, but he shivered under the grim, accusing glare of the doors.

Careful screamed, "*Flee!*" but *Need* shrieked, "*No! Must have!*" and refused to be dissuaded.

As Terry vacillated, the sky above him split open. He rushed up the steps, ran past the low sign that read *St. Joseph's Episcopal Church*, and raced to those hateful, scowling doors. He yanked on each handle in turn until one weighty door swung toward him. He rushed inside and pulled the door closed after him.

Terry was immediately engulfed in the foyer's dense, oppressive darkness.

Narthex, he reminded himself. *That's what mama called it.*

He shook his head. The church had a lot of funny words.

Vespers. Acolyte. Diocese. Liturgy. Gablet.

Terry slowly exhaled and alternately fisted his hands and flexed his fingers—a coping mechanism for anxiety. As his heart slowed from a mad gallop to a more sedate canter, he shuffled toward a bearing wall, placed a splayed hand upon it, closed his eyes, and waited. Waited for the old building to speak to him. He felt the thundering rain on the narthex roof, followed by the jolt of a terrific gust rattling the heavy doors, the pounding of droplets as they spattered against the grimy stained glass over the narthex entrance, and the temperature as it plummeted.

Terry stiffened. Somewhere in the building, old timbers groaned and moved under his fingers. Eventually, though, he convinced himself of the church's emptiness and sighed with relief.

Ahead of schedule. Safe. For now.

He tiptoed through the swinging doors leading from the chilly narthex into the nave, the long, narrow, and cavernous seating portion of the church. He had attended this church with his mother years ago when they first moved to the city, and he recalled the nave's layout.

The layout of *this* church wasn't all that different from the *other* church, was it?

The other church?

The muscles in his shoulders tensed as he tried to remember. Remembering was hard, but hadn't his mother taken him to a different church when he was a very little boy? He had a vague recollection of the two of them creeping out the back door of their house on a Sunday morning.

"*Shhh! Tiptoe!*"

"*Why?*"

"*Daddy is sleeping; don't wake him up!*"

Terry shuddered. Bad things happened when Daddy woke up. *That* he remembered. But in the end, it never mattered how quiet or cautious they were. When his father sobered up, he, without fail, cursed, ridiculed, and punished them both.

Terry was intimately acquainted with cursing, ridicule, and punishment. Being different from the other little boys at school, he'd often been bullied and beaten. But the ostracism of his schoolmates was mild compared to what he endured at home under his father's "loving" hands.

A faint, familiar *ping* sounded far back in his head. The ping burgeoned and birthed a strident ringing. If Terry didn't act quickly and decisively, the noise would overwhelm him.

Stop it! Daddy's dead! Can't hurt us anymore.

Terry's father had died when he was still that young boy. Although he couldn't recall the actual event, the memory of his mother breaking the news to him was quite clear. According to her, his father drank himself into his usual state of oblivion but never woke up. Terry watched his mother's mouth slowly form the words so he could see them. And since he thought he should be sad that his father was dead, he tried to be . . . even though inside he was bubbling with relief.

His mother took him away not long after that. They moved to this big city, to the house and neighborhood where he still lived. He'd been relieved when his mother no longer made him go to school, but his mother did take him to church at Saint Joseph's on Sunday, and he'd been glad of it   for a while. Yes, for a while Terry believed no one would ever again beat him as cruelly as his father had.

He shivered. *I was wrong about that.*

Off to Terry's left, just inside the gloomy nave, two tiny flames flickered in the votive candle rack. He sniffed to sample the air. The place smelled as it always had: mildew mingled with incense. Those intertwined fragrances called up vivid scenes from his childhood. Some of Terry's memories were good . . . although the good ones were inevitably eaten up by the ugly ones.

He had been all of twelve but tall for his age when Father Sweeny, St. Joseph's stern senior rector at that time, caught him in the choir loft, hiding in the nook adjoining the organ's casement. The priest had shouted at Terry, but when Terry was slow to respond, the priest became enraged. Showing surprising strength for a man far past his prime, the priest dragged Terry down the stairs and into a side room off the narthex. There, the man yanked off Terry's shirt and lashed him with a yardstick. Over and over until it snapped in two.

Terry had been too terrified to return to the church after the beating. His mother cajoled, even tried to insist, but Terry dug in his heels and refused to go. And although the priest died this past December, Terry remained frightened of the old man. He could still feel the wicked sting of the yardstick on the bare, tender skin of his back, could see the man's wide mouth hurtling accusations Terry *could not hear.*

The terror and pain of that punishment had lodged deep in his heart, and as Terry peered around the shadowed nave, fear began to rise within him. His mouth dried up. He trembled. His eyes darted back and forth across the church. They landed on the two candles in their red sconces, their dual flickering glows instantly ominous—far too suggestive of the gleam in the mad priest's eyes.

Terry blinked to clear his vision, but blinking did not help. Instead of candles, he saw Father Sweeny's angry face.

Fright burst from Terry's throat in guttural gibberish. He slapped a hand over his mouth to bottle up the sounds. Force them back inside.

Must not make the noises! he shouted to himself. *Must not make the stupid noises!*

Once, twice, and again, he slapped his face and his head. He slapped himself repeatedly—the way his father used to slap him when he made the noises.

It was then that one of the two voices inhabiting Terry's thoughts whispered a kindly reminder to him: *The old priest is dead, Terry. He will not be coming back. He cannot come back.*

The other voice, a voice of cold, hard logic, a voice that demanded Terry's obedience, stepped in.

You are not stupid, Demand insisted, *and you are hardly defenseless. Don't forget it.*

Terry finally agreed. *I am not dumb. I am not defenseless.* He was not defenseless. Not when he had his own monster residing inside, a monster with a mind and will of its own.

He calmed when the first voice, *Careful,* the one that often sounded like his mother, added, *Go upstairs now, Terry, but be careful. Always careful.*

Yes. Always careful. Do not ruin it!

In the far rear corner of the nave, a steep flight of stairs led up to the choir loft. He felt his way along the wall to the steps. Climbed them lightly. Crouched on the landing at the top of the darkened staircase. Waited for his senses to acclimate.

Barely breathing he crept forward, low to the floor.

The choir loft hung suspended over the width of the nave and had a railing all the way across it. From the railing to the back of the loft, the floor sloped gently upward and supported the tiers of pews from which a choir used to sing. When the church's overhead lights were on as they were during the liturgy, figures standing in the loft could be seen from below, particularly from the altar and front of the church. With the church darkened as it was now, however, the odds of being seen were nearly negligible.

Terry's caution did not care about facts: It took no risks. It understood that even in darkened conditions such as these and with the church seemingly deserted, he should never—must never—chance being seen.

Yes, he was terrified of being caught again, but he was more afraid of other things, and rightfully so. He was afraid of that over which he had no control, things *Demand* said the monster inside might make him do.

Like before.

Oh, Sara!

Terry shook off a shiver. Still crouching, he scuttled across the loft under the concealment of the railing and paused, centered on the loft's four rows of pews. He stared through the gloom toward his objective. Although he could not quite make *it* out, he knew exactly where it was. The pews had no center aisle, but on the loft's highest tier, directly beyond the choir pews, it waited for him, a relic of this church's former glory days, back when the church had served a modestly affluent congregation within a modestly prosperous community.

Terry understood nothing of the organ's exceptional provenance. He had no idea that the prized instrument was the sole reason the church had not been abandoned as quickly or easily as the neighborhood had been. He had no knowledge of its three manuals (keyboards), its assortment of stops, or its foot-operated swell sheets and bass pedal boards.

What he *did* know was that, behind the organ and against the loft's back wall, stood a great wood casement. The casement housed the electrical mechanisms supplying the air that gave the organ's pipes their tremendous voices.

The pipes!

He had studied them minutely in those weeks before Father Sweeny found him in the choir loft, had counted them more than once, never getting the same number twice. What he knew with certainty was that more than a thousand pipes crowned the organ's casement, pipes ranging from the slim and sweetly fluting all the way down to the huge and powerful bass and baritone. And while the organist and the organ itself faced away from the congregation, the pipes—*oh, those blessed and magnificent pipes!*—pointed their mouths toward the congregation. Like a host of angelic beings, they proclaimed their praise into the nave's great, cavernous expanse.

The pipes were why Terry had come. He had ignored *Careful's* warnings to satisfy his craving desire for the pipes. Only his need for them mattered in this moment.

On all fours, he crept up the narrow aisle between the loft's far side wall and the varnished wooden pews, then made his way across the back wall toward a shadowed alcove. A thin, jutting partition perpendicular to the organ's casement formed the third side of a three-sided niche: back wall, casement, partition. The partition screened the door that opened into the casement whereby artisans knowledgeable of the organ's workings might enter to repair or maintain the mechanisms. The door into the casement was locked, but Terry could not have cared less.

He stepped into the alcove, released the breath he'd been holding, and turned to the wood that surrounded him on three sides. Its waxy fragrance was his to savor and enjoy. Inhaling the pungent scent, he pressed his cheek to the casement's soft, pitted grain, let his fingertips roam across it, stroking, sighing, and softly crooning with simple delight. Years ago, he had found he could rest here, could take its offered solace and lay down his battles, if only for a few short hours.

After Terry had leaned against the wood's coolness and soaked up its comfort a while, he sensed the glossy pipes beckoning to him. They urged him to touch and stroke them. Yes, he loved to reach above his head and stroke the tapered ends of the magnificent pipes within his reach, especially the largest pipes of the array. But more than the delight of their satiny sheen under his hands, he ached to feel their might flow through his fingers as the organist played.

Careful. Be very careful.

Careful? Yes. On no account did he wish to disturb the organist, his agent of bliss, especially now that he'd discovered she came here each Saturday to practice. He wanted nothing more than to arrive before she did, hide himself here, and sink into her music.

But he knew better than to lose himself in the music or slip too deeply into ecstasy. If he made the noises, horrible consequences would follow—as the old priest had taught him.

Since that beating, Terry had not dared to return to the church. The very thought was far too terrifying, too intolerable. He had believed so until the previous Saturday when his glance passed over the woman as she jostled by him, toting a stack of music. He'd been astounded when a jolt of recognition struck him.

This woman had been St. Joseph's organist!

Was she still?

In a single, unanticipated moment, the craving in Terry's heart reignited. Shutting out the cries of *Careful* in favor of *Need's* siren song, he turned and trailed behind the organist until she led him to the church he'd avoided for so long. He watched with dismay as she went inside. He longed to follow her, but he was too afraid to pass through the glowering doors guarding the church. He dithered for some time before working up the courage to slink up to the doors and slip through them.

Yet, once those doors had closed behind him, he calmed. And when he placed his hand upon one of the narthex's walls, he felt her music reverberating under this fingers. Except . . . as welcome as the distant pulsations were, they were not enough.

Not nearly enough.

So, giving in to his desires, he had slipped into the nave, crept up the darkened staircase to the choir loft, and crouched on the landing to study the woman from the shadows. Within the small yellow circle thrown by the lamp, with her head slightly back, she played. He could feel some of the pipes' song through the wood landing, yet he fretted because he longed—he *yearned*—to touch the pipes themselves. He ached to press himself against them, caress their cool, satiny finish, and feel them as they sang.

Nothing in his narrow, lonely life had ever rivaled that happiness.

Afterward, and through the following week, he'd agonized over his growing hunger and weighed his *Need* against his fear. He thought. He planned. He ignored *Careful's* dire warnings. He made his decision: The very next Saturday, he would arrive at the church ahead of her.

Today was that day.

With his heart pounding in his throat, Terry stood in the alcove he had not visited since the day the old priest caught and beat him. He shuddered, fearful the priest might again find him.

But when he beat me it was years ago . . . wasn't it? And he's dead now, isn't he?

He couldn't say how long ago it had been, though. He frowned and wondered if he didn't sometimes muddle the past with the present. Worse, he suspected he did not always distinguish between what was real . . . and what was not.

He shoved his anxiety away. He was *here*. Nothing else mattered. Safely hidden within the alcove, awaiting the organist, tears stood in Terry's eyes. Yes, he would need to restrain himself when she began to play, because the pipes possessed the power to seduce him. Cause him to make the noises. And if Terry were to accidentally betray himself to the woman? He might lose control of the monster lurking in his head—and he did not want that! Nor did he want to lose this day's glorious pleasure or further opportunities in the weeks ahead.

How he *hungered* for the pipes and their ability to drown out the persistent torment in his head!

He winced. Just acknowledging the shrill, sharp trill that resided far back in his skull was enough to awaken it. Within seconds the faint hum increased in volume and pitch. The ringing grew louder, higher, more piercing, until it exploded into a mad kaleidoscope of pings, buzzes, and clanging gongs.

Clutching his aching head, Terry groaned. He alternately squeezed his skull and beat his head with his palms again and again and again. When he was panting and dripping sweat, the riot retreated . . . but only to wait in grim abeyance.

Terry exhaled . . . and froze in consternation, some sixth sense jangling a warning. He crept from the alcove to the front corner of the casement and peered around it. Spotted a jiggling beam of light slowly moving up the staircase.

MARY ALICE WAITE trudged up the unlit staircase, one hand sliding along the banister while grasping the small flashlight that guided her footsteps, her opposite arm curled around a stack of music covered in loose, waterproof plastic. The infernal rain had slickened the plastic, and her grip on her precious music was tenuous at best.

She rested her chin atop the pile to prevent a heavy volume of Bach from sliding out from under the plastic and spilling its pages down the staircase. Tightening her grasp, she ascended to the choir loft one staggering step at a time, all the while grumbling under her breath against Father Benjamin, the priest appointed to replace the departed Father Sweeny.

Mary Alice, single and too soon middle-aged, pressed her bloodless lips into a tighter line as she recalled the young priest's grinning, smooth-cheeked face. *Sixteen years I been St. Joseph's organist. Sixteen years!*

The unmistakable aroma of Noxzema face cleanser clung to her clothing like another woman's perfume might, not that she cared what anyone thought of her in that regard. There had been a man in her life once, but he had exited as quickly as he had entered, a mere ripple in the empty sameness of her life. Her music had been and was the sustaining constant in an otherwise lonely existence.

And a purely volunteer organist I been for the past how many years? Not a penny for my services since they erected that wretched expressway over us, after which our congregation shriveled like an apple left on the tree all winter.

She had not even received the church's usual small monetary gift last Christmas thanks to Father Sweeny's inconsiderately timed death.

Paid or not paid, for sixteen years without fail, she had played for every Sunday worship service, evensong, and feast day. And for sixteen years when she arrived to practice, she had switched on the lights in the narthex, the nave, the stairwell, and the choir loft, lights that brightened her mood as well as the gloomy church.

It had taken the smug new priest a mere two months to declare it economically necessary to cut back on St. Joseph's utility usage. Quoting facts and figures that befuddled Mary Alice, he announced that the parish was eliminating all nonessential use of lights. Starting with her.

"It is not as though you don't know every inch of the stairs to the choir loft after all these years; however, I will personally supply you with a pocket flashlight to ensure your safety. Why, the church's lighting fixtures are so out-of-date, we actually burn more electricity warming them up than we do for the hour you practice—can you believe it?

"And once you are seated at the organ, you will have the music lamp, will you not, Mary Alice?" he'd coaxed, his roguish smile beaming down at her.

"*Miss Waite*," she'd ground out, offended by his casual address. Yet, he seemed not to notice her correction.

Still smiling and so *disgustingly* certain of her approval and agreement, he'd given her no opportunity to respond. Patting her thin arm with the patronizing self-assurance of blind, insensitive youth, he moved away, murmuring something about "potholes in the parking lot," leaving Mary Alice in stunned, angry silence.

Mary Alice knew from long experience that many people in authority—lovely, educated, privileged, and self-important people—were accustomed to running roughshod over those they deemed lower than themselves. In their arrogance, those lofty individuals presumed the right to impose their will on the plain and unassertive. Mary Alice had experienced it all her unchanging years.

"And what about trippin' in the dark, I ask? But do I ask? Why, no, not a word in edgewise with that one! Can scarcely carry m' music w' both hands, yet here I be in the dark, music in one hand, a-hanging on to the banister for dear life with the other, and the tread coming off these steps just a-waitin' t' trip me up. Carry a pocket flashlight, says he? A grand idea! Shall I be carryin' your precious flashlight 'tween my teeth I ask? But no, not a blessed word from my lips afore that one gallops off on his *high horse*."

Two steps from the landing at the top of the staircase, the stack of music shifted. As her hand on the banister shot out to rescue the load, she lost her grip on the flashlight. It bounced down the steep ascent, cracking and breaking to pieces as it tumbled on its merry way. Mary Alice pressed her hip into the banister to keep from tumbling after the flashlight. As she slowly caught her breath and regained her balance, she leaned forward and peered above her, hoping the tall windows of the nave below might provide faint guidance.

"Not a bit of it," she grumbled.

No, the sun was imprisoned behind a wet, gray ceiling, unable to pierce the storm's roiling mist, let alone the soot-stained glass windows of the nave. Sighing, because autumn was depressing and her life was as drab as the weather, she inched her way up to the loft's landing. Relieved to be on solid, familiar footing again, she felt her way up another three steps to the organ and switched on the music lamp. A smallish puddle of light landed on the music rack. It wasn't much, but it was enough.

Here her grumbling left off, and the brightest hour of Mary Alice's week began. She was unhurried in arranging her music "just so" and in adjusting the bench to her satisfaction. She even forgot her one-sided quarrel with the young priest as she perused her selections for Sunday liturgy. She automatically put out her left hand and toggled the switch that powered the organ.

TERRY, ONE HAND on the casement, shivered with anticipation when the mechanisms within the casement hummed, warmed, then breathed in and out. When the woman put her hands to the keyboards, he sucked in a breath, and the pipes trilled, warbled, and reverberated with increasing intensity.

Terry sighed and screwed up his face as his pleasure intensified. He swayed back and forth, both arms stretched above his head, splayed fingers spread upon the pipes within reach.

The woman's transition into the piece's powerful next movement sent him higher still, mounting toward ecstasy. The pipes' vibrations surged through his body, rocking him with glorious joy. Soaring, soaring he flew, lifted above despair and beyond. The marvel of it filled him with a rapture that coursed up and down his limbs. His mouth opened, and he sang out his primal, rasping praise—

Cold fear jerked him back to reality. The organ's wondrous song had fallen away.

What had happened? Why had she stopped playing? Terry was dimly aware of a faraway bellow lingering high up in the vaulted rafters. He shut his mouth on the sudden and alarming realization that the dying, scraping note had come from his own throat.

I wasn't supposed to make the noise!

Had the woman heard him?

Heart hammering, Terry crept from the alcove and peered around the casement. The woman at the organ trembled in the faint glow of the lamp.

"Who . . . who is it? Who's there?" she called.

He watched her strain to see into the choir loft's darkness.

Again the woman called urgently, "Who's there?"

Flee! Flee! Careful screamed.

Terry wanted to obey, but the woman was between him and the single exit from the loft.

I'm caught! No way out! No way out! No way out!

At the apex of his dread, all Terry's hopes crashed to the ground. Its wreckage lay strewn across his pathetic future. Decimated. Utterly destroyed. Even if he managed to escape from here today, *Careful* would not allow him to return. He would never again experience this precious hour he so deeply and desperately loved.

The weight of Terry's loss was crushing; it shook him to his core. His hands and fingers twisted together in a futile effort to calm his rising panic.

Careful screamed again, *Run! Run quickly! Before it is too late!*

Yes, must flee. Must try to escape.

He wrapped his arms about his middle, hugged himself, and nodded, slowly building up his resolve. Finally, he stepped out from the alcove and made himself creep along the back wall, then past the pews, determined, if needed, to rush past the woman and make his escape. He hunched down and crept across the width of the loft, slowly getting closer to the staircase.

Almost! he told himself. *Hurry!*

But Mary Alice, sensing the shadowy presence shifting toward her, slid from the organ's high bench. In a dither of fear, she stumbled for the staircase.

Groped for the banister.

Missed it.

Terry, only feet behind her, gaped in stunned disbelief as Mary Alice toppled from the landing and plummeted down the steep flight of steps. He shifted from foot to foot in horrified agitation for several moments, before following her down.

She rested on her back at the bottom. Unmoving. Her head thrown to the side in a grotesque and unnatural manner. And like his mother's eyes had been when he found her on that terrible morning, this woman's eyes were wide open. Soft but sightless.

Terry fell to his knees beside her, overcome with distress and sorrow. He hadn't intended to scare the organist, held no animus toward her, no wish for her to die—quite the opposite! He prized and admired her. *Desperately needed her.* It grieved him that he would never again experience the joy her music had given him.

He wept over her. Mourned her demise. Moaned in anguish and tried to tell her, "I'm sorry! I'm sorry! Didn't mean to scare you. Didn't mean to hurt you!"

Terry knew his words were incoherent to others; he'd never been able to make the right sounds, only disgusting noises. Still, as he wept, he poured out his heart to her, "My fault. My fault. My fault. I'm stupid. Always wrong."

He swiped at his tears and looked with regret upon the woman's empty expression. He reached out one hand and caressed her forehead.

He was gently smoothing her hair when *Demand's* arch and haughty voice broke through his terror.

Her death is your fault. You must pay for your wrong.

Demand issued his no-nonsense instructions. He minced no words: What Terry was to do, how he was to do it.

Blood. Your blood is forfeit, because only blood can pay.

Pacing around the woman's broken body, Terry whined, "Please! Please don't make me! I don't want to. It will hurt!"

But *Demand* brooked no argument. He commanded. Terry had to obey. *Or else.*

With fearful reluctance, Terry straightened the woman's head, then her body, dress, and legs as much as he dared. One leg was angled in a direction nature never intended it to go, and the idea of straightening it made Terry want to puke. Instead, he placed the woman's arms by her sides so that she almost looked like she was resting. Except for the leg.

He turned to run from the church—

Blood. You must pay.

Terry vacillated. Shifted from one foot to the other.

Your fault. You must pay.

Finally, he swallowed down his nausea and shucked off his hoody. He reached into the pocket of his jeans, and removed a thin, folded blade. He slowly opened the knife.

Knowing how it would sting. How much it would hurt.

For many minutes, he resisted . . . but eventually, he did as *Demand* commanded him.

The two cuts to the inside of his forearm were deep and stung fiercely. Then the blood welled, dribbled, and flowed from his arm, blood sufficient for the task before him. Shaking hard, Terry approached Mary Alice and stood over her. Let the twin rivulets run down his left arm and hand to join and flow from his fingers onto her peaceful face.

Within moments, the woman's features were obscured.

Terry took a step back. Tears ran down his cheeks. "I'm sorry," he sobbed.

You must stop it.

Terry tried to sniff back his tears.

You must stop it!

He glanced down. The blood had continued to flow from his arm, had run down his jeans and onto his left shoe, forming a puddle on the floor. He felt a wave of nausea pass over him.

Stop it! Stop it now!

Terry finally understood. He whipped off his t-shirt, used his knife to cut and fold thick pads that he placed over the cuts. Holding his arm and the pads to his side, he sliced the remainder of the shirt into long strips that he bound around his forearm and tied. The two cuts were deep, hard to close. He used nearly every scrap of the shirt to staunch the flow.

The slashes burned. He felt sick. Queasy.

Aching loss clutched at him, but the pain in his arm was stronger. The cuts burned and throbbed, and he wondered if they would heal on their own or if he would need to stitch them up like when he was little and had fallen on broken glass and the doctor had stitched up his knee. Terry shivered. He was cold, shaky, and weak.

He used the last bit of his shirt to wipe the blood from his pantleg and shoe. Then he slipped his hoodie on over his bare chest and arms, tucked the bloody fabric into his pocket, and considered what he must do next.

As if on cue, his sense of loss reasserted itself.

Sorry I will never hear you play again, organ lady.

No more music. No more pipes singing through my fingers.

He left the church weeping.

CHAPTER 3

SUNDAY, OCTOBER 1

HAWKE WAS DRESSED and on his way out the door to church when the phone rang. He whipped around and grabbed the cat before he shot out the door between Hawke's legs. Kicking the door closed behind him, he put the cat down and picked up the phone.

"Detective Hawke."

"Hey, Rick. Dov. Glad I caught you. Patrol called in a suspicious death at St. Joseph's Episcopal Church, far south end of town. We're on call this week, so . . ."

Hawke sighed. *Downside of being a homicide detective? Murders don't care what day it is.*

"Medical examiner on scene?"

"On her way."

"I'll meet you there."

So much for church or football.

Again.

HAWKE AND MAYER spied a patrol officer standing post in front of the church. They showed their badges and stepped into St. Joseph's narthex. Another officer directed them into the sanctuary where they found the ME and the body in a rear corner at the foot of a staircase. Although the overhead lights in the cavernous room were on, the ME's assistant had fired up a portable bank of lights and positioned them over the scene.

The officer who had been first on scene greeted them, then tipped his head toward the body. "Deceased is one Mary Alice Waite. Found her ID in a little purse in her pocket. Other than going through her pockets for ID, we have not disturbed the body or the scene. The parish priest tells us the deceased is the church organist."

The detectives drew near and studied the body while the ME worked. Dried blood marred the deceased woman's features and a puddle of the same had coagulated on the floor not far from her head.

"Substantial amount of blood," Dov muttered, "but I don't see a source."

"Because there isn't one," the medical examiner answered as she swabbed the deceased woman's hands, then bagged the and tagged the evidence.

"How's that possible?" Hawke demanded.

Dr. Lucinda Rodríguez glanced up, smiled, and winked. "Hey, Rick."

Everyone in Homicide Division knew Rodríguez was sweet on Hawke—including Hawke himself. Most of his coworkers couldn't understand Hawke's reluctance to date her . . . or anyone recently, for that matter.

"You have COD?"

"Preliminary cause of death is a broken neck at the C4 vertebrae. Death would have been immediate, 'C4, breathe no more' being a truism and all. She has other broken bones, too; look at the angle of her left leg. She probably fell from the top of the staircase with multiple impacts on the way down —which is curious, considering she looks 'laid out,' clothes nice and tidy . . . except for her leg."

She remembered something. "Oh, yeah. The officers also found, photographed, and bagged bits and pieces of a flashlight, most of it around the body. One or two pieces on the stairs, and I found a few bits under the body when I turned her."

"Why a flashlight?"

"Apparently, the rector wouldn't allow her to turn on any of the church's overhead lights to practice for Sunday morning service. Budget cuts. Gave her a flashlight to navigate the staircase."

"A flashlight she had to have dropped either before or as she was falling, since you found pieces under her body."

"Right. That notwithstanding, this case is odd. If I considered her injuries *and only* her injuries, they are entirely consistent with a fall down a steep flight of stairs. But how to explain our pesky little anomaly, the dried blood on her face and this puddle? I've turned the body every which way, looking for a bleeder. *Nada*. If she'd been found like this without the blood? I'd rule it an accidental death."

Somewhat hesitant, she added, "I've noted very fine traces of something else near the unexplained pool of blood. The traces look like salt crystals. My guess is dried tears. I've taken samples. Need a microscope to be sure."

Dov frowned. "Someone stood here and cried over her but didn't call an ambulance?"

"And you think that's the strange part. You're cute, Mayer. Let's go back to the dried blood, shall we? First, note *where* the blood dried: There's this puddle and what looks like a couple of shoe smears, but the only blood on the body is on the woman's face. Second, note *how* the blood dried on her face. Directionality of the spatter tells us the blood was poured or dripped from directly above her from a height of eighteen to twenty-four inches."

She lifted one brow. "I'll bet you drinks after work it's not her blood, Rick."

Hawke didn't rise to the bait. "Then who does it belong to?"

Miffed by Hawke's indifference, Rodríguez's attitude cooled. "That's your job, not mine. I've taken samples and will have the blood type for you tomorrow. If you find a suspect, I'll be able to either match the blood to him or rule him out. And I'll let you know about the other residue."

Hawke lifted his chin. "What manner of death will you rule? Accident or homicide?"

"Homicide only if she was pushed—but good luck proving she was or wasn't, either way. Still, like I said, I can't rule it an accident, due to the blood. For now, the manner of death is undetermined."

"Have you been upstairs?" Dov asked.

"Not my bailiwick. I do bodies."

"TOD?" Hawke queried.

"Liver temp says eighteen to twenty-two hours ago, so between 2:00 and 6:00 p.m. yesterday. The rector is over there. You'll want to speak to him, I presume, and I need to finish here." She pointed to the opposite side of the nave, her dismissal clear.

They found the young priest wringing his hands. He kept repeating, "Look what I've done! I wouldn't let her turn on the lights. Too expensive, I said . . . It's my fault. Oh, God, what have I done?"

After they completed their interview, Hawke asked the priest to turn on every light in the church so they could properly canvass the scene. He and Dov started on the stairs and worked their way up to the choir loft.

Dov leaned over the loft's railing and peered out into the nave. "This place is like a mausoleum. Imagine being up here with only a flashlight. Downright spooky, if you ask me."

"Agree."

"Since the priest ordered Mary Alice not to turn on the lights, that puts her in this loft practicing for Sunday service by only the light of that lamp." He pointed to the still-lit lamp over the organ. "Pathetic," he muttered.

He fiddled his fingers in the air in imitation of playing a keyboard. "So, she finished up her rehearsal and on her way down the unlighted stairs, dropped her flashlight, and subsequently took a fall?"

"You're forgetting the blood, Dov, and I'm not buying the 'she finished up' part either. While she might leave her sheet music on the organ's music rack until morning, would she leave the music lamp on overnight? I don't think so. I mean, what would the priest say to that?"

Dov joined Hawke by the organ. He scanned the open book of music and turned a page. "Looks like she left in the middle of a piece." Without much thought, he reached out and pressed one of the organ's keys.

A high reedy note resounded above them.

Dov snatched back his hand and stared at Hawke. "She left the organ on. Someone else was here, probably *right* here, and she ran!"

Hawke's eyes narrowed. He stepped down from the organ platform, walked to the railing, and put his back against the railing, centering himself on the loft. His gaze swept from one side to the other, over the two blocks of choir pews, before fixing his attention on the organ.

The organ was also centered on the loft, and most of the pipes, in various banks, were housed in a wood casement behind the organ. The front of the casement had a carved grill work that exposed parts of the pipes in an artistically pleasing manner, much like a shadow box.

Hawke's eyes followed the pipes as they emerged from the top of the casement, rising until they peaked in height according to their individual pitches. The largest pipes, however, were mounted to the walls outside the casement and on both sides of the organ.

Without moving, he studied the columns of bass pipes on the left side of the organ not far from the staircase. Sturdy shelves bolted to the wall and stuffed with rows of hymnbooks protruded from under the largest pipes. Nodding, he switched his gaze to the right side of the organ where a second course of enormous pipes mirrored the large pipes on the organ's left side.

There. A narrow partition protruded from the casement wall.

He jogged up the far aisle, crossed over to the casement, and peeked around the partition's edge. He saw that the partition screened a locked door that, presumably, provided access to the casement itself.

Hawke stepped into the niche. "Dov, go sit on the organ bench."

Dov shot him a curious look but did as asked.

"Can you see me, Dov?"

"Well, no. You're around the corner of the casement and behind that partition thingy."

Hawke stepped out of the alcove and edged two feet toward the far wall. "How about here?"

"Ah. Now I can see you."

"As I thought. Come over here?"

Dov joined his partner, and Hawke pointed.

"See this little niche? Inside the niche and immediately outside of it are the only places in the loft not visible from the organ."

Dov backed up, cleared his throat, and looked from the organ to where they stood. "I think I get it. If our guy had come up the stairs *after* Miss Waite started playing, and if he threatened her, she would have run this way. Except," he concluded, voice flat, "there's nowhere to run in this direction. Instead, our guy, whoever he is, had to have been hidden in this cubby before she arrived. When he came out, she ran for the stairs but . . . it was unlit. Dark. She could have fallen in her haste."

"And what does this scenario tell us?"

Dov faced his partner. "Well, if we have our facts right, it tells us a couple of things. First, if our suspect was determined to arrive before Mary Alice did, it means he had to know *when* she would be here."

"And second?"

"He waited until she was playing to attack her."

Hawke rubbed his jaw. "You're implying he hid up here in order to commit a crime, Dov. We don't know if there even is a crime."

"Why else would he hide up here?"

"Seems obvious to me."

"Oh?"

"He wanted to listen to her play."

Dov shook his head. "Kinda weird, though, don't you think? I mean, how loud do you think it had to be inside that alcove?"

"Very. He'd be up close and personal with the largest pipes too. Not possible from the other side with those shelves in the way."

"So why didn't he just listen from downstairs? Nice acoustics and all. Why hide in the alcove?"

"I'm more interested in why he came *out* of the alcove. If we knew that, perhaps we'd know whether Miss Waite ran from him and fell or if he pushed her . . ."

"Right, because there's no obvious motive to her death. No rape, no violence, no robbery. Just the weird bloodletting thing."

Hawke mulled over Dov's words. "The weird bloodletting thing . . ."

When he didn't finish, Dov shrugged. "Maybe our bleeder didn't like the selection Miss Waite was playing, you know?"

He snarked at his own humor, and Hawke stared at him for a moment, as if actually considering what he'd said.

"For heaven's sake, I was joking, Rick. What's running amok in that head of yours?"

Hawke rubbed his chin. "Haven't figured it out yet, Dov, but let's recap, shall we? What do we know for certain?"

"Uh, we know someone was inside this church when Mary Alice died—an unknown individual, 'the bleeder.' We *assume* that someone was up here before Mary Alice arrived, and we figure that someone was hiding in that niche over there. Since she left the organ and lamp on and her music out, we think the person in the cubby startled or threatened her, after which Mary Alice fell down the stairs."

"Correct. Now, what *don't* we know with certainty?"

"We don't know if Mary Alice fell while running from our bleeder or if the bleeder pushed her."

"In other words, even with our assumptions, we can't tell if we have a homicide or an unfortunate accident."

"Yeah. That about sums it up."

"Not quite. We don't understand the blood part, and it has to mean something, something connected to Mary Alice's death." Hawke sank into his own thoughts, picking away at something he wasn't able to dig out.

Yet. Haven't dug it out yet.

Finally, he glanced at his watch. "Come on, Dov. We'll ask the crime techs to fingerprint the loft, then head back to Homicide and write up our notes. After that I'd like to salvage at least a few hours of this Sunday."

CHAPTER 4

MONDAY, OCTOBER 2

HE WALKED AWAY from the bus station, and moved deeper into the downtown area, searching for the boarding house where, they said, he had a reservation. He had practically nothing to his name, only the little money they'd given him, maybe enough for a week's rent, plus the clothes he wore including the light jacket on his back. He desperately wanted to get out of the weather and find a warm place to sleep.

They had promised him a job too, although it might be part-time at first. They told him to show up early tomorrow and prove himself willing to work hard. As the biting wind tore at him, he hunched down inside the jacket and wrapped his arms around his chest—for all the good it did.

She took my life, took it all! Took everything I sweated and slaved for. Took it and disappeared. She thinks I won't find her, but I already have. I have connections, and they traced her for me. She's right here, in this filthy city. I will find her soon enough. And when I do? I will dish out to her everything she's earned.

It was a familiar refrain. He'd muttered it under his breath, had lain awake in the dark and said it aloud, let it run rampant in his head for years.

She lives in this town, but they didn't know that when they gave me a bus ticket here. I need time to get settled and situated. Then I'll scope out her routine. Pay her a little visit when she least expects it.

He squinted at the street sign on the corner. Pulled the address out of his pocket. Searched down the street and spotted the blinking vacancy sign.

He sighed with relief when the landlady showed him his room. "Nice," he muttered, feeling warmth radiating from the wall heater. The room had a hotplate too. Good.

He shelled out a week's rent, all the money he had except for ten dollars. *Man's gotta eat. Ain't no chow line here.*

"Today is Monday. That mean's your rent is due every Monday no later than noon, and I do *not* take excuses," the old battleaxe said. "If you haven't paid on time, you're out. Plain and simple."

"Sure, sure," he agreed. He just wanted her gone so he could get under a hot shower to warm up. Then he could lie down to sleep.

"GOOD MORNING, ALL. I'm Sharon Richmond and this is *Morning Line*, the city's first choice for news, weather, and traffic. International headlines this a.m. cover widespread flooding in northern India and another outbreak of rioting in Soweto. Local headlines include the FBI capture of a terrorist wanted by Interpol in connection with several suspected Islamic bombings. Also? A bizarre death on the city's crime-ridden south end.

"*Morning Line's* guests this day include Shane Corning, wildly acclaimed star of Broadway's newest hit show, *The Edge*, and Dr. Grace Warner, a practicing physician and psychiatrist making her mark in the fields of otolaryngology and family therapy for the hearing impaired.

"But first, with today's top local stories, here's Bradley Dennison. Bradley?"

The tanned face of the blond veteran newscaster filled the screen. "Thanks, Sharon. Two altar boys at St. Joseph's Episcopal Church, Atlas and Marchand South, received a terrible shock when they arrived prior to Sunday morning service and discovered the body of St. Joseph's longtime organist, Mary Alice Waite, age 44, at the bottom of the staircase leading to the choir loft. It is believed that Miss Waite had been in the loft Saturday afternoon practicing music for Sunday service, as was her habit and, at some point, fell down the staircase to her death.

"So, what is giving the police pause? According to a source wishing to remain anonymous, a person or persons unknown to the police *rearranged* Miss Waite's body after she fell, leaving her on her back in respectful repose. Then the unidentified party subsequently dripped or poured *a significant amount of blood* directly onto Miss Waite's face.

"Since the ME insists Miss Waite was deceased immediately prior to the blood being applied to her face, and given Miss Waite had no bleeding wounds, this strange twist indicates that Miss Waite was not alone when she perished and has left the police asking three questions: Whose blood, why the bizarre ceremony, and did Miss Waite fall to her death . . . or was she pushed?"

Dennison looked into the camera. "The medical examiner has yet to publish her findings, but our source tells us that, given the blood ritual, 'death by accident' must be ruled out. More on this curious story as it develops.

"Meanwhile, Ibrahim Azize, the suspected Islamic terrorist captured by the FBI last Sunday, was arraigned in court . . ."

Grace unconsciously sighed as the newscaster finished his report on the strange and as-yet unresolved death of St. Joseph's organist. The makeup woman bending over her glanced at the monitor and nodded her agreement.

"I've worked in the news environment for two decades, hon, so you might think I've seen it all, right? Nope. Turns out, people are plain *weird* and getting weirder by the day. Why, on any given day, something stranger than the previous 'strangest thing' crops up. Believe me when I say we'll probably never run out of weird people making even weirder news."

The woman swiveled the chair so both she and Grace could scrutinize her work in the mirror opposite her station. "Color is good. A bit more on the lips, I think." Back around again. "Look up, please."

Grace tilted her head up and parted her lips slightly. She fixed her green-gold eyes on the woman's smock but her thoughts were focused on the up-coming interview.

"Keep in mind, Gracie," Dr. Bill had advised last evening, "you have only a few minutes on these talk shows. Your goal is to leave a positive impression, not lecture the audience."

She nodded her head as she recalled his words.

"Steady, please." The makeup woman added a last touch and backed away. "Okay, that does it, Doctor. You look great, but may I offer a suggestion? If I had hair half as luscious as yours, I'd flaunt it, you know? Something less severe? If it's important to present yourself as a doctor, wear a white coat and carry a stethoscope. In my humble opinion, you're too young to wear your hair pinned up behind your head."

Grace glanced in the mirror as she stood up. Her nearly black hair was swept into glistening perfection off her high forehead and over her ears, then coiled and pinned at the nape of her slender neck. But too severe? Grace already knew that.

I'm twenty-nine, but I still spend half my time trying to convince people that I'm old enough to be a doctor.

She was escorted to the green room where she shuffled through her notes and kept a cursory watch on the program's progress. The monitor showed Sharon Richmond conversing intimately with a handsome actor. The volume was down; nonetheless, his charisma and charm emanated from the screen. Sharon, exuding familiarity, leaned her lithe body toward his.

Grace shook her head and tried to calm the surge of nervousness that numbed her lips. She hoped her words wouldn't falter or crack under the tension.

I cannot compete with that kind of charisma. I am out of my depth on a show like this. Lord, please help me!

The green room door shot open and the stage manager swept in, a young man whose frizzy blond hair receded from his forehead. He approached Grace, projecting boundless enthusiasm.

"Dr. Warner? Why, don't you look wonderful! Listen, I'd like to get you onto the set now. You don't know how absolutely excited we are about your segment today—terrific people angle, know what I mean? Our audience will rave over it. Lovely dress too."

He ran his eyes down her in a knowing, practiced manner. Grace felt a nervous giggle rise in her throat and swallowed hard.

"Yes, just perfect," he purred, steering her onto the set. "And here's your seat. Dave will get you wired up. Oh, Dave? Yes, this is Dr. Warner. Beautiful, isn't she?" he gushed.

Grace blushed and licked her lips, but Dave appeared bored to death as he attached and adjusted her microphone.

"Now Doctor, you relax and look right into Camera B as Sharon prompts you. Be perfectly natural. You'll be great, really!"

The frizzy stage manager then left her alone on the set under the harsh lights. Technicians moved outside the perimeter of the cameras. A moment later, Sharon Richmond, suave and entirely at ease, strode to her seat, shook Grace's hand and sat down.

The interview commenced immediately.

"I'd like to introduce Dr. Grace Warner, Chief Operating Officer of the Upton-Warner Clinic, renowned for its excellent work in hearing disorders and, more recently, in family therapy for those with hearing loss and their families. Dr. Warner, welcome to our show today. I must say, I'm intrigued by your clinic. I have never heard of a clinic that approaches both hearing impairment and its impact on family dynamics. Can you tell us more?"

Grace smiled and relaxed. "Thank you for asking about us, Sharon. Upton-Warner owes its genesis and success to my father, Glen Warner, and his partner and my mentor, Bill Upton. My father died some years ago, leaving Bill to carry the clinic's torch alone. I say alone, because I was in high school at the time. Eventually, I graduated med school and completed my residency in otolaryngology—that is, a specialization in disorders of ear, nose, and throat or ENT—and joined Upton-Warner's practice.

"I am here today to talk about what Dr. Upton and I see as the future of Upton-Warner. Our clinic, in addition to serving the medical needs of the hearing-impaired community, also recognizes that many individuals in that community struggle with the ongoing mental, emotional, and social challenges of hearing loss. And whatever the individual struggles with, their families do also. Upton-Warner's family therapy services provide support and coping strategies for both the individual and their family."

Sharon sat back. "Wonderful! Please continue?"

The trepidation slipped off Grace as she launched into an account of her work. "Thank you. As of today, Upton-Warner employs three physicians specializing in otolaryngology and hearing disorders, two audiologists, two speech therapists, an allergy specialist, and two family therapists—including myself.

"You see, to further our family therapy services, I returned to school and completed a second specialization, this one in psychiatry. I spend half my working time seeing patients with structural hearing disorders and performing related surgeries. The other half of my time, I direct the family therapy side of our clinic."

Sharon leaned toward Grace in much the same way she had with the famous actor earlier in the broadcast, and Grace experienced a sudden frisson of foreboding.

"Dr. Warner, during our phone conversation earlier this week, you revealed your fascination with a fairly new term in psychiatry, *psychopathy*. I must tell you how interested I am in your explanation of this term and its treatment. Would you care to expand on this field?"

Grace blanched. *What in the world!* The newscaster's off-topic question threatened to derail the whole purpose of Grace's interview.

Well, I am not going to allow that.

Firming up her tone, Grace answered, "*Sharon*, Upton-Warner conducts individual and family therapy for those coping with hearing impairment, *not* psychopathy. I would prefer to discuss the ways in which our clinic is helping the hearing-impaired community in our city and state."

Grace thought her attempt to pull their conversation back on track would work, but it didn't even slow Sharon down.

She kept on as if Grace hadn't spoken.

"Dr. Warner, I believe you told me how, early on in the field, psychopathy was termed 'sociopathic personality disturbance,' and that more recently its definition was changed to 'antisocial personality disorder,' then shortened to simply 'personality disorder.' You said, and I quote, 'Key traits of a personality disorder are lack of empathy, low impulse control, manipulative and deceitful behaviors, and it also shares characteristics with narcissism.'"

"None of this applies to—"

Sharon bulldozed ahead. "Dr. Warner, you also said, and again, I quote, 'Persons exhibiting the traits of psychopathy often have *criminal tendencies*.' Thus, what interests me most is how psychopathy intersects with criminology and applies to police work."

"But that's not—"

"For example, just four years ago, the FBI opened its National Center for the Analysis of Violent Crime, a specialist department within the Bureau. A year later, this new department added what is called the Behavioral Analysis Unit, specialized criminologists who use behavioral analysts to assist in their criminal investigations. These criminologists are also known as 'profilers.' Tell me, would you characterize yourself as a profiler?"

"Would I what?" Grace dropped the notes into her lap and folded her hands, her fingers gripped tight. "No, Miss Richmond, I would not. While I likely share similar training with FBI profilers, and while it *is* necessary for therapists to accurately diagnose their patients, I don't consult with law enforcement—"

"But could you do so if requested? I ask because earlier in our broadcast we reported on the curious and worrisome death of Mary Alice Waite, right here in our city. She died as a result of a fall down the stairs in her church, yet the police cannot say whether she fell or was pushed. That said, someone else, *someone unknown*, had to have been with Miss Waite when she died or just after, because this unidentified individual poured blood on Miss Waite's face."

Grace gaped at the information, and Sharon leaned toward her. "How would *you*, as a psychiatrist, interpret this bizarre ritual, and what sort of individual would do such a thing?"

Grace sat up taller. "As I said, I do not consult with the police or—"

"I am asking your professional opinion, Dr. Warner."

Grace lifted her chin. "Miss Richmond, I cannot make a diagnosis without direct observation and interaction with a patient; furthermore, I would be remiss to even discuss the possibilities."

She hesitated, momentarily caught up in the details of the case. "I *can* say that the application of blood has significance in the history of every human culture. Thus, one could speculate that whoever applied the blood to the deceased did so with personal or cultural significance in mind."

"This significance you speak of, would it or would it not project malice toward the deceased?"

Grace, upset with herself for getting sucked into Richmond's salacious agenda, shook her head. "Let me repeat myself and be clear: It would be impossible and irresponsible to attempt such a conclusion without further information."

Richmond smirked over her partial success. "Thank you, Dr. Warner. And now a word from our sponsor."

As the bright lights around Grace died, a young Asian woman directed her off the set.

"Hi, I'm May Miller, Sharon's assistant. Thank you again for appearing on *Morning Line*." The young woman left Grace at the studio exit and walked away.

Grace left the building and moved toward her car on automatic pilot. Inside, she trembled with self-loathing. *Why did I add that bit about personal or cultural significance? It opened me up to Sharon's follow-on question. Oh, Bill! You would never have made such a mistake. Why did you insist on sending me to do this interview?*

～

TERRY WAS DREAMING, the quiet so tangible that he smiled in his sleep. Peace! For long, refreshing hours he'd slept without torment. As the dream began to fade, he realized he was waking up, but he didn't mind because his head was so wonderfully quiet.

He opened his eyes and slid from his bed. *Quiet!* He reveled in it. When he stood, however, his arm began to ache where he'd cut it. He could feel his pulse pounding in the slashes across the inside of his forearm, and he experienced a touch of apprehension. Terry went directly to the little bathroom in his corner of the basement to look at his arm.

When he'd returned home last night, he pulled out his mother's meager first aid kit and her sewing basket and set them on the kitchen table. He soaked one of his mother's needles and some black thread in a small dish of alcohol. Then, as awkward and painful as the task had been, he'd stitched the two cuts together as best he could, swabbed the wounds with more stinging alcohol afterward, and finished off the job using the gauze and tape he had on hand.

I need more supplies, he realized. *Need them today.*

He was concerned about infection. The cuts had been so deep! He hissed as he pulled up his pajama sleeve and unwrapped the gauze he'd wound around and around his arm. As he feared, the underlying pads were soiled, the cuts oozing through the pads—and oh how his arm ached! He took a bottle from the medicine cabinet, shook out two aspirin, and dry-swallowed them. Rewrapped the soiled pads on his arm.

Must go to a drug store this morning.

At least the quiet remained. Smiling, he returned to the kitchen. He flicked on the black-and-white television and glanced absently at the ticker-tape headlines scrolling across the screen while making oatmeal on the hotplate. Always news and flashy talk shows in the morning. He liked cartoons better. Old, familiar reruns too. He hated the "soaps" with their infighting, backbiting, and—he jerked his thoughts away from their dangerous shift and turned back to the TV.

He was putting bread into the toaster when the anchorwoman handed off the news to the male reporter. A moment later, he blinked in surprise at the closed captioning at the bottom of the screen. The male newscaster was reporting on the death of St. Joseph's organist! Her name had been Mary Alice? Terry hadn't known her name until now. His interest piqued, he waited to see if more on Mary Alice's death would appear.

He poured his oatmeal into a bowl, buttered and bit into his toast. Sighed. He was so relaxed!

The newscaster finished, and the camera returned to Sharon Richmond who began to interview a woman, some kind of doctor. She looked quite young and licked her lips.

Self-conscious, Terry thought. *Nervous.*

The doctor was talking about some kind of family therapy—Terry didn't understand what family therapy was—when Sharon Richmond interrupted her. She leaned toward the doctor. The captions always lagged behind the actual conversation, so Terry saw the doctor's discomfort before the words on the screen told him why.

"Would you characterize yourself as a profiler?"

Profiler?

Terry leaned in and followed the scrolling captions. Saw the doctor drop her notes into her lap and clench her hands together. She was still speaking when Richmond interrupted her.

Why, that Richmond woman is asking about Mary Alice . . .

And by association, about *him.*

"How would you, as a psychiatrist, interpret this bizarre ritual, and what sort of individual would do such a thing?"

Bizarre ritual? What is a ritual? Terry leaned closer, not wanting to miss anything interesting as the captions crawled across the screen.

The doctor answered, "As I said, I don't consult with the police or—"

"I'm asking your professional opinion, Dr. Warner."

Here, the doctor showed some spine and pushed back. Terry nodded his approval. He didn't like bullies either. He'd had his fill of them in school.

"Miss Richmond, I cannot make a diagnosis without direct observation and interaction with a patient; furthermore, I would be remiss to even discuss one."

She paused, momentarily caught up in the details of the case. "I *can* say that the application of blood has significance in the history of every human culture. Thus, one could speculate that whoever applied the blood to the deceased did so with personal or cultural significance in mind."

Part of the sentence flew over Terry's head, but he knew the word "significance." Sort of.

She's saying that what I did with the blood had meaning. He thought for a moment. *I think she's right, even if I don't really get it.*

If he had paid for Mary Alice's death, why did he still feel guilty for frightening the woman and causing her to fall down the stairs?

He returned his attention to the screen as Richmond spoke and the captions followed, "This significance you speak of, would it or would it not project malice toward the deceased?"

The doctor sat back, clearly frustrated. "Let me be clear: It would be impossible and irresponsible to attempt such a conclusion without further information."

Malice toward the deceased? Terry knew deceased meant dead. He did not know the other word, malice. He hadn't finished school, but he could read, although lots of words eluded him. Writing was harder because spelling did not come easily to him.

One of his clueless teachers had told him to *sound out the words*. When Terry rolled his eyes in sullen disdain, the woman had rapped his head with her knuckles.

Cursing that teacher under his breath, Terry reached for the thick book he kept on his table and looked for the letter "M." He ran his finger painstakingly down the pages and found the word he was seeking.

He sat back, appalled. *A desire to cause pain, injury, or distress to another.* Deeply troubled, he shoved back his chair and stood. Stared across the room, eyes unfocused. *Malice means you hate someone, doesn't it? But I didn't hate Mary Alice, and I didn't mean to hurt her!*

A prick of pain brought his hand to his forehead. The whine slowly rose in volume, and a thrust of fear set him pacing up and down the small room.

Demand whispered to him, *They have no right to judge you. They are unfit to understand your feelings for the woman and her unfortunate demise.*

Demand drew closer and spoke clearly. *You must tell them.*

Terry stopped pacing. He tried to recall some of the words he'd read on the screen during the interview. When they came to him, he scrawled them on the tablet he kept by his dictionary. It was not enough, though. How would he get the rest?

The house had an old phone mounted on the kitchen wall upstairs, but it hadn't worked for years. Then he remembered the heavy book someone dropped on his front porch every year. He didn't know where the book came from, but he dutifully threw out the old one his mother kept in a kitchen drawer and replaced it with the new one.

Would it help?

He took the stairs two at a time to find out.

DOV SWITCHED ON the division's television and ran through the available stations, settling on *Morning Line* and Sharon Richmond's assured expression as she passed the news over to Bradley Dennison.

Dov turned up the volume. "Here we go, Rick."

Hawke's desk was set in the corner farthest from the elevator, apart from the other cubicles that were lined up, cheek by jowl, in multiple rows across the division floor. The corner wasn't much of an improvement over the other cubicles on space or privacy; it was more a stab at giving the department's senior detective the privilege to concentrate with fewer noises and interruptions—not, in actuality, an advantage to be sniffed at, given the busy floor's acoustics.

As Hawke sauntered to the television, a soft smile touched Dov's lips. After more than three years as Rick Hawke's partner, he believed the man to be the consummate detective with more brains, intuition, and dedication than anyone he knew. He was a good friend too, even if they didn't share the same worldview and often butted heads in that arena.

Hawke was tall and imposing, with a head of unruly brown hair. Of course, those weren't the features people recalled from their first encounter with Hawke. It was his typically impassive expression along with the deep crease scribed across the bridge of his nose and below his left eye that snagged and fixed their attention, not his hair, height, or soft brown eyes.

The scar, which predated Dov by close to a year, had finally lost its glaring redness. Dov hadn't known Hawke's former partner, Steve, still didn't know all the details of the guy's death. The only thing Rick ever said was that he was grateful to have survived. By rights, he added once, he shouldn't have.

All that aside, the tire iron that split his face that fateful night had left him with a fearsome expression. And on occasion, Rick would joke that while his face scared little kids, it scared some adults too—and in their line of work, "scary" could be useful.

Dov laughed to himself. Rick played a pretty awesome 'mean cop,' and didn't even break a sweat.

The other detectives in the division regarded Hawke with varying degrees of cautious admiration. Opinionated and ruthlessly tenacious to the point of obsession, Hawke was difficult to work with. Most of his coworkers admired his devotion to the job; at the same time, some felt insecure because they refused to put in the long hours he regularly did.

"Fact is," they rationalized around the water cooler, "Hawke doesn't have a wife or a family. He can afford to be married to the job, whereas we have actual lives and responsibilities off-shift."

On the other side of the same coin, not one of Hawke's coworkers would want to find themselves the hunted suspect of an investigation he led. Also on the flip side? Those same coworkers would, in a heartbeat, pick Hawke to back them up in a tight spot.

Bradley Dennison concluded his summary of Mary Alice Waite's death. "Since the ME insists Miss Waite was deceased immediately prior to the blood being applied to her face, and given Miss Waite had no bleeding wounds, this strange twist indicates that Miss Waite was not alone when she perished and has left the police asking three questions: Whose blood, why the bizarre ceremony, and did Miss Waite fall to her death . . . or was she pushed? The medical examiner has yet to publish her findings, but our source tells us that, given the blood ritual, 'death by accident' must be ruled out. More on this curious story as it develops."

Dov gaped. "Hey! We didn't release any info about the blood!"

Hawke scowled at the screen. "Meddling journalist. He just told the world, including our bleeder, that we haven't a clue who he is or what his intentions were."

"Someone from the ME's office or one of the patrolmen from the scene had to have blabbed," Dov said. "Any chance we can figure out who?"

"Unlikely," Hawke growled. "Too many possibilities."

Dov eyed his partner. He knew how tired Hawke was, how hard he'd driven himself to investigate his CI's intel. He knew that Hawke struggled with black moods at times, and while work was Hawke's usual panacea, extreme fatigue made him more prone to those spells.

Dov cleared his throat. "McCormick wants our report by noon. I don't see any problem finishing it up by then." It was a temporizing statement, intended to engage his partner. Draw him out.

Hawke didn't even hear him.

HAWKE TURNED INWARD. He was thirty-eight years old, in the prime of a demanding but personally satisfying career. The academy, hard work, and years of volunteer overtime in a squad car plus intense study and exams had gotten him kicked up to Homicide, which had been Hawke's goal.

Sure, he'd pushed hard. He'd worked every kind of dirty job that came down the pipe, too, and asked for more. Why? Because he enjoyed the challenge. Over the years a reputation had attached itself to him, and now the chief regularly assigned him the sticky, high-visibility cases for which he'd proved himself best suited.

In fact, Hawke consistently turned down promotions that would take him away from the action. The reason was simple: The action is what he craved.

To most people, Rick Hawke seemed a satisfied, self-contained man. He knew better. And, as much as he didn't want to admit it to himself, he knew he was tired. *Been burning the candle at both ends for too long.*

When he glanced up, Sharon Richmond was interviewing a woman doctor. Dov reached the knob to turn it off just as Sharon sprang her loaded question on the unprepared doctor. Hawke pivoted toward the screen.

"Hold up. I want to see this."

He and Dov watched the rest of the interview, which ended with Richmond's question, "This significance you speak of, would it or would it not project malice toward the deceased?"

The doctor, tamping down her temper, shook her head. "Let me repeat myself and be clear: It would be impossible and irresponsible to attempt such a conclusion without further information."

"Interesting, huh?" Dov asked.

"Perhaps."

GRACE'S TAXI DROPPED her at the main entrance of the ten-story Physician's Annex opposite City View Hospital. She glanced up at the sky bridge that linked the two buildings at their fifth floors.

Lord, is it wrong of me to wish I could be as high above the responsibilities weighing on me as those people are above the expressway below them?

She received no answer, so she took the elevator to the seventh-floor suite Upton-Warner occupied and went straight to the offices she shared with Bill Upton.

The receptionist, whose office was sandwiched between the two doctors, slid Grace a look of wry sympathy. "He's expecting you."

"Thank you, Linda."

Grace closed Bill's office door and plopped into her usual chair. "It was awful, Bill. One shot at a really big break for the clinic, me praying I wouldn't screw up, happy and relieved the interview was going well, and then *that woman* ambushes me."

She was too upset to keep her seat. She swept across the width of Bill's carpeted office and back, close to tears. "You know, I have to hand it to Sharon Richmond; she truly is the consummate 'journalist.' I'm pretty sure she'd expound on air while watching her own mother drown: 'Mom, can you share with our viewers how drowning makes you feel?' And after Mommy Dearest has gone down for the third time, she'd turn to her viewers with a regretful sigh and close with, 'As difficult as that scene may have been to watch, please know that we here at *Morning Line* are committed to bringing you *all* the breaking news!'" She scowled. "That harpy is nothing more than a self-seeking opportunist."

Grace presumed Bill wouldn't answer right away. He'd known Grace all her life and probably realized it was better to let her blow off steam before he spoke. He tapped the ash from his pipe and smiled in sympathy.

She recognized that long-suffering expression. "I'm sorry, Bill. I shouldn't have dumped on you like this."

"It's all right, Gracie. It's why you keep this old man around."

"Just try *not* being 'kept around' and see how fast this clinic unravels, you old bear."

Grace stepped around his desk and planted a kiss on his thinning hair. She dropped her hand to his shoulder, and he patted it.

"Just so. Which puts me in a position to remind you of the raft of patients waiting to see you after lunch, so I suggest you pull yourself together. And Grace, a word to the wise about this morning? You did the best you could, given how you were ambushed. That said, we don't want to blow this incident out of proportion, especially in light of the fine, tight job you managed to jimmy into the interview."

"Was it good enough? Will it help the clinic . . . or will it hurt us?"

"Frankly, if I had hearing issues, I would call Upton-Warner today. The other? The way Richmond twisted your specialty interests to suit her penchant for the dramatic?"

"It was vile of her."

He stroked her hand gently. "Yes, I must agree, but you held your own against a pro—and pretty well, if I do say so."

Grace sighed. "Thank you, Bill."

She left Bill's office feeling a little better. She walked past Linda into her own office, selected a bottle of cold water from her refrigerator, pulled the combs out of her hair, and massaged her temples where the tension seemed tightest. Her dark hair swung down to her shoulders and waved naturally. Slumping into the corner of her office couch, she stared at the portrait hanging behind her desk. The faces of her parents stared back.

"Hello, Mom and Dad. I sure wish you were still here."

"Dr. Drake on line 1, Dr. Warner," Linda announced via the intercom.

Grace picked up the extension. "Yes, Willard?"

"Tough interview, but you did well, given the situation. Lunch? I have a shoulder available, should you need a good cry."

"Not today, but thanks for the offer."

Willard Drake was okay in small doses, but she wasn't convinced the man possessed any topics of conversation beyond his work and the state of the clinic. Even after seeing each other on a casual basis for six months, Grace felt no deepening affection for the man, nothing other than a growing surety that they were better suited as colleagues rather than anything approaching romance. She hoped Willard would figure out the same.

Just then, Grace recalled the release form she'd signed at *Morning Line*. It allowed them to rebroadcast any part of her interview at their discretion. She exhaled a cleansing breath, sat down at her desk, and told herself the hard, cold truth: No one had pried open her mouth. In the course of *two sentences*, she'd screwed up. Plain and simple.

If they rebroadcast that interview, it's on me . . . and I should have known better than to take Sharon Richmond's bait.

CHAPTER 5

HE'D RAMBLED MOST of the day, threading his way through the crush of walkers, going nowhere in particular, always alone and never "seen." Staying on the move was how he kept the pain at bay, but it never worked entirely and not for long. Nothing did.

Even the joy he'd experienced at St. Joseph's, listening to the organ the past two weeks, would fade under the raucous pain. He could hear it now, far away, making its way into his head, slowly ramping up.

He wound down an alleyway, clenching the folded blade in the palm of his hand. In this neighborhood, he never knew when he might experience an unpleasant encounter, and he felt safer with the knife's cold weight in readiness. If only his wits weren't dulled by the constant jangle inside!

He rarely experienced *good* emotions, nice ones that made him smile. The exception was when something reminded him of Sara and the soft, wispy feelings he'd had for her. She had been kind and sweet to him. Not in a man and woman kind of way—he'd only been ten years old, after all, and she several years older than him. But she'd been generous, had let him come and listen while she played, as though she understood what it meant to him to be welcomed. For whatever reason, her kindnesses had touched something vital down deep inside of him, a place that was now numb.

He recalled with a sigh the whooshing song of the pipes at St. Joseph's. The pipe organ had made him remember and mourn for Sara even though she was long dead.

Dead . . . and he had killed her.

Terry hung his head and wept until the frosty voice of *Demand* interrupted his grief.

The pipes at St. Joseph's are not the only pipes in the city.

Terry's spirits lifted. Brightened. *The city has other organs?*

If you look, you will find them.

He nodded in eager agreement. *Yes. I should look.*

GRACE WAS UNACCUSTOMED to having a free morning . . . and she didn't much like it. Frowning, she stood behind her desk, sorting a stack of mail.

Junk, not junk. Magazine. More junk. Junk . . . not junk? She picked up an odd envelope and studied it. The envelope's paper was yellowed with age. The address on the envelope, written in a childish hand, puzzled her.

Lady doctor
Uptown Warner
1672 Plainview Bulvard

No specific addressee and three spelling errors. City, state, and zip code missing. No return address.

"It's a wonder the post office delivered this," she said aloud.

She slid the tip of her letter opener under the envelope's seal and removed a sheet of what looked like Big Chief tablet paper.

"Goodness, haven't seen paper like this since grade school."

She scanned the words scrawled across the sheet, and her heart skipped a beat. Scarcely breathing, she muttered, "Is this what I think it is?"

She grabbed her telephone book, found a possible number, hoped whoever answered could forward her call or at least point her to the right person, and dialed. After muddling her way through several city police departments, she was finally connected to the right place.

"Homicide Division. Detective Nelson speaking."

"Good morning. I would like to speak to the detectives in charge of the . . ." She was speaking to a homicide detective, but she wasn't sure how to characterize Mary Alice Waite's demise.

"Investigating the death of Mary Alice Waite?"

"Yup. Hold, please." She heard a muffled Detective Nelson shout, "Hawke! Call for you. Line 2."

A brisk voice picked up. "Detective Sergeant Hawke."

"Um, good morning, Detective Hawke. My name is Grace Warner. This morning I received a letter—a note actually—that I believe pertains to the death of Mary Alice Waite. I would like to bring it to you, if I may."

"Absolutely. How soon can you be here?"

She smiled, suddenly glad of the morning's cancelations. "Within the hour. I'll leave shortly."

"We're on the fourth floor. We'll be expecting you."

HAWKE IMMEDIATELY RECOGNIZED the woman the desk clerk pointed toward his desk: the doctor from Sharon Richmond's *Morning Line* show. She was medium height with thick, dark hair pulled back into a fashionable chignon, carrying a briefcase. She was also younger than he'd expected. Surely too young to have completed med school plus the additional years of training necessary to hang out a second shingle as a clinical psychiatrist?

"Dov, our visitor's here."

Dov joined him. "Hey. Isn't she—"

"Yup."

As their visitor approached, he asked, "Dr. Warner? I'm Detective Sergeant Hawke. This is my partner, Detective Mayer. Thank you for coming down."

Her brows lifted. "I don't believe I told you I was a physician when I called."

"Practicing physician and psychiatrist. Medical license first, trained psychiatrist second, with a focus on personality disorder, I believe? We saw your interview on *Morning Line*."

His disarming smile, the one he used when addressing the public, was accompanied by his left eye's annoying tick. It was caused by residual nerve damage . . . or so he'd been told.

Her gaze passed over his face, pausing only momentarily. "I see."

"Let's chat in our conference room, shall we?"

Once they were seated, he asked, "You said you received a letter regarding the death of Mary Alice Waite?"

She placed her briefcase on the table and withdrew a manila file folder. Passed it across to him.

Dov scooted toward Hawke as he opened the folder. The folder's contents, both the single sheet of paper from a kid's writing tablet and the envelope it had arrived in, had been placed inside clear plastic carriers.

Hawke was mildly impressed with the care Warner had taken to preserve the evidence. The scant content of the note interested him too.

> I dint meen to
> skare her

"Huh. What do you make of this, Dov?"

Dov slid his eyes toward his partner. "A kid?"

"Maybe." Hawke glanced across the table. "What do you think? Written by a child?"

She shook her head. "I don't think so."

"Mentally challenged, perhaps?"

She weighed her words before she answered. "Arrested development is a possibility, but certainly written by someone with enough self-awareness to take responsibility for his part in the woman's fall . . . and enough sense of right and wrong to confess to what happened. In my opinion, the author is neither a child nor a mentally challenged individual but something else."

"Why? What's your reasoning?"

"My reasoning comes down to the matter of the . . . blood ritual." A shudder rippled through her body.

"You called it a blood ritual. Does that mean you know what the blood on the deceased woman's face signifies?"

She sighed and didn't answer immediately. When she did, she said softly, "If I were to offer you my professional opinion, we should agree first that I am not a trained profiler."

"You made that clear during your interview—not that it mattered a whit to Sharon Richmond."

She huffed. "Noticed that, did you?"

Hawke found himself grinning. "I am a dee-*tec*-tive, after all, Dr. Warner. Got the badge and junior decoder ring to prove it. On the other hand, Sharon Richmond is about as subtle as a tax audit. And we agree to your condition."

She grimaced and asked, "Do you . . . have photos of the scene?"

"I'll grab them, Rick." Dov quick walked to the door, leaving Hawke and the doctor alone.

The woman studied her hands; Hawke, intrigued, studied her.

"I want to thank you again for bringing this note to us, Dr. Warner."

"Of course."

After a long silence between Hawke and the doctor, Dov returned. He placed two photographs in front of Warner. She glanced at them, swallowed several times, then picked them up one at a time and studied them more closely.

Hawke waited a full minute before asking, "Any idea what the blood is about?"

She glanced up. "Please repeat your question?"

"Any idea what the blood is about?"

"The ritual's purpose, you mean? Not the slightest. However, if I were to comment on the source of the blood, I'd say the individual cut his forearm and allowed the blood to run onto the woman's face. It's quite a lot of blood, in fact, so the cuts had to have been fairly deep. Frankly, I doubt that *a child* or someone with diminished mental capacity would be capable of cutting himself that deeply, nor would they have formed a purpose for dribbling the blood onto the woman's face."

"So, you think an adult did it?" He watched her as he spoke because her eyes were fixed on him.

She replied, "Most likely a socially stunted adult with a patchy education."

Hawke picked up the plastic carrier and studied the envelope. "The writing is pretty juvenile."

"I'd say elementary school age," she was quick to reply. "Contrarywise, the note's *content* says the author is older. A child of, say, nine or ten might experience regret but would lack the sense of accountability of a young adult."

"Explain, please?"

"As I said, a child of nine or ten might experience guilt or remorse, but a child that age likely lacks the sophistication necessary to write a note of explanation or apology unless prompted to by a teacher or parent. Also, while the note expresses regret for scaring the woman, it also says it was not his *intention* to scare her or cause the fall."

"No malicious intent, then."

"I should think he was rather horrified when she fell."

Hawke said softly, "And here you told Sharon Richmond you don't profile or consult with the police."

She blushed. "My profession may give me something of an advantage over most people, Detective, but I do not have the specialized training of a behavioral analyst. I would be hard pressed to work up a profile on this individual. I merely felt it my duty to bring this note to you."

Hawke smiled. "Your professional 'advantage' could be just the leg up we need, Dr. Warner, and would it be such a bad thing for you to provide us with your insights? Who knows? You might point us in the right direction."

He was mildly surprised when she smiled back. Tentatively.

"If . . . *if* you find yourself needing my opinion, I might be amenable."

Two "ifs" and a "might," but Hawke would take them.

"Thank you, Dr. Warner. May we have your contact info? Then Dov will see you out."

HE FINALLY HAD a day off from his job, so he took a city bus to her neighborhood and got off half a mile from the address scrawled on the scrap of paper in his pocket. He sauntered on, nice and easy, and found her place without too much difficulty.

As he stared at the house standing at the address he'd been given, he felt like he'd been kicked in the gut. *Abandoned!* Doors and windows boarded up, missing roof shingles, the yard a neglected mess, and one side of the crackerbox structure gang tagged.

And I was worried about my shabby appearance? Afraid I might raise the concerns of her neighbors? Ain't nobody around here raising "concerns" about nothing, he sneered to himself.

Looking more closely at the general state of the housing development, he experienced a further stab of dismay. More houses than just hers had their doors and windows boarded up. Those that weren't boarded up were broken out. Every yard was overgrown with weeds. Trash and debris lay where the wind had scattered them.

Mass exodus. Nobody lives here anymore.

Maybe that wasn't entirely true. He counted three houses on the block that might be occupied. He walked to the closest occupied house and knocked.

The man who opened the door looked him up and down. "Don't have money or food to spare."

"Not looking for a handout," he answered easily. "Just want to know about the woman who lives in that house." He pointed and the man glanced that direction.

"Far's I know, no one lives there," he answered. "Most everybody 'round here moved out." The man shut his door and locked it with an audible click.

Keep trying. Somebody's got to know something.

His knock at the second house he tried wasn't answered. At the third house, far down the block, the woman who answered shrugged. "Last I knew, the lady who lived there was really sick. Didn't know her all that well though and haven't seen her in a coupla years. Figured she must of died."

He stared at her in disbelief. When she closed the door in his face, he turned away but his feet refused to move.

He was still in shock at finding the house where she had lived abandoned. Boarded up. A ruin. But what stung the worst were the words, *"Last I knew, the lady who lived there was really sick . . . Figured she must of died."*

No! She's supposed to be here!

His big celebratory plans, every nuanced minute of how he'd repay her and every degree of pleasure he'd extract from her, were instantly as dead as she was.

His immediate problem, what was most difficult to control in the moment, was his craving *need*. It hadn't gone away. Not in the slightest. Sure, he'd been forced to keep it under control for years. He'd used the detailed, intricate plans he'd constructed to keep it at bay, but his need had not diminished.

And now, with the news that *she was dead*, his need leapt into full flame. He gasped; it felt like he'd struck a match to a gas burner and couldn't find the shutoff valve.

The fire in his gut roared and refused to be denied.

He fantasized briefly about turning about and knocking again. The woman would come to the door a second time. He would smile to disarm her, ask for directions, and at that moment force his way inside.

Not in broad daylight, dummy; you're smarter than that.

No. He must stifle those thoughts.

For the time being.

CHAPTER 6

INSIDE AND OUT, the Claremont's fading beauty bore testimony to the grand gilded era during which she was built. Yes, without question, the theater stood as a proud, regal dowager of the period. Perhaps she was eking out her last years in thinly disguised shabbiness, but the old lady still boasted of one great, redeeming feature: an ornate, hand-crafted organ, one of the most respected on the east coast.

The majority of theater organs still in service were of lesser quality, either in the construction of the organ itself or in the inferior acoustical design of the building that housed it. The indifference was understandable, given that the principal usage of a theater and its organ during that era had been low-priced stock shows such as vaudeville, melodrama, minstrel, and so forth. Yes, a few theater owners, espousing the American adage, 'bigger is better,' had paid for overlarge organs, but the Claremont's idealistic architect had conceived a true concert hall built for and dominated by an organ to rival its European counterparts, most of which resided in churches.

The architect's peers considered him odd to aspire to such excellence for a mere stock theater. However, their sniffs of disdain did not discourage the Claremont's designer. His theater was built to his exact specifications: as high as wide, and its length two times its width. In addition, the theater's ceiling panels high above the floor were meticulously canted to maximize the theater's acoustic properties.

The organ's body occupied the theater's stage-right corner, but the pipes? Those jewels ascended in sized order, to the untrained eye like so many members of a gleaming and visually inspiring metallic choir. The central harmonic sub-bass pipes stretched their thirty-two vertical feet toward the ceiling, flanked by the sixteen-foot pedal pipe complement. The pipes of the great, swell, and solo manuals assumed their relative positions on either side of the massive pipes, rank upon rank and tier upon tier, commanding every eye.

The concert at the Claremont that evening was a benefit espoused by the city's society elite; the organist performing that night, Donaldo Menti, an acknowledged world-class artist. Accordingly, ticket prices were astronomically high, tax-deductible, and entirely sold out.

The ladies of the city's high society paid homage to the theater's onetime elegance by donning their priciest jewelry and sleekest furs. The gilded lobby provided the perfect stage for the women to flaunt their unabashed wealth and display their finery before open admiration or veiled envy. These paragons of sophistication floated to and from animated knots of acquaintances, while their gentlemen paraded the lobby and mezzanine levels in uniformly fine evening wear.

Society doyenne, Esther Grunbaum, was the sort of matronly leading figure whose impressive proportions mirrored her personality. She positively shimmered in ankle-length green lamé and, not unlike a wave of pulsating emerald Jell-O, she swooped and billowed through the lobby from guest to guest. Frothy, silver-white hair gathered high upon her head furthered the impression of an ocean whitecap, her ebb and flow towing societal flotsam whither she willed.

Esther was loved by those who knew her. Those unfamiliar with her determination to "do good" sometimes mistook her drive for arrogance or snobbery, but they were wrong. Esther was one of those women whose character was above reproach and whose husband, Arthur, knew she embodied the proverbial heart of gold. The strength of her character and influence had guided the social lives of a good part of the city's wealthy into productive veins for decades, and her close attention kept money flowing in the right direction, in particular toward her favorite charity.

A RETRACTED FIRE escape ladder and catwalk hung suspended from the theater's stage-left exterior wall over the alley. A second ladder led upward from the catwalk to a landing and a theater fire exit door. Inside, the fully draped exit opened onto the mezzanine between the lobby and the second-floor balcony.

Terry had already tested his route into the theater and made certain earlier that day—while the custodial crew left a stage door unwatched—that the curtained fire exit doorway on the mezzanine level would open from the outside tonight. The exit's latching mechanism, embedded in the door's narrow edge, was simple to tape open. His plan would work because the Claremont was in violation of several ordinances, including alarms that should blare—but did not—when fire exits were opened.

During a not-so-thorough security check later that day, a cursory glance at the visual position of the door's lock would tell security that the door could open only from the inside.

And after all, who would try to enter from the outside at that height?

Terry never considered such arrangements difficult. Whenever he needed something, by trial and error, he always found a way to achieve his ends. Like the door in the lobby vital to getting to his destination. He'd wandered into the theater yesterday morning while the cleaning crew was working and had, literally, "gummed up" the works: He'd closed the door with himself on the hallway side of the door, then shoved a wad of well-chewed gum into the deadbolt's receiver—enough gum that the bolt would catch on the edge of the receiver but not far enough that his thin blade couldn't nudge it back. He knew, because he'd locked and unlocked the door several times before leaving.

Most of the remaining day he spent restlessly trudging the unfamiliar downtown area. He was out of his own neighborhood and uncomfortable, but he persisted in making the unfamiliar area less so, should he need to disappear into it quickly. Occasionally he pulled the wadded newsprint from the pocket of his hooded jacket and reread the society section article about the concert. The article featured a large photo of the revered organ. The photo had caught his attention, and the organ in the photo made him sweat with hopeful anticipation.

Before dark, he took the bus across town to his house. On his bed he arranged an ancient tuxedo he'd found at Goodwill. He figured the suit, although threadbare, would pass muster. He washed in the sink and scrutinized the hollow reflection in the mirror as he shaved. He couldn't gaze at the reflection for long though, because he didn't recognize the person staring back at him. Abruptly, he changed his mind about washing his hair. Drying and combing it meant more time in front of the mirror, and the stranger staring out at him frightened him.

He dressed instead. The pants were loose, and he had to punch a new hole in the belt to hitch the pants up around his waist. The jacket was little better. Its sleeves left his wrists dangling by a couple of inches. He shrugged. The distance from the theater's mezzanine to the building's basement stairwell was not far and would put him under anyone's casual 'once-over' for only a few moments.

The ache in his arm gave him pause. The cuts were knitting, but his stitches had been amateurish and uneven. Several of them pulled painfully when he stretched his arm. He dry-swallowed two aspirin, and hoped he wouldn't tear the stitches too badly getting into the theater.

At 7:45, he approached the alley behind the theater with care. Security was always tight where rich people wore their wealth around their necks and dangling from their ears. The guards would have closed the theater in the early evening and done a complete sweep of the building from balconies to basement before stationing their men. That said, security's focus was to guard against possible thieves, not a simple concert crasher.

He crept down the alley alongside the theater, watching for security guards. When he was relatively certain the coast was clear, he climbed upon a dumpster, leapt up, and grabbed the first rung of the set of retracted fire stairs. They were, as he already knew, locked in place from above. His arm screamed as his weight stretched and tore the stitches holding his cuts closed. Motivated by the pain, he moved quickly, hand over hand, until he could set his feet upon the rungs of the retracted ladder. He climbed the rest of the way up to the catwalk, and then, more slowly, up the second ladder toward the mezzanine's fire escape door on this side of the building.

At fifteen minutes before the concert began, a slight breeze fluttered the heavy drape covering the mezzanine's fire exit. He emerged, blending into the press of people rushing to take their seats, threading his way confidently through the crowd, down the steps to the lobby and toward the corridor off which the basement stairwell could be found. A few disinterested glances were all he expected.

He hadn't planned on Esther Grunbaum.

TO ESTHER'S PRACTICED eye something about the young man's appearance was unacceptable. He moved alone down the stairs, against the upward flow of traffic, greeting no one, his face expressionless. Furthermore? He had *greasy hair*. Who attended a gala of this caliber with dirty, foul hair?

Smiling and nodding to her friends, her gaze followed him. As he reached the lobby, she noticed that his suit was crumpled and ill-fitting—not at all appropriate for an event of this stature. Fixated on the man, she frowned and lost track of the conversation. When, instead of entering the concert hall, the young man slipped through a lobby side door, she gasped.

That door led to the corridor by which one could approach the offices where the evening's box office take was being counted. The offices were supposed to be guarded but . . .

"Arthur!"

Art broke off mid-sentence and blinked at her interruption.

She pointed. "Arthur, I wish to you to fetch a security guard. Quickly! A young man who does not belong here just came down the stairs and has gone through that door toward the offices!"

Art obediently scouted out the nearest guard and turned to tell his wife he would fetch him, but Esther had never been the type to wait on another's actions. She had already sailed across the lobby before the door closed and gone through.

No one was going to steal from her kids!

She hurried down the corridor until she reached a junction. Ahead were large numbers of dressing rooms; to the right, lay the offices. Esther was nonplussed to hear soft footfalls down the hallway to the left, moving away from the offices.

Odd.

Frowning again, she followed the sounds and soon came to the corridor's end and a single doorway on the right. Opening the door cautiously, she saw a landing and peered down a dimly lit stairway.

To the basement?

Still convinced her suspect was up to no good but certain her husband and a security guard were directly behind her, she stepped onto the landing. She heard the echoing scuff of a shoe far below as the door hissed closed after her.

MOMENTS LATER, Art and two guards burst into the theater's main office to the confusion of the manager, bookkeeper, and the two guards with them. The manager and bookkeeper were calmly counting the ticket receipts.

Looking around in flustered puzzlement, Art demanded, "Where's my wife?"

HAVING REACHED THE basement level, Terry hurried past row after row of towering shelves stuffed with props grimy and cobwebby with age. He skirted the boiler room and pressed on. Above his head, aged and dust-laden timbers groaned under the weight of the full auditorium.

Then Terry found himself beneath the theater's stage, compassed by a multitude of wheels and pulleys rusted with disuse. Finally, where the auditorium and the stage met at the far edge of the building, he spied the door that would give him access to the organ's massive cabinet. He pulled on the antiquated wood door. It turned on surprisingly well-oiled hinges to reveal a ladder-like flight of wood steps, and Terry knew he would soon be within the bowels of the beautiful instrument, surrounded by its workings and mechanisms . . . and its glorious pipes.

What might not have been immediately apparent to anyone else was that the organ, unlike the rest of the theater's basement, was tended regularly and with proper care. Not a speck of grit or dust could be found inside the organ's cabinet to foul the instrument's intricate workings—to which Terry hardly spared a glance. He had eyes only for the clustered ranks of pipes mounted to the theater's walls, the tapered ends of the largest pipes just out of his reach. Oh, how he longed to feel the organ's music as it boomed and bellowed through them! If he kept climbing up, he'd soon be able to touch them.

Applause shook the building around him, and his heart thundered in sweet agreement with the audience's approbation. The concert was about to begin!

Terry climbed up the ladder, hands outstretched above his head, fingers splayed upon the backs of the largest pipes, his cheek resting on one tapered tip—until the first notes swelled and burst him free of his silent prison.

Pure, unadulterated joy! Such wonder! All clanging, shrilling, nauseating darkness fled away, and he was adrift in painless bliss.

There was only peace . . . and Sara.

"WHAT ARE YOU doing?" Esther stood at the foot of the ladder, calling in vain to the young man above her, the strains from the organ too overpowering for her to be heard. She covered her ears as the music intensified and glared at the man's pantlegs.

Why, this suit is quite old, she realized.

"I said, *young man!* What is your business here?"

He could not hear her over the organ, and appeared to be utterly unaware of Esther's intrusion.

Esther lost her patience, summarily stepping up a rung, just close enough to tug his pantleg and secure his attention. As he revolved slowly, her righteous indignation confronted eyes filled with sorrow and disappointment . . . followed by rage.

Esther swallowed on the realization that she may have acted rashly.

She stumbled while stepping down, caught herself and regained her balance. She hustled as quickly as she could out the cabinet door. Her breath came in great gasps as she shouted, "Help! Please help!"

The music was so loud that it prickled her skin like the pattering of hail upon a roof, while the booming pedal bass notes rumbled, rattled, and shook her chest. Esther, jogging as fast as her gown's tight skirt and her generous thighs would allow, glanced back.

He stood in the doorway to the cabinet, watching her vain flight. He raised a fist and opened his mouth wide to a guttural, unnatural scream that the bellowing organ swallowed whole. Esther hurried on, certain the man would be following behind her, drawing closer.

A sharp stab lanced Esther's chest. She rushed ahead, anyway. Suddenly, she felt as though she'd hit an invisible obstacle. Her forward progress, as ponderous as it was, abruptly halted.

She swayed and reached for the nearest wall, but wasn't close enough. She panted for air yet could not draw breath, and the piercing stab in her breast dug itself deeper, all the way into her chest. It flung iron cords about her heart and squeezed. The pain—the agony!—was unbearable. It drilled into her left jaw, radiated across her shoulder, and shot down her arm. Helpless, the dim basement growing dimmer still, she sank onto the cold, filthy floor, her heart jumping and pulsing erratically before dropping to slow ineffectual beats.

Slowing further. A single blip. Another. Barely again.
Nothing.

The man stood over her, but Esther no longer feared him, nor did she hear his croaking sobs. Had she been privy to his thoughts, she would not have comprehended his sorrowful protests or to whom he spoke.

I didn't mean to! Sorry! I'm Sorry! followed by *No! I don't want to! Please . . . please don't make me!*

ART AND THE TWO security guards accompanying him checked the remainder of the offices along the hall. Each door was locked, yet Art insisted that all doors be opened one by one and every room or office searched while he waited in the corridor, clicking his fountain pen with staccato agitation. He exhaled as he heard prolonged, enthusiastic applause and the opening strains of the organ.

Esther was supposed to introduce her friend, Donaldo. Boy, is she gonna be disappointed, he thought with growing exasperation.

Art and the guards reached the corridor junction, and still found no sign of Esther.

Art looked to his right. "What's down that hall? What's there?"

"Dressing rooms down the length of the auditorium. Beyond that, the stage entrance. But we have guard checkpoints down there."

Art pointed across the junction. "And there?"

"Storage, coupla closets, and a door to the basement."

"Guards?"

The senior guard, a tall lanky man by the name of Galen, shook his head. "Nope."

"Let's go," Art insisted.

He and the guards crossed the junction and walked briskly down the corridor. This branch of the hallway was far shorter than the office corridor. The guards rapidly opened and closed several closets and small storage areas, then arrived at the door off the end of the hallway.

Galen, chomping a piece of gum between his jaws, opened the basement access and pointed his flashlight down the stairs. "You think she woulda went down here?"

Art shook his head doubtfully. "I don't know. I mean, she saw this guy and followed him, but I didn't even see him myself, you know?"

Galen cracked his gum and stared at Art, his skepticism apparent. "Right."

"We should check the dressing rooms next."

Galen sighed. "Yessir. Stan? Lead on."

"Yeah, Boss."

Stan, husky and middle-aged, headed for the corridor junction and turned left. Art and Galen followed. They worked their way down the hall that ran the length of the auditorium, checking every dressing room as they went. Finally, they reached a door at the end of the hall. Stan opened the door, and they were confronted by a large Black man, similarly uniformed, seated on a stool.

Galen, with hands on his hips, peered beyond the seated guard into the more modern staging mechanisms. "Hey Phil. You-all seen a lady down here?"

"Nope. Nobody here but us boys. What kinda lady?"

"This man's wife." Galen jerked his head at Art. "He says she saw some guy open the door from the lobby into the office corridor. Says his wife followed him. Now we can't find her anywhere." He cracked his gum impatiently.

"Isn't that door kept locked before and during a show? How could some random guy just walk through? And what's this lady's business following some shady dude anyways?" Turning his gaze onto Art, the seated guard inquired suspiciously, "What I mean, *sir*, is what's your wife's concern in this matter that she should follow some shifty-looking stranger?"

Put on the defensive, Art flared back. "For your information, my wife organized this entire shindig. She heads the committee to raise money for the hospital and came up with the idea of this concert because Donaldo Menti is an old friend of hers. They went to school together. He wouldn't be even playing here tonight except for her." Then with uncharacteristic harshness he ordered, "Listen you guys, get off your lazy backsides and find my Esther, or I'll make certain you never work here again!"

Shrugging, Galen suggested, "Guess we'll try the basement then. Phil, you stay at your post and keep your eyes peeled. C'mon, Stan."

The two guards, with Art trailing behind them, returned to the basement door and descended the stairs then stared around themselves at the bottom of the staircase. The basement was cavernous, studded by dusty and webbed support pillars and beams throughout. Dim, yellow bulbs hanging at regular intervals revealed sheeted props and rows of floor-to-ceiling shelves of stage relics. The moist odor of mildew was pervasive. Together the three men began circling around the debris. The organ music seemed to come from both overhead and the back of the basement, rendering communication difficult.

Fifteen minutes of wandering among the piles of props and furniture left the three of them grimy and chilled. The guards were ready to call it quits.

Art himself was trying to stem the rising uneasiness in his stomach, because there was no way Esther would have missed introducing Menti. Not voluntarily.

"Look you guys, finish searching down here. I'm gonna go upstairs and see if she's turned up. Be back in a few."

Galen and Stan exchanged sarcastic looks behind Art's back as he lumbered toward the stairs. The guards then threaded their separate ways through the basement and converged at the boiler room.

"Just that area over there left, Galen." Stan pointed in the direction of the far wall.

The black man nodded and glanced down, suddenly interested. Away from the boiler room's more regular traffic the floor was considerably dirtier. A coat of soot and dust showed a hint of marring here and there and one smear that could have been a footprint. More obvious were several thin, uniformly spaced streaks, two to three inches in length.

"Hey, Stan." Galen pointed at the floor.

Stan glanced down. "I'm thinkin' high heels. You?" He looked to Galen for confirmation.

Galen's gum-chewing jaws slowed. He jerked a second nod and without a word unsnapped and pulled his gun. Stan didn't have a gun, so he trailed behind Galen. By the illumination of the hanging bulbs they followed the scuff marks.

A long sustained chord, overrun by applause and cheers, signaled the end of a musical piece when the two guards found Esther Grunbaum. She was lying on her back in a state of peaceful repose, her hands at her side, the length of her green lamé dress tugged down and smoothed over her ankles.

One might even have initially believed she was merely resting except for the filthiness of the floor on which she lay . . . and for the blood dribbled upon her face and puddled beside her.

Stan, mouth hanging open, stared at the scene as though mesmerized, but Galen, choking on his gum, turned aside and retched.

HAWKE AND MAYER, called out to the scene at the Claremont Theater, met up in the lobby. Mayer was *not* a happy man.

"First dinner out with Lisa in months," he grouched. "I finish my salad, the waiter plops a sizzling sixteen-ounce ribeye in front of me, and *off* goes my pager! Man, if looks could kill, Lisa's glare would have reduced me to a sizzling chunk of meat to rival that steak."

Hawke liked Lisa Mayer. He also knew her pretty well. "You're lucky you escaped alive and unscathed. I assume you ordered her the most decadent dessert on the menu, paid the bill including tip, and called a cab for yourself?"

"Does Santa wear a red suit?"

"You don't celebrate Christmas. Don't you mean, 'Does a dreidel have four sides?'"

"Duh; I'm Jewish, not blind. And Lisa is probably scraping the last bit of Death by Chocolate Cake—plus a scoop of vanilla ice cream—off her plate as we speak."

As they descended the stairs to the theater's basement, Hawke added in a bland voice, "Glad to hear you handled it. I mean, I've finally got my latest partner broken in and would hate to go through the tedium of breaking in a new one."

"You can shut it right there, Hawke." Grumbling to himself he added, "You've finally gotten me broken in, huh? Been with you how many years? Three, going on four? Yeah, man, I just *love* working with this egotistical jerk."

Far down in the bowels of the theater, the detectives encountered a scene too like the one at St. Joseph's. The presence of Lucinda Rodríguez, medical examiner, only added to the surreal déjà vu.

Standing clear of the body and the small pool of blood beside it, Hawke nodded at Rodríguez. "COD?"

She sighed. "All the obvious signs of a simple heart attack except . . ."

"The body appears to have been staged?"

"That and the bloodletting."

"Bloodletting. That a technical term?"

She shrugged. "It's an accurate term. No way this blood is from the woman's body or got here accidentally. I'll have more after I—"

"After you finish the autopsy. Got it."

"You're missing the best part," she added.

"Oh?"

The ME gestured toward a nearby wall. There, across its grimy face, and looking for all the world like it had been scrawled by a finger dipped in blood was a single word: *Sorry*.

He sighed. "Better and better."

Hawke scanned around the dusty area, and his eyes fixed on a small open door. He wandered over to it, bent, stepped inside, and stared up the ladder-like steps.

Dov joined him. "Not a homicide but there's a note of regret and a pool of blood that ain't the deceased woman's. Too many similarities not to be connected to St. Joseph's, Rick."

Hawke pointed through the doorway. "Yet another similarity, Dov, and probably our most important clue to date. Take a look—but touch nothing."

Mayer stepped through the door and looked up the ladder. "What is this contrap—" He halted in the middle of his question. "Are we looking up at the underside of a pipe organ?"

"We are. Let's get the print guys in here."

CHAPTER 7

FRIDAY, OCTOBER 13

WHEN DOV ARRIVED at his desk the next morning, his partner was already hard at work. Dov cracked a wide yawn. "'Morning, Rick."

Hawke grinned at him. "You sleep on the couch last night?"

"Nope. Lisa was passed out cold when I came in—I'm thinkin' *'drunk on chocolate'* as opposed to 'death by chocolate.' I just eased myself under the covers and dropped off. She never budged, and I left this morning before she—"

Chief McCormick stuck his head out his open office door and barked, "Hawke! Mayer! Get in here."

Hawke sent a shrug to his partner and got up. The two of them sauntered into the chief's office. "Chief?" Hawke asked.

McCormick was on his feet, pacing, his coffee mug in hand. Lowering his voice to a harsh whisper so the whole division wouldn't hear him, McCormick spit out, "It is *one thing* for an obscure, middle-aged spinster to die under accidental albeit suspicious and strange circumstances—some one-off event that dies a natural death. We work the case, get the best results possible, no complaints, right?"

Hawke and Dov nodded in unison. They knew what was coming.

"But last night's *disaster?* The city's monied society—including the city's highest elected officials—knew Esther Grunbaum. You think I haven't heard from half the attendees of that benefit last evening *and* from the mayor and district attorney? My phone is so hot it could fry bacon. Listen to me: This woman had friends in high places. Read my lips! *High places.* Not one of those friends is going to buy our standard 'we cannot comment on an ongoing case' line for long. Nope. And I guarantee you the screaming won't die off until we provide real answers to this mess." He waved his arm and muttered, "This weird, creepy mess."

He continued with irritation, "Arthur Grunbaum is an extremely wealthy and influential man, and trust me, he can afford to scream a lot. That man can *hire it done*, if you catch my drift." McCormick slammed his mug down on his tall file cabinet, launching some of its contents into the air. The chief's face above the tight collar of his uniform glowed a dull umber.

Dov watched Hawke stare dispassionately as coffee from McCormick's mug trickled down the cabinet to the carpet.

Hawke murmured, "You're telling us that we are to give this investigation precedence over actual homicide victims? An investigation that has all the hallmarks of a heart attack and is suspicious at best?"

Hawke didn't bother to soften the criticism he telegraphed to McCormick, and the implied rebuke wasn't lost on the chief.

If possible McCormick's volume increased. "When you find Esther Grunbaum's *murderer*, you'll have the Waite woman's killer too, Detective, so knock that ugly 'justice for all' chip off your shoulder. I'm adding Browning and Percival to your team. Put in as many hours as it takes and get me something to settle the city's nerves—and I need that something *now*, Detective Sergeant Hawke. Got it?"

McCormick was undeniably an old-school cop, politically savvy and hard as nails. He scooped up the stack of headlines on his desk and dropped them in Dov's arms for effect. "If we don't find answers, the people with clout in this town are going to make life very unpleasant for me—and that means *you*."

Hawke's lips curved with the mildest tinge of disrespect he could get away with. "I can tell you this right now, Captain, for what it's worth."

Dov lifted his eyebrows when Chief McCormick rasped, "I'm not taking any of your lip today, Hawke. If you have something to report, do so."

With his hands in his pockets, Hawke answered concisely. "Yes sir. The *main* commonality between the two cases is that our bleeder, bloodletter, whatever you want to call it, likes his organ music loud. *Very* loud. Right up close and personal."

Dov felt a little shiver run down his back at the word *personal*.

But McCormick wasn't in the mood. "You think an organ's volume has bearing on this case? The kids in my apartment building like their rock and rap at decibels guaranteed to burst brain cells, but it matters that *this* guy likes his music loud? Get out! Get out of my office, Hawke!"

No doubt about it now, the chief was yelling.

On leaving McCormick's office, Hawke smiled and nodded at the detectives across the floor as they stopped pretending they hadn't been listening in on McCormick's tirade. They grinned, dispersed, and got back to their business. The desk officer snickered and sent Hawke a thumbs up.

Hawke lifted his chin in acknowledgment. Then his feigned good nature dissolved. "Browning! Percival! With me." Dov could tell Hawke was anything but pleased that McCormick had hung two mismatched millstones around his neck—one inexperienced, the other lazy and lackluster at best.

The two men fell into line behind Dov and followed him across the floor to Hawke's semi-isolated cubicle. Pointing to Percival, Hawke said, "You and Browning get a print team back over to St. Joseph's. This time around, I want every square inch of that organ's pipes within reach of a man's hands dusted. When you're done, have the print team compare their take to prints pulled from the Claremont's organ pipes. Put a rush on it courtesy of Chief McCormick."

Hawke dropped into his seat and drew it up to the desk. "By the way, you two are assigned to me exclusively and exhaustively until we solve these cases. Or had I already given that away?"

The detectives laughed easily, but when Hawke glanced up they saw zero humor on his face. Percival pushed his glasses back up on the bridge of his nose, his nervous tell. "Understood, Hawke."

"Good. I'll be moving the both of you to desks closer to mine. Take care of shifting your stuff as soon as I make those arrangements." Hawke turned to Dov. "Mayer, see if Mr. Grunbaum can meet us at the Claremont. Round up the security guards who found the body as well. I want to go over the scene again, just the way it happened. That's all. Get busy."

The three detectives exited Hawke's corner cubicle. and Dov made his calls while thumbing through newspaper accounts of the Claremont case. He smiled to himself. Hawke had called him Mayer in the presence of Browning and Percival. Not Dov, but Mayer. And he never missed, not Hawke.

When Dov had transferred to Homicide Division, he hadn't randomly drawn Hawke as a partner. Nope. Chief McCormick had imported him from uptown, brought him in like a mail-order bride specifically selected to partner with Hawke.

At that time, nearing the four-year mark now, Hawke was struggling with coming back to work, had found it difficult to reclaim his edge following his stay in rehab . . . after his longtime partner, Steve Binder, had been laid to rest.

Hawke's coworkers had experienced their own difficulties upon Hawke's return. To be accurate, Dov knew the entire division had borne with Hawke's short temper and suffered through two abysmal attempts to match him with a new partner. After several months, Chief McCormick realized a more creative approach was called for.

Someone unknown and untried was in order, a moldable individual, preferably someone sufficiently ignorant of Hawke's foibles. Mayer, standing as tall as Hawke's shoulder, forty pounds lighter, and about eight years Hawke's junior, hit the lotto jackpot.

"You're young, Mayer," McCormick told him ahead of time, "yet you have already demonstrated that you have the aptitude and makings of a decent detective. That's all well and good, but in this partnership, we require someone willing to watch and contribute *when asked*, whose ego and self-confidence won't be easily shaken, and whose temperament can roll with Detective Hawke's abrasive manner. I won't sugarcoat this for you: Partnering with Hawke will be anything but a cakewalk. It'll be difficult and unrewarding for a while. But . . . if you can sit tight and wait him out, if you can earn his trust, I don't think you will regret it. And in the end, you'll learn from the best we have."

Dov accepted the assignment and quietly transferred to Homicide Division. Hawke looked him up and down, then ignored him. Dov expected no more. What he hadn't anticipated was how the entire division would hold him at arm's length and, with blatant skepticism, adopt a wait-and-see attitude toward him as the new partnership unfolded. Before long, Dov was positive the other detectives had laid bets on how long he'd last.

But Dov had walked into the situation with his eyes wide open. He went to work quietly, did what was asked of him, kept his own counsel, made no demands on his partner, and deferred to Hawke's seniority and experience. Either Hawke would eventually put forth the effort to make the partnership work or Dov would—when he'd exhausted all attempts to pierce Hawke's brick walls—wave the white flag and skulk back to the precinct he came from, grateful that his skills as a detective were improved by the experience.

Still, as the succeeding days and weeks dragged on, nothing changed for the better. Hawke's disregard and the department's standoffishness wore thin. Near the end of six incredibly difficult months, Dov was ready to throw in the towel. He'd even convinced himself that the problem had to be on his end.

The next morning, Dov stood beside Hawke's desk. Told him he was sorry he couldn't cut it, couldn't meet Hawke's expectations. Dov let Hawke know he'd filled out transfer papers, and he wished Hawke well with his next partner. He would tell Chief McCormick he was leaving before the end of the day.

With surprise, Dov had watched Hawke's jaw harden. "If you think I'm going to stomach yet another break-in period with some kneejerk rookie from downtown, you're wrong, Mayer. I'll fight your transfer."

Fight was unquestionably the expression on Hawke's face.

Dov's mouth must have hung open in astonishment because Hawke looked away, mumbling words Dov had to strain to pick up.

"I'm sorry I haven't made your transition easier. You've been doing well and . . . I'll try to be . . . more collaborative."

Dov was shocked into muttering, "I'm what? Doing well? Really?"

"Don't let it go to your head."

"Uh, okay. Thanks . . . I think."

Dov wandered back to his desk in shock. It took him the rest of the morning to work through Hawke's response, but at the end of the day, he tore up his transfer papers.

Overnight he also changed his approach. He stopped treating Hawke with unmitigated deference. He thought aloud when he had an opinion, addressed his partner as Rick, and ignored the outraged glares Hawke trained on him.

He furthermore made his presence known to the division—which may have been a mistake since it opened him up to the "seasoning" ridicule of the other detectives.

"Looks like our little 'Dove' has finally cozied up to his 'Hawk,' huh?"

"My money's still on Hawke. Ten bucks says bird of prey takes down dove, leavin' nothing but a mouthful of feathers and a little grease spot on the floor."

Astonishing Dov again, Hawke took exception to the ribbing, particularly the mocking misuse of Dov's name. He came out against it.

Openly.

"Listen up. Detective Mayer is my partner. You may refer to him as Mayer or Detective Mayer," he'd stated quietly. "Got it?"

Hawke's quiet statements had a way of taking on a life of their own, and Dov grinned at the memory. Their partnership had jelled at that point, eventually becoming warmer than most working relationships. He supposed Hawke may have realized he'd have to quit grinding up and spewing out partners at some point and decided he could live with Dov. In any event, soon after Hawke's proclamation, maybe as a private joke, maybe as a sign of camaraderie with his partner, Rick had taken to calling him Dov—but never when another detective or police officer was within earshot. Not ever. When anyone else was nearby, Hawke called him Mayer and only Mayer.

Dov grinned to himself. The guy never forgot and never got it wrong.

That left Dov puzzling over just one facet of his partner's personality: the guy occasionally let slip some mention of his Christian "walk." As a Jew—and a nonreligious Jew at that—Dov didn't "get" Hawke's faith. Religion was the antithesis of *Detective* Hawke's sharp-edged exterior. Furthermore, as a hardened skeptic himself, Dov rarely let a Christian reference from Hawke go by without poking fun at it.

Dov wanted his partner to recognize his "faith" in Jesus for the religious delusion it was and surmount it. Get over it. Shuck it off!

At the same time, he had to admit that there was a part of himself that wondered if there was actually anything of substance to his partner's belief. Either way, Hawke's Christianity was the man's single remaining enigma, the paradox that had Dov stumped.

Doesn't mean I'll stop pushing back when he spouts that junk.

Dov watched Browning amble his way and hoped his desk wasn't the detective's destination. Fortyish, at least twenty pounds overweight, and after fifteen undistinguished years in a squad car, Browning had somehow managed to make detective grade. Dov had heard it rumored that Browning's brother-in-law, an assistant D.A., had swung the favor for him. Favor or no, Browning was not and never would be prime detective material. Fact was, the man had a penchant for cutting corners and a reputation for holding grudges.

Percival, though, shows possibilities. I'd say he's about where I was when I joined Homicide, Dov thought. *He'll learn fast enough. Browning, on the other hand, without some seismic shift in attitude, will never cut it. I can only imagine how thrilled Hawke is to be saddled with him.*

To Dov's disgust, Browning made himself comfortable on the corner of Dov's desk. "The society pages are full of this Miz Grunbaum's good works —oh, I see you're reading 'em. Well, you know that news gal, Sharon Richmond? Did you see she's milking this story for all it's worth? She did a report on *Morning Line* today with a clip from last week's interview with that lady doctor."

Dr. Warner has my sympathies, Dov thought.

Browning frowned. "Say, what's the deal with reprinting the scene at St. Joe's? The tech guys already did their thing. Seems like a waste of time to send 'em back for another round."

Dov folded the newspapers away and made himself patiently explain. "Hawke noticed that the nearest parts of the big pipes in the Claremont had smears on them, like maybe our bleeder had put his hands on the pipes and run them up as far as he could reach. We may not get any decent prints from the Claremont due to smearing, but what if the guy did the same thing at St Joe's and the techs are able to pull off something usable? That's why Hawke wants the tech guys to recheck the St. Joe's pipes for prints wherever they are mounted low enough to be touched. Get it?"

Browning considered Dov's words, then smiled with agreeable condescension. "Sure, sure. Pretty weird though. Well, Percival and me, we're outta here. Meeting the tech guys at the church." He jerked his thumb at the door, signaling his partner to get going.

After Browning left, Dov called Arthur Grunbaum. "Mr. Grunbaum? Detective Mayer here. I apologize for the inconvenience and timing, but are you available today to meet Detective Hawke and me at the Claremont to go back over the scene?"

"I'll make myself available. What time?"

"Since your schedule is flexible, I'll get back to you shortly with that. Thank you."

Next, Dov called the company that had provided security for the gala at the Claremont. The clerk who answered transferred him to the day manager.

"Yeah, sure. I've got contact info for the two guards you want. Let me get it for you."

The manager returned to the phone soon and reported, "Here we go, Galen Truett and Stan Wallace. Looks like they are both on the clock right now."

"We'd like to speak to them. May I know when their shift ends?"

"They get off at two o'clock."

"Can we call them at this work site? We'd like them to meet us at the Claremont after their shift ends."

"I suppose . . . but only if you keep it short. We don't want our guards distracted from their work."

"We'll keep your concerns in mind."

Dov called the two guards and spoke to Truett, who said he and Wallace could meet them after their shift ended. Dov dialed Art Grunbaum back with the meeting time, then wandered over to Hawke's corner. "Grunbaum and the guards will meet us at the Claremont, 2:30."

"Good."

GRACE WALKED INTO Linda's office and tried to smile. "Dr. Bill in?"

Linda hated to see her normally bright employer down in the mouth. "Not yet, Dr. Warner. Would you like some coffee before getting started?"

"Yes, please. Has Mr. Galt checked in for his appointment?"

"No, but he will shortly. He's always on time, and you're a bit early." Jesse Galt was a regular, and had become a personal friend to Bill Upton. Linda smiled back at Grace, trying to infuse her expression with assurance. "Looks like another full day for you."

Grace nodded and turned toward her office door.

Linda sighed. After the public's initial reaction to Dr. Warner's interview last week, things had returned to normal quickly. They'd even picked up a few patients from the publicity. None of the clinic's staff members had expected *Morning Line* to air a rerun of Sharon Richmond's interview with Dr. Warner after the discovery of Esther Grunbaum's body . . . until this morning.

Linda figured Dr. Warner had seen the repeat and taken it hard. A closet Shakespearean with a love for *Romeo and Juliet*, she muttered, "A plague on your house, *Morning Line*."

GRACE SEATED HERSELF behind her desk and glanced through her schedule for the day. Linda was right—it was going to be full. She evaluated again the forty-five-second segment from *Morning Line* and told herself that the damage was small and should pass. Regardless, she had too many irons in the fire to waste time worrying over its effects: Patients today through 2:00, afternoon hospital rounds at 3:00, staff meeting at 4:30, and three surgeries first thing tomorrow morning. Linda knocked on her door and handed her a steaming cup of coffee.

"Mr. Galt in Exam 2, Dr. Warner."

"Thank you, Linda."

Grace took the coffee with her when she stepped into the bright examination room and greeted the plump but lively senior.

"Hello, Jess. How are you today?"

"'Mornin,' Dr. Gracie. I certainly feel a lot more like steppin' out than the last time I was here."

While checking him over she humored Mr. Galt with the running dialogue he loved. He was a retired math teacher who lived alone. Grace had found him to be a sensitive, intelligent man, always laughing and cheerful. Dr. Bill even played chess at Jesse's apartment twice a month.

She swung the light up and out of the way. "Jess, the swelling in your ears has subsided; did you complete your antibiotic regimen?"

"Sure. You know I wouldn't quit it just 'cause I was feeling better."

"That's good, but I always need to ask. You can use your hearing aids, now that it won't be painful to wear them."

"Well, won't that be super," he drawled. "Now I won't be able to pretend I can't hear Mrs. Casey knocking at my door six times a day."

He deadpanned it, and while Grace tried to hold in her laughter, she failed miserably. Her response earned her a colorful, five-minute description of Mrs. Casey's latest attempt to snare him. It was long-standing pursuit: Jess doted on the attention, but he wasn't about to get caught.

TERRY SLEPT FITFULLY that night. The fresh cuts on his arm ached and caused him to toss and turn. When he got up, he made a pot of coffee. While he waited for the pot to perk, he swallowed more aspirin, removed the wrapped gauze from his arm, and examined each of his wounds.

His stitching job on the two new cuts was better than his job on the first two. The newly stitched wounds were oozing some, and he felt a bit weak from the blood he'd paid out for the woman's unintentional death last evening. He was actually more concerned about the older cuts.

He hadn't done himself any favors by jumping up from the dumpster to grab the fire escape ladder and pull himself up. The effort had torn several of the stitches on those older cuts, and he didn't think he could properly restitch the places where the thread had ripped through his skin. Instead, he carefully applied strips of adhesive tape to pull the torn edges together.

This morning, those torn bits were red and hot to the touch. The possibility of infection worried him.

They will heal in time, as will the new cuts, he tried to reassure himself, *but maybe I should eat a bigger breakfast to build back the blood I've lost.*

As for his usual problems? *Peace.* He reveled in the silence! Missing the second half of the concert hadn't bothered him as much as he'd thought it would either.

He pulled out eggs and bread, then switched on *Morning Line* and dragged the cart the small television sat on close to the stove. He was surprised when he saw that Sharon Richmond was handling the news today.

Slowly, he realized why.

The woman's presentation was hard and fast, more suited to an evening news broadcast. Using as much visual impact as she could muster, she reported on the death of the woman last evening, incorporating file film of the Claremont and its organ and footage of the covered body of Esther Grunbaum being placed in the ME's vehicle.

Solemnly, Richmond concluded, "With cause of death yet to be determined, one cannot but wonder if the city is witnessing the work of a serial killer. Certainly the ritualistic taking of these two innocent women's lives is indicative of some hidden reasoning, but police have not as of today . . ."

He frowned at her image on the screen, and a low whine started behind his eyes.

ART GRUNBAUM AND the two guards were waiting for Hawke and Mayer in the Claremont's lobby when they arrived. They shook hands all around, then Hawke told them what they wanted.

"We'd like you to walk us through last evening, verifying as many of the details as possible. Mr. Grunbaum, would you show us, please, where you and Mrs. Grunbaum were when she noticed the man she followed into the basement?"

"Right over there." Art pointed to a spot in the lobby. "We were talking to friends when Esther pointed him out to me—although I didn't actually see him."

"You say she *pointed* him out. Could you stand where you were and show us in which direction she pointed?"

Art walked across the lobby and thought a moment. "I was here. Esther was . . ." He took a few steps. "Esther was here. She pointed . . ." He frowned. "Actually, she pointed at the door over there that leads to the offices, but what she *said* was, 'A young man who does not belong here just came down the stairs and has gone through that door toward the offices.'"

"He came down the stairs?"

"That's what she said."

"How hard would it be to enter the theater through the box office entrance?"

"Easy, if you had a ticket; difficult, otherwise. See, those tickets were mighty pricy, which was kind of the point of the evening. We were raising money for the children's wing of City View Hospital. That children's wing is Esther's pet charity."

Hawke turned to the guards. "So, if our guy didn't come through the main entrance, how would he have gotten in?"

Galen, hands on his hips, his jaws working a piece of gum, shook his head. "We had every stage entrance manned. Without a stage pass? Not getting in. Only other way in was through those doors." He pointed to the lobby entrance.

"Then how did the man get upstairs in the first place? What's up there?"

"Mezzanine and second-floor balcony. No entrances; only fire exits."

Stan nodded. "We checked all the fire exits when we came on shift. Made sure they were locked."

"How many fire exits up those stairs, Stan?"

Stan looked to Galen for confirmation. "Four?"

Galen nodded. "Two on the mezzanine level, two on the balcony level."

"Show me."

The five of them climbed the stairs to the mezzanine. Galen led them first to the stage right fire exit. He swept aside the curtain that draped the door. "See this?" He pointed to the bar on the door. "When the bar is out, the door is locked."

"Is it alarmed?"

"Uh, don't think so. This place is kinda old. Probably behind on safety requirements."

Hawke pushed through the door and found himself on a catwalk. He closed the door behind him, heard the lock engaged, then tried to pull the door open. It didn't budge. Galen opened it from the inside.

"Next?"

Galen took them to the stage left side of the mezzanine, swept aside the curtain, and pointed to the bar.

Hawke pushed out the door and closed it behind him. Waited for the lock to engage. It didn't. He hauled the door open.

Galen's mouth opened. "What the—"

Hawke squatted and, without touching the locking mechanism, studied the door's edge. "Someone taped the bolt so that it stayed retracted inside the door. This is how he got in."

Stan reached for the door's edge to get a better look; Dov's hand shot out and grabbed the guard's arm.

"No touching, please. In fact, we need the three of you to stand back while we take a look."

Dov followed Hawke out onto the catwalk where they stared down into the alley. Hawke's chin jutted toward the alley floor. "Think you could jump up, grab the ladder, and haul yourself up?"

"Maybe if I stood on that dumpster I could."

"We need the print team again. Our bloodletter may have left prints."

"I'll make the call," Dov said.

While they waited for the print team to arrive, they walked the rest of the scene with Grunbaum and the two guards, then thanked them and sent them off.

Fingerprinting the mezzanine door, locking mechanism, and the entire fire escape took a while. It was close to five o'clock by the time the print team finished.

While Dov drove, Hawke pondered their findings. "I have questions about our bloodletter, Dov. Like, are pipe organs some kind of fixation for this guy? And, if so, why?" He chuckled. "Hey, I think we know someone who might be able to answer those questions."

"Oh? Wouldn't happen to be a pretty young doctor, would it?"

THE SCENE AT THE Claremont nagged him mercilessly. Maddened him to distraction. *How could that fat broad's death so closely resemble that other . . . incident from long ago? How could it?*

Well, it couldn't, so it has to be a coincidence. A really nasty coincidence.

He gnawed on his knuckles in an effort to gain control of the furious burning in his gut.

And yet I know what I saw.

"Can't be. That's . . . crazy talk."

"Crazy" was a word he feared. They'd tried to pin "crazy" on him a time or two, but he'd been too smart for them and their shrinks.

"It's a coincidence trying to *make* me crazy—that's what it is! Well, I'm not gonna think on it anymore, and that's that."

Still, he salvaged a pile of recent newspapers from the boarding house's trash, and read everything he found in them on Esther Grunbaum's death.

"Yeah, yeah. Same junk, over and over. Fat broad with lots of money. So what?"

The doubts stuck with him, though. *How could that rich society snob's death so nearly mimic that other . . . scene?*

CHAPTER 8

GRACE TACKLED HER Monday morning patients at a dead run. She ate her brief lunch with Sam O'Toole, the clinic's allergy specialist, and worked steadily afterward until the afternoon staff meeting. To her relief, no one at the meeting mentioned the rebroadcast of her interview from *Morning Line*.

But as she stepped into Linda's office after the meeting ended, two men came to their feet.

"Dr. Warner," Linda apologized, "these gentlemen are detectives. They arrived half an hour ago to speak to you, but you were in your meeting. I told them you would be finished about now."

"Thank you, Linda. I am familiar with them."

Grace turned a questioning look on the men.

The taller officer, Detective Hawke, spoke. "Dr. Warner, remember us? Detective Sergeant Hawke, Homicide Division, and my partner, Detective Mayer. May we have a few minutes of your time?" He smiled, but the smile didn't reach his eyes.

She stared at his face and found herself analyzing the damage that ran under his left eye and across the bridge of his nose. Her examination bumped into his slightly amused expression.

She quickly recovered. "Yes. Of course. Would you care to follow me?"

Grace led the way into her office. She waved them to the two short sofas, took the seat behind her desk, and folded her hands on it.

"Please take a seat."

Instead, Detective Mayer stood quietly off to the side while Detective Sergeant Hawke slowly circled her office, perusing her degrees and wall hangings.

"Did you take these, Doctor?" He indicated a framed photo grouping, three black and white snow scenes.

"Yes, I did. Please sit down, Detective Hawke." She picked up a pen just to give her hand something to do. Frankly, she was beginning to feel a bit intimidated, her sitting but the two men standing—chiefly the senior detective whose studious examination was sucking the air out of her office.

"Nice contrasts—35mm.?"

"Yes." She was teetering on the edge of defensiveness, when he finally sat, taking up the entire loveseat to her left. Detective Mayer remained standing. When he grinned friendly like at Grace, she calmed a little.

"Thanks for seeing us without an appointment, Dr. Warner," Hawke began. He rummaged in his suitcoat and pulled out a notebook. "We're now investigating two suspicious deaths, the first one eight days ago, the second last night. Sadly, both these deaths have striking similarities."

"A second death? You mean like that . . . other one?" The pen in her hand tapped a light staccato on her ink blotter.

Hawke's eyes searched her for a moment. His response was softer.

"Yes, quite similar to the death of Mary Alice Waite. The conversation we had when you brought that note to us was very helpful, so we were hoping you could help us out again. Answer a few questions that might relate to your field."

Grace relaxed. "If I can, Sergeant."

HAWKE CAN BE *mighty smooth when he wants to be*, Dov noted, amused. *Good looking woman, too. Fantastic hair, beautiful eyes. Rick has to have noticed, right? I mean, the man isn't blind. Lisa would definitely want him to give it a shot.*

He and Lisa didn't know which was harder these days—finding an available woman who would look past an initial introduction to Hawke's normally abrasive manner or, if she got past that point, getting him to return her interest.

"See, I'm wondering," Hawke began with a speculative tone, "why an individual would want to stand beside a massive pipe organ during a concert. When I say *beside*, I mean directly against the pipes themselves. Touching them. I'm wondering if such a person might do so because they are deaf or nearly so."

Interested, Dr. Warner asked, "Touching the pipes? Which size pipes?"

"The largest ones."

She lifted a slender hand and smoothed the dark hair covering her ear, then stood. "Come with me," she said.

Dov followed Hawke who trailed after her into the receptionist's office, then across the hall into what he assumed was an exam room. It wasn't; it was actually more of a classroom.

"Please sit," the doctor said, shifting into teaching mode.

The chairs in the room faced a wall filled with a number of colorful charts. She stood beside a chart depicting the anatomy and composition of the human ear.

"Hearing loss presents in two types: sensorineural and/or conductive. *Sensorineural* loss is caused by damage to the tiny hair cells in the inner ear that conduct sound to the brain. *Conductive* loss occurs when there are problems in delivering sound energy to your cochlea, the hearing part in the inner ear. Common causes of conductive hearing loss include blockage of your ear canal, a hole in your ear drum, problems with three small bones in your ear, or fluid in the space between your ear drum and cochlea."

"Okay," Hawke replied. "That seems simple enough."

"It isn't. Loss can include either or both of these types—a mixed hearing loss—and can vary significantly from one ear to the other. A hearing test looks for both types of loss and presents its outcome in a chart called an audiogram, but the test also helps to define the frequency at which that loss exists. *Hertz* are the units of frequency recorded in an audiogram. Those units can be visualized as notes ranging from low pitch, 125Hz, to very high pitch, 8,000Hz. The higher the frequency, the higher the sound."

Dov blinked, trying to absorb her lesson. Hawke nodded, his attention fixed on the information.

Dr. Warner moved to another chart on the wall.

Her ring finger is bare, Dov observed, pleased.

"This is an example of an audiogram. The Y axis represents volume; the X axis lists the frequencies tested. The blue line is the right ear; the red line is the left ear. Notice that at higher frequencies, the volume had to increase in order for the left ear to hear the test sounds. Volume tells us the severity of the loss, but notice on this audiogram that the same severity of loss does not occur in the right ear."

"Could you elaborate further, Doctor?" Hawke scribbled on.

"Sure. Let's talk about speech. Speech occurs at higher frequencies, so hearing loss in the higher frequencies affects the ability to hear or understand speech. And not all speech occurs at the same frequency: For example, consonants register in a higher frequency than vowels. An individual with high frequency loss in the consonant range may hear vowels but struggle to hear consonants. Often, individuals with this level and type of loss will find background noises distracting, even maddening. They may struggle to hear conversation in a crowded room or need to turn the television's volume higher to hear the actors speak.

"But as to why your suspect would seek out the bass end of a pipe organ?" She thought briefly. "Let's assume for a moment that this individual has profound hearing loss. The more profound the loss, the less *all* frequencies are heard. However, perhaps—*perhaps*—this person has some measure of residual hearing at the low end of the frequency spectrum, and *perhaps* only at extremely loud volumes."

Hawke nodded slowly. "That makes sense . . . but why would he need to place his hands on the pipes?"

"Ah. Because conduction hearing occurs in two ways: air conduction and bone conduction. Normally, sound passes through the airwaves, enters our outer ear and is conducted by the ear's hearing mechanisms to the middle ear, then inner ear, then to the brain. Air conduction loss describes the inability of sound to reach the inner ear, which occurs when the middle ear structure itself is damaged.

"The causes of such damage are many and diverse, such as deformity at birth, chronic and/or acute infection, otosclerosis, long-term exposure to any extremely loud noise, a blow to the head that harms the ear's structures, like a skull fracture.

"Bone conduction, the second method of conduction hearing, is when sound vibrations are conducted via cranial bones, including the three small bones in the ear, directly to the inner ear."

The doctor faced the two men. "I'm going to step out onto a limb here and suggest that your person of interest places not only his hands on the pipes, but may also place his forehead, cheek, or the side of his head on the pipe in order to feel the pipes' vibrations and to possibly better hear the pipes' sounds."

She smiled. "I hope this information helps you."

"Indeed it does," Hawke responded. "Just one more thing, Doctor."

Oh brother, Dov thought. *Here he goes with the Columbo impersonation.*

"The other similarity we observed at the second scene was the same blood ritual that we found at the first scene."

"Oh! Oh, dear." Her response was immediate and unguarded.

"Yeah, exactly. So, given two of those 'blood rituals,' what is your sense that we could just be dealing with a nut job?"

Dov winced. *Nut job? Way to ask, buddy.*

She flushed, obviously displeased with how he'd framed his question. "Detective Hawke, we don't use 'nut job' or other denigrating slurs here. A person with hearing loss living in the hearing world deals with enough anxiety, rejection, and fear without being called a 'nut job.'"

Hawke inclined his head. "You're quite right, and I apologize. If I may rephrase my question? Is there any chance our person of interest, in addition to having hearing loss, is also suffering from mental health issues?"

Only partly mollified, Dr. Warner exhaled, pursed her lips, and replied, "There is a small—*very small*—possibility for hearing loss or hearing abnormalities to be psychologically induced or that the loss is caused by a combination of physical and psychological factors."

"You're saying hearing loss can be imagined?" Hawke asked.

"I didn't say imagined. I said psychologically induced—although, to be strictly frank, it is quite rare. But I must say," she paused to consider, "that the behaviors exhibited in your first scene *are* rather bizarre, especially when you factor in this-this *blood* thing."

Dov nodded, *I'm with you, lady.*

Hawke nodded. "I have to agree. And, if I might ask for a clarification?"

Dr. Warner nodded.

With a thoughtful tone, Hawke said, "During your interview with Sharon Richmond, you defined the term 'psychopathy' or personality disorder and you said that one of the traits listed as common to such an individual is narcissism. Could you define narcissism in the context of psychopathy and how this trait might apply to our "bloodletter," as we're calling him?"

The doctor stared at Hawke with something akin to surprise mixed with respect.

Dov chucked to himself. *Bet you didn't think us knuckle-draggers capable of a vocabulary containing words longer than two syllables, did you, Doc?*

Then she stiffened and answered, "All of us, to one degree or another, have a dose of narcissism in our personality. I can tell you, categorically, that the individual who wrote that note does not suffer from *abnormal* narcissism. Abnormal narcissism is marked by excessive preoccupation with oneself and one's own needs, such as exemplary or superior appearance, intellect, or reputation. Obviously, the writer of this note doesn't fit the definition of abnormal narcissism."

"Good. That was my take, too, when I looked up personality disorder at the library and stumbled a bit over 'narcissism.' But then I encountered a term entirely new to me: gaslighting. Again, in the context of personality disorder, could the author of this note be gaslighting us, misdirecting our perception of him? See, I have to wonder if he might be toying with us."

The woman's lips parted in astonishment. "I . . . goodness. You've certainly given more thought to the note than I have."

"More thought to the note's author, actually. When we're establishing an idea of who we're dealing with, every supposition we form has to be meticulously challenged. Otherwise, we're the ones likely misled or misdirected. Sent down the primrose path, so to speak."

"I had no idea detective work could be as rigorous as you've described. Let me think how to best put my response to your question."

As Dov and Hawke waited for her to formulate her answer, the woman's left hand gently kneaded her forehead. Then she looked up.

"Gaslighting is verbal and emotional manipulation. It is one individual telling a second individual that their perceptions of objective reality—a reality they can clearly see and evaluate for themselves—are erroneous, invalid, or flawed. The victim of gaslighting is generally in some sort of subordinate position to the one doing the gaslighting. Their subordinate position makes it difficult to assert themselves against the narcissist.

"A truly wicked narcissist takes great pleasure from mentally and emotionally toying with and torturing their victim, which is the narcissist's objective. Based on my dissection of the note, the author is not gaslighting. He is more likely to be the object of gaslighting rather than the perpetrator."

"Interesting!" Dov said quietly.

Hawke slapped his notebook closed. "Thank you, Doctor. We appreciate the time and clarity you provided. Of course, we'll have to wait and see how it all shakes out."

"Is that all, then?" Grace stood up, too.

"That's it. You've been a big help. Thanks again."

"Then may I ask *you* two questions, Sergeant?"

"What? Uh. Okay . . . shoot."

"How did you receive your injury, and are you suffering any residual effects from it?"

She's not the least bit apologetic, Dov thought. *No, this is clinical for her. Strictly professional curiosity.*

Once again, Hawke's left eye twitched.

"I received my injury while in the line of duty. For a while my doctors were worried about my eye, concerned the retina had detached, but it came through all right, and none of the breakage has affected my sight or hearing. Zero residual effects."

Not entirely true, Dov thought. *That tic is a surefire poker tell—because when you're under stress, you have no control over it.*

Dov wondered if the doctor had overheard his internal musings, because her eyes narrowed, and she asked Hawke, "So you didn't have surgery to reconstruct the sinus and nose?"

Hawke snorted. "Does it look like I've had reconstructive surgery? And by the way? That's three questions."

Dov was used to Rick's dark brand of humor but the lady doctor wasn't. Color flamed her face.

Rick, on the other hand, went on as if he hadn't noticed. "They cleared the bone fragments at the time of the incident. I guess I never got around to getting the 'cosmetic' part done."

"I see."

"Most people find it difficult not to."

The doctor reddened further, and Dov sighed to himself.

Well done, you Neanderthal.

He and Hawke left through the side entrance, the evening breeze carrying the faint aroma of burning leaves to their nostrils.

"Whoops. Forgot my notepad, Dov. Be right back."

Dov had the car running when Hawke returned a few minutes later.

"Took you long enough. And it's not like you to forget a notebook," Dov remarked, "or fail to notice how attractive that doctor is." He changed lanes and moved into the flow of the freeway.

"Who says I failed to notice? Asked her to dinner tomorrow."

"Just now?"

"Yeah."

"And you forgot your notebook? Riiight. Nice one. So what'd she say?"

"About what?"

"C'mon. About dinner."

"She said no."

"Seriously?"

"Seriously."

"Gee, tough break, Rick."

"Shut your face, Mayer."

GRACE RETRACED HER steps through the lobby out to the parking lot and started her car. She was still a bit astonished by the detective's offer of dinner. She'd said no, of course.

First of all, the man was intimidating—and she thoroughly despised feeling vulnerable Still, he'd been surprisingly pleasant when he asked, and slightly disappointed when she turned him down.

If I'm being truthful, it was flattering, but . . .

Yes, *but*. The more important reason she'd declined his offer had to do with her recent and deeply held decision to stop dating men uncommitted to God—Willard Drake holding the spot at the top of that list.

I said I wanted to draw closer to you, Lord. Wanted to become more committed to your word. You immediately convicted me in this area, and I'm grateful. I won't go back on my decision.

She was surprised to experience a shade of regret. "No," she whispered to herself. "No compromises and no regrets."

She found herself praying aloud, "Lord, I know that if it is your will for me to marry, it must be to a godly man—a strong, mature follower of Christ. I just want you to know that should you never send such a man my way, I will not settle for a merely decent man. Even if I am to remain single all my life, I will continue to trust you . . . and I will choose to be content."

HE GATHERED UP all the newspapers he'd collected with accounts of Esther Grunbaum's death. That whole scene had freaked him out but good, but he was okay now. Ready to toss the newspapers away and put the coincidence behind him.

Out of the blue, a snippet he'd overheard in his employer's break room floated to the surface of his mind. "What was it? Oh yeah. That guy they call Bowman. He and Galen were talking about Esther Grunbaum."

He searched his memory for what Bowman had said. "Something about a dead organist?"

And blood on the woman's face.

"A woman organist?" He stared at the folded newspapers in his arms. Sat down and searched page by page through each one, pulling out all the articles on the Grunbaum woman.

"I thought I read all of them," he muttered. "Did I miss one?"

He hadn't missed one, but he had neglected to read one article on Esther Grunbaum's death thoroughly. Toward the end, it referenced a similar event, the demise of one Mary Alice Waite, *the organist* at St. Joseph's Episcopal Church—nearly two weeks prior to the death of Esther Grunbaum.

He froze, shell shocked. *No way*, he told himself.

In a frenzy, he tore through the papers, hunting for articles concerning the death of the church organist, but none of the papers he'd scavenged went back two weeks.

I need a library.

He hotfooted it over to the closest library branch and searched out newspapers going back several weeks or months. Sure enough, didn't take him long to find multiple accounts of the organist's death.

He read every article he could lay his hands on. A couple of them mentioned that early morning news program, *Morning Line*, its host Sharon Richmond, and her coverage of the organist's death.

He skimmed another article and its mention of a female doctor who specialized in the treatment of ear, nose, and throat illnesses, including hearing impairment. The article included the doctor's name and a head shot of her.

"Who cares?"

He went back and reread the specifics of the organist's death, his finger tracing the lines that detailed how the body was found: precisely laid out, arms to the side, blood dribbled across the woman's face.

Exactly the same.

The same as that Grunbaum woman.

The same as . . . but how is that possible?

It's not!

CHAPTER 9

"WE PICKED UP THE print analysis from the pipes at St. Joe's, Sergeant. You were right about them!" Excited, Percival pushed up his glasses and hurried on. "More prints than you can shake a stick at. Look at this."

Dov saw that, in addition to the analysis report, Percival had asked for copies of the lab technician's photo spread. Holding out a close-up of a lab photo to Hawke, Percival pointed out the dusty smudges covering one section of pipe.

Dov also noted Browning hovering close to Percival's shoulder. The moment Percival took a breath, Browning elbowed his way in. "If you put all fifteen shots together, it looks like the guy was finger painting on those babies. What gives, Hawke? You know?"

"What about the prints themselves? Get anything useful?" When Hawke addressed himself to Percival, Browning's mouth turned down.

Hey, Browning! Hawke dislikes bullies, and despises lazy detectives, Dov telegraphed to the older detective, but apparently the man's receiver was not on. *You'd better start doing your own work, and stop trying to take credit for your partner's efforts.*

"Several solid fingers and some great partial palms, Hawke," Percival answered. "Didn't get a hit in the system, but we already know our guy isn't a pro. I mean, no gloves, right?"

"What about the prints taken from the mezzanine fire escape at the Claremont?"

"Should have them this afternoon. Think they'll be a match?" Percival waited hopefully for Hawke to respond.

Instead, Hawke sat in lowering concentration—and Dov could only guess where his partner's head was at. *Maybe rehashing our interview with Arthur Grunbaum and the two subdued security guards?*

When Hawke didn't respond, Browning sniffed in disgust. "Come on, Percy, we can talk to the air elsewhere." He whispered an aside to Dov, "Feel free to call us should the almighty Detective Sergeant Hawke deign to communicate with the rest of us slobs."

Dov hid a grin and threw himself into Hawke's old folding chair after the detectives walked away. Browning would be livid if he knew Hawke's candid opinion of him. Just as well he didn't know. Browning might be an incompetent detective, but he was a tenacious, vindictive grudge holder, and Dov didn't want Browning undermining Hawke behind his back

Hawke continued to stare into the air past the stacks of notes and files overflowing his desk, his expression stony.

The other guys in the division just haven't figured out how Hawke ticks, Dov reasoned. He, on the other hand, had learned to gauge the man's moods and didn't take them personally. As a matter of fact, Dov felt like he was getting pretty good at exploiting Hawke's vulnerabilities, while he doubted the other guys even realized Hawke had any.

But boy, oh boy, did he!

Watching him through half closed eyes, Dov said casually, "Too bad about last evening, huh, Rick?"

Just wait . . . wait for the bait to drift into the current . . .

Hawke jotted a note. "What?"

Jig the line ever so lightly.

"I said it's really too bad."

"What's too bad?"

"About Dr. Warner."

"What about her?" Hawke looked up suspiciously.

Nibble, nibble.

"That she wouldn't go out with you." Dov picked a stray thread off his sleeve. "But no big deal, right? And not all that surprising."

It took a few minutes but eventually Hawke responded. "What's that supposed to mean?"

"You know. Just that I figure the two of you probably don't have much in common."

Hawke turned his attention back to his files. "She said she was busy."

"Oh. Sure. Got it."

Gently flick the bait back upstream. Let it slooowly float down with the current.

Dov could hear Lisa's amused voice in his ear. "Rick is entirely too self-sufficient for his own good. But you, Dov? You know what buttons to push to get that stick-in-the-mud's goat. Do it, babe. I can't wait to see what happens next."

Hawke was rereading his notes and nursing a cup of cold coffee. Dov felt the proverbial elbow of his wife land between his ribs.

"You can be a charming guy, Rick. Occasionally."

Rick was trying hard to ignore him, but Dov was a patient angler. Sooner or later . . .

Ah! Here we go.

"She didn't say she wouldn't go out with me. She has a meeting every Tuesday evening."

"Oh! So you asked her for another evening, right?"

"Hmm?"

"You invited her out another night?"

No answer.

"Never mind, Rick. I mean, women like her usually have guys lined up around the block. Besides, she's intelligent. You know, cultured. Not your league."

Hawke's head snapped up. "Don't you have reports to file, Mayer?"

Shoot. Lost my bait.

"Right. On 'em now."

MIDAFTERNOON, PERCIVAL, *sans* Browning, showed up at Hawke's desk with the fingerprint report from the Claremont's mezzanine. Dov joined them.

"Not a single print, Hawke, not even on the tape he used to retract the deadbolt. All the print team found were smudges. Guy had to have worn gloves. And as suspected, no usable prints on the organ pipes."

Hawke nodded. "Thanks, Percival."

An hour later Hawke dropped a folder on Dov's desk. "Take care of this before you leave, Dov?"

Dov spoke to Hawke's back. "Sure, Rick. Headed to the gym?"

Keep it casual, Dov. Keep it casual.

"Nope." He shot a challenge over his shoulder. "Home to shower and change. Then dinner. With Grace Warner."

"Oh. That's nice." Dov kept his face perfectly bland, but inside?

Fresh caught and pan-fried, he thought with a wicked grin. *Wait until Lisa hears this!*

GRACE TOOK A CAB and was early to the restaurant. The longer she waited, the more nervous she felt. *It's just dinner*, she told herself for the third time. *Just a meal.*

Grace had been disconcerted when Detective Hawke called her this afternoon. More than that, she'd been staggered by the words he'd spoken across the line.

"Dr. Warner? Detective Hawke again. Listen, I left something out of my dinner invitation the other day."

"Oh?"

Oh, did you really?

He'd gone on in the same matter-of-fact vein.

"Yes, I neglected to ask if you were a Christian. You see, I'm only interested in dating women who are as serious about their relationship with God as I am."

Stunned, she'd muttered, "And you are? Serious, I mean."

"I am. Went through a rough patch a while back, but . . . somehow Jesus saved me and pulled me through it. Yanked, hauled, towed, lugged, dragged me kicking and screaming—all the above. I'm on the other side of that difficult patch now. Fully committed to Christ. You?"

The man was nothing if not to the point.

She'd found herself saying, "As it happens, yes. I am also a committed Christian . . . with definite convictions regarding dating."

"I thought I sensed something the morning you brought us that note. And after you turned me down Monday evening, I just wanted to make sure it was because of your weekly Tuesday meeting and not because I hadn't declared my faith in Christ to you."

"All right, then. What's your life verse?"

"My life verse?"

"Your go-to Scripture. The one that more or less speaks to your walk with Christ. Do you have one?"

He thought a minute. "I've never had it explained like that, but yeah. I think I do. It's Proverbs 19:21: *Many are the plans in a person's heart, but it is the LORD's purpose that prevails.* It tells me that God has a purpose in mind even when what I have planned is something totally different, even perhaps the opposite of what I wanted. I had to lean on that promise a lot while I was recovering from . . . you know, the tire iron tattooed across my face."

Grace's smile was half grimace. *Recovering from a tire iron across the face? I suppose that resonates with me. It also underscores the fact that this man is immersed in a violent profession, which is, frankly, intimidating and off-putting.*

When she first picked up Hawke's call, she had thought it a blatant, last-ditch attempt on his part to secure a date with her. But even now that she knew he was a Christian? It was still out of character for her to jump into a date with someone she hardly knew let alone a man so . . . Aggressive? Blunt? Unpredictable? All of the above?

"Dr. Warner? Are you still with me?"

"Um, I am. Yes."

"May I buy you dinner this evening?"

What in the world had possessed me to say yes?

Grace was still debating within herself why she'd agreed to see him when she caught sight of Hawke entering the restaurant.

She told herself for the umpteenth time, *It's just dinner. Don't flip out.*

"I DISLIKE FIRST DATES," Hawke began as they looked over the menus. The restaurant was classy enough for a date but unstuffy enough to be relaxing. "I eat here a couple times a month. I can recommend the shrimp or prime rib. What sounds good to you?"

She studied the selections. "The shrimp then, because you can vouch for it. What did you mean about first dates?"

"Just that they're a pain in the neck for both parties. I mean, you're so busy trying not to make a fool out of yourself that you forget to have a good time. Makes the evening awkward, to say the least, made worse because if you do screw it up, there won't *be* a second date."

She frowned at him like he'd lost his mind. "I think I see your point," she responded, her body language telling him she had *no* idea what he was babbling on about. And he could tell she was uncomfortable just sitting across the table from him.

Once more into the breach, he told himself. "So, Dr. Warner, if it's all right with you, I'd like this evening to be merely two people getting to know each other over a nice dinner. That way we can skip the first-date scenario. Is that okay?"

She stared for a long moment at the crease across his cheek, stretched and whitened because he was smiling like a fool, before she replied, "For the life of me, I cannot figure you out, Detective. I mean, what kind of line is 'skip the first date scenario'?"

He pretended innocence. "And here I was hoping to bypass the hard work of making a good first impression. That way we can avoid a lot of needless posturing."

His eyes still held their humor but he figured she also saw a slight challenge in them.

No, wait. She has that off balance look again and is studying her hands.

He was pleased when she glanced back up and replied. "All right, since you put it that way, I agree to your terms: A nice dinner without the awkwardness of a first date. It would be a blessing, Detective."

He could almost hear her challenging him: *And I'll just be myself, too, thank you very much.*

"Great!" He turned as the waiter approached and kept talking. "Hey, if you're interested, I thought we might take in a movie after dinner. Has to be a decent one showing somewhere, right? And by the way, my friends just call me Hawke, if that's more comfortable than Detective."

She glanced up and wrinkled the bridge of her nose.

It was so quick and cute that he laughed outright. His laugh brought up an answering blush, but she managed to chuckle too.

The waiter hovered and they ordered: salads, fresh shrimp pan seared in seasoned butter, steamed asparagus, and hot bread.

The waiter left them again.

"But what is your first name?" She wanted to divert the attention from herself. "Just 'Hawke' is a bit . . . "

"Boorish? Like me?" He saw her unspoken agreement and laughed again. "Hawke is all my manners deserve, but my first name is Rick. Richard, actually."

"Richard." She turned it over on her tongue. "Is it all right if I call you Richard?"

Her thick black hair gleamed in the candlelight, and a stray strand curled down the nape of her neck. That soft wisp of hair mesmerized him.

"Sure. Richard is fine. I already know your first name: Grace."

"That's right; you watched my interview with Sharon Richmond."

"Yes. I like your name—uh, what I mean is that it suits you."

Good grief, Hawke! Try not to make a fool out of yourself just to prove your awkward "first date" theory is spot on.

"Uh, Grace, alternatively, we could catch the symphony, if you would prefer music to a movie?"

"No, I'd prefer the movie. I haven't been in a while so I won't have seen any of them."

Just a trifle too quick, Hawke thought. *Make a mental note: doesn't care for "highbrow."*

Lord, I'm grateful!

After dinner Hawke purchased a paper and they sat in his car, perusing the movie selections. When he asked her preference, she suggested the same comedy he had tentatively chosen. Their agreement seemed to bode well, and the theater was practically empty on this cold weeknight, giving them a wide choice of seats. Hawke sat them a little closer to the front than the back, and they laughed in easy companionship through the show, sharing a bucket of popcorn and sipping sodas. It was simple fun with no subtleties or hidden agendas.

Afterwards, when he saw her to the door of her townhouse, they'd somehow already agreed to see each other again the next evening. Unaccountably relaxed and at ease, Hawke found that he wanted to kiss her goodnight—just a peck on the cheek—but he discarded the idea when he remembered how his pastor had stressed that even casual intimacies should be saved for engaged couples.

Lord, I sure have a lot to unlearn.

She offered him her hand. "Richard, thank you. I enjoyed myself tonight; It was lovely, actually. And I'm looking forward to our *third* date—since we skipped the first one."

They laughed. She stretched up to brush her lips across his cheek. He kept his hands at his side and bent to her, knowing she'd never reach his cheek otherwise.

She went inside, leaving him standing on the porch . . . wondering where this might go.

CHAPTER 10

THURSDAY, OCTOBER 19

HAWKE CLIMBED OUT from under the covers and sat on the edge of his bed, groggy. It was 5:00 a.m. and chilly in his apartment. He shivered then recognized that the usual racket of street noises seemed muffled and distant.

Striding to the bedroom window he pulled back the drape. A carpet of snow blanketed his view, and more was falling, heavy and silent. It was way too early in the fall for snow, but last winter had provided so little precipitation that they'd been in drought the rest of the year. At least, since it was too early for snow, the white stuff wouldn't hang around long. When it melted, the ground would drink up the moisture like a thirsty sponge.

For a few minutes he stood there, enjoying the clean and tranquil sight and thinking about Grace Warner. One date, and he was already intrigued by her freshness and the absence of worldly sophistication. He hadn't expected that. He'd gone out with far too many casual, worldly women after his partner died. He'd assuaged his pain with their pretensions and his own. More than enough to kill his appetite for pointless dating.

Maybe Grace was different. She did say she had serious convictions about dating.

Well, so do I, he thought. *Huh. I'll bet she's enjoying this unexpected snow.*

As well as a bright mind, Grace had a sensitive nature, and surprisingly, they hadn't run out of things to talk about. *She's a photographer with a gifted eye. Has a great sense of humor. Intelligent but not conceited. Belongs to a good Bible-teaching church. Talks about her walk with God as naturally as she talks about her work.*

A car turned the corner under his window, its rear tires sending up a fantail of wet snow. Before evening all this beauty would be reduced to crusty, blackened debris piled up beside the roadways. Such was city life.

Turning away, he threw his workout clothes and his shaving kit into his gym bag, then grabbed the garment bag holding a fresh suit and shirt. But as Hawke opened the front door, his cat, Ontario, did his best to slip out through the crack. Hawke dropped his gym bag, snagged the cat, and slammed the door before the brown-striped feline could make good his escape.

Ontario yowled and hissed and scrabbled to get down. As he released the cat, Hawke questioned why he'd bothered to rescue the stray—a miscreant if ever there was one. Maybe it was because, as moody and independent as this cat behaved, his presence was the only company of sorts Hawke's apartment had witnessed since he moved into it. Perhaps, too, his apartment felt empty and lifeless because Hawke spent as little time as possible in it. Certainly no creative hand had taken part in decorating the place; he'd merely shifted the collection of furniture and household items gathered over the years from his old digs to this location and called the sorry, masculine out-come "home."

He scanned the living room, taking stock. One corner was allocated to a bench press and several piles of weights. The television conveniently swiveled toward the bench or the sofa, and when he came home from work, the back of whichever chair was handiest sported his shoulder holster and revolver. Not that he was a slob. Neat stacks of magazines sat on the end tables and he vacuumed regularly. The place was occupied, yes, but did he live his life here?

Not really. The fridge hadn't had a week's supply of groceries in months, a prerequisite for actual cooking, so he ate out or ordered in regularly. That left sleeping, and at least he did sleep here.

Still, the place felt depressingly empty, so when the mongrel cat turned up at his door a while back begging for food, he'd let it in. Over the ensuing months, they'd formed an alliance of sorts: mutual dependence tempered with mutual antipathy.

Hawke sneered at the cat. *Frenemies. That about sums up our relationship.*

Four years ago his life hadn't been this way. He'd had buddies over, had entertained regularly. But that was before he'd acquired his permanent facial reconstruction. Before he'd lost his partner and best friend in one horrible moment.

Hawke sighed. He set his gym bag aside. Rinsed and filled Ontario's dishes. Made a clean getaway while the cat was occupied with his food, jumped in his department loaner, and headed for the gym.

He meant to push himself hard today, starting with a long warm-up at the row machine. Twenty minutes on that, then he stretched out thoroughly and attacked his free-weight program. Not too many years ago he was still concentrating on bulking up. Now he worked out just to maintain his current level of fitness.

After a thirty-minute free-weight routine, dripping but pleased with the 'burn' he was feeling, Hawke hit the indoor track. Running was the toughest part of his regimen. It took a great amount of self-discipline to alternately jog and sprint five to six miles on a regular basis. But especially as he approached forty, Hawke knew that letting himself go would diminish his effectiveness as a detective. So, he worked out hard and denied himself desserts and sugary snacks to keep the weight he carried tight and hard. Unfortunately, with the long hours he worked, the temptation to let his regimen slide was always lurking in the background.

Six miles later, chest heaving, he slowed to a walk and cooled down. When he hit the shower, the jets of hot water that pummeled the muscles in his neck and shoulders felt marvelous.

He found himself standing under the stinging spray praying. *Lord Jesus, I am grateful. Grateful for this new day, grateful for the new mercy you pour over me each morning, and grateful that you brought me out of the deep pit I fell into after Steve died.*

He thought a moment. *Would you tell him hi and thank you for me? You and I both know I wouldn't be talking to you right now if Steve hadn't been bold enough to speak openly about you, persistent even in the face of my ignorant anger.*

He blew out a long breath and cranked the hot water up a notch. *Lord, I'm especially grateful on this cold morning for hot running water.* He surprised himself when he added, *And I'm grateful for Grace Warner. Please bless her this day.*

DOV GOT IN FIRST and was hard at work, when Hawke breezed by his desk.

"'Morning, Dov."

"'Morning, Rick. How was dinner?" Dov didn't mention that Hawke was fifteen minutes late—a phenomenon so rare, Dov had considered asking a patrol officer to do a wellness check.

Hawke gave him a thumbs up.

Dov smirked. He even let Hawke see him smirk.

HOMICIDE DIVISION WAS always busy, day or night, but after a brief lull near dawn, the shift changed and business again picked up steam. From his desk, Hawke leveled a perfunctory glance over the crowded floor and its officers. They wore the same harassed expressions they'd worn yesterday. Most of them sipped or gulped coffee from stained mugs, grimly determined to get a start on the day's work.

But before Hawke jumped into the tasks at hand, he took a clean sheet of paper, and in small, precise lettering, wrote out the words of Proverbs 19:21. He cut the verse to size and pinned it to his bulletin board.

Hawke swiveled his chair and beckoned to Dov.

"Grab Browning and Percival, will you? We'll have a little confab in my corner."

"Sure thing, Rick." Dov squinted at his bulletin board. "That's new. What is it?"

"A Scripture from Proverbs. Apparently, I have a life verse."

Dov snorted. "Sure you do. Do you also have a death verse? And if so, is your death verse anything like a death wish?"

"Haha. Very funny."

Dov headed down the aisle to grab Browning and Percival. When the four of them were crammed into the close quarters of Hawke's cubicle, he laid out his instructions.

"We have a lot of pressure coming down on us because of Esther Grunbaum's standing in the community. As much as I don't like my priorities getting shuffled by the size of someone's bank account, in the end we have to do the job we're assigned. What the mayor and the commish want from us is a quick resolution to these puzzling cases, and we're going to give it to them. Got me?" He received three nods of acknowledgment.

"I think we can all agree that, aside from the blood thing, *the evidence* tells us the deaths of Mary Ellen Waite and Esther Grunbaum were unintentional. As such, we shouldn't have another incident with the same M.O., am I right?"

"Right, Hawke," Percival answered. Browning and Mayer nodded again.

"Right. So, our task is to identify our mystery bloodletter in short order, and I've been puzzling out how best to do so. The fact is, there's no way to sugarcoat the way forward. It's going to cost us time, effort, and dogged persistence. In plain language, the four of us are going file diving."

Groans followed his pronouncement, but Hawke was having none of it. "Suck it up, *detectives*. This is the job, and we *will* do it to the best of our ability."

Three sets of resigned eyes waited for him to continue.

"We'll start by compiling a list of search terms, and frankly, it will be a short list. Also, as you know, our division has only two years of cases on our computer network. Sure, we can wish *all* the city's police files were on the network, but the cold reality is that after we've completed a thorough search of our network, we'll have to move on to paper copies, and they reside in evidence lockup in the basement. That means we'll need to requisition files from evidence, have them brought up to us or fetch them ourselves, check each case against our criteria, take them back to evidence, and check them back in."

"Date parameters on the case files, Hawke?" Dov inquired.

"Dr. Warner says our bleeder isn't a kid but is likely a teen or a young adult, so let's say 1969 forward, okay? That gives us a twenty-year span."

"How many, Hawke?" Browning asked, frowning.

"How many what?"

"How many case files do we check?"

"Are you not listening? *All of them*," Hawke answered. "Every case on the network and every case on the premises, dating from 1969 forward."

Browning opened his mouth, then snapped it shut.

"After we've exhausted our review of the city's case files, we'll move on to other law enforcement entities—state police, county sheriffs, county and state lockups, and so on—in an outwardly expanding radius."

Three pairs of eyes pleaded silently.

He ignored them.

"In addition, we will send short, concise bulletins to other law enforcement agencies asking for their assistance and cooperation. We'll follow up with phone calls. Cordiality and *good will* from our team to these other agencies will help grease the skids, so I cannot emphasize enough that we had better turn on the charm, gentlemen. Just a single LEO who recalls a case with even a single similarity to our two cases could break things wide open. And, of course, we'll include the feds in our bulletins, just in case this guy recently transferred his bloodletting 'franchise' to our fair city from another state."

His tone toughened up.

"Let's talk criteria now. The deaths of Mary Ellen Waite and Esther Grunbaum have two commonalities that we'd expect to find in related cases: bloodletting and organs—and I'm not talking bodily organs. That means we search for any case or report that involves or mentions some type of blood ritual and/or any file containing the word 'organ,' meaning the musical kind. Blood, bloodletting, blood rituals or fetishes, pipe organs, organ music, music fetishes? Any further suggestions?"

Percival spoke up. "What about notes? The bleeder left a note at the second scene and sent a note through the mail after the first. We could add the words regret, apologies, and notes. I realize those are vague, but . . ."

"Won't hurt to include them. Any further terms? No? All right, but if you think of additional terms, don't hesitate to bring them to the team.

"Now, let's talk assignments. Percival, I want you to compose and send the bulletins, including our search terms, and I want those bulletins sent today. Join us in reviewing case files after you've sent the bulletins, but early next week, start following up on the bulletins."

"I'm on it, Hawke."

"Good. Mayer, you will search our network today using our search terms; I will review the cases your search returns."

"Got it."

"Browning, you will hit the evidence lockup as soon as we finish here. I want you to submit and monitor the file requisitions so that the lockup delivers a steady flow of boxes each day. If they can't deliver them as fast as we need them, you grab a hand truck and fetch them yourself."

"Yeah, got it." Browning shuffled his feet and muttered to himself, "Because I became a detective for this."

Hawke pretended he hadn't heard and said to the team, "I'm sorry I can't requisition more bodies to get this done, but the division budget is stretched as tight as a drumhead."

"Gee, I wonder how much your replacement ride will cost our division budget," Browning grumbled.

Hawke eyed him for a long moment, before adding softly, "Prepare yourselves to arrive for work each morning *no later* than 7:00 a.m. Expect to be here until 7:00 p.m. or beyond. And decide *now* to work with a will, because I will not tolerate complaints or grumbling."

The lack of enthusiasm radiating from his team was about as understated as a brick to the head.

"This, gentlemen, is basic police work. It's what the public pays us for, so let's get rolling."

"Sure thing, Hawke." Percival turned docilely to leave.

Browning, his mouth tight, sucked in his paunch and stalked away.

Hawke stared after the man, his eyes glittering unpleasantly. *Keep it up, Browning. The day you push me too far is a day you will regret.*

The four of them got to their tasks. Dov ran their queries through the department's network by way of Central Processing and compiled a list of case files for Hawke. Hawke, in turn, pulled up the files and read through them.

By ten o'clock, Hawke had finished his review of possible cases off their network.

"You have any more for me?"

"Nope. That's it," Dov told him. "Anything in those cases fit the bill?"

"Not even close."

About then, puffing and red, Browning lugged a hand truck loaded with boxes out of the elevator and onto the division's floor. He sauntered over to Hawke, "Filled out the paperwork down in evidence. Got the first load of files by the elevator, a second load waiting downstairs. Evidence will bring up more boxes before they leave for the day. Where do you want me to park this load?"

"How about you stack the boxes beside your desk. Each of us will retrieve a box and take it to our desk."

Browning went for the hand truck parked near the elevator. As soon as he arrived at his desk, Hawke helped him unload it. While Browning returned to evidence for the second load, Hawke and Dov grabbed a box off the stack and set to work.

Percival, from his terminal, had composed the bulletins and asked that the recipients reply if any cases in the last twenty years, 1969-1989, were a match to the conditions included in the bulletin. He sent his bulletins about the time Browning returned a second time from evidence lockup with more boxes.

The rest of the day and into the evening, the four of them opened and reviewed every case file in their selected boxes. Around 1:00 p.m., Browning returned to Evidence to bring up a third load, and Evidence, as promised, delivered several more loads at 5:00 p.m.

The team was dog-tired, bleary-eyed, and partway through the five o'clock load when Hawke sent them home. Weary as he was, a late dinner with Grace Warner was only an hour away.

The prospect energized him. He hurried to his apartment to shower and change.

GRACE DEPRESSED THE girl's tongue and shined a bright light down the child's throat. The back of the girl's throat was red and raw, and an ugly pus pocket swelled behind and to the left of the epiglottis.

No wonder the kid's throat hurts when she swallows, she thought.

Next she tenderly palpated the seven-year-old's neck and underjaw. Lastly, she shined the light into her patient's ears and watched while she blew compressed air into each ear to test the movement of the tympanic membrane. The right ear drum moved slightly. The left ear drum did not move at all. Rather, the drum's bulge was impossible to miss.

"Thank you, Chrissy. How about some spray on your throat to make it feel better?"

Fearful, the petite child looked to her mother.

"Cherry flavored," Grace coaxed.

Chrissy opened her mouth.

She sprayed the anesthetic onto Chrissy's painful raw throat and turned to the girl's mother.

"Chrissy does indeed have an infection, Mrs. McEnerny, likely strep. We'll treat it with antibiotics. However, and undoubtedly the reason your pediatrician sent you to us, Chrissy's eustachian tubes are filled with fluid. The pressure of that fluid against her eardrums is the source of her recurring earaches, but that is not the only issue this fluid is causing."

Reaching up the wall behind her, she drew down a colored chart. "This tube here behind the eardrum is the eustachian. It connects with your throat and sinus cavities. When you get a cold or infection, drainage from your sinuses can back up and collect in these tubes. See, when I blew air into her right ear, the drum failed to vibrate adequately. But when I blew air into her left ear, the drum failed to vibrate at all. This tells us that the space behind the drum is plugged with fluid.

"Based on a year of recurring earaches and infections, I would say the fluid has been building up in Chrissy's ears for some time. At this point, it may be quite congealed, something like glue."

"Would that cause Chrissy hearing trouble? Lately we've scolded her for not paying attention." She looked a trifle guilty.

Grace nodded in sympathy. "It absolutely could affect her hearing. It is the other issue we need to discuss. Even though we can clear up the infection in her throat, it will likely recur. You see, curing the infection will not necessarily dry up the fluid—that sometimes takes months—meaning the fluid itself becomes a breeding ground for renewed infection, perpetuating a vicious cycle, Mrs. McEnerny. Does that make sense?"

"Are you saying the fluid needs to be removed?"

"Yes, that's right. I suggest that we treat the infection with antibiotics, but also schedule Chrissy for a simple procedure. During the procedure, I will insert a tiny tube in each ear and gently suction out most of the fluid. The tubes will remain in her ears, allowing air and drainage to clear up remaining fluid. Eventually, as the holes in the drums heal and close, they will naturally push the tubes out."

The woman sighed anxiously. "Will Chrissy have to stay overnight?"

"No, it is an out-patient procedure. She's anesthetized, of course, but the procedure doesn't take long. We will allow her to leave about an hour after she awakens. Believe me, the procedure is very common. I do some most every week."

"What if we don't have the surgery done? My husband's insurance isn't all that great."

"Mrs. McEnerny, you brought up Chrissy's hearing. I have no doubt that when we're finished it will return to normal, but you do need to understand that a long-term infection can cause permanent hearing impairment. To let this condition continue untreated is inviting serious consequences. In fact, I would say Chrissy's left ear drum is in danger of rupturing. We should act quickly."

The mother caressed her daughter's hair for a moment then replied, "I understand. Let's go ahead."

"Good. I will have you meet with my nurse to schedule the surgery. On another note," Grace continued thoughtfully, "have you ever wondered why Chrissy has so many runny noses? Her chart says you've had her to Dr. Cole, let's see, twice last winter and five times this summer and fall. If I'm not mistaken, allergies are at the root of all of this, predisposing her to these infections. Find and treat the allergies and you'll have a much brighter, healthier child."

Grace's nurse came in and helped Mrs. McEnerny make an appointment for Chrissy's procedure and a second appointment to be 'scratch' tested by Sam O'Toole, the clinic's allergy specialist.

Grace washed her hands, thankful to be leaving after a long day. It was later than she had hoped, but she still could soak in a hot bath and take her time dressing. She wanted to look good for her second date with Richard.

She laughed aloud. "Nope. We skipped the first date, so I guess we've already had our second date. Straight on to the third!"

She was glad Richard had a quirky sense of humor under his gruffness. And he was a Christian! Committed *single* Christian men were hard to find in any shape or form. Still, she wasn't altogether comfortable with Richard . . . yet. But she was definitely interested.

When she'd met him and he'd introduced himself and his partner to her, she instinctively sensed that across some undefined line he was probably a very dangerous man. That had put her on guard.

I certainly said 'no' quickly enough when he asked me out!

Then perversely, she'd been pleased when he'd called her to explain he was a Christian and to ask her out again. They never had gotten around to discussing much about his work or how he'd been injured. Professionally she wondered about it, as well as just being naturally curious. However, as deftly as he'd fielded her questions about it, he had posted an 'off limits' sign around that aspect of his life.

She finished reflecting on the evening and smiled. *It was*, she admitted, *the most I've enjoyed being with a man in a long time*.

HAWKE PICKED HER up at 8:00. The dinner rush was waning, so the hostess was able to seat them immediately. The restaurant had a three-piece band and *a dance floor*—additions Grace stared at, askance. And when Hawke asked her to dance, she declined. Replied with an emphatic, "No, thank you. I don't dance. Never learned."

So what was his reply? "Not to worry, Grace. I'll dance for both of us. Come along for the ride? I won't let you down—promise."

She was terribly self-conscious, but he was encouraging and somehow got her laughing at herself. Then, suddenly, she found it easy to follow his lead. She even tripped over his feet less often. They danced through several songs while waiting for their dinner to be served. When she finally confessed that she was enjoying herself, he grinned, gratified.

They lingered over coffee and watched other couples dance, neither willing to call it a night although it was later than advisable, what with work the next day. Instead, they talked and smiled and danced once more. This time

Richard held her closer while they swayed together to the music, his face against her hair, her cheek resting below his shoulder.

That was when the gun under his left arm pressed into her, and she started. He loosened his hold. "Sorry about that."

Mulling it over, she realized he probably wore a side arm continually. It was his job, after all. She chose to ignore it because the evening's mood was too wonderful to spoil.

They didn't leave the restaurant until half past eleven. By then, the temperature had dropped. A light snow skittered across the windshield, and the companionship of the evening slowed to a quiet reticence. At Grace's door Richard wordlessly drew her close, filling her with his warmth.

For a long moment he stared hard into her face. Grace wondered if he thought she'd find him repugnant. Undaunted, she stared back.

When he kissed her, it was deliciously slow and tender, and Grace thought her heart would stop.

"Can I see you again Saturday evening?" His voice was rough.

She wanted to protest that Saturday evening was a *very* distant two days away. Instead she managed to murmur, "I would like that, Richard."

"I'll call you."

"Yes."

With the snow dropping silently upon them, Richard held her, but there was nothing left to say. Like a couple of shy, high-school teens, they were wordless.

CHAPTER 11

FRIDAY, OCTOBER 20

THE BUS SWAYED as it turned the corner. His employer's office wasn't far from the next stop. Hopefully, they would have work for him today. He rubbed his eyes and yawned. He hadn't slept well, had tossed and turned.

His need was scratching inside his head, begging him to let it out. And all night he'd dreamed of the vast number of possibilities before him.

I live in a big city now, he'd realized, *with endless opportunities.*
Endless?

Yes. All I need to do is keep my eyes peeled. Seize the moment when the perfect prospect presents itself. And eventually, when I have all my ducks in a row? That's when I'll finish the job I botched. And this time? She will die.

He thought ahead. *Good plans require resources. I'll need more money. Probably a car. Yup. Need to stay on my toes and keep my eyes peeled. Soon. Yes, very soon.*

He stifled another yawn as the bus came to a shuddering stop. He stepped out of the bus's warmth into the cold and crossed the street, setting a brisk pace for his employer's office.

WHEN HAWKE DISMISSED them late Friday evening after logging long, tedious hours Thursday and Friday, his small team was reduced to grouchy, red-eyed fatigue. Worse, their file search seemed about as pointless as a snipe hunt. To date, every possibly related case they'd looked at had been ruled out.

Hawke reminded them, "Remember, we only need to find the one right lead."

Dov yawned and pulled on his coat. "More like the one right needle in a haystack. 'Course, there's the unpleasant possibility that the circumstances of our two cases are novel, and we won't find anything related to them."

"We'll hit it again Monday morning," Hawke ground out. "For now, enjoy the weekend. I sincerely hope I don't have to drag your sorry-looking faces in here before then."

Hawke drove himself to his gym, grateful it was open until midnight. He was stiff and weary from sitting over piles of file folders all day and badly needed to stretch and work the kinks out of his shoulders and neck. While he drove, the futility of the situation set in. If they never stumbled over a related case, how could he and his team possibly unravel the mystery surrounding the deaths of Esther Grunbaum and Mary Alice Waite?

What really grated on him was the fact that neither woman had been murdered, yet the pressure coming down from Esther Grunbaum's wealthy and influential friends had forced Hawke and his team to set aside actual homicide cases, cases with real victims.

"I hate politics," he mumbled aloud.

It was after nine o'clock when he reached the gym, and the only bright spot ahead this weekend was Grace. Thank goodness, he'd see her tomorrow evening!

Shoot, if it wouldn't be so late when I finished here . . .

"No, I'm beat, and I haven't called her about tomorrow evening yet like I said I would." He changed into workout clothes, threw his suit into a locker, slammed the locker door, and stalked onto the gym's track.

He warmed up and ran a fast five miles, pushing himself mercilessly. Then, as difficult as it was, he stretched until his neck and back released. Exhausted, he showered and dragged himself home. The only thing he did before crawling into bed was feed Ontario.

THE CANNOLI SENT over for the party were especially good. Wanda knew they were because she had sampled one, and it had melted like glorious cotton candy in her mouth.

She selected a second pastry shell and eyed the stiff cream piled inside with something approaching lust. Saliva ran into her mouth. She swallowed, then held the dessert to her nose and inhaled appreciatively.

Rich food was a craving Wanda indulged whenever possible, something her ample figure advertised. She probably would have scarfed down the second cannoli right then and there, but she worried her client might notice if two of the delectables went missing. With regret, she returned the pastry to the crystal platter and continued supervising her catering crew as they set up for the party. Still, she had a hard time getting her mind off the temptation she'd left on the table in the kitchen.

Wanda's servers were mostly college kids who worked for her part-time. They showed up at 4:30. An hour later, the security team took their stations. By six o'clock guests began arriving. Wanda's servers shuttled in and out of the kitchen under her watchful eye, transporting platters of food to stock and restock the buffet or moving among the guests with silver salvers, offering tall, fluted glasses of champagne. Wanda glided continually between the kitchen and the party area, never missing a thing, making certain she remained on top of every aspect of the event.

More than one young server felt the bite of her tongue that evening. She didn't abide members of her team flirting with each other or security or, for that matter, in any way frittering away their time. They probably didn't like Wanda's toughness, but by golly, the party's hostess, Mrs. Armistead, *did*. Events came off without a hitch when Wanda took charge of them!

Take that sulky delivery boy she'd scolded. Maybe she *had* used the rough side of her tongue on him but one thing she refused to countenance was an attitude of sullenness from hired help. The way he'd stared at her following her harsh dressing down had made her even angrier.

"Be glad I'm not reporting you to your boss," she told him, wagging her finger under his nose.

The party was a short affair as parties go, lasting only until half past nine. Wanda put on a fresh pot of coffee to be ready when the last of the cleanup was complete. She never left until the kitchen was spotless and her two regular, full-time employees had packed up all the crystal, china, and serving pieces into the catering truck and driven off.

A hot cup of coffee and a few minutes gossip with Mrs. Armistead's housekeeper would rest her aching feet, then she would head home. Back at her apartment she'd curl up in bed with a juicy book and the cannoli she'd salvaged from a guest's plate.

The pastry was untouched so why should I waste it?

Closer to midnight than she'd hoped for, Wanda left by the back door, the housekeeper locking up behind her. Mrs. Armistead had been pleased with the party and, in addition to the sizable payment, had tipped generously. Wanda carried the money in her handbag—along with the cannoli wrapped in a napkin and tucked into the deep recesses of her purse's side pocket.

Wanda hummed with satisfaction and began to relax. She had parked her own car in the alley behind the Armistead's yard so there would be more room out front for the guests' vehicles. Exhaling slowly, she wound her way through the draped patio furniture and down the length of the over-large garage. She thought fondly of the book waiting for her at home . . . and the yummy treat in her purse.

Thank goodness I have Saturday off! I'll stay up late reading, then sleep in tomorrow.

Wanda believed she had the gift of intuition. That belief was reinforced when she stopped abruptly. She didn't know why she'd stopped, yet every hair on her neck and arms stood to attention.

The garage loomed alongside her, but she really couldn't see anything else in the dark nor did she hear anything out of the ordinary. She was both puzzled and anxious at the same time. After a long moment she started on her way again, leery and a bit slower.

It was when she cleared the end of the garage that she knew for certain someone was stalking her. A rushing motion behind her caused her to shriek. *Loudly.* Wanda might have been bulky, but she was also sturdy, and in her fear-fueled response, she swung her heavy purse around with all her weight behind it.

She connected with a shapeless form in the night and heard a male *umph* as her purse landed.

Wanda went on screeching for all she was worth. Lights blinked on in the big house, a neighbor's dog howled along with her, and her assailant fled. By the time Mr. Armistead and his live-in driver arrived, Wanda was shrieking in the dark alone, hard put to convince them that she'd actually been in danger.

The police arrived in due course, and Wanda gave them her statement. With nothing else to do, the police shrugged and left.

Wanda could tell that Mr. Armistead doubted her story—she saw how he looked at her. He probably couldn't envision anyone wanting to ravage *her*, a dumpy, middle-aged caterer. He likely had forgotten *the money* she was carrying.

Nevertheless, he and his driver saw Wanda to her car, and Wanda fled home to her apartment, more insulted than shaken at this point. Someone *had* been there! Someone *had* tried to assault her! But her own defensive actions had robbed her of the proof.

Well, she was safe, wasn't she? Yes, but humiliated too, because neither the police nor Mr. Armistead or his driver believed her story. And, no doubt, when word got out, she'd hear snatches of whispered remarks among a few of her smart-mouthed servers.

At least, I still have an evening's enjoyment to look forward to, she consoled herself.

She changed into a warm, serviceable nightgown, fetched her book and purse, and crawled thankfully into her bed. She opened her purse's wide side pocket to retrieve the cannoli. Down at the bottom her eager fingers sought her expected treat. Instead, they found a flattened pastry and a napkin soaked in smeared filling.

She threw her ruined dessert, purse and all, against her bedroom wall.

HE PLUNGED THROUGH the dark, empty streets, angry and frustrated. Why had this night gone so wrong for him? He'd been so certain of his plan! After reading everything he could find about Mary Alice Waite—and after the incredible revelation that had fallen into his lap—he truly believed his luck had changed.

He'd looked forward to this night, had shivered with unholy expectation over it. He desperately needed a vehicle and more money than what his job provided, so after he'd given his need what it desired, he had intended to take the woman's car and replace its license plates with freshly stolen ones. More-over, he'd counted on the money she'd been carrying to see him through the coming month.

But instead of that sweet sense of power, that stirring, thrilling sensation of *total control* that he craved, the woman he'd targeted had *not* crumbled under his hands, had *not* begged for her life. No indeed—she'd shrieked like a banshee and beaten him off.

Beaten him off? He'd gotten away—without her catching sight of him—by the skin of his teeth!

Bottom line? He'd failed.

So, you're a tad rusty, old boy, a bit out of practice, he told himself. *Don't have a cow over it—you'll have better luck next time.*

Next time? But would there be a next time?

Of course there's a next time. All you need is a slight adjustment, a little "tune up," so to speak. Why, you've been constrained for far too long! It's time to let yourself go. Feed the monster. Let him stretch and limber up. Give him breathing room.

He closed his eyes. Inhaled. Exhaled.

That's right. Fill your lungs! Let your true self out to play.

"Yeah, my time is still ahead. It's coming. Gotta let my true self have its own way."

He breathed deeply and pushed on.

CHAPTER 12

HAWKE RANG THE bell to Grace's townhouse. It was ten o'clock in the morning. A damp and frigid wind was blowing straight off the Atlantic, freezing him where he stood.

He had no business showing up at her place uninvited. He knew it. Knew it was stupid of him. But when his body clock awakened him at his usual early hour, he'd lain in bed, wide awake, wondering and scheming how he might wrangle an entire day spent with Grace. Waiting for a decent hour to call in case *she* was actually enjoying a few extra hours of sleep and loath to take that rest from her.

The moment nine o'clock rolled around, he reached for the phone . . . and stopped short. Tossed around the insane idea of just dropping by. Now here he was, standing on her doorstep. Uncertain. Definitely *not* invited. And auditioning for the role of Icicle of the Year.

He shoved his hands deep into his pockets and, out of habit, glanced up and down the street, making mental note of the cars parked nearby and a few hardy souls braving the cold.

A gust hit him. *Man, this weather is frigid!* He shivered and stomped his feet. *Frigid? Probably an apt description of the reception you'll get, if she even opens the door.*

He sighed. *You know what, Hawke? You're an idiot.*

Grace's place was a corner unit in a row of side-by-side townhouses. He rang the bell again, scanning the other units in the row. Obviously, her neighbors were intelligent folk; *they* were indoors, but no, not *him*. No, he was slowly freezing on her porch because apparently the woman was not home. But where would she be on such a miserable morning?

Cold and impatient, he pressed the doorbell a third time.

Hey, what is that?

When he'd pressed the doorbell, he'd heard it ring inside, but he also thought he saw, from beneath her closed living room drapes, a faint flash of light. On. Off. On. Off.

He rang the bell again. Same thing happened.

That's weird . . .

To his surprise, he heard her coming. His mouth dried up, and he experienced an immediate and fervent hope that she wouldn't be upset.

"Who is it?" Her voice was soft and muffled.

He caught movement through the peephole. "Hawke," he barked.

You sound like a cop making a bust, you dolt.

He faced the peephole, cleared his throat, and tried again. "It's Richard."

"Richard? I thought . . ."

"Grace, I hate to rush you, but may I come in? It's freezing out here."

"What?"

"May I come in?"

A pause, then, "One sec."

She unlatched the door, held it open, and gestured for him to come through.

Shaking his head as she closed the door behind him, he broke into apology. "I'm sorry, Grace. Totally inconsiderate of me. Should have called first, but I just . . ."

He grinned sheepishly and came clean. "I didn't want to wait until this evening to see you. Can I buy you brunch? Take you to a museum?"

She'd recently been in the shower. She was wrapped in a pale yellow chenille robe and had been towel drying her hair. It curled around her shoulders, a moist, deeper, darker brunette than usual because of its dampness. Her face had that fresh-scrubbed shine, and she watched him intently.

A moment after he finished speaking, her mouth curved into an amused smile.

Wow, Lord! She has a terrific smile.

"Do you mind if I get dressed and dry my hair first?"

"What? Sure. By all means." He breathed deeply. Happily. "This is great."

Still smiling, she asked if he would like coffee while he waited.

He nodded. As she headed for the kitchen, he added, "Just black, please."

By the swinging doors leading to her kitchen she turned. "Cream or sugar?"

He tilted his head and blinked slowly. He smiled and answered, "Just black. Thanks."

Hawke chose a seat on the couch, impatient for her return. He couldn't stop thinking about how her hair looked curling softly across the collar of the yellow robe. When she returned, he even managed to touch her slim fingertips as she handed him the cup and saucer. They were warm and delicate compared to his oversized paws.

Then before she reached her bedroom he called to her, "Be sure to dress warm, Grace. It's more than nippy out there."

She closed the door on his suggestion.

He sipped his coffee and speculated aloud, "So that's how it is."

He took stock of her place. Lots of muted color, soft lines, and comfortable furniture. Not overly feminine, but it had warmth, and he liked it. He knew the swinging doors opposite the living room went into the kitchen; he guessed a bedroom and a bathroom were down the hall where Grace had disappeared.

Yup. I hear a blow dryer.

Fifteen minutes later she bounced out of her room, bright in a bulky-knit pullover sweater and jeans, looking more like a teenager than a doctor.

"Okay! I'm ready for brunch and a museum."

With an answering smile, Hawke patted the couch next to him. "Could we talk first?"

She was instantly wary. "Talk about what?"

He was gentle. "Please?"

She sat, but across from him, still wary.

He began again, "Grace, you didn't tell me you have hearing loss." It was a statement, not an accusation; still she flushed.

"Is it any of your business?"

Her defiance startled Hawke. He was stung, not quite able to keep it out of his answer.

"Well, no . . . I suppose it isn't. I guess I wanted you to know that it doesn't matter to me. You don't need to keep it from me."

"Oh."

That one syllable held a breath of relief.

He grinned to defuse the tension. "Hey, I'm the one who barged in, unannounced, and promised you brunch and a museum. Shall we? Let's get out of here before we laze away the day."

They were quiet while he drove. He parked near the restaurant he had in mind for brunch, but they didn't go inside immediately. Instead, they walked in the chilly air. And talked.

"I didn't have my hearing aids in when I answered the door. Gave me away, didn't it?"

"Yup."

"Most people aren't as perceptive as you are, Richard."

"'Perceptive' is sort of in my job description."

They were tolerably warm as long as they walked. Hawke had Grace's hand nestled in his and tucked deep inside his coat pocket. He realized he liked having her hand in his.

"A detective has to pay attention to everything, not just what a person says, but how they say it, and what he or she avoids saying. That attentiveness becomes second nature. A detective lives by what he or she notices."

Or pays a price, if he doesn't.

"Are you good at your work?"

He snorted. "They say I am—whomever 'they' might be. They also say other things about me, but I'd rather you didn't listen to them." A moment went by before he added, "Would you tell me about your hearing loss, Grace? I'd like to know."

They walked on, still silent, before she grudgingly spoke.

"I lost much of my hearing when I was nine years old. Caught the measles. Plain old measles! Silly, huh? People aren't aware of the possible side effects of childhood diseases, the damage they are capable of inflicting. My case caused a severe inflammation in my inner ears."

She stopped. "How technical do you want me to get?"

"I'll let you know if I'm going under, Doc."

She chuckled. "Got it. Well, inside the ear canal, beyond the drum and within the inner ear is a round, shell-shaped organ called the cochlea. It's the nerve center of hearing. The cochlea is filled with fluid and lined with audio sensitive 'hair cells.' When the cochlea's fluid flows over these tiny hair cells, they detect sound vibrations and convert them into electrical signals that the brain interprets as sound.

"My case of measles caused an inflammation in my inner ear known as viral labyrinthitis. It destroyed many of these vital, sound-conducting cells resulting in 'sensorineural' damage and hearing loss. Since those cells do not reproduce themselves, the loss is permanent."

"But you're not entirely deaf."

"Not *quite* profoundly deaf, but I'm likely more impaired than you think, because if the loss had occurred when I was much younger, my speech would not have developed normally. It was a blessing that I was nine and not, say, two years old when I caught the measles. Otherwise my speech might be markedly different. Follow me so far?"

"Yup. Go on. I'm interested."

"Okay. I should add that these audio sensitive cells in the cochlea are specialized—that is, they are responsible for receiving and interpreting different audio *frequencies*. Upper-frequency or higher-pitch interpretation cells are located first in the cochlea. Lower frequency cells are farther inside. In my case, the sensorineural damage—nerve deafness in lay terms—took out most of my high- to mid-range hearing frequencies. I believe I explained frequency to you and your partner when you came to the clinic?"

"You did."

"Ah, but I may have not mentioned that loss in the upper frequencies is the most common form of impairment. All people experience some upper frequency loss as they age, but some experience more loss than others. Unfortunately, most *speech* occurs in the mid to upper frequencies, so without my aids I would miss *all* conversation. My aids offset most but not all of my conversational impairment, so I had to learn to compensate, to read lips, and to determine from context what certain words are. It is a continual guessing game with no respite."

"Then how did you hear me through your front door?"

"I didn't. I saw you through my extra-large peephole and watched your mouth." She giggled. "Watched you shiver and dance up and down on my porch."

Her giggle turned into a laugh. "I took pity on you."

"Color me grateful! Please continue?"

She was animated now, her fingers unconsciously gripping his.

"Richard, when I'm wearing my hearing aids, I can hear your voice. Thankfully, you have a deep, mellow voice that is easier for me to hear than, say, a woman's voice. You see, every spoken word—actually every *phoneme*, the smallest unit of speech—has a different tone and pitch. Take the word 'steeple.' The long 'ee' is high, while 'ple' is lower and shorter, and the 'st,' which is the first phoneme in steeple, has yet a third frequency.

"With my severe sensorineural damage, even while using hearing aids, I might hear only the second half of a given word spoken by a high-pitched woman's voice. I have to guess if she is saying people, steeple, or Peter, for that matter. You cannot imagine how difficult it can be to follow conversation when, in the best of settings, only fragments of words are audible.

"And conversations in group situations? Oh my; they are the worst. Sounds get muddled up together and lost in the white noise—the room's background atmosphere. So much garbled input to interpret!"

She glanced at him for his reaction.

"You said you read lips."

"Yes. I read lips, use American sign language, and employ any and every strategy available to a hearing-impaired person in order to navigate the hearing world, to try to fit in and not feel excluded. It is no wonder many profoundly deaf individuals choose to withdraw from the hearing world altogether and live exclusively, or nearly so, with others like themselves."

Hawke said slowly, "I had no idea. I suppose I can understand, then, why the family therapy arm of your clinic is important."

"*Vital.* For many it is vital." She released a tired sigh, and they were again quiet for a time.

Hawke squeezed her hand, and she turned to him. "What about music?" he asked.

"Sadly, I cannot enjoy a lot of music. I remember a few tunes from my childhood before I lost hearing, but perhaps you can understand how difficult it was as I grew older to develop an appreciation for something that most of the time is, well, either noise or just not there. You know, they just don't make much bottom-heavy stuff. Tuba solos, anyone?"

Definitely not opera or symphony, Hawke conceded to his own relief.

Another thought hit him. "Wait. That's why you'd never been dancing?"

"Actually, I can hear the lower parts of rhythm, particularly when it is loud and pounding, but yes, that's one reason why. I suppose the other reason is that I have always been too self-conscious to put myself out there. Do you know what, though?"

There was a breathy softness to her question.

"What?" Hawke asked. "Tell me?"

"I have never had as much fun as I had the other night when you danced with me."

"Really?"

"Really."

"Good." He was pleased. Practically elated. "Want to do that again?"

"Definitely."

The skies grew suddenly darker, but not because it was late in the day. Rather, storm clouds were building, and along with them was the sense of more snow hanging heavy in the air. They walked faster, retracing their path to the restaurant.

"There's another aspect to hearing impairment you should know, Richard. It's called *tinnitus*. For varying reasons, strange sounds often plague hearing-impaired individuals. They may describe their tinnitus as a shrill ringing, chiming, whining, buzzing, or rasping either in their ears or elsewhere in their head. Tinnitus varies from person to person and can present as mildly distracting or loud enough to drive a sane person crazy. Incessant tinnitus is why many hearing-impaired individuals eventually sink into depression and withdraw. Give up."

She paused and added, "All these issues are why Upton-Warner's support and therapy system is so very important. We don't want our patients to lapse into depression and give up on life."

"You didn't do that," Hawke observed. "You went to college and medical school. You have your clinic and a thriving career. You function as well as any hearing individual."

"Yes, but only because I had the understanding and support I needed: my parents, until they died, and after they passed, Dr. Bill—especially, Dr. Bill. He was there for me through the horror of my parents' deaths; thank you, Lord!"

Made curious by her fervent response, Hawke asked, "Who is Dr. Bill, Grace? I can tell that you're close to him, but what is the relationship?"

"Bill Upton was my father's good friend and was like an uncle to me. He and my father founded Upton-Warner. But then my parents died in a car crash. I was a hormonal fifteen-year-old terrified of my own shadow. Bill had never married, had no children, and was in his late fifties when he found himself responsible for me. Dear Bill! I cannot imagine how hard it was for him, having to cope with a devastated teenager."

Hawke could hear the tightening in her throat as she continued. "He gave me his time and care. Pulled me back together. Helped me look to my future and helped me finish high school. Together, we decided that I *could* do college and med school, even a second specialization, with the goal of eventually coming to work with him at the clinic.

"We have a full staff now, specialists in overlapping fields, and Dr. Bill serves primarily as our administrator. The clinic is finally developing a solid reputation, too, but it has taken many long years of hard work. I've either never had the time or never taken the time to do much else."

"The total career preoccupation of the eighties," he said softly, "yet you hardly look old enough to have shouldered so much responsibility. Just how old are you, Grace? I mean, if you don't mind my asking." He added the last with an apologetic inflection.

Grace chuffed a laugh. "If there's one thing I'm learning about you, Richard Hawke, it is to expect the straightforward. But not to worry; I rather prefer it."

Laughing again, she added, "How old am I? I'm hanging on to the last months of my twenties. Not that 'hanging on' will do any good."

"Seriously? You're twenty-nine? You don't look it."

"So I've been told, but you can't be that much older than I am," she shot back.

"Me? I look old by virtue of wear and tear."

"Fair's fair. I told you my age."

He chuckled. "Okay, I give. There's nine years difference between us. Doesn't sound like a big gap and I suppose it only matters if I point out that you caught the measles the same year I shipped out for Vietnam."

"Now the rest. I bared my soul, after all," she insisted.

"So you did. Well, not unlike you, since the day I mustered out of the service, I've poured my life into my job."

He told her about his time in law enforcement, then talked about his father and mother, recently retired to Florida. "I have two brothers, both married with kids. One brother is an accountant in Jersey, the other is a Marine lifer. Me, I'm just a cop, but that's what I have wanted most of my life."

With her free hand Grace gently traced the scar on his cheek and across his nose. For an instant she thought he was going to flinch but he held himself still as she smoothed the line with her fingertip.

Hawke hesitated and then asked the question she'd been expecting.

"Does it bother you, Grace?"

"Does what bother me?"

"Nice deflection, Dr. Warner. Thank you."

"You're welcome. Are you going to tell me about it?"

"Not much to tell. Homicide Division was working a joint investigation with Narcotics. My partner Steve and I posed as drug dealers from Florida because we weren't known to the dealers in town. We lured a local bigshot gangster and his crew into buying a large quantity of cocaine from us. We wanted the gangster for murder; Narcotics wanted him for trafficking. Win-win."

He hesitated, not wanting to continue.

Grace stared at him, anxiety marring her expression. "Richard?"

He nodded. "Yeah. It's bad."

Heaving a sigh, he continued, "We had SWAT and a large police contingency standing ready to take them down as soon as the money changed hands. We popped our trunk, showed them the product, they popped their trunk, showed us the money. But at the last possible moment, a new guy on the bigshot's crew piped up, said he recognized me as a cop, and pulled a gun.

"A battle ensued. We had the numbers, so the end result was never in question, but getting there was . . . costly. Devastating. Steve and I managed to jump the big shot and take him to the ground. The guy's lieutenant, however, pulled a tire iron from their trunk. Steve never saw it coming. I did and managed to twist away just a little before the blow connected. That's it—a matter of an inch or two saved my life, but . . . Steve took the hit across the back of his neck and died twelve hours later."

She swallowed. "Do you . . . feel responsible?"

He thought for a moment. "Yes. *If* I hadn't been recognized, *if* I'd let Steve take down the big cheese by himself, and *if* I had watched our backs instead of helping him . . . well, a lot of ifs. The 'ifs' have about owned me ever since."

Grace whispered, "All things work together for good for those who love God . . ."

"Right. I've quoted that Scripture to myself a hundred times. I have finally come to the settled realization that what Steve has *in the here and now* is the best 'good' any of us will ever know. He's with Jesus! Given the chance, he would never choose to come back. That, however, doesn't keep me from wishing God hadn't taken him when he did."

He snorted. "On the other hand, I doubt I'd be a Christian if Steve hadn't died."

"Oh?"

"Steve talked to me about Jesus. Daily. Incessantly. *All the time*. Me? I argued, resisted, and mocked." Hawke chuckled. "It's a lot like Dov and me. I talk about Jesus, he argues, sneers, and scoffs. Anyway, that rough patch I told you I went through? It brought me to my knees, so I will praise God forever for the five years I had Steve in my life."

They were quiet for a while. Then Hawke sort of shook himself. "Want to ask me anything else? I'm an open book—whatever you want to know."

She nodded. "All right. Have you ever been married?"

"Me? No. You?"

She shook her head with slow regret but managed to smile. "No."

Hawke smiled back. "I'm not sorry that I haven't been married . . . yet."

"Care to explain?"

He squeezed her hand inside his pocket. "As you've no doubt figured out, life has beat me up and spit me out a few times. But that last beatdown? It came close to taking me out in more ways than one."

He shook his head. "If I'm being honest, I must admit that I allowed a crusty shell to grow around me while I healed from the inside out. That 'shell' is something the Lord needs to change in me, and I want him to. But, back to marriage? I have come to a place in Christ where I believe that marriage is 'one and done.' No do-overs. I choose to trust God for his best for me, and I choose to wait for that . . . someone to come along."

They paused at a corner and faced each other. He added, "I might be babbling . . . or does any part of what I've said resonate with you? Can you . . . relate?"

She swallowed. "What, that your life has been a series of beatdowns and can I relate? Actually, I think you've pretty much summed up my life too."

Cold, brittle snow fell around them, some of the flakes sparkling on her upturned face. They stared at each other, searching the other's heart as deeply and humanly as possible, until Hawke had to look away lest he pull her into his arms.

Finally, he murmured. "For the record, Grace, your hearing loss doesn't mean diddly to me; I admire you immensely, and I wouldn't want you to think otherwise."

She said nothing for a long moment, then replied, "You did say being perceptive was part of your job description." Her smile was a tad crooked and something other than snow glistened on her lashes.

Hawke answered softly, "But I'm not on the job when I'm with you, am I? Feel free to remind me. A good wallop should work."

She nodded. "I will take your suggestion under advisement."

They crossed the intersection making for the restaurant, their joined hands, warm in his coat pocket, keeping them close.

CHAPTER 13

Thursday, October 26

"DETECTIVE HAWKE, THIS is Arthur Grunbaum; Mr. Grunbaum, Detective Sergeant Rick Hawke." McCormick made the introduction, his voice even. It was the superfluous gesture of McCormick's hand that told Hawke the chief had a lot riding on this conversation.

"Yes sir; Mr. Grunbaum and I have met. How are you, Mr. Grunbaum?" Despite the expensive cut of his suit, the man didn't look good.

"Mr. Grunbaum would like an idea of the progress we've made in our investigation, Hawke." McCormick eyes bored into Hawke's, threatening him while at the same time imploring him to placate their influential visitor. Without uttering a word, McCormick was granting Hawe a measure of latitude.

And I'll take it, Hawke told himself.

"Certainly. Mr. Grunbaum, if you would care to step over to my desk, I'll go over our progress with you." Hawke caught the glimpse of relief on his captain's face. He hoped McCormick's feelings would remain unchanged after Grunbaum left. Hawke led the man across the floor to his corner niche.

"Please have a seat, Mr. Grunbaum."

The man squinted at the sparsity of Hawke's office area and, with reluctance, settled onto the ancient folding chair. The noise level from the main floor was only slightly less for the chest-high wall partway around the cubicle.

"This is where you do all your . . . work?"

"Yes sir, this is it." Hawke smiled wryly and Grunbaum caught his meaning.

"I see." Grunbaum coughed to cover his dismay. "So what can you tell me, Detective Sergeant?"

Here comes the hard part, Hawke thought. *All I need now is a top hat and a white bunny.*

"Sir, based on common elements found at both scenes and other findings, our working theory is that the individual who provided the blood for the, ah, *rituals*, suffers from profound hearing loss and is likely socially stunted."

Grunbaum's brows lifted. "Oh? And how did you come to those . . . rather explicit assumptions?"

"Before I answer, I will need some assurances from you."

"You have evidence you haven't revealed to the public, is that it?"

"One small but central bit, yes. However, in order to show it to you, I need your word that you will not speak of this evidence to anyone else. *Not anyone.*"

Grunbaum slowly nodded. "All right. You have my word."

Hawke opened the folder on his desk and slid a plastic-encased sheet of brownish paper from it. He handed the paper to Grunbaum, then watched the man's reaction as he read the scrawled message. Hawke would not, however, show Grunbaum the envelope the note came in.

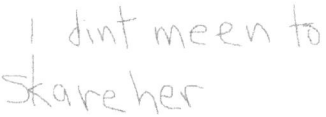

"This . . . this note? Looks like a kid wrote it."

"At first glance, it does. However, we have an expert who tells us it is from an adult, but an individual damaged or stunted in some manner."

"How did you come by it?"

"It came through the mail, but not to us—and I cannot reveal the recipient's identity."

Grunbaum continued to stare at the paper. "I see. So . . . this note, is it referring to that church organist?"

"Yes, the timeframe in which we received the note tells us that it does."

"But it's not from a child?"

Hawke nodded. "That's what we believe. As I said, we have an expert resource, someone with the credentials to advise us, who insists that, although the writing and spelling are childish, a child lacks the level of remorse and responsibility expressed by the note."

"Then you're saying the organist's fall down the stairs actually *was* an accident despite the . . . blood."

"We believe so. Our working theory is that the 'bloodletter,' as we've decided to term him, was in the nearly dark loft only to listen to Miss Waite's organ rehearsal. At some point, Miss Waite became aware of the man's presence and felt threatened. When she made for the stairs, she dropped her flashlight, lost her balance, and fell. The bloodletter followed her down the stairs and stood over her body."

Hawke took the note from Grunbaum and put it back in the folder. "In addition to the puddle of blood, the ME found traces of dried tears on the floor next to Miss Waite's body. The tears coupled with the note tell us the bloodletter experienced remorse."

Grunbaum stared down at his hands. "That note painted on the wall near my Esther? By extension, you're saying Esther's death wasn't intentional either, that she died of a heart attack . . . because she chased that young man?"

Hawke nodded. "The ME's report tells us your wife had advanced cardiovascular disease, undiagnosed. If we follow our working theory, that the bloodletter was there only to listen to the concert, then it stands to reason Mrs. Grunbaum's death was due to overexertion . . . after which our bloodletter painted the word 'sorry' on the wall near her body."

He added, "I, too, am very sorry for your loss, Mr. Grunbaum."

Grunbaum had folded in on himself. "But who is this person she chased that evening? And why was he in the belly of that organ? You say he was there to listen, but I don't . . . I don't understand."

"This is where the second half of our theory comes into play: We believe the bloodletter is hearing impaired. We found an abundance of finger and palm prints on the largest pipes of both organs—the organ at St. Joseph's and the organ at the Claremont. The bloodletter had his hands all over them. Our expert tells us that an individual with profound hearing loss may be able to hear the lowest pipes and might gravitate to them to feel their vibrations."

Hawke added, "Our advisor suggests that the bloodletter likely finds great joy from what little of the organ music he is able to hear."

Grunbaum lifted his grieving eyes. "Esther didn't know, didn't realize—how could she! If she had . . ." He sniffed. "My Esther was the most compassionate woman I've ever known. If she had realized the guy was nearly deaf and went to such extraordinary lengths just to listen to the concert up close, she would have made arrangements for the guy, tickets practically under Menti's nose, new evening wear, dinner after—the works! You have no idea."

"A tragedy all around," Hawke murmured.

Grunbaum wiped his eyes. "But none of this explains the blood he put on her face. What is that about?"

"Still a mystery. But unless we identify and interview the bloodletter, it's possible we may never know. The best we can do at present is to presume—and accurately so, in my estimation—that there was no malice intended at either scene."

Grunbaum slowly nodded. "And you want me to quit publicly busting your chops."

Hawke chose his response carefully. "The detectives working this case and other cases are mere public servants, Mr. Grunbaum. *All* of our work is important, but as you can see by our surroundings, our budget has limits."

Art Grunbaum bent his silent scrutiny on Hawke for a good minute. "You're saying you need to put this case to bed so you can move on to other cases."

"Yes, but entirely because the evidence in these two instances tells us there was no actual crime, only terrible, tragic misfortune."

Grunbaum sighed. Picked imaginary lint from his trousers. Shook his head again at Hawke's meager work space. "I . . . I'll make a statement to the press thanking you for your service. Will that take the pressure off?"

"It should. And we'd certainly appreciate it, sir."

"Call me Art."

"Thank you, Art."

Lord God, Hawke prayed silently. *I have no idea how you orchestrated it, but you have just managed to defuse this entire situation. Thank you!*

The man withdrew a slender cigar from his suit coat. Idly Hawke estimated that Grunbaum's suit probably cost in the neighborhood of his monthly salary and the cigar about a day's pay.

Art rolled the cigar between his fingers "Stinking habit. Gave it up years ago . . . for Esther."

He stood abruptly. "Thank you for your valuable time, Detective."

Hawke walked the man through the division's narrow aisles. They shook hands at the exit. Turning back, Hawke caught sight of Chief McCormick studying him from his doorway.

CHAPTER 14

SATURDAY, OCTOBER 28

IT WAS COLD. *So painfully cold!* The late afternoon air was brittle, and every breath he drew felt like shards of glass piercing his throat and lungs. Furthermore, the lightweight jacket he wore didn't even begin to keep the wind's painful bite from penetrating his bones.

He thought of the warm room and bed he'd lost—all because the old biddy he'd rented from 'didn't care for his tone.' Well, that and the fact that he'd been reduced to paying by the night and couldn't come up with the scratch for tonight's rent, let alone Sunday night's. His job owed him pay, but he couldn't collect it until Monday. And because the landlady refused to give him credit, he had no bed and no place to shelter from the cold and damp.

Not tonight. Not tomorrow. And I need a winter coat bad—real bad. I won't survive the night without one.

Pedestrian traffic was thick and hurried, and as he sauntered slowly down the street that old, familiar compulsion tickled him. He needed a good coat, but he needed that *something else* "real bad" too.

Disappointment still vibrated within him over his failure the night of the catered party a week ago yesterday. *If I'd taken down that fat broad nice and quiet-like, I'd have all the money I need, but nooo. Somehow she sensed me behind her and sent up a scream that like to shred every tire on the block.*

Worse than losing the money he'd counted on, the reassurances he'd repeated to himself had grown stale, and that needy, insistent voice in his head would *not* shut up.

Let yourself go, it chanted. *You gotta let your true self out to play.*

My true self? He'd fantasized about what he would do to the fat woman once he had her on the ground. Just thinking about using the homemade shiv in his pocket made his hands tingle and itch.

Stop it! I failed. I'm no better than the street trash camped out under the expressway.

He watched the people as they passed him, followed them with jealous eyes. They brushed by him with sightless stares or detoured around him, eyes fixed ahead—all of them moving toward warmth, comfort, and security. Any one of them would have the price of a warm jacket on them, but not for him! He thought about panhandling, but he was too proud and too angry to beg. Too suspicious of people's disdain.

He worried briefly over his job. The little he earned barely covered the cost of his room, and they had only given him two shifts this week. He knew why: The people he worked with got nervous around him; they watched him out of the sides of their eyes. They probably didn't think he noticed but he did. He noticed lots. Like how the other guys got all the hours except when they had so many events that they even pretended to be glad when he came in.

He acted like it didn't bother him, but it did. *Oh, yeah, it did.* If it wasn't for the panic he felt over sleeping outside in this frigid weather, he'd never go back.

Foot traffic thinned and steps quickened. Looking around he realized it was nearly 5:00 p.m. Stores were closing up, employees heading home, the cold intensifying, and yet he would be left on the street all night!

A barrel-chested man marched out of a secondhand store and shook his dust mop into the biting wind. Before he went back inside, he turned over the sign in the door window. *Closed.* On the corner the streetlights flickered on while another shop's lights went out. The descending night was colder already. His persistent banging on the door of the secondhand shop summoned the barrel-chested man.

He peered at him through the glass. "Sorry. We're closed."

"I know, but I need a coat real bad. I'll freeze tonight if I don't get one." He plucked at his thin jacket and shrugged sheepishly.

After looking him up and down, the man unlocked the door. "Sure. Got some good, thick ones. Right over here, this rack. All of us got to stay warm, right?" He smiled, open and friendly like, as he turned to face his customer. "How about this one? Try it on."

He slid his arms into the sleeves. "Shoulders are too tight."

"Well, I got a larger one here, costs a little more. How much do you want to pay?"

"Pay?" He wasn't thinking right. Those annoying phrases repeating in his head were drowning out everything else.

Just let yourself go. Let your true self out to play.

"Shut up!" he hissed back.

The store clerk heard and frowned. "What'd you say? Hey, man, don't give me no disrespect. I don't take lip off anybody. You want a coat or not?"

"I didn't. I mean—" He stared around, then bolted. The clerk's hand grabbed at the coat he still had on and jerked him back.

"I knew I shouldn't have let you in, you bum. Gimme my coat and get outta here." He pulled on the jacket's snug sleeve.

The words clanged in his head and a deeper need, *an urgent compulsion* raised its fearsome head.

The clerk shook him hard. "Gimme my coat and don't come back here. You understand?"

He wriggled out of the tight sleeves and dropped the coat to the floor.

"I said, you understand me? Get outta my store and don't come back!"

The compulsion grew. A red haze stole over him and took control. His hand reached inside his pants pocket. When he stepped forward and slid the shiv into the clerk's side, the man's snarl slipped and he gaped, slightly puzzled, then gasped as the pain ripped through him. The clerk's hands instinctively scrabbled for the knife but the blade slashed his fingers as it jerked out and plunged in again and again. His mouth opening and closing like a fish out of water, the clerk slowly crumpled to the floor.

Even while the shop owner was dying, he began to arrange the man's body in a peaceful pose. Then he dipped his knife into the puddle forming on the floor and, standing over the clerk, stared with disinterest as the blood dripped off the tip of the knife onto the man's dying eyes. He took his time. Flicked blood onto the man's face for good measure.

Only blood pays.

"Now, where was I? Oh, yeah. I need a coat, a good one. And somewhere warm to sleep tonight. Maybe somewhere in here?"

As if he'd done nothing out of the ordinary, he relocked the shop's door and wandered past the racks of clothing, working his way toward the back of the store. Behind the counter and register, he spotted the door to an office and break room combo. When he checked it out, he found it had a coffee pot, a microwave, a desk, and an old camp cot with a wool army blanket strewn across it. A tiny half bath opened off the room too.

He washed his shiv and tucked it back into his pocket. Then he made himself a pot of coffee, two packages of ramen noodles, and a bag of microwave popcorn. With his hunger blunted, he wandered the store, looking at what was available. He rechecked the front door to make sure it was locked. The sign on the door with the store's hours read *Closed Sundays.*

Hey. Tomorrow is Sunday. I can sleep here as long as I want. No one will be coming to evict me until Monday morning. Gotta have a good coat by Monday.

He went about selecting one. The clerk had been right: he had some good coats hanging on the racks, but the best-looking specimen was lying across the counter by the register. It was dark green, thick and warm and plenty big. He even found a pair of matching insulated gloves in one of its pockets and a knit watch cap in another.

He sighed with simple contentment as he put the coat on over his old thin jacket. Eventually, he turned out the lights, laid himself down on the cot, and pulled the blanket over himself, coat and all.

~

HE SLEPT HARD that night, and on Sunday he loafed away the day, filling up on popcorn, ramen noodles, and a couple of candy bars he found in the desk.

Early Monday morning, after fortifying himself with more coffee and noodles, he emptied the register, stuffed a couple packages of ramen noodles into the deep pockets of his new coat, and locked the shop door before he closed it behind him. The morning was bitterly cold and windy, but he hardly felt the freezing wind through his new coat, gloves, and hat.

He was happy this day. He would collect the pay owed him. With his pay and what he'd taken from the register, he'd be able to hand over a couple of weeks' rent to the old biddy. Two weeks' rent on his warm room! Or . . .

Or maybe I don't have to go back to that old battleaxe. I might have enough to do a monthly rental down the street. Cheaper by the month, you know. And groceries. Need me some cans of chili and stew.

A whole month to save up for the next month's rent!

Yeah, but gotta get ahead of the game. Figure how to get a car, too, if I expect to take my lovely bride for a ride in the country.

No worries, his compulsion gloated. *See what happens when you let your true self out to play? Everything lines up perfectly. So just be yourself. Your* true *self.*

Reveling in his good fortune, he muttered, "Guess it pays to be my true self. I *will* be myself from now on, never you fear. Not gonna get caught this time neither."

He chuckled. "I *for sure* ain't goin' back to prison. Nope. Not me."

CHAPTER 15

MONDAY, OCTOBER 30

HAWKE AND MAYER studied the body as the ME and crime scene techs did their thing. Browning looked around, anywhere but at the body; Percival read aloud from his notes.

"Vincent Delano, widowed, lived with his son, Rudy Delano. Rudy was gone over the weekend on business, Friday afternoon through late Sunday evening. He thought his father was in bed when he came home last night. He didn't realize he was alone in the house until just this morning, around 8:00 a m."

"Son found the body?"

"Yup. He tells us his father should have closed the store Saturday evening and come straight home."

"TOD?"

"According to liver temp, around closing time Saturday," Dr. Rodríguez muttered.

"Been pretty cold the last few nights," Dov added, "but the lights in the store were off, thermostat turned down when the son got here about two hours ago. Like the guy had closed up shop, but . . ."

Hawke nodded and refocused on the scene. "But someone was still inside the store. Maybe hiding, waiting for him to close."

"Not seeing anywhere to hide in here," Dov replied, "Dead body and empty register. The usual hallmarks of a robbery gone bad, except . . ."

Neither of them wanted to say the words aloud. Nevertheless, certain facts hung in the chilly room like the vapor that puffed from their mouths.

Vincent Delano lay on his back, his body neatly arranged, his hands at his side in peaceful repose. Nothing else about the man's body bespoke repose, however. He'd been stabbed multiple times, and the killer, while Delano was bleeding out, had dribbled blood onto the man face.

The scene was too reminiscent of Mary Alice Waite and Esther Grunbaum to be ignored. Too deliberately reminiscent.

"Definitely homicide . . . this time," Rodríguez muttered.

"Kinda figured," Hawke said.

"'Cause the body looks like a pin cushion,' Browning snarked.

Hawke frowned in Browning's direction and gently massaged the dented bridge of his nose. Cold weather dried his skin, made the scar pull and itch, and sometimes the broken and remodeled bones of his nose and cheek ached. Didn't help that he'd been hunched over stacks of files since 6:00 a.m. until they'd been called out just after 11:00 a.m.

He and Dov left Browning and Percival to finish up at the scene and rode back to the station in sober silence. It wasn't until they pulled into the parking lot that Dov spoke up.

"The person who did this?"

"Yeah, I know. The scene was staged. Whoever murdered Delano had to have either seen Mary Alice Waite or Esther Grunbaum's body in person or been shown photographs of the crime scene."

"Are you saying you don't think our bloodletter killed Delano?"

Bits of conversation between Hawke and Art Grunbaum floated through Hawke's mind.

The best we can do at present is to presume—and accurately so, in my estimation—that there was no malice intended at either scene.

You're saying you need to put this case to bed so you can get on to other cases.

Yes, but entirely because the evidence in these two instances tells us there was no actual crime, only terrible, tragic misfortune.

"Wait. This *was* a crime. Two crimes. Murder and robbery."

"What's that?" Dov asked.

"No, our bloodletter didn't do this."

While they took the elevator up to Homicide Division, Hawke's thoughts detoured abruptly. He'd worked all day Saturday, mostly to keep himself occupied because Grace had been called to perform an emergency surgery, the result of a bad traffic accident. Hawke had seen his share of bad accidents back when he was on patrol: Kids with smashed-in faces from hitting the windshield because their dad or mom decided to drive drunk. The cars always had seatbelts, of course. They just weren't used, *of course.*

Grace had done the initial repair work on the boy's broken nose, cheek bones, and the orbit around his left eye. "My job was to repair or remove the worst fragments so the kid could breathe. A cosmetic surgeon will follow up and make better repairs than I can."

Still, the surgery had taken hours. Afterwards she was too exhausted to go anywhere, emotionally as well as physically. "My feet and shoulders ache. All I want is a hot bath and my bed," she explained.

Sunday morning, they met for early service at Grace's church. Afterward, they drove north out of town where they were surrounded by clean, crisp air and thick stands of trees frolicking in fall colors interspersed with early snow. They had time to talk but were mostly quiet.

Comfortably quiet. Together.

When an old-fashioned café off the beaten track caught their eye, they stopped for lunch. Later, when they were getting back into town, they shared dinner in a hole-in-the-wall diner.

Hawke hadn't thought about work once all day. But while they rested over the weekend, someone had killed and robbed Vincent Delano, then staged his body to look like Esther Grunbaum's and Mary Alice Waite's.

Hawke and Dov grabbed coffee, then returned to Hawke's cubicle. He forced himself to get back to business. "Go through this with me, Dov."

Dov nodded, attentive. This was usually good.

Swallowing a hot gulp of what passed as coffee across the fourth floor, Hawke began. "First fact: Mary Alice Waite's death was accidental—the bloodletter as good as told us that—and Esther Grunbaum's death was a fluke. How do we know this? Because there's no way our bloodletter could have foreseen that she would follow him into the basement, nor could he have foreseen that Mrs. Grunbaum would have a heart attack."

"And don't forget he wrote 'Sorry' on the wall, Rick."

"Right. Fact two: In both cases, the bloodletter posed the dead women in serene, respectful positions, and followed up with the blood ritual—by cutting himself.

"Fact three: Our bloodletter was in the basement of the Claremont for the same reason the audience was seated in the Claremont's auditorium: to hear the concert. The only difference is that our bloodletter prefers to listen up close and personal—*hands-on* personal. Same with the organ at St. Joseph's. Our guy was in the choir loft to hear Mary Alice Waite rehearse, not hurt her. Point is, in both cases, he was on scene *for the music*. Period. No malintent on his part. With me so far?"

"Yeah, I think so. Go ahead."

"Two cases, identical in all respects."

Hawke lifted his mug to his mouth and took a gulp. "But when we get to Mr. Delano, we immediately run into aberrations. No organ concert, no music of any kind, not even a radio in the room. Furthermore, the assailant stabs Delano repeatedly, so now we have a homicide, not an accident or natural death."

"Don't forget it's a robbery, Rick."

"Have not forgotten. In fact, only two things tie these three cases together: posing the body and the blood ritual. But you know what? Even those are different." Hawke laid photos of the three bodies in a row and gestured at them. "Let's play the game, 'which of these is different'?"

Dov studied them only seconds. "Delano's. A lot less blood on the face, and the spatter is wrong . . . like . . . like he dipped his knife in the blood and *flicked* some of it onto Delano's face."

"Right. Because this killer is not our bloodletter. Our bleeder guy cuts himself and dribbles his own blood on the dead person's face. *This* guy cut Delano and shook *Delano's* blood on the guy's face, not his own, and the ME's report will confirm it."

Hawke shook his head. "I tell you, Dov, if I thought this case was related to our bloodletter, this important deviation tells me it isn't."

"So why did Delano's killer copy the blood ritual, Rick? They have to be connected somehow, don't they?"

Hawke closed his mouth with a snap, stared at the photos, and was quiet for a long time.

Dov squirmed. "Rick?"

"You're right, Dov. A connection has to exist. I just don't see it yet."

"So, what's next?"

"What next? We keep excavating files and keep running bulletins. We keep at it until we find that connection."

Dov sighed. "Swell."

Monday, October 30

"GRACE? THIS IS Hawke. Have a good day?" He was so weary he just wanted to hear her voice speak his name.

"Hi, Richard."

I love the sound of my name on her lips.

She continued, "Mondays are pretty hectic, but I managed to get away by 6:00."

"That's not too bad. I'm clearing off my desk right now."

"It's after nine o'clock!"

"Tell me about it. Another body turned up this morning, this one definitely a homicide."

"A murder!"

"Yes, but this victim was a man. Despite the differences between the cases, the publicity will get ugly."

"You and your team are already working so much overtime . . . " Her voice conveyed sympathy and concern.

"Our only option is to dig for possible connections through association, common *modus operandi* and the like, and a search like that is tedious and time consuming. Anyway, I do realize it's too late to see you tonight, but could we have a late dinner tomorrow? A little Italian or Greek?"

"How would you like to eat at my place instead? It won't be a gourmet meal, but it'll be homecooked."

"That's the best offer I've had all day, believe me. But don't you have your group thing?"

"My 'group thing' is canceled for Halloween."

"Halloween?"

She chuckled. "Look at your calendar, you big lug. Tomorrow is the last day of October. Can you get away by say, seven o'clock?"

"I'll make sure of it. See you then, Babe."

"Babe?" There was laughter in her throat, and it kind of clutched at his chest and jiggled around inside—not at all an unpleasant sensation.

"I apologize. That said, I did warn you about my rough edges. Think you can do anything with me?"

"The question is, Richard, would I want to?" There was just enough smugness to draw a weary grin from him.

"You mean I'm perfect the way I am, and you wouldn't change a thing?"

"Don't tempt me to respond except to note that *I* have the good sense not to try." She was laughing aloud now.

"You're a sharp woman, Grace."

"Hmm. Rough vs. sharp. We sound like low-grade sandpaper."

"Ah. I appreciate your sharp mind smoothing out my rough edges. I like it." He sighed. "Grace . . . I'm looking forward to seeing you tomorrow evening."

"Me too, Richard. Sleep well tonight."

The dial tone cut in and Hawke found himself smiling vapidly into the dead receiver and wishing he had someone other than Ontario to go home to.

SARA CAME TO Terry in his dreams that night. Gentle. Accepting. Never mean or impatient. The other kids at school were invariably cruel, but Sara was always kind, even though she often seemed sad.

She said we were friends.

She hadn't known that she was his *only* friend, but she was. She even understood his need to touch the organ's pipes while she played. She had learned a few words in sign language and would sign to him, "Thank you for keeping me company while I play the organ."

He wasn't quite certain she meant "keeping me company," because she used a sign that could also mean "safe." *Thank you for keeping me safe while I play the organ?*

He squirmed in his sleep. *I don't want to think about that.*

In his dream, her brown hair floated in soft curls about her face and shoulders and her mouth curved sweetly. He sighed in painful joy until . . . until Mrs. Currys' tight, agitated words edged in.

"Stay away from Sara, do you hear me? Stay away from my niece, do you hear me, boy?"

Sara smiled on, undeterred by the rebuke. He grinned back, confident in her friendship.

"Stay away from her, do you hear me?" The voice was fainter, fading.

"But Sara likes me. She's nice. Nobody is nice to me except Sara."

Of course the question, *the accusation* returned at that point. It always did. He asked the same question whenever Sara came to him in his dreams.

Why Sara?

Why did I kill you?

He had but one answer. *It couldn't have been me.*

It had to have been the monster inside me.

He did it.

CHAPTER 16

TUESDAY, OCTOBER 31

"HEY, HAWKE? SINCE it's Halloween and our two 'pipe organ' cases are cooling down, could we knock off early tonight? By early I mean our regular quitting time, five o'clock? Gotta help Lisa hand out candy."

A hopeful Percival hovered nearby. Browning loomed behind him, resentment glittering in his eyes. Hawke knew he was going to have trouble with the older detective sooner or later, likely before too long.

Another issue for another day.

He sniffed. "Our pipe organ cases are cooling down? Really, Dov? Given Vincent Delano's manner of death and its unmistakable copycat connection to Mary Alice Waite and Esther Grunbaum, you think those two cases will just fizzle out on their own? You think the political axe hanging over us is likely to go away?"

Dov sighed. "Look, Hawke, I know the pressure hasn't lessened, but at least the press has moved on to other stuff. Also? Lisa and I haven't spent an evening together in nearly two weeks, and our home life is getting a little tense. I'm not asking for the moon, just a normal evening off. You know, purely with self-interest at heart—like to save my marriage."

Hawke stared down at the file he was reviewing. "I get it. Sure. Go ahead." Hawke's tone was neutral.

"Thanks!" Dov started clearing up his desk, but the other two detectives waited, Browning shifting from foot to foot.

"You guys also. Beat it."

"Later, Dov. C'mon, Percy." Browning was halfway to the door.

A fidgeting Percival, however, lingered outside Hawke's cubicle. He exercised his nervous habit, pushing his glasses up his nose, while he waited for Hawke to say something.

Hawke tried to ignore him, but the guy didn't go away.

"What?" he finally rasped.

"So . . . you're going to stay late anyway, Hawke?"

"I'll be here another hour."

Percival nodded. "I'm not married. Got nothing else going on. I'll keep you company." He trod over to his desk, and went back to work.

He didn't see Hawke's tight smile of approval.

GRACE OPENED THE door to him, and he said, "*Boo!* Trick or treat."

She giggled. "Where's your sack, little feller?"

He waggled his brows with mock threat. "I was looking for one big enough to haul *you* home in but they were all out. Had many trick or treaters yet?" He peeled off his coat and handed it to her.

"Half a dozen from the neighborhood, all whom I know personally." She gestured at a bowl of Tootsie Pops next to the sofa. "Most parents go with their kids these days and take them before it grows dark. Myself? I won't open my door if the 'kids' ringing the doorbell are as tall as I am."

"And I'm relieved to hear it." When he moved to help himself to one of the suckers, she smacked his hand and indicated the kitchen doorway.

"Dinner first. I thought we'd eat in the kitchen. Do you like Mexican?"

"I like," he interrupted, catching her arm gently, "you. I haven't seen you in weeks—no, *months!*"

"Pretty sure we saw each other two days ago. You know. For Sunday worship and the entire rest of the day?"

"Well, I've been waiting an eon to do this again." He kissed her softly on the lips and pulled back after just a moment.

Lord, he is so careful and gentle. Thank you.

"Yes, I like Mexican food," he murmured, "and if I can get work off my mind, I might even be decent company while we eat."

She'd set the table in a corner nook and placed a fat, drippy candle on it. "*Señor*, your seat."

She tied on an apron and opened the oven door.

He spied the entrée and chortled, "Stuffed peppers? I'm down with that." He pointed at the covered dish already on the table. "And what's this?"

"My own recipe: rice with melted Monterey jack, chopped peppers, sour cream, and other spices. To go with the stuffed peppers." She placed the flat pan near his plate, then retrieved a salad from the fridge. "You can eat up as soon as we bless the food."

She sat across from him. Hawke bent his head and prayed. "Lord, I cannot tell you how grateful I am for this food, for time with Grace, for this respite from the work you've given me to do. I thank you in Jesus' name. Amen."

He grabbed the serving spoon for the rice, plopped a serving on her plate, then two servings on his plate.

"You're fast!" Grace laughed. She set a stuffed pepper beside the rice on his plate.

"Growing up with two brothers, the three of us were always vying for food. We scarfed dinner down so fast, I'm surprised my mom and dad didn't starve to death."

He sampled the rice, then the stuffed pepper. "Great, Grace, really great."

"Salad?"

"Yes, thank you."

"If your mama had three boys like you to feed, she must have had a grocery bill as long as my arm."

"Longer. My brother Thad is an inch taller than I am."

"He must be the Marine?"

"The Marine *accountant*. And let me tell you something: *Nobody* messes with his books."

She chuckled. "Richard, you are actually so different from what I thought when we first met three weeks ago."

"You bring out my good side. Apparently there is another me, 'The Dark Side.'"

"Ooo, I'm scared."

She studied him while he ate, watched the lines of fatigue relax and the tension melt away. Thought how ruggedly handsome he really was and, beneath the hard exterior, as gentle as a lamb.

"You're the cop that everybody has a story about," she said out of the blue.

"Hmm?"

"Oh, I have my sources, primarily two gossipy previous schoolmates, one who works at City Hall, the other an attorney here in town. They talk about you in hushed tones, like you're a serving of James Bond with a side of Rambo." She hesitated, then added, "They whisper things about you."

His gaze sharpened. "What things?"

Wishing she'd kept her mouth shut, while still needing to hear him respond, she said, "The line of broken hearts in your rearview mirror, for one. Didn't line up with what you told me about dating only . . . Christian women."

He looked down at his plate. "I'm not proud of those stories, but they aren't wrong. It was before I gave my life to Jesus, and I was desperately trying to fill a God-sized hole with whatever I could find to stuff in there. Turns out, nothing fills a God-sized hole except God."

She nodded. "I get you."

"Anything else?"

She sighed. "They may have whispered phrases such as 'blood bath' and 'taking out the Mob.' Neither of them could believe I'm seeing you . . . socially."

"And?"

"What makes you so sure there's an 'and'?"

Hawke finished his rice while he waited. Grace fiddled with her food.

"Fine, Mr. dee-*tec*-tive. They warned me about your reputation for being cold-blooded."

"You should know. I scared you half to death when I asked you out."

She flushed. "What makes you think that?"

"Are you kidding? Grace, your face registered terror."

"No fair using your police tricks!"

"No tricks. You read like a book. And Grace, it's good to remember that first impressions are usually right."

She shivered. "What, that I was right to be wary of you?"

He took her hand, rubbed her fingers gently. "Nah. What you saw that first day? That's me being the best detective this city has to offer. Yet, because I'm tough and unrelenting while pursuing the facts of a case, a lot of 'regular' people, mostly people who have no clue how violent and wicked this world can be? They plain don't like me. On the other hand, the bad guys have developed a healthy respect."

Grace hesitantly ventured further. "As an example, one of my friends brought up those terrorists killed or captured about a month ago. She said that you not only took part in that raid, you were the one who hunted them down and uncovered their 'nest.'"

"Yes. I carry a gun and I hunt bad guys, Grace. It's my job."

"I suppose I worry that it's dangerous . . . carrying a gun and hunting bad guys."

He didn't answer, just watched her.

She stabbed a bite of salad, embarrassed. "Well, of course it's dangerous. Stupid comment. I'm sorry."

"I prefer to focus on the lives my actions save. You know, 'serve and protect'?"

She stared intently into his eyes. "Do you actually save lives, Richard?"

"Yes, I do, most often by removing from our streets those, such as those terrorists, who intend to kill innocent civilians. But to be honest with you about my job and all it implies, it comes with both the good and the ugly. Does that bother you terribly?"

"I confess it's a bit scary."

"But do *I* scare you?"

She paused and considered. "No. I believe I'm starting to feel . . . safe with you. Comfortable and easy."

He smiled and raised a wicked eyebrow, breaking the tension between them. "I could change that."

She snort-laughed into her hand. "Coffee? I'll put on a fresh pot. After dinner we could sit in the living room and watch a movie. Eat popcorn." She got up and moved toward the counter, but he caught her hand, tugged her to a stop.

"Deal—if you'll sit by me on the sofa."

"Okay . . . but only if there's no . . ." Her cheeks reddened.

"No inappropriate touching or groping?"

Her eyes narrowed. "Exactly. If I have to fight you off, I'll report you—to your *pastor*."

"Yikes! I'm asking for nothing more than the companionable closeness necessary to share a bowl of popcorn. Scout's honor."

"All right." She giggled low in her throat and Hawke liked the heightened color washing her cheeks.

Then the low ding-dong of her telephone sounded, accompanied by a blinking yellow light coming from the living room. She answered from the extension on the kitchen wall.

"Hello? Oh, hi Willard. Yes, I have company as a matter of fact. Umm, no, you don't know him. Friday? Oh, that's right. No, I hadn't forgotten. Just slipped my mind momentarily. Yes. All right. See you then."

Hawke didn't ask but she volunteered anyway.

"Willard Drake. One of the doctors from the clinic."

"Problem?"

"No. He calls occasionally. And we go out . . . occasionally. We have a conference coming up. He called to remind me."

"I see."

They put the coffee on and did the dishes. Hawke insisted that he wash because it was her kitchen and she knew where everything went. They didn't talk further about his job. When the dishes were finished, the pot of coffee was ready.

"Here's your coffee. Black as night." They moved into the living room and settled on the couch. She switched on the set with the remote. "I have cable and run the closed captioning option. Will the dialogue on the screen bother you?"

"Don't worry about me. Even if it did bother me, I would tell myself to get used to it."

She smiled. "And do you like movie classics?"

"Love 'em. *Guns of Navarone*, *Mutiny on the Bounty*, *Run Silent, Run Deep*."

"Military obsessionist! I was thinking more along the lines of *Pride and Prejudice* with Lawrence Olivier or *Jane Eyre*. Not your shoot 'em ups."

"I can handle them, too. I like *Pride and Prejudice*, probably because of Greer Garson. Love the way she plays her character, but the book is even better—all that insightful, verbal sparring."

"You've read the book?"

"Yes'm, ah surely hev. They done larned me t' read in school," he said, grinning. "I read voraciously, Grace. One of my favorite pastimes."

She pointed at the television. "Look, it's the old *Phantom of the Opera*."

"Please!" Hawke held his hands in front of his face in mock horror. "I cannot handle another psycho with a pipe organ! What else have we got?"

"We have an episode of *The Twilight Zone*."

"Lucky us! More weird stuff."

"I think they're running a scary movie theme for Halloween. How about *Rear Window?*"

"Hitchcock? I can roll with that."

He was replete and actually getting drowsy in the candlelight. He nuzzled her hand and stroked her fingertips across his stubbled chin.

"Richard."

"Hmm?"

"Don't go to sleep. You'll miss the movie."

"I won't." His eyes sagged.

"You will, too."

"Just a cat nap. Wake me up in a while?"

"Okay."

Young and svelte, Grace Kelly swung through Jimmy Stewart's darkened apartment and peered out his apartment's back window with him and watched the shadowy activity in the windows across the courtyard.

Hawke's head slid onto Grace's shoulder. She smiled when his low snores rumbled faintly in her ear. She kept watching the show until it ended and the credits rolled across the screen.

"Richard."

No reaction.

"Detective Hawke."

"What?" He sat up, wide awake and fierce.

"Movie's over."

He calmed. "Oh. Was it good?"

"You just slept for an hour and a half, mister."

"Am I in trouble?"

"Not a bit, but it's time to go home."

"Home? I just got here!"

"Three hours ago. Pack it up and move it out, copper."

He stood and stretched. "Sheesh. I must have needed that, Gracie."

"I think so, too." She held his coat.

"That was the best dinner I've had in a long time, Grace. Thank you. I'm sorry I went to sleep."

"I'm not. I got to listen to all your deep, dark secrets while you dreamed."

"Uh, I don't think you did, or you'd have me on the other side of that dead-bolt right now—just kidding, of course. Can I call you tomorrow?"

"Uh-huh."

They kissed with mutual restraint and parted. Hawke waved to her from the driveway. He felt more relaxed and rested than he had in months.

"Dr. Warner, you should wear a label: *Danger: Habit Forming*," he mumbled to himself.

The cold whipped him and stung his face.

He scarcely noticed.

Was it possible that the frozen place in his heart, numb for so many years, might thaw? He'd been alone in the icy wastelands of regret far too long.

CHAPTER 17

"DELANO?" HAWKE GLANCED up from his desk. He'd arrived at work twenty minutes ago. *And I'm only half awake*, he realized.

"Yeah, Rudy Delano, son of last week's homicide. I interviewed him. He's on my phone, says he wants to come in and tell us something further." Dov gestured toward his phone.

"Sure. Tell him to come on in." Hawke returned to his work. The details of other cases were being sadly neglected while they plowed through years of case files—not to mention he was supposed to be working with the DA's office to prepare his testimony for the upcoming trial of Ibrahim Azize and the surviving members of his captured organization.

The man Dov seated beside Hawke's desk an hour later was young, perhaps twenty-five, his dark hair thinning early. His face wore the pinched, gray look Hawke and Mayer associated with grief.

"Mr. Delano, thanks for taking time to come down and see us," Hawke began. "We understand how very difficult this is for you. We certainly appreciate anything you can tell us that might assist us in our investigation."

The man, struggling with the anger that often accompanies loss, blurted a curse word. Making an effort to curb his emotions, he drew a long breath. "Sorry. Not myself right now. Kinda want to hit something or someone, you know? Because it's just not fair, *not decent* what that . . . *person* did to Dad." He paused, jaw working.

"We know," Hawke agreed with a little more sympathy in his voice, "and you nailed it. That's what murder is; it's wrong and indecent. And when it happens to good, kind people, it's plain obscene."

Delano stared at Hawke, evaluating him. He muttered, "I suppose you guys know something about that."

"We do, and we're being truthful when we say you have our deepest sympathies. But you said you have something related to your father's death, Mr. Delano?"

"Yeah, well, it's my dad's store. I checked it, you know, to see if anything other than money was taken, and like I told the officers at the time, as far as I could tell, nothing was missing or vandalized. At least I was pretty sure at the time. We've been busy . . . the funeral yesterday and all. Anyway, I finally remembered."

"Remembered what?"

"Dad's winter coat. He bought a really nice one recently, see? But he didn't need it when they . . . took him away, so I never thought about it until this morning. Anyway, he wore it to work that day, so it should still be at the store, right? Except I can't find it anywhere."

He looked expectantly from Hawke to Dov and back but they stared at him with blank expressions. Finally Delano blurted, "So the creep who killed him *took his coat*, right?"

Hawke slowly smiled. "Can you give us a description of this coat, Mr. Delano?"

"I can do better'n that. Here's a picture." He unfolded a page from the Sears catalog, laid it on Hawke's desk, and jabbed the image with his finger. "Exactly like this one. Hunter green, lined, size 44."

Then he asked, "Will this help catch my dad's killer, Detective?"

Fingering the page, trying hard to keep his expression neutral, Hawke replied, "This is good, Mr. Delano. Very, very good. Just about the best lead we have to date. Thank you."

The man nodded, satisfied. "By the way, you should know that Dad's name is printed on a tag sewn inside the right sleeve." He opened his mouth, closed it and finally added, "I hope you catch this creep, Detective Hawke, I really do."

While Dov ushered Delano out, Hawke scrutinized the map of the city hanging to the left of his desk. He stuck a red pushpin in the map to mark the shop where Delano had died. After a few moments, he added two more red pins.

"Look here," he motioned when Dov came back. "Delano's store is nowhere near St. Joe's, but the store and the Claremont? Too near each other to be happenstance. See, the Claremont," he ran his hand over to the pin, "is only five blocks from Delano's thrift shop. Both in the same class of neighborhood, an older but respectable part of town. Many thriving small businesses, lots of apartments, some high-end homes. Couple of schools. Solid, working- and middle-class people."

Dov picked up on his line of thinking right away. "Whereas St. Joe's is run down, lots of boarded up businesses and houses, and a large homeless population."

"Exactly." Rubbing his chin Hawke thought aloud. "You know, city people tend to work in the neighborhoods they live in and are familiar with. And even though the benefit at the Claremont was hoity-toity and exclusive, it makes me wonder how many people from this same neighborhood may have worked some aspect of that large event."

Dov nodded. "Sure. Caterers, bartenders, florists, cleaning crew, security, ticket takers, ushers. The list goes on, but we've already interviewed everyone."

"Ah, but which workers, before the ME removed Esther Grunbaum's body, would have had opportunity to view the scene in the course of their duties?"

"Huh. Well, since she died in the Claremont's basement, it has to be a fairly short list, Hawke. Like, the theater owner, the theater manager and his assistant, the rent-a-cop security guys who helped Mr. Grunbaum look for his wife, their supervisor from that night, and members of the cleaning crew?"

Hawke still studied the map. "To start with, we need to compile an exhaustive list of everyone who laid eyes on the scene in the Claremont's basement before the ME took Mrs. Grunbaum's body away. I want names *and* addresses, because one of these individuals lives near both the Claremont and Vincent Delano's thrift shop."

He nodded to himself. "Dov? Have Browning and Percival check downstairs with dispatch. I want us to review every 911 call and every officer response for the past three weeks." He pointed to the two pins marking the Claremont and Vincent Delano's shop. "Any 911 calls and officer responses that fall inside *this* neighborhood."

Hawke picked up the page from the catalog. "One more thing: It's cold outside, Dov. If our man is on the street, he will be wearing his new coat. Issue a citywide 'Be On the Look Out,' particularly targeting that neighborhood. Every beat cop gets a blown-up photocopy of this jacket. If our guy is out there, we stand a real chance of pulling him in."

"Right." Dov took the catalog page and familiarized himself with the cut of the parka. "I'll call dispatch and take care of the BOLO myself."

HOURS LATER, HAWKE dialed a number he'd only recently committed to memory. "Hey. How are you?"

"Hello, Richard." Her warmth was welcoming. "Just getting some supper. Warmed up in the tub first when I got home. It's freezing outside! You?"

"I've been at it all day and suddenly realized how late it was. We were handed a decent lead today and it's kept us busy. I need to drag myself home for some sleep so I can reappear here tomorrow morning by 6:00, but tomorrow is Friday. Can I take you somewhere special tomorrow evening?"

"I'm afraid not, much as I'd love it. Most of the clinic's staff is attending a conference in Boston this weekend."

"*What?*"

Good grief, Hawke. You sound pathetic!

"I'm sorry; I completely forgot to mention it to you. Do you remember when Willard called the other evening? He was reminding me of the flight time. I was going to tell you, but then you fell asleep watching the movie and it slipped my mind until after you'd left. We'll be gone through Monday afternoon."

"The whole weekend?" Hawke felt irrationally let down. "When do you leave?"

"Tomorrow evening about 6:00."

"Could you squeeze in lunch tomorrow?"

"Oh, Richard, I just can't. I'm sorry."

"I could pick you up at noon—curb to curb service."

Laughing at his salesmanship attempt, she replied, "But how can you get away for a couple of hours in the middle of the day when you can't even get yourself home at a decent hour in the evening?"

"By working all weekend to make it up and to keep myself from missing you."

"Oh." She barely breathed it.

Hawke shifted his approach. "Since you're going to be gone all weekend, and I have you on the line right now, may I reserve some time in your very busy schedule next week before you're all booked up? How about saving me a slot Tuesday night?"

"Have my group Tuesday night."

"Well Monday then. Or will you be too tired just getting back from your trip?"

"Um, I already have company coming for dinner."

"Anyone I know?" He attempted to sound casual, but rebuked himself instantly. *Why do I wonder if it's another man?*

"No one you know, but someone I'd like you to meet. Care to join us?"

"Uh, sure."

"Seven, then." She paused. "I'm really glad you called, Richard."

"I'm glad I did too. Be safe on your trip. See you Monday evening then, seven o'clock."

"See you then."

He hung up. "Three days in Boston with Dr. Willard What's-His-Name who takes her out occasionally? Fine. Great. No, *really*—it's fine."

He snorted. "Sure it is."

He clocked out, ran five miles at the gym, drove impatiently, and scowled at the cat before crashing into bed. Even then he lay awake for an hour, muttering to himself.

CHAPTER 18

HAWKE DIDN'T HAVE time to miss Grace: He and his team caught their first real break Friday afternoon.

Hawke, along with Dov and Browning had made slow but steady headway through the mountains of case files found in the department's evidence lockup, every case dating from twenty years back to present day. Percival worked tirelessly alongside them, but he also spent hours on the phone each day speaking to law enforcement departments throughout the state and region, following up on the bulletins he'd issued.

Around four that afternoon, Hawke saw Percival take a call, then stand to his feet and pace his cubicle while he spoke and listened. Twenty minutes later, while Percival was on the same call, he buzzed Browning to join him. Soon after, Hawke observed Browning hovering over the fax machine like a hen brooding over her chicks.

Around 5:00 p.m. the two detectives converged on Hawke's cramped domain with Dov in tow.

"Got a minute, Hawke?" Percival's voice betrayed suppressed excitement.

The three of them, Percival, Browning, and Dov, pulled folding chairs into Hawke's cubby to hear Percival's report.

The younger detective cleared his throat. "I just spoke at length with one Clive Nightingale, retired detective from Brockport, a small town upstate. The guy is eighty-three now, suffering with congestive heart failure, thus short of breath. It took time and a lot of effort on his part to convey the details of his only unsolved case."

"Speed it up, detective," Hawke growled, feeling his hopes rise to do battle against the long odds.

"Roger that, Boss. Okay, so in 1968, that's twenty-*one* years ago, the little hamlet of Brockport suffered a tragedy that shook its citizens pretty hard. A young girl by the name of Sara Curry was found murdered in her aunt and uncle's garage."

Percival plopped a faxed sheet on Hawke's desk where the four of them could see it. Hawke held down the curling edges of the slick paper and studied dark, shoulder-length hair framing a pair of soft eyes that gazed at him with sweet expectation.

"Ah, the innocence of youth," Dov muttered, cranking his neck to study the grayscale image.

"Right," Percival agreed. "Fourteen when she was murdered. She'd been orphaned the previous year, after which she came to Brockport to live with her father's brother and his wife, Ron and Ebbe Curry. The Currys' neighbors were pretty much unified in their testimony that Mr. and Mrs. Curry were tickled pink to have Sara."

"Testimony?" Hawke raised an eyebrow.

"During the inquest, and I'll get to that shortly. The Currys had no kids of their own, so they considered Sara a real blessing. She was affectionate, studious, and wholesome. Musically inclined too. When she was killed, the Currys were devastated."

"Suspects?"

"Just one initially. At the Currys' insistence, the police brought in a young neighbor boy for questioning. The aunt and uncle, aunt in particular, were vocal about this kid's infatuation with Sara. In particular, the kid always hung around while Sara took lessons and practiced—*get this*—the pipe organ over at the town's Catholic church."

Hawke sat up straight as a cold shiver coursed down his back.

"*No way*," Dov breathed, echoing Hawke's unspoken sentiments.

"Right? According to Sara's school chums, this kid idolized the girl, and Sara, for her part, was uniformly kind and tolerant of the boy's fascination. The same teens from Sara's sphere said the Currys quickly developed a strong antipathy toward this kid."

"Why? What did he do to earn their disapproval?"

Percival shrugged. "As far as Nightingale found, he'd done nothing other than appreciate Sara's friendship and her music. Nightingale did learn that the kid was a loner and was bullied at school."

"You're describing the perfect setup for obsession," Dov murmured.

"That's what the police thought . . . at first." Percival shifted his notes and took a satisfied swig from a can of Coke, totally enjoying the moment . . . until Hawke started tapping his pen on his blotter.

Percival recalled himself in a rush. "Okay, so the police interviewed this kid but got nowhere fast. Why? Because the kid was *deaf* and what limited speech he had was garbled. Difficult to understand. Also, he was only ten years old."

"What? *Ten?*" Hawke rubbed his jaw and moved his head side to side. *Too young*, he protested inside. *Too young to be a cold-blooded killer*.

"Yup. *Ten years old*. In order to properly interview the boy and establish his whereabouts and state of mind at the time of the murder, the police brought in a male officer fluent in sign language. Turns out, the kid couldn't sign much better than he could speak. Wondering how the kid managed school in such a state, the officer tried several approaches. He reported observing that the kid could, to a limited degree, read lips.

"All that aside, the officer wrote in his report that he couldn't find a way to connect with the boy—either because the kid was too broken up over the girl's death or, as the officer was starting to believe, because the kid was extremely uncomfortable in the presence of a *male* police officer."

Interesting, Hawke thought.

"The officer suggested that the Brockport police call in a child therapist for the hearing impaired—a competent *female* therapist who both signed and specialized in the emotional and psychological struggles of those with hearing loss."

"Sounds like a description of Dr. Warner, Hawke," Dov observed.

It does, Hawke realized. He nodded for Percival to continue.

"This therapist, a woman, began seeing the kid two hours a day, hoping he would be able to tell her what he knew about Sara's death. What was plain to her was how devastated the boy was . . . devastated and something more. According to Nightingale, she felt the boy was deeply conflicted—over what, the therapist didn't know.

"But before the therapist got any further, one of Sara's girlfriends, accompanied by her parents, showed up at the police and delivered a bombshell.

"Seems Sara had confided to this friend that her dear uncle Ron had been making passes at her—buying her little gifts, often touching her, and trying to get her alone, away from his wife. Sara told her friend a week before the murder that her uncle had gotten particularly handsy with her. Well! That put a whole different slant on the investigation, even if the friend's information was hearsay.

"However, when the police searched the Currys' home, they came up with nothing incriminating in the slightest. Furthermore, Mr. Curry seemed to have an airtight alibi—said he was out of town on business the morning Sara was killed."

Percival looked at his notes. "That sent the police back to square one, and they shifted their focus back to the kid."

"Hold up. Tell us about the murder itself," Hawke demanded.

"The girl was stabbed, multiple times."

"How many times?" Hawke asked.

"Twenty-three separate knife wounds—chest and neck—plus thirteen defensive wounds on her hands and forearms."

Dov shook his head. "That takes a *lot* of rage."

Hawke nodded. "Rage or malevolent pleasure. Was she violated?"

"Detective Nightingale said the girls' blouse was sliced, of course, and her sleeves torn. However, the girl was not sexually assaulted. Nightingale came to believe that Sara struggled and fought so hard, the assailant began to cut her in an effort to subdue her. They were in the Curry's garage, after all, and even though the Curry's residence was somewhat removed from its neighbors' homes, if the girl began screaming, people in homes nearby might have heard her."

"I can't see how a ten-year-old kid would be physically capable of overcoming a teenager," Dov said quietly. "Seems a stretch."

"Exactly," Hawke answered. "Medical examiner's report?"

Percival turned back to his notes, "The ME said Sara's body was definitely moved post mortem. Repositioned."

He placed another sheet in front of Hawke, an image of the body and paused for effect. "Mrs. Curry found Sara lying on her back, eyes closed, arms to her side . . . with a copious amount of blood from what they assumed were her wounds dribbled onto her face."

Hawke thumped a fist on his desk. "This is it. Has to be."

"I agree, Hawke," Percival said. "But there's more—"

Browning jumped in, eager to add to the report, "During the inquest Mrs. Curry continued to insist the boy killed Sara, but like Mayer, the police also thought it unlikely that a scrawny kid his age could overwhelm a girl six years older than himself. Nevertheless, Mrs. Curry mounted a personal campaign against the kid, which included public screaming fits, if you can believe it. She became so enraged, she had to be restrained during the inquest."

He shook his head, chuckling cynically. "The uncle, on the other hand, was calm and cool during the inquest. Hardly a flicker of emotion from him."

"Until," Percival interjected, recapturing the narrative, "until the police broke Curry's alibi. They proved he'd returned home hours earlier on the day Sara died than what he'd told the police."

"So he did it?" Dov asked.

"He claims he was out for a walk when she was killed, so most everyone came away from the inquest believing he was guilty. Their belief was cemented when, two days later and just as the police had decided to arrest the guy, Curry hung himself. Mrs. Curry found him dangling in the same garage where Sara was killed. She promptly sailed straight off the edge of reality and resided in a state institution until her death, five years back."

"And the boy?"

"While all this was going on, the child therapist continued seeing the kid—and this is where Nightingale says the case took a strange turn. The therapist, recognizing the behavioral cues of abuse in the kid, insisted he receive a physical exam. To do so, the police took him out of school without his parent's knowledge.

"What the doctor who performed the exam found was horrific. Multiple bruises, welts, scratches, and cuts in various stages of healing. The x-rays were worse. They showed extensive bone remodeling, arms, back, chest, and head. Incontrovertible proof that he'd been beaten repeatedly."

Hawke spoke up. "You said the therapist thought the kid was devastated and something else?"

"Yeah. Devastated and *conflicted.*"

Dov asked, "Are we talking cycles of abuse? The kid was abused and, even at ten years of age, had developed violent tendencies? Are we talking about a . . ."

He turned to Hawke and asked, "When Sharon Richmond interviewed Dr. Warner on *Morning Line*, what area of psychiatry did Dr. Warner say she had an interest in?"

"Psychopathy. Used to be called antisocial personality disorder. People with this disorder are also known as sociopaths."

Dov snapped his fingers. "That's it. Lack of empathy. Low impulse control. Manipulative and deceitful behaviors."

Percival shook his head. "Nope. Not this kid, apparently. The therapist said he was certainly *not* a sociopath. The kid became distraught whenever they spoke of Sara—and he invariably signed the word 'friend' to the therapist along with a sentence the kid insisted Sara herself had signed to him."

"Sara knew sign language?" Hawke asked, surprised.

Percival shook his head. "Not according to her friends, and yet the police found a library book on American Sign Language in her bedroom. They think she may have taught herself a few words and phrases for the kid's benefit. You know, the basics like *hello*, *please*, *thank you*, *yes*, and *no*."

Percival signed the words as he spoke them.

Dov grinned. "Way to go, Percy. Did you just learn those?"

"Nah. Learned them ages ago. My cousin is deaf."

"Show off," Browning grumbled.

Dov ignored him. "But didn't you say the kid told the therapist Sara had signed an entire sentence to him? What was it?"

"Nightingale told me to keep in mind that Sara wasn't fluent in sign and may have composed this wording of the sentence herself. When the boy signed Sara's sentence to his therapist, she told the police the sentence read, *Thank you for keeping me company while I play the organ*—except, when the therapist repeated the phrase aloud and the boy watched her mouth, he shook his head and tried to correct her translation by repeating the same three broken, croaky words over and over.

"The therapist tried several times to repeat his words back to him, but he always signed the word *wrong*. Finally, she tried asking him, 'Do you mean *keeping me safe?*' and the kid signed the word *yes*. Emphatically."

"Thank you for keeping me *safe* while I play the organ? Sara saw this boy as her protector while she played the organ *in a church?*"

"*Safe* is what the boy insisted Sara *said* even though she *signed* the word *company*. Unfortunately, this is also where everything started to fall apart."

"Great," Dov growled.

"Yeah, just *peachy*. What happened next, Percival," Hawke demanded.

"Once the report on the boy's physical exam came back, social services and the police investigated the boy's home. His father must have gotten wind of the visit, because he made himself scarce before they arrived. They interviewed the mom, and she was patently terrified, afraid to tell them anything, which made them believe she, too, was being abused.

"However, when they told her they were required by law to remove her son from the home, she cracked. Told them that the dad regularly beat on and berated both her and the boy."

"Berated?" Hawke asked.

"Pretty rough stuff. According to Nightingale, the level of verbal and physical abuse heaped on her and the boy was off the charts—her, for producing 'flawed offspring;' the kid for *being* that flawed offspring. Finally, after they had counseled the woman for hours, they got her to agree to take the boy and go to a shelter. A place where they would be safe."

Percival sighed. "Turned out to be a colossal mistake."

Hawke tried to prepare himself for what was coming. He knew it wouldn't be good and found himself praying silently.

Lord? How can the people you created in your image do such horrible things to each other, especially to children?

"What happened, Percy?" Dov asked softly.

"The dad found the shelter and broke in during the early morning hours. Took the boy and his mother hostage. We don't know what all that . . . jerk said or did to them during the seven hours he had them, but Nightingale believes a lot can be extrapolated from the hospital reports on the mom and boy . . . afterward.

"When it was all over, the dad was in police custody—somewhat worse for wear, courtesy of two overzealous officers—while the boy and his mom were hospitalized, the boy near death. The hospital released the mom after a week in care, but her son remained in ICU for a month before being transferred to a county rehab facility. Nightingale says the kid suffered severe head trauma and had little to no memory of the hostage event."

Percival reviewed his notes. "The dad was arraigned on two counts each of kidnapping and attempted murder, plus criminal trespass on the shelter. He was denied bail. Nightingale said he figures the mom made her plans right after the guy was denied bail, because the day the kid was released from rehab, she split. No one ever managed to trace her or the boy."

"And the father? Where's he?"

"Upstate. Twenty years into a thirty-year sentence."

"So who killed Sara Curry?"

"Remember when I said earlier that Detective Nightingale was eager to convey the details of his only *unsolved* case?"

"What? You mean the uncle didn't do it?"

"Unknown, but Nightingale figured Mr. Curry had to have hanged himself for a reason, right? And because of that one unknown factor, Nightingale kept digging. Eventually, he found two women in the town where Curry grew up who went on record to say that the man was a serial molester, that he had garnered himself a considerable reputation for groping little girls and young women while he was in high school and beyond."

"And?"

"And *zilch*. The Police found nothing further than the groping in Curry's background and nothing at the time of Sara's murder to suggest Curry killed her. The man likely killed himself due to fear his dirty little secret was about to come out."

"And the boy's father?"

"The police found no proof that he killed Sara either. End of line."

Percival closed his notebook. "If we were to, somehow, crack this twenty-one year old case, Detective Nightingale asks that we let him know. Preferably before his time runs out . . . and he's getting short on that."

Hawke pursed his lips. "Names?"

"Surname Gretzky, father's name Marek, mother's name Aneta, maiden name Walas."

"And the boy?"

"Terry Gretzky. He would be close to thirty-one years old today."

Percival laid the remaining faxed documents before Hawke with the finesse of a gourmet chef presenting his special entrée.

"You said the boy was a suspect for a time. Did the police obtain his prints?"

"He was never charged, so no."

"What about the father?"

"I'll ask Brockport PD to send along his prints and see if we get a match to what we gathered at St. Joe's. 'Course you know the print team got nothing from the Claremont or Delano's shop."

Hawke stood up and clapped the young detective on the shoulder. "Good work, Percival. Uh, you too, Browning. I need some time to soak in this info. As you were."

Browning and Percival left. Hawke walked toward the television and coffee station. He began slowly pacing the open area, his head down.

Dov waited near the television, silent and patient—until his silence and patience petered out at the same time. "Rick. Hold up. Tell me what you're thinking."

Hawke nodded and said, mostly to himself, "I think we should schedule a consult with Dr. Warner ASAP, because . . ."

"Because?"

Still talking it out to himself, Hawke answered, "Because we have three cases, only one of which is a homicide. Because those three cases and the murder of Sara Curry have a single, unique factor in common: the blood-on-the-face ritual. And because I believe the evidence in our three cases suggests we're seeking *two* individuals—and I'd bet my badge those two people share a nasty little secret."

"But if Terry Gretzky is the first person, who's the second?"

Hawke looked up. "We'll know for certain when you confirm that Marek Gretzky was released from prison quite recently. Get the exact date of his release while you're at it, Dov."

"You serious? The man has a dime left on a thirty-year stint!"

"You'd better believe I'm serious. I'm convinced that *Marek Gretzky* is Vincent Delano's killer—who dripped Delano's blood, not his own, on the guy's face—but Gretzky's son, Terry Gretzky, is our bloodletter. Furthermore, my gut tells me that something utterly perverse is buried between Terry Gretzky and his father. Whatever that secret is? It's more disturbing than all the disturbing stuff we already know about this wretched family—something that has shaped Terry's life to date and, most significantly, now puts his life in danger."

Dov's mouth suddenly went dry. "I'm on it."

Hawke returned to his cubicle and grabbed his phone. Dialed Grace's number.

"Upton-Warner Clinic, Linda speaking."

"This is Detective Sergeant Hawke, Homicide Division. I need to speak to Dr. Warner."

"I'm sorry, sir. Dr. Warner is out of town until Monday."

"Right! She's at that conference," he murmured to himself.

"Yes, sir. May I take a message?"

He exhaled. "Yes. Please tell her to reach out to me at her earliest possible opportunity."

TWENTY MINUTES LATER, Dov stood beside Hawke's desk. "How did you know?"

"Tell me what you found out."

Dov sighed and read from his notes. "Marek S. Gretzky was released from prison Monday, October 2, just shy of five weeks ago. He was released early for earned 'good time' and given a bus ticket to his choice of location in our fair state. Care to guess his destination? Yup. Right here."

He looked up. "The timing of his release means he couldn't have been in the city when Mary Alice Waite fell down the stairs at St. Joe's, but he *was* in the city when Esther Grunbaum had a heart attack in the basement of the Claremont."

"More to the point, he was here when Vincent Delano was murdered." Hawke watched as the light slowly dawned on his partner.

Dov muttered, "Delano was stabbed multiple times in the chest . . . like Sara Curry."

"Yup. Like Sara Curry." Hawke headed for his desk.

Dov followed behind him. "Tell me what you've figured out?"

Hawke's pen tapped out a staccato rhythm on his desk known only to him. He stared at Sara Curry's grainy image and furrowed his brows. "Terry Gretzky. Quiet, sensitive. Moderately intelligent but bullied and treated like he was stupid or 'retarded' by his school peers. Why? Because his speech was garbled and because Terry's teachers were more blind than he was deaf. Makes you wonder what an accurate diagnosis and some specialized care might have done for the kid. But I imagine his ignorant, bigoted father would have put the kibosh on that."

He sighed. "And poor little Sara? Recently orphaned and grieving, she was dropped into an unfamiliar town among total strangers. She made a few friends, but she likely still felt alone in her sorrow. Perhaps she recognized a kindred suffering spirit in Terry and perhaps it's why she took the time to get to know and appreciate him."

Hawke's pen stilled. "And maybe Terry, this wounded, misunderstood boy, at age ten, developed a crush on Sara. Ever suffer a crush, Dov?"

"Yeah. Utterly miserable experience. Can totally commiserate."

"Oh? What happened?"

"You've met Lisa, haven't you, Rick?"

Surprised into laughing aloud, Hawke tossed a wad of paper at his partner.

He continued, "Then there's Aneta Gretzky. The moment she saw a viable avenue of escape from the horrors she and her son endured, she whisked our boy Terry away from Brockport to start a new life."

"Don't blame her a bit," Dov said with some heat.

"Nor I, but on Terry's side of the equation? When Aneta Gretzky took him and ran off to parts unknown, the kid was still suffering a world of hurt including head trauma. Physically and mentally abused and degraded at home on a regular basis. Misunderstood by his teachers and ostracized by his school mates. Nearly beaten to death by his own father and left with residual brain damage? To top it off, *Sara*, the girl he loves and his only friend in the world, murdered. Poor kid."

His voice dropped off and Dov waited patiently.

"I wonder," he muttered.

"Fill me in, Rick?"

"I wonder what went on in that domestic violence shelter while Marek Gretzky held his wife and son prisoner for seven hours. We know he beat them both, but surely Gretzky wasn't silent during that time. What did he *say* to Terry while he alternately hit and choked him?"

He abruptly stopped and turned to Dov. "Reach out to Nightingale and ask if he or another officer overhead anything during those long hours Marek Gretzky held Aneta and her son captive. I want to know what that sicko said to Terry, what Terry had to 'hear' by reading his father's lips."

"On it," Dov answered as he spun on his heel.

"Percival! Browning!"

"Coming," Percival answered.

"You two. City hall. Aneta Gretzky, maiden name Walas, moved here twenty-one years ago. Find out where they lived or still live. Property records, utility bills, and so on. Get a warrant for her finances, and *get me an address*."

"You got it, Hawke!" Percival answered.

Even Browning nodded and said, "We'll find 'em," no trace of simmering resentment in his eyes or in his tone.

As they left, Dov came flying back to Hawke's desk. "Forgot something the warden told me."

"Spit it out."

"Marek Gretzky left a letter in his cell. He'd chiseled some mortar out of his cell's brick wall and slid the letter between two bricks. Crammed bits of the chipped mortar in after it. Guards noticed the broken mortar and found the letter when they tossed the cell after he was released. Do we want it?"

"And how! Have the warden overnight it to us—no, have him fax it immediately, then send the original."

"Will do."

With his team working leads and with no reason to continue the case file search, Hawke found himself staring at the faxed photo of Sara Curry. He carefully picked it up and pinned it alongside the city map.

"What do you know that we don't, Sara?"

He began boxing up the folders stacked on his desk, then went over to Percival, Browning, and Dov's desks and boxed up their files. Stacked the boxes and returned them to the basement. Half an hour later, he heard the fax machine chugging out paper.

"Hawke? I'm on hold with Brockport PD. Can you grab that fax?"

"Sure," he called to his partner.

The fax was from the warden's office, a cover sheet followed by a single page. The creases of twenty-plus years were evident even in the facsimile of the letter, the text brutally blunt.

Marek,

You killed our son. You beat him every day of his life until you beat him to death. He died suffering and in pain, but he's out of your reach now FOREVER. And just so you know? I had his body cremated, and I scattered his ashes to the wind so that your presence could never defile his resting place, not even your shadow.

I filed for an expedited divorce last month. My attorney will serve you final papers this week. I have a court order that allows me to sell our pathetic home and pocket ALL the money in compensation for the horrors Terry and I endured at your evil hands. I will leave Brockport a FREE woman, and you will NEVER see me or control me again.

May you rot in your prison cell for decades and in hell thereafter.

Aneta

Hawke shook his head in amazement. "She told him Terry died? Nicely played, lady. No con gets out of prison and goes looking for the ashes of a dead son . . . but he might want to confront his ex-wife."

Dov appeared. "Nightingale can't think of anyone still alive who was privy to what Marek did or said to his wife and son during the time Marek held them captive in the DV shelter. Sorry, Rick."

"It was a long shot, I suppose. This, on the other hand, says a lot." Hawke showed him the faxed letter.

"Wow. Harsh."

"Better than he deserved. We just have to figure out how he knew to come *here* straight out of prison, how he found out Aneta had settled here. And I'm really hoping Percival and Browning find us an address, because Marek has already been here five weeks. If he knew exactly where his former wife lived, he may have already paid her a visit. On the other hand, if we're fortunate enough to find either Aneta or Terry before Marek does, we'll need to hustle them into protective custody ASAP."

Hawke arranged a short meeting with Chief McCormick to bring him up to speed.

"You think the deaths of Mary Alice Waite, Esther Grunbaum, Vincent Delano, and Sara Curry have some shared meaning?" McCormick asked.

"The single commonality across all four deaths is the blood ritual." Hawke took a deep breath. "It's my belief that two people, Terry Gretzky, our bloodletter, and his father, Marek Gretzky, suspected killer of both Vincent Delano and Sara Curry, know what the blood ritual means or portends. Now that we've identified these two, we hope to find them shortly."

A knock on the chief's door interrupted them. Dov stuck his head into the chief's office. "Got Percival on the line. Needs to talk to you."

"Go ahead, Hawke. We're done here," Chief McCormick said.

Hawke picked up the call at Dov's desk. "What do you have?"

"Nada, Hawke. Checked everything under Gretzky and Walas. Even tried Gretzky under a bunch of various spellings. Also called the utility companies while here. Same result."

Hawke ground his teeth, but something Percival had said was tooling around somewhere in the back of his head. "Wait. You tried different spellings of Gretzky. Did you try different spellings of Walas?"

"Huh. Did not think to check for different spellings of her maiden name. We should do that right away only . . ."

"Only what?"

"Only City Hall and the utility companies? They all closed at five o'clock."

Hawke glanced at the clock hanging over the coffee bar. It read 5:05.

"Swell."

"We'll be waiting at City Hall when the doors open Monday, Hawke. Promise."

"Thanks, guys. That will have to do. You can go on home now."

He stared at the clock but he no longer saw it. What he saw was a young boy, just a child, deaf, bullied at school, and abused at home. What would that make the grown Terry Gretzky? He mentally went through the scenes at St. Joe's, the Claremont, and Vincent Delano's second-hand shop. And he listened to Grace's voice.

"*As I said, a child of ten might feel guilt or remorse, but a child that age isn't likely to write a note of explanation. Also, while the note expresses responsibility for scaring the woman, it also says it was not his intention to scare her or cause the fall.*"

Hawke nodded to himself. "No way Terry Gretzky is a killer. That kid is a victim."

HAWKE CHECKED OUT for the day. It didn't thrill him that he was off work relatively early in the evening while Grace was halfway to Boston. With gritty determination, he planned his weekend around dinner with the Mayers, workout time at the gym, every chore he'd pushed to the side while hunting Ibrahim Azize over the last several months, and church Sunday.

After a meal at a café frequented by off-duty cops, he went home and sorted his laundry. Ontario, usually standoffish, rubbed up against him often enough to let Hawke know the cat was feeling neglected.

"Yeah. Me too."

GRACE SIGHED DURING takeoff. Willard Drake's non-stop monologue while they waited on the busy tarmac for their clearance had given her a headache. Her mistake had been in arriving after he did to catch the late afternoon shuttle to Boston. He'd already commandeered the block of seats purchased by the clinic and arranged seating so she was in a window seat hemmed in by him.

A long weekend loomed ahead with him showering her with similar attentions.

I should tell him I'm no longer interested in dating him. What I'd really like to do is tell him about Richard . . . but that would be presumptuous of me.

It was far too early for either of them to make a declaration of love to the other.

Willard was trying to say something to her now and Grace felt justified in waving him away, indicating she couldn't hear over the whine of the jets. Besides maintaining good relations at work, there were other complications to speaking her mind too emphatically.

Dr. Bill. For some perverse reason, Bill considered Willard Drake the epitome of ear, nose, throat medicine. *Yes, the man is just about that,* Grace grudgingly conceded. His patient list was larger than hers and growing.

Bill also considered Willard an exceedingly well qualified prospective son-in-law: He had even hinted at Upton-Warner continuing through the generations—meaning through the children she might have with Willard. Not that Bill had ever pressured her; he wouldn't do that. But Grace, by allowing her on-again, off-again relationship with Willard to drag on rather than severing it decisively, hadn't put those expectations to bed.

That's on me, Lord. You told me months ago to date only godly men. But Willard and I were so casual, I hadn't actually placed him in the "dating" column.

All that was before Richard. Before her dating status mattered one way or another. Before these feelings she had for him had taken root in her heart.

Dear Bill! You will meet Richard Monday evening. And if you don't see my heart for this man right away, I will spell it out for you.

She exhaled to calm her frayed nerves. *Oh, Richard! How I wish you were beside me right now. How I wish we were leaving the city together, going anywhere together, just to be there. Together.*

Then she found herself, eyes closed, praying. *Lord, you know I am weary, tired to the bone; you know Richard is too. But can I tell you something? The idea of having this man's company all to myself for a few uninterrupted hours sounds like heaven on earth.*

Please be with him and keep him safe for me? He has a difficult and dangerous job.

Thank you.

❧

"HELLO, LISA. YOU'RE looking good." He hugged Dov's wife and she buzzed his cheek, withdrawing in mock horror.

"Good heavens, Rick! Give up shaving? You've grown enough stubble there to sand the varnish off that ancient rocking chair Dov dragged home."

"You've been planning to refinish that old piece for the past two years, Lisa. I thought Dov bought that special for you."

"He bought it all right, gave it to me two years ago this coming May— on Mother's day, to be exact. But am I ready to enter motherhood? Don't think so. Not just yet."

"I quit. Won't say another word."

Dov and Lisa's disagreement about when to start a family dated back to Dov's purchase of the chair. Apparently Lisa was still holding out for more time before getting pregnant.

"Say, I thought you were bringing someone tonight, Rick. I certainly cooked enough."

"That sounds like Dov's version of events, Lisa. You recall how uptight you get when certain in-laws start hinting around about events that portend more deductions on the Mayer IRS returns? I feel the same when Dov starts pushing me to date."

"Sorry, Rick; I'll butt out. Say, listen," a quick change of subject, "want to come for Thanksgiving dinner?"

"Thanksgiving?" He looked blank.

"Yeah, you know, when the pilgrims invited the Indians to share in the harvest the first year they were here? We generally celebrate it on the fourth Thursday in November?"

"I didn't realize how close it was."

"Less than three weeks. What do you say? Or do you have plans to go to your folks?"

"No, not leaving town. I usually work Thursday and Friday that week. A lot of guys ask for the day off so I sub for them." His "I usually work" was a bald-faced bluff. He had one and only one plan in mind for Thanksgiving and it involved a certain woman, for the entire day, no interruptions.

"Well, let Dov know if you decide you'd like to come."

"Sure. Thanks, Lisa."

Lisa Mayer, just thirty years old and five-foot-nothin', was exactly what the doctor had ordered for Dov. Lisa was small but definitely feisty, and even gave Hawke a run for his money on occasions when they'd gotten into heavy discussions. She was, Hawke admitted, a really great girl in every respect and loved Dov with a passion that made her husband shake his head.

"What'd I do to deserve someone like her, Rick?" he'd utter in amazement. Then again, Hawke had heard him say the exact same words in total disgust once or twice too.

"C'mon. Burgers are ready," Dov called from the kitchen.

They played a little three-handed rummy after dinner until Hawke started yawning. Lisa put the cards away and got his coat.

"You're a barrel full of laughs tonight, Rick. Get a good night's sleep, okay?"

"Sorry. Been burning it from both ends."

"Don't I know it? You have sent my husband home dead on his feet every night since you started this file chase."

"Yeah, well, thanks for the dinner."

"Sure. Next time, bring a friend."

"Lisa . . ."

"It just popped out. Won't happen again."

"Sure it won't."

Driving home and feeling more alone than he'd been able to feel in years, Hawke began thinking about bringing Grace to Dov and Lisa's next time. To his surprise, he found that he wanted to. More than that, he wanted an end to his loneliness even if the pain of Steve's demise would always be with him.

Along with the guilt.

CHAPTER 19

"GINGER! COME BACK, Baby! Don't run away from Mama, Sweetheart."

He watched the white toy poodle, absurdly garbed in a fur-trimmed red knit sweater, sniff around the alley's mouth. Saw the moment the dog found the tantalizing tidbit he'd left for it.

He sneered to himself, *What kind of airhead dresses up their dog and, furthermore, is dumb enough to let her little rat off its leash?*

Huh. Works for me.

Despite the chill in the air, many people were out walking, probably because it was Sunday afternoon and the sunniest part of a cold day. They weren't the kind of people who might pose a threat to his plans, though. Not in this neighborhood where prostitutes, pimps, and pushers outnumbered the ordinary, decent residents too impoverished to move elsewhere.

He'd chosen the woman when she passed the alley walking her dog. The dog meant she lived nearby; it also meant she might pass him a second time on her way home. He eased into the shadows of the alleyway and let the dog come to him—or rather to what he carried in a napkin tucked into his jacket pocket.

"Ginger! Come back, I say!"

Ignoring his mistress, the poodle raced to where he leaned against the alley's brickwork.

Such is the power of freshly fried bacon!

"Ginger! Please come to Mama, baby!"

Ignoring his mistress's calls, the dog circled him, sniffing and salivating. He pulled out the napkin, broke off a piece of the bacon, and tossed it to the dog, who snapped it up and sat, waiting expectantly for more.

"Oh Ginger, you naughty, naughty girl!" The woman who came into view was world-wise and hard-bitten, far past her prime, her hair overbleached, her face caked with yesterday's makeup. He took note of her pudgy hands and the several gaudy rings on her fingers, had fingered her earlier as a "pro" who'd seen better days and let herself go.

When she spotted him, she stopped, ran an appraising eye over him, then approached with swaggering boldness.

"Hello there. I'm Trixie. And you are?"

He didn't answer; kept his eyes down.

"Dogs are a wonderful judge of character, don't you agree?" she asked.

Hands on her hips, she struck what may have, at some point in her younger years, been an alluring pose but was, at her present age, patently grotesque.

He almost laughed but schooled his features at the last moment.

"Don't be shy. I won't bite."

When he still didn't answer, she sauntered forward. "You look like you could use a good meal and some company. It's cold outside and it'll be dark soon. Would you like to come home with Ginger and me? We could show you a real good time, Ginger and me. Won't cost you much. Just a few twenties."

He let himself smile.

The woman smiled back, snagged her prancing dog, and beckoned to him. He followed her down the street, keeping a discreet distance between them. No one seemed to take note anyway; they were intent on their own business.

He followed her into an old but halfway-respectable apartment building. The place had seen better days. The doorman's stall stood empty, and the elevator was broken, forcing them to walk up three flights to her apartment.

She glanced over her shoulder at him once or twice, smug in her assessment of him. From under her arm the poodle watched, its black eyes bright with hopeful anticipation.

Oh, if you only knew, he thought with a smirk.

HOURS AFTERWARD, HIS immediate appetites appeased, he spent a comfortable night in the woman's apartment, got up early, pillaged her refrigerator and cupboards, and fixed himself a hearty breakfast before leaving. His "close encounter" with the woman had gratified his cravings . . . for the time being. It was now time to set his trap and wait for his prey to blunder into it.

To catch the specific prey one has in mind, one must use the most fitting bait.

He stuffed the woman's car keys into his pocket on his way out. Under his arm, he carried a bulging plastic bag and a small wrapped package, both fresh from the woman's refrigerator. As he closed the unlocked apartment door behind him, he left a trail guaranteed to rate a police response and the eventual arrival of the *right* detective.

He carried the bag down the stairs, squeezing out its contents along the way. He completed his task, unwrapped and placed his surefire, can't-miss bait in the middle of the sidewalk, then sauntered down the street and dropped the empty bag and wrapper into a conveniently located trash bin. After that, using the woman's keys, he entered the apartment's damp basement parking garage, and sought out her car.

"A green Ford," she'd whimpered.

He found her old beater, drove it out of the garage and down the street a block. Flipped a U-turn at the intersection, pulled up across the street and a few doors down from her apartment where he'd have a good view, then settled in to wait for his prey to come sniffing around.

All things considered, no one—even in this neighborhood—was likely to ignore a severed human hand on the sidewalk and the trail of blood leading from the street directly to the woman's apartment door. He yawned and kept watch as the sun came up and the earliest of the neighborhood's morning walkers stopped, gawked, and pointed. Within a quarter of an hour, the first police unit arrived.

HAWKED STARED OUT the apartment window. Curious onlookers had gathered around the police cordon. Children played in the street, heedless of the drama, except to point at the police cars and officers with their uniforms and guns.

Here I am again, Lord. Working on a Sunday when I should be—and would rather be—in church . . .

Dov cleared his throat. "Same MO as Vincent Delano, Rick . . . except for the obvious calling card."

The woman's severed hand left on the sidewalk, her dead fingers sparkling with the faux gems of several cheap rings, had been impossible for her neighbors to ignore. As impossible to ignore as the puddle of blood in which the glittering hand lay and the deliberate trail leading to the victim's apartment.

"I'm sure glad this case is cooling down, aren't you?"

Dov sighed. "You're not going to let that go, are you?"

"Not likely."

Rodríguez waited, arms folded in sober silence, while the crime techs finished up before giving the order to remove the body. As she directed her assistant and the gurney toward the door, Dov had to dance sideways to avoid putting his foot in a slick of blood.

"Same MO as Vincent Delano with the exception of the hand and *that*." He jerked his thumb to the wall where a toy poodle's limp body hung, impaled to the wall with a steak knife. "That's beyond perverse."

Hawke grunted. "Confirms we're dealing with the same guy who killed Delano . . . and most likely Sara Curry too. This is someone with a lot of anger and cold-blooded calculation. Suggests he's escalating."

"The press is sure going to jump all over this, especially when *that* gets out." He again gestured toward the body of the poodle. "I expect tomorrow's edition of *Morning Line* will run an especially sparkling commentary, courtesy of Sharon Richmond."

"You're probably right."

"You know, Rick, Richmond's producers ought to jerk a knot in her neck. I mean, her coverage is inflammatory, like she *wants* to egg this guy on."

"You're not wrong." He took a last look around. "I think we're done here. Want to grab lunch?"

Dov slid his eyes toward the wall and grimaced. "You're hungry after *that?*"

"A man's gotta eat. C'mon. I'll let you buy."

"Well, well. What a surprise."

"I think you meant to say, 'What a privilege.'"

"Hardy har har."

FROM INSIDE TRIXIE'S old Ford, he kept track of the number of responding police officers, the ambulance and paramedics that followed, the arrival of the ME on scene, and finally, the appearance of two detectives.

He'd been waiting for them to show. Surely, given the tantalizing breadcrumb he'd left on the sidewalk and the scene inside Trixie's apartment, the police would dispatch the detectives already assigned to investigate the knifings?

Nice to see you again, detectives. FYI? We'll be joined at the hip for the foreseeable future . . . although you won't have a clue. I'll dog your steps, learn your schedule, and follow you to where you live and eat. Why, one might say that I'll be stuck like glue on you!

He laughed at his little rhyme. *You won't shake me, gentlemen. Nope. I'll be your little alter ego until you lead me to my wife . . . so I can finish the job I apparently left undone all those years ago.*

CHAPTER 20

MONDAY, NOVEMBER 6

HAWKE WAS AT HIS desk early Monday morning. Dov sauntered in fifteen minutes later. They put their heads together to sharpen their testimony for the upcoming trial of Ibrahim Azize.

Hawke found himself twitchy and distracted from the task at hand. He glanced regularly at the division's wall clock. Percival and Browning were likely standing on the cold steps of City Hall, waiting for the doors to open. Hawke was praying his detectives would find property records for whichever alias Aneta used when she moved to the city.

"You're jumpy this morning," Dov observed.

"I'm hoping we find Aneta and Terry Gretzky today. Preferably alive."

Dov nodded sagely and lifted one brow. "You praying on it?"

Dov's loaded question wasn't a surprise or a one-off. It was one more gauntlet in their yearslong dialogue: Dov, a cynical, nonobservant Jew, regularly sniping at and challenging Hawke's faith in Christ; Hawke, clinging to a Savior he'd grudgingly surrendered to a month or so before Dov's arrival.

Hawke's progress in his faith had been incremental and ponderous. The only thing his coworkers were aware of was that Hawke's usual brusque and surly behavior had gone downhill and into the toilet following Steve's death . . . and remained there. It had improved after Hawke's surrender to Christ with such agonizing slowness that they hardly noticed.

My fellow detectives have no idea how bad it got after Steve died, Hawke thought, *or how deep was the despair I fell into. No one does—my fault, though. I wore my anger like armor, so how could anyone have sensed the anguish that gripped me? No one was aware of the things I did while desperately trying to appease my distress. I hid my shame and guilt so well, they never suspected the bouts of drinking, the women I used . . . or the nights I stood on the edge of that dark abyss, service weapon in hand, a smooth-talking demon on my shoulder insisting it was perfectly all right to "let go."*

McCormick may have wondered. He had likely speculated.

At any rate, after Hawke had shredded his way through two prospective partners, it was McCormick who forced Hawke to see a grief counsellor.

"Keep the appointment or turn in your badge and gun, Hawke."

The ultimatum had jolted him.

But if I'm not a detective, then who and what am I?

The therapist ran through the stages of grief, spouting them in with offhand, matter-of-fact ease. Hawke could tell she was bored with her work and had explained the "stages" theory multiple times. He threw them back in her face.

"I'd say I'm stuck in the anger stage, wouldn't you agree?" he queried softly, his eyes locked on hers.

The woman, chancing a deeper look at Hawke, was instantly nervous, aware of the rage lurking behind his mild speech, a violence coiled and ready to spring, only needing a halfway adequate reason to detonate. Any reason at all, really.

Amused, he watched her lick her lips and rush to appease him.

"Yes, I can see your, er, anger. What I might recommend—"

"And doesn't the grief literature insist that everyone grieves at their pace and in their own way?"

She nodded slowly, knowing precisely where he was headed, undoubtedly relieved that he would be exiting her office shortly.

"Then why don't you *get off my back* and let me grieve?"

Hawke had no way of knowing what she reported to Chief McCormick, only that the chief left Hawke alone and partnerless for the next couple of months . . . partnerless and off all active cases.

Beached. Like a dead or dying whale.

"Desk duty until I say otherwise, Hawke."

It was during that low, humiliating period that Hawke finally listened. Listened to Steve's long-suffering voice in his head as he explained who Jesus was, why he came, what he did for humanity on the cross, what he calls each person to do in response.

Apparently, all those times he'd turned a deaf ear to his partner's earnest preaching, Hawke's subconscious had recorded and stored up the entirety of Steve's religious blather. And apparently that "blather" came with a self-charging battery, because night after night, Hawke had lain in bed unable to escape Steve's sincere words and helpless to resist another Voice, this one whispering, "Come to me, Richard Hawke, and I will heal your heart."

More than a month later, skinny, dark-haired, dark-eyed Leshem Dovid Mayer, about as imposing as a lox and cream cheese bagel, walked quietly up to his desk, introduced himself to Hawke as his new partner and, without waiting for Hawke's reaction, started unpacking his stuff into the nearest empty desk, about three cubicles from Hawke's Batcave in the corner.

No prior notice from McCormick, no announcement to the division floor, no hoopla from the other detectives.

The day Dov reported for duty in Homicide Division, McCormick lifted Hawke's desk duty restriction.

At the beginning of Hawke and Dov's partnership, Dov played the role of passive spectator and obedient lackey. But eventually, as their partnership found a bit of solid footing, Dov showed Hawke he had a keen mind and a can-do attitude. He also spoke freely of his disbelief in God and had no qualms about voicing his contempt.

New to his Christian faith and unschooled in the Bible, Hawke was unable to fully articulate what Jesus was doing in him. Still, Hawke felt compelled to respond to Dov's little digs, a compulsion that drove him to search his Bible and to pray.

Great. Now I'm Steve and Dov is me, Hawke sighed, *and I'll never be the Christian Steve was.*

In the nearly four years since Dov became his partner, Hawke had grown in his walk with God. Looking back, he saw how he'd changed. Those changes notwithstanding, he still had more rough edges than he could count.

Yeah, so I've grown—from wretchedly bad to merely wretched. Super.

"Um, Lord? I really need you to . . . fix me. Do a greater work in me," was his recurring plea, often accompanied by the repeating line of one of his go-to Christian songs: "Change me on the inside, change me on the inside, change me on the inside."

Right. 'Cause I'm never going to change on the outside unless you change me at my core, Lord, so please . . . please plant your word deep in my heart. He knew the hours he dedicated to Bible study *were* changing him . . . just line upon line and precept upon precept, here a little, there a little. *At the speed of near-frozen molasses.* For him, spiritual growth was a sluggish, frustrating process that demanded diligence, tenacity, and immense patience. He *had* the diligence and tenacity, but—*big surprise*—patience was always in short supply.

Lord, please grant me patience . . . and I want it right now!

He took a deep breath and answered his partner's question. "Yeah, I'm praying on it."

"Huh. So, you actually think Marek Gretzky hasn't already tracked down his ex and his son? Hasn't already offed them?"

"Doesn't matter what I think. The Bible says God knows the end from the beginning. He already knows what the man has and hasn't done."

"If God knows it all, then what's the point in praying?"

Hawke felt his temper creeping up his throat. He stuffed it down into submission, where it belonged. "The Bible says, 'The prayer of a righteous person is powerful and effective.'"

"So now you're a righteous person? Don't forget I *know* you."

"I don't claim to be righteous in and of myself—and we've been over this before, Dov. Jesus, who *did* live a blameless, sinless life, lives in me.

Because Jesus loves me, he has clothed me in *his* righteousness before God. When God looks at me, he sees his Son and his Son's righteousness, not my sins or my pathetic attempts to live a righteous life."

"That doesn't answer my question. What's the point in praying if God already knows what's going to happen?"

"God's foreknowledge doesn't nullify humanity's free will or invalidate Jesus' command to pray to his Father in his name or to ask and keep on asking. My prayers can touch God's heart, move him to alter circumstances and even nudge people in the right direction."

Dov snorted. "Sounds like circular logic to me."

"Sure—until the undeniably miraculous occurs. How about we circle back to this discussion after we close this case? And just by way of clarification? Situations that require much prayer often get worse before they get better."

"Worse?" Dov's eyes narrowed. "If that's the case, I'm not sure I want you praying."

"Like you have anything to say about it."

HAWKE'S PHONE RANG just after nine o'clock that morning. He jerked the receiver off the handset. "Hawke."

"Hawke, it's Percival! Great news—we have an address!"

Hawke stood up, waved Dov over, then spoke into the phone. "Good work. You and Browning get back here ASAP. We'll be assembling a team by the time you get here."

He hung up and addressed his partner. "Dov, I need multiple printouts of Marek Gretzky's prison photo and one copy of whatever photo you can find of Aneta Gretzky."

As he turned toward the chief's office, he added, "Oh. And grab a photo of Grace Warner if you can find one."

He beat a path to Chief McCormick's office, knocked once, then barged inside.

"Chief, got an address for Marek Gretzky's ex. We need a warrant to enter the house and SWAT authorization since we may encounter a hostage situation." He dropped the jotted address on the chief's desk.

"Good. Judge Bailey is aware of the situation and is prepared to issue the warrant as soon as I provide the address. Have someone from your team pick it up."

"I also request a temporary duty transfer for that officer down in Community Outreach. The one who knows sign language. Need him for this action."

McCormick studied Hawke. "Tell his CO I'm requesting the officer's help. Today only."

He picked up his phone and dialed. "Chief McCormick here. I am authorizing SWAT to assist Detective Sergeant Hawke in the apprehension of a possible murder suspect. Immediate action."

McCormick didn't need Hawke to brief him on the details of the impending action; the man trusted that Hawke knew what he was doing. Instead, the chief hung up and fixed Hawke with a hard look. "You know how badly we want this guy. Good hunting, Detective."

"Thank you, sir." Hawke was already moving toward the door.

Chief McCormick and the entire division would be rooting for Hawke's team to locate Marek Gretzky and arrest him. Hawke and his team wanted nothing less. But deep inside, Hawke continued to pray and wrestle over his concern.

When they took Marek Gretzky, would he have already killed his former wife? And would Gretzky have discovered that *his son* was still alive? Would he have killed him too?

Lord, I'm asking you to protect that young man. He has already suffered so much.

TWO HOMICIDE DIVISION vehicles, the department's SWAT mobile command center, and several police units parked out of sight, about a block south of the address Percival and Browning found. Hawke deployed two of the PD units to plug both ends of the alley behind the target. The SWAT team was fully armored; Hawke's team wore armored vests. The PD officers were to secure the perimeter of the scene and remain clear of the action.

Hawke and his team (including one Officer Turley, a sign language expert), the SWAT commander, and the SWAT team leader moved closer on foot until they had an oblique view of the front of the house.

"Boarded up," Browning mumbled, "like the rest of this dump of a neighborhood. Nobody been living there for a long time."

"That's not what the post office told me when I called," Dov answered back. "Mail carrier delivers bills and whatnot regularly. The mailbox is always empty the next time he comes. Gas and electric to the house are on too."

"Huh. You don't say."

"Oh, but I do say. Not everything is what it appears to be, Browning. Keep that in mind."

Browning's mouth bunched up at Dov's mild rebuke, but Percival's answer was excited.

"Hey, if someone's living there, maybe those boarded-up windows and doors are just camouflage. You know, to blend in with the other abandoned houses? To make people *think* no one's living there?"

"Solid reasoning, Percy," Hawke said quietly.

Percival beamed. Browning, from behind his partner, scowled, then cut his eyes to the younger man, with something like grudging respect.

"What's the play here, Hawke?" the SWAT commander asked.

Hawke trained a pair of binoculars on the house's front door. "The front door *looks* like it is boarded up, but I suspect it isn't. Focus in on the door and let me know how it looks to you."

Both the SWAT commander and the team lead swept their binoculars across the house and zoomed in on the front entrance.

"Huh. I see what you mean," the commander said. "Rather than nailing boards to the doorframe, kinda looks like someone attached plywood to the screen door but left a few inches of overlap to make it *look* like it's nailed to the doorframe. Good enough to fool the casual observer."

"That's what I'm seeing. Now, if it were *me* hiding inside, I'd wouldn't leave myself only one exit. I'd like to send Mayer and Percival down the alley to the back of the house. Have them cover the back door while we breach the house from the front."

"What about a third exit, Hawke?" Percival asked.

Hawke cast his eye on Percival. "What would you suggest?"

Percival, put on the spot, froze, then quickly recovered. "Uh, send six guys total up the alley. Two on the rear, two on either side of the house. Breach from the front and let whoever is inside choose their exit. We'll have all of them covered."

Hawke glanced at Dov, who nodded. "That's our play, then."

He addressed the SWAT commander. "Detective Mayer will take Detective Percival up the alley to cover the back door. Please direct four members of your SWAT unit to accompany them, two each to take up positions alongside the house. Detective Browning and I will then accompany your team to breach the front door. The six on the rear and to the sides will be ready should we chase someone out."

The SWAT commander and team leader nodded their approval.

"One thing more. I want us to check out the front door before we breach and see if it can be unlocked and opened without commotion. If it can, I want to enter first."

The team leader started to protest Hawke's plan; Hawke held up his hand to forestall him.

"I want to remind everyone involved in this action that we may encounter one of two very different situations. The first possibility, if our murder suspect has already been here, we'll find two bodies, and our suspect will be long gone. *But*, if he has not yet located this place, and if this house is occupied as we believe it is, those occupants are *victims*, not suspects. In that instance, I'd much prefer a soft entrance. We don't want to startle the occupants into making a knee-jerk defensive move against us."

Neither the SWAT commander or the team leader cared much for that approach. The team leader huffed and locked his jaw.

Hawke persisted. "All I'm asking, initially, is that we try to open the front door quietly rather than bash it in. Do you have someone who can pick the lock?"

The team leader huffed a second time. "Yeah, but you need to wait and come in after my team clears the place."

"Look, if we encounter the victims alive, they should see me first—me and Officer Turley, who knows sign language. See, one of our victims is deaf, and a bunch of guys all in black, brandishing weapons, would undoubtedly freak him out. On the other hand, you've all seen the prison photos of Marek Gretzky. If we encounter him, you guys have the ball."

The team leader slowly nodded. He didn't like it, but he understood Hawke's logic. While he radioed orders to his squad, Dov and Percival headed down the alley behind their target.

Hawke motioned to Browning. "You and Turley are with me. Stay behind me, keep your muzzle pointed toward the floor, and unless I ask you something, keep quiet and say *nothing*."

Browning's lip curled, and he nearly spoke . . . until. Until he saw the look in Hawke's eye.

Taking a breath, he nodded. "You got it . . . Boss."

The corner of Hawke's mouth tipped up. "Thank you, Detective Browning."

The man wasn't stupid; it was the first time Hawke had referred to him as Detective Browning. He nodded and fell into line.

Ten minutes later, with Hawke, Turley, and Browning following the SWAT team, the first team member unlocked and opened the "boarded up" screen door, then unlocked and gently nudged open the target's front door. He signaled for the team members to enter, and they glided into the house's living room, making the barest of sounds. They swept the kitchen, bathroom, and two bedrooms. They encountered no one and found no sign the house had been lived in or recently visited. A carpet of dust lay everywhere . . . except where scuffed prints led from a closed door near the washing machine to the back door.

A member of the SWAT team gestured to a faint light showing under the closed door. "Basement," he mouthed.

The team lined up at the top of the basement stairs. The team leader gestured for the SWAT member who'd pointed out the light under the basement door to reconnoiter. So clean and quiet were his movements, Hawke thought the man a ghost. He disappeared down the stairs and out of sight. Moments later, he reappeared.

"One male Caucasian. Young, early thirties. Alone." His forehead wrinkled. "I don't think he noticed me, even when the bottom step creaked."

Hawke breathed a sigh of relief and holstered his service weapon. "That's our victim, Terry Gretzky. Browning, run outside and grab me a couple bits of gravel, will you?"

Browning returned, and Hawke slipped the pebbles into his breast pocket. Beckoning for Turley to follow him, Hawke made his way down the stairs. As reported, the bottom step creaked, but the figure across the basement to his right continued what he was doing. When Hawke reached the bare concrete floor, he took in the basement's unfinished layout.

One far corner had been turned into a makeshift living area: bed, sofa, table and a single chair, refrigerator, hotplate, and a television on a rolling stand, all positioned atop a large carpet remnant. Hawke felt like he'd been dropped into a scene from decades past. Every last furnishing, from the ratty orange-and-yellow flowered sofa upholstery to the harvest gold refrigerator was dated. Even the daytime soaps on the television were in grainy black and white.

A gangly man eating from a bowl faced the tv, his attention fixed on the captions flowing across the screen. Hawke scanned the basement for Terry's mother, Aneta. His gaze slid over a section of wall, stopped, returned to the one word scrawled in heavy letters:

Mama

As he took in the body-sized cement patch beneath the word, something in Hawke's heart clenched. *God have mercy—Terry buried his mother here!*

Hawke shook himself and turned to Turley. "Listen up. We believe Terry is deaf and has only limited sign language and a partial ability to read lips. You'll need to employ both. When he turns around, he's going to be afraid and defensive. Be ready to sign and speak 'hello' and 'friend.' Maybe 'don't be afraid.'"

Turley squared his shoulders and nodded.

Hawke drew close to the living area. He retrieved a couple of pebbles from his shirt pocket and tossed one toward the young man. It pinged off the television screen.

The man leapt to his feet and whirled to face them, a switchblade in his right hand. The blade snapped open with a sharp *snick*. He shifted from foot to foot and moaned, his fear evident.

Hawke noticed how the man's bandaged left arm hung by his side, so Hawke lifted both hands and kept them up, palms forward, while Turley signed and spoke aloud what he signed. But nothing Turley said or did seemed to reach the man: His fear was building.

"Turley, tell him my name. Tell him I want to help him with his injured arm."

Turley pointed at Hawke. He spoke and spelled out Hawke's name and message in sign. It didn't help. The man lifted the hand holding the knife to his head; he began to pound his head with his clenched fist. A harsh groan slipped from his mouth. The groan rose into an agonized shriek. He dropped the knife and repeatedly slapped his open hand against his face and his head.

When the man switched to pounding his forehead against the concrete wall, Turley gave up. More than a little freaked out, he yelled over Terry's screams, "I don't know what else to do, Detective Hawke! I did my best!"

"I know you did. Listen, run upstairs and find Detective Mayer. Be quick about it. Tell him we have Terry Gretzky and need Dr. Grace Warner here ASAP. Dr. Warner, got it? Tell Mayer to send a unit, Code 3, to fetch her."

He sighed. "And radio for an ambulance, 10-96."

10-96: Police ten code for 'mental subject.'

TURLEY LEFT, AND Hawke moved to where Terry was hitting his head against the wall. He checked that the knife he'd dropped was still on the floor. Hawke reached his hand toward the distraught man and placed his palm on Terry's shoulder.

He wasn't surprised when Terry flinched and shied away, his forehead skinned and bloody. His eyes skittered around the room, desperate for an avenue of escape. Hawke again raised his hands, palms out.

"Terry."

He wiggled one hand to get Terry's attention. As soon as the man's eyes shifted to him, Hawke said again, "Terry. Terry, look at me."

The man's eyes jinked away, then slowly slid back.

"Terry."

Terry's eyes blinked and fixed on him.

Hawke pointed to himself. "Hawke." Pointed to Terry. "Terry." Took a breath. Pointed toward the word on the wall. "Mama."

Terry blinked again. His eyes teared up.

Hawke moved closer. He again gently reached his hand toward Terry's shoulder—but the man shied away.

Hawke waved to reclaim the guy's attention. "Sorry," he said.

Deliberately and slowly, he added, "I. Will. Not. Hit. You. I. Promise."

Then he sat down on the floor, cross-legged. Terry stepped away and eyed him with distrust.

"I. Will. Not. Hit. You. I. Promise." Hawke repeated, grateful Terry had not returned to shrieking and pounding his head against the wall.

Behind him, Hawke heard Turley inching his way back down the stairs. "Officer Turley, if you could move a little quicker without further freaking out our friend here, I think we might manage to converse a bit while we wait on Dr. Warner."

Turley's hands signed and he spoke the signed words aloud as he came closer. "Friend. You are safe. We will not hurt you."

When Turley reached Hawke, Hawke gestured for him to sit down beside him. "Uh, I'm kinda worried about that knife over there, Detective Hawke."

"Yeah, I get you." He pointed at the knife, then at Terry, back to the knife. Nodded.

Terry shuffled to the knife, picked it up, folded the blade. Set it on the table. Then, to Hawke and Turley's joint astonishment, Terry walked over to his bed, pulled the covers back, and crawled in. Turned on his side and pulled the blankets over himself, including his head.

"Huh." Hawke rubbed at the scar under his eye. "Officer Turley, pull back to the stairs and keep an eye on our . . . friend."

EVEN WITH LIGHTS flashing and sirens blaring, forty minutes passed before a PD unit delivered Grace to them. By then, Hawke had explained the situation to his team and the SWAT commander.

He sent Dov to fetch the first aid kit from their ride and dismissed SWAT with, "We've got this covered now. Please thank your team for the assist." He had Percival and Browning convey the same message to the PD presence. When they were gone, that would leave his team and Turley alone at the house with Terry.

And Grace, he thought.

He had to restrain his fervent impulse to pull her into an embrace when she stepped through the doors. Instead, he just said, "Grace. I am beyond glad you're here."

"You've found the bloodletter?"

"We think so, yeah. You missed quite a lot over the weekend, including a murder yesterday we think was committed by the same individual who killed Vincent Delano. On the positive side? Friday after you left for your conference, we got a callback on the BOLO we issued to law enforcement entities across the state and region. A retired detective in Brockport, upstate, filled us in on his only unsolved case, a twenty-one-year-old murder."

She was astounded. "Twenty-one years? That long ago?"

"Hard to believe, huh? But because of that one detective, we now know about the bloodletter's horrible childhood and how, all those years ago, his mother brought her ten-year-old son here to escape her abusive husband. The kid's name is Terry Gretzky, except he's not a kid any longer, at least not physically. He's around thirty-one and, from what we can tell, he's been living alone in the basement of this house for some time."

"What about his mother?"

"She died, of what, I can't say, but Terry interred her in the wall of the basement. And you were right. He is profoundly deaf."

He detailed his and Turley's interactions with Terry. "When Officer Turley and I went downstairs, Terry was watching an old black and white television. Although sound was off, he didn't hear us, didn't notice us. When we did get his attention, I had Turley sign to him that we were friends and would not harm him, Instead, Terry flipped out and pulled a switchblade on us. A minute later, he began to moan like he was in pain. He dropped the knife, held his head, beat it with his fists, and screamed. He then started banging his head against the basement wall."

Grace nodded, her expression thoughtful and serious.

"I sent Turley upstairs to have PD pick you up and call an ambulance for Terry. While Turley was upstairs, I got Terry's attention, pointed to my mouth, and said my name and his name several times. He watched my mouth, and he calmed down some, stopped hurting himself. When Turley came back, I pointed at the knife Terry had dropped on the floor. He picked it up, folded the blade, and set the knife on the table.

"After that, Terry sort of withdrew. He crawled into his bed and went to sleep. I have Turley keeping an eye on Terry from the stairs. As far as we can tell, he's still sleeping. It's like he got so overwhelmed, he just checked out."

"You may be right. I . . . I'll go down there. Do you think he will recognize me? Know who I am?"

"He has that television, and I have no doubt he watched your *Morning Line* interview with Sharon Richmond. It's the only way he would have known where to send you that message. By the way, the TV has some kind of device attached to it."

"A telecaption adaptor?"

Hawke shrugged. "Never heard of such a thing." He added, "Grace, I'm really hoping you can find a way to communicate with Terry, because we believe his father is the murder suspect we're seeking."

"His *father?*"

"Marek Gretzky. Convicted of nearly beating his son to death when the kid was ten, possibly causing some form of permanent brain damage. Marek was sent up for thirty years but was released last month for good behavior. We also know he was given a bus ticket when he left prison. Want to guess where that bus dropped him?"

"No," Grace breathed. "Not here!"

"Sorry, but yeah. He came here. We know he arrived in town after the death of Mary Alice Waite but before the death of Esther Grunbaum— meaning also before the murders of Vincent Delano and a former prostitute by the name of Trixie Lawson."

Grace shivered. "She died yesterday, yes? I read the details in this morning's paper. Absolutely horrible—pathologically so."

"Then you know Delano and Lawson's CODs are nearly identical. Those CODs are also nearly identical to the murder of a fourteen-year-old girl, Sara Curry, but for which Marek Gretzky was never charged. Sara's stepfather hung himself, which the police considered a confession. Marek, on the other hand, was convicted of the attempted murder of his own son."

"His own son? Terrible!"

"No kidding. Furthermore? His wife wrote him a letter after he entered prison, saying their son died from that beating."

"To protect him?

"That had to be her intention."

"But why would she do that if he was in prison for thirty years?"

"I think she feared the day her husband would get out of jail and come looking for her—only to find out she'd lied to him and that his son was still alive. See, that man carries an abhorrence for Terry's disability. He blamed his wife for bearing him a 'defective' child, and he hated Terry for being that child.

"Now, let's say Marek Gretzky is our murderer, and let's say he finds out his son is still alive. I think I can safely say that twenty years of hard time will not have softened this man's heart toward Terry. Thus, I am greatly concerned for Terry's well-being."

Hawke stretched his neck where the muscles were tight and aching. "By the way? Terry's left arm is bandaged, but he isn't using it. If he will let you, I'd like you to take a look under those bandages. I had Turley take our first aid kit downstairs."

"You think that's where he cut himself in order to dribble blood on Mary Alice Waite and Esther Grunbaum's faces?"

He sighed. "Yeah, and I sure wish I understood that part of this mess. Grace, we need to stash Terry where Marek Gretzky cannot get at him but where he can receive the help and treatment he needs. I can think of several safe places, but I doubt Terry's state of mind would tolerate the confinement; his paranoia makes him an extreme flight risk. And if we were to lose him, we might never find him again. I have an ambulance waiting right now. Can you suggest somewhere we might take him?"

She thought a moment, then murmured as if to herself, "He's going to need intense treatment. If I and others in the clinic are to care for Terry throughout the day, we would need to keep him close by. He will need brief but regular interactions with us followed by evaluations, tests, and therapy. He may even require light sedation initially to control his anxiety. I want to personally oversee his care and meet with him often throughout the day until he begins to know and trust me and our staff better. Only then can we expect to make real progress."

She looked at Hawke and added, "You've been to Upton-Warner. Do you recall that the physician's building housing our clinic is just across from City View Hospital?"

"Where that pedestrian walkway crosses the expressway?"

"That's it. The sky bridge connects the Physician's Annex to the hospital, and here's my point: City View Hospital has a small but secure mental health wing for emergency patient observation. The wing has two security guards 24/7 and two sets of automated locking doors controlled by trained personnel at a checkpoint within the wing. Only authorized persons are allowed in or out.

"Terry would be safe from his father in that wing and close enough for us to treat him. I can arrange for the hospital to admit him; however, in order for him to go willingly, he and I need time to establish a connection."

Hawke frowned. "How much time?"

"At a minimum, several hours."

CHAPTER 21

HE LURKED BESIDE a deserted house across the street. Hidden within a tangle of overgrown shrubs, he watched the action unfold.

My idea to follow the bumbling gumshoe was spot-on! I may have lost sleep keeping him under watch, but I was certain he'd eventually lead me to my treacherous wife.

Ha! My useless wife? Instead of bearing me a son I could mold into a man, that inept excuse of a woman saddled me with a freak of nature. The whole world will be better off when I finish her.

Marek Gretzky tucked his chin to his chest. He'd been quite amused when the detective and his trusty sidekick led him to the same abandoned house he'd already visited. He laughed up his sleeve at the SWAT and police presence—for what? To raid an empty house? He found the overblown SWAT scenario absolutely hilarious.

But after the detective and SWAT team entered the house and they remained inside, he stopped laughing.

What are they doing in there? And why would they need an ambulance? It didn't even have its siren on when it pulled up.

Ten minutes later, the SWAT team emerged from the house and gave every indication of standing down. The detective, on the other hand, did not appear.

What did they find that would keep them inside for going on an hour? He experienced a shiver of uncertainty, and that uncertainty irked him and rankled . . . threatened to snatch away his good humor and his control of the situation. Yet what could he do but wait?

Marek's chin jerked up. A police unit, lights flashing, screeched to a stop across the street. An officer flung open the curbside rear door and helped a woman out.

Who's she? He squinted. *She looks vaguely familiar.*

Marek studied her with slitted eyes that followed her into the house. He reached for the faint memory of a newspaper article . . . and an accompanying photo. He attempted to tease out the details, but they were patchy at best. *I only skimmed that article but . . . didn't Sharon Richmond from* Morning Line *interview this woman? Something about the death of the church organist?*

He growled in frustration. *What was the woman's name! More importantly, why would the cops bring her here?*

HAWKE RELIEVED TURLEY and escorted Grace down to the basement. He pointed out where Aneta Gretzky's body was interred, the word Mama etched over the cement. Terry was still in his bed, so Grace wandered through his small living area, studying the artifacts of his equally small life.

"Richard."

Hawke turned to her.

"I need you to wake him up. Gently, if you please."

Hawke slid the covers from Terry's head, placed his hands on the man's form, and jostled it lightly. Grace stood where Terry could see her when his eyes popped open.

She smiled and signed to him. Aloud she said, "Hello, Terry. Do you know who I am?"

Terry sat up. When he saw Hawke, he drew back. Hawke wisely moved several feet away. He pulled the chair from the dining table, moved it outside the carpet that bounded Terry's "home" and sat on it.

GRACE NUDGED TERRY to get his attention. "Terry, I need to talk to you. Shall we sit on the sofa?"

Gesturing to him, Grace got up and moved to the sofa. He followed but glanced nervously at Hawke, who responded with his "hands up" gesture and stayed put.

Grace soon realized Terry's comprehension of sign was low, and his ability to read lips not much better. Although he alternately watched her hands and her mouth, she often had to repeat herself. When their conversation got going in earnest, Grace said to him, "Terry, we know you did not hurt the woman who played the organ at the church."

Terry ducked his head and appeared sorrowful.

"We know you did not hurt the other woman at the Claremont."

Tears trickled from the young man's eyes.

Grace took Terry's hand in hers and squeezed it. Terry stared at her and exhaled. His indecision was palpable, but he did not pull away. For years, the only human touch he'd experienced was his mother's. Grace hoped Terry's need for connection would help her breach his fear and distrust.

"Terry, I am sorry your Mama died. You have been alone for a long time. You must miss her terribly."

The man broke completely. He bent over and sobbed. After a moment of consideration, Grace put her arms around him and gently cradled him there.

She lifted her face to Hawke and said, "Breakthrough. Thank God."

An hour later, having told Terry—to his utter astonishment—that his father was alive, and having explained why his father was a danger to him, Grace convinced him to come with them to a safe place, a place where he would have books, puzzles, games, and plenty to eat and where he could sleep without being afraid.

Then Grace opened the first aid kit Hawke had given her and asked the man if she could tend to the scrapes on his forehead. He tolerated her doctoring, so she asked if she could look at the wounds on his arm. When he nodded, Grace undid the awkward wrap around his arm and peeled back the soiled bandages.

She grimaced at what she found, looked up at Terry and said, "You need medicine, Terry. You have an infection."

She was gratified when she received her first spoken response from him. Even though his voice was rough and his words garbled and nearly incomprehensible, she managed to pick out a few of them. Something along the line of, "I did my best, but it was not good enough," was what she gathered.

She signed and spoke back, "I know you did your best, but we should go to the safe place and get medicine. Please pack a few things to take with you. Whatever you need most."

Terry pulled his pillow out of its case and began adding items to the pillow case. While he did so, she and Hawke put their heads together.

Grace sighed. "In an ordinary counseling situation, my behavior toward Terry would be markedly different. To prevent patient confusion over my role and to limit a patient's dependence on me, I would establish and maintain proper therapist-patient boundaries. But, given Terry's fragile state and the danger remaining in this house presents, I ignored those professional boundaries. Terry needed the comfort of a friend, and I felt it was the right and necessary thing to do. It was . . . what Jesus would have me do."

"Because his only relationship was with his mother and she died?"

"That about sums it up. Can you imagine having only one human connection in your life and, in an instant, having no one at all? His mother, out of fear that her ex might one day be released from prison and come looking for them and in order to protect Terry and give him the skills to survive without her, ingrained in Terry a fear of all others. Her mandate to him was, 'Be careful at all times. Let no one see you.'"

Grace sighed. "Basically, she taught him to live an invisible life."

"Knowing that, do you think you can convince him to get in my car?"

"It will hinge on how much he trusts me. Perhaps if I get in the car first, he will follow."

"Good, because something in my gut tells me we need to get him away from here, pronto."

MAREK WAITED AND waited, pacing up and down behind the shrubs that screened him from the four men on the sidewalk across the street. One of them he recognized as the detective's partner. *Partner Pig*, he snickered. *Haha!* Another was a uniformed police officer. The remaining two men had the same general appearance as the detective's partner: cops, but not beat cops. Most likely also detectives.

But the woman whose name he couldn't recall and the detective he knew as *Richard Hawke* remained in the house, presumably with *his wife*.

His fury and frustration built with every passing minute.

What are you doing in there, Detective? What lies are you telling my wife? Doesn't matter what you do. You cannot save her from me.

I just need to get shut of your guard dogs.

He debated walking up the sidewalk toward the four cops, acting like he belonged in the neighborhood. He fingered the blade in his pocket and ran the scene in his mind.

I could take two of them before they reacted, maybe a third. But all four? One of them would manage to pull a gun and shoot me.

So he waited. And waited.

After an interminable length of time, the detective he knew as Hawke appeared on the front porch and spoke to the uniformed cop and three detectives. The detectives peeled off immediately. He had hopes of taking down the uniformed officer left behind and making his way inside—until the cop followed Hawke into the house.

Only two cops inside with my wife, but they're both armed. And if they heard me sneaking into the house, I would lose the advantage of surprise. No. Better to wait.

He resumed his impatient watch and was glad he had when, minutes later, two vehicles pulled up to the curb. Two detectives were in one car; Hawke's partner was driving the other. The uniformed cop emerged from the house and got in the first car. Hawke came out next, and behind him was the woman and . . . a gaunt stranger cradling his left arm. The stranger saw the cars and hung back.

He frowned. *Who is that? And where's my wife?*

The woman, patiently smiling, coaxed the man into following her down the cracked sidewalk to the second car.

Why can't I remember that woman's name?

His inability to recall her name bugged him. He dug deep to retrieve information he'd only skimmed over, but nothing came to him. The woman slid into the back of the car driven by Hawke's partner. After much hesitation, the man cradling his arm climbed in after the woman.

At that precise moment, the single crumb of information he'd been fishing for floated to the surface of his thoughts: *Grace*. Yes! But not any old Grace. No, it was *Dr.* Grace something or other.

He muttered to himself, "And didn't that article say this woman doctor treats 'the hearing impaired'?" He snarked at that. "Hearing impaired, my left foot! Fancy name for deaf imbeciles."

Click.

Like the first tile in a row of precisely placed dominoes, that single fact tipped over . . . and other tiles fell, one after another, until the trail of fallen facts reached its conclusion.

Both vehicles pulled away. Left him standing with his mouth ajar.

The stranger holding his injured arm. The fearful man who got into the detective's car with the woman doctor . . . who treats deaf blockheads.

The enormity, *the sheer stupidity* of his blindness, sent a shockwave down his spine all the way to his shoes.

"But he died—and I am *not* crazy! She told me I killed him!"

Shaking all over, he gave himself up to the only feasible possibility—no, the *only* possibility. Period.

He laughed under his breath, scarcely believing what it meant.

It meant she lied, you fool. You should never have believed a word that witch said.

"But how? The dimwit's just a boy!"

You mean he was a boy twenty-one years ago.

Twenty-one years ago he'd beaten his son to death. After a year of judicial delay and languishing in county lockup, he'd been found guilty and spent the next twenty years in the state's penal system.

"If my dead son were still alive . . . why, that would make him thirty-one years old."

The realization hit him harder. Like a freight train.

"That grown man was my son?"

Disgust at his own ineptitude quickly followed.

I never actually entered the house when I scoped it out weeks back. The place was boarded up, evidently not lived in, and the neighbors seemed to agree. And yet, by not breaking into the house and checking it out for myself, I screwed up.

My wife **and** *my son? Living in that house, only yards from me while I stood on the sidewalk. And what did I do? I squandered the simplest of opportunities to take them both.*

He slowly grinned. His newfound knowledge stole his breath away, caused his heart to skip and pound.

"Yup, you told me a lie, *Dearest*, an out-and-out lie. But *karma*, Baby. Yup, what goes around, comes around—and trust me, Sugar: *I* am the karma coming 'round to you."

He clamped his teeth together. Set his jaw. "No matter. Nothing will keep me from my task now. I will dispatch my wife . . . and the imbecile son I thought I rid the world of, two decades back."

Still muttering, he retreated to Trixie's car, peeled away from the curb, and raced through the neighborhood. Even when he spotted the car driven by Detective Hawke's partner far ahead of him, recriminations dogged his thoughts.

He trailed after the detective's car, staying far enough behind to escape their notice, all the while rehearsing what he now understood. However, something about the scene where his son had gotten into the detective's car bugged him.

What was it?

The question plagued him until he merged onto the expressway and was forced to push it aside to navigate the traffic. It had been twenty-odd years since he'd driven, after all. The volume of cars and trucks roaring past and around him across five lanes was nerve-racking. He managed to stick with the detective's car, though. He followed it until it reached the city center, took an off ramp, and disappeared into a parking garage.

He took the same off ramp and skimmed the sign at the garage entrance.

Physician's Annex Parking

He rolled into the garage and glided slowly along, head swiveling left and right. He spotted the detective's parked vehicle on the second level, immediately scanned around, seeking movement, and caught a glimpse of the elevator doors closing. He gunned the engine, braked alongside the elevator, and watched the indicator rise and stop at the seventh floor.

Slipping the car's transmission into Park, he walked around the car to peruse the sign listing the building's physician groups by floor. In bold letters, the seventh floor line listed its occupants.

Upton-Warner Clinic:
Ear, Nose, Throat Specialists
Audiology and Allergy Services
Speech Therapy
Family Therapy for the Hearing Impaired

Hold on, there. I need to be smart about this. I have no business on the seventh floor, so taking the elevator there would not be smart. I'd stick out like a sore thumb.

He pulled into a parking spot and turned off the engine, got out and walked to the open-air edge of the garage to think. Across the wide expressway a large red neon sign blinked on and off.

City View Hospital
Emergency Services

He glanced up and caught sight of a pedestrian overpass connected to the physician's building. His eyes followed the overpass across the expressway. To the hospital.

The freak has something wrong with his arm, and they gotta get it checked out, right?

The truth smacked him upside the head.

Something wrong with his arm? Of course! Just like I taught the poor fool. Oh, this is rich, just rich.

Laughing to himself, he walked over to the elevator for a full look at the sign listing physician groups by floor. The fifth floor had what he was looking for:

**Pediatrics, Pediatric Oncology,
Snack Bar, Pedestrian Sky Bridge
to City View Hospital**

"Snack bar, eh?" He pressed the elevator "up" button.

At that very moment, the unease niggling at the back of his mind came roaring to life.

Hey! Where's my wife?

HAWKE DIRECTED DOV to an empty parking slot on the second level, and the four of them headed for the elevator. People were waiting for the car, and others soon arrived before the car did. When the elevator doors opened and those waiting crowded in, Terry began to exhibit anxiety. Grace shook her head, and Hawke told those getting on that they would take the next car up.

Apparently, Terry had never been in an elevator. He squirmed and rocked from foot to foot as the doors closed, but when the car jerked and flew upward, amazement wreathed his face. At the seventh floor, they stepped out into relative calm. Grace said hello to several patients she recognized, but she didn't linger to talk; she asked Dov and Hawke to pull Terry aside and wait with him while she spoke to Dr. Bill.

She returned some minutes later. "Had to let Bill know what was going on and ask Linda to reschedule my afternoon appointments."

"So we're off to the hospital now?" Hawke asked.

"Yes. The sky bridge on the fifth floor will take us across. The secure ward is on the hospital's fifth floor too, but Admissions is at ground level. We'll go there next to have Terry admitted."

They again boarded the elevator. Getting out at the fifth floor, however, presented a problem: A crush of pediatric patients and their families stood waiting for the car, and Grace couldn't convince Terry to leave the elevator and walk into that crowded and unfamiliar environment.

Hawke held the elevator doors, lifted his badge to those waiting, and said to them, "City Police. I need you good folks to step back and to your left, please. Clear a path—quickly now."

Once they had an opening, Grace took Terry by the hand, tugged him away from the elevator, and quickly moved toward a pillar that was out of the flow of patients and family. At Grace's request, Hawke and Dov agreed to walk ahead of Grace and Terry and run interference for them.

"The sky bridge is that way," she pointed. She still had Terry's hand in hers, although his was the tighter grip. As soon as Hawke and Dov moved forward, she tugged Terry along behind them.

Then the sky bridge was before them, a wide, arched, glassed-in corridor spanning the expressway. Hawke and Grace did not slow as they entered the pedestrian overpass, but kept Terry moving forward—until he shook loose from Grace's hand, shuffled to one side of the bridge, and stared with wonder at what he saw.

He's not getting too close to the windows, Hawke thought. *He doesn't know if he might fall off the edge or not.*

Terry gaped at the view spread before him—all ten lanes of the expressway below, building after building on both sides, and a pollution-hazy vista culminating in a far mountain range. A deep, guttural belly laugh burst from his mouth. He turned to Grace, pointed, and gabbled with excitement.

Hawke grinned at Grace. "Haven't the foggiest what he's saying, but it's good to see him happy."

Grace smiled back. "It is indeed."

After several minutes, they got Terry moving again, took the elevator down to ground level, and soon arrived at the emergency and urgent care wing of the hospital. Grace spoke at length to the intake nurse, then she came back to them.

"Due to our unique situation, they are going to put Terry at the top of the queue. Let's find some seating until they call us, but not near other people, if possible."

"What about there?" Dov asked, pointing nearby. "Just the one guy with his nose in a magazine."

"Perfect. As soon as we have Terry sitting and comfortable, I'll step away. I need to meet with an administrator about the billing for Terry's admission to the hospital's secure ward."

HE'D TAKEN A SEAT in the Admissions waiting area, close enough to overhear patients speaking as they signed in, then he picked up a magazine, and pretended to read it. With his face in the magazine, knit watch cap pulled onto his head, and a thick scarf he'd found in the hospital gift shop wound about his neck, not a soul could tell what he actually looked like.

When Detective Hawke and his partner showed up, the woman doctor right behind them, he could hardly believe his lucky guess had panned out.

He sneered at the woman from behind his magazine.

Holding my son the freak by the hand. How fitting . . . for an imbecile.

He perked up when the woman murmured to the detectives, "I need to meet with an administrator about the billing for Terry's admission to the hospital's secure ward."

He kept his head down so no one would see him smile.

Later, after they'd left to take his son to the so-called "secure ward," he returned to Trixie's car.

The police left the house without my wife, but they took my imbecile of a son with them, no doubt because of his arm. Well, if they left the dummy's mother behind, this is my golden opportunity.

He returned to the abandoned neighborhood, parked where he had parked before, and again peered through the overgrown bushes at the house where his wife lived. It was night now, and the sky was very dark. Only three lights were visible in the neighborhood. None came from the house he watched. Feeling confident, he stole across the street and up the porch. He had a crowbar in one hand and a flashlight in his pocket. He needed the crowbar to get the front door open.

Except, he hadn't needed the crowbar. The "boarded up" screen door swung open effortlessly under his hand.

Twenty minutes later, he left the house and made his way to Trixie's car on slow, clumsy feet, more shaken than he'd believed possible. After checking each room in the house and finding absolutely no sign anyone had lived in those rooms for years, he stared down the steep steps into the dark basement, suddenly anxious about what he would find.

And he'd found it all right. A large, body-sized patch on the basement's cement wall, a single word scrawled across the patch.

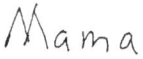

CHAPTER 22

THREE DAYS HAD passed since Terry was admitted to City View Hospital's secure ward. Hawke called Grace each evening to get an update on Terry's progress. Those daily reports opened a window into the intense battle being waged for Terry Gretzky's sanity and future.

"Terry is still quite anxious and distraught, Richard. Imagine being thrust into an alien and restrictive environment after living alone and apart from other people most of your life. Medication is helping him as are my several visits each day, and we are slowly making headway. Now that I am a familiar face, he looks forward to my visits. I have also introduced him to others on staff at the clinic, and he is beginning to accept them.

"And, oh! Terry is brilliant! He has his own, creative way of navigating the world that demonstrates he is mentally capable of solving complex logistical problems. At the same time, he's vastly ignorant of the majority of places, things, and experiences we take for granted. And emotionally and socially, he's somewhat a child. This is the greatest hurdle we face. Why, you ask?"

Hawke smiled. "Er, right. Tell me?"

"Well, you said that prior to age ten, Terry was bullied and misunderstood at school. Given what he's also been able to tell us, we now know that after his mother left Brockport and moved him here, still recovering from the near-death beating his father dished out, she further isolated him.

"She did not enroll him in school, and she made him promise to never stray far from their neighborhood. Thus, he grew into physical adulthood entirely without the usual breadth of social connections and group interactions most of us had. Those interactions, as we grew up, provided feedback loops to our behaviors and taught us social and cultural cues, norms, and standards. Terry had none of those experiences."

"She sequestered Terry to protect him," Hawke commented.

"I agree. Sadly, she likely didn't realize how much the isolation stunted him. Going forward, the two greatest impediments to Terry's social and emotional growth will be his communication deficiencies and his need for a group of friends and role models who will be his extended family, so to speak."

"Makes me think of the church," Hawke replied. "A good, bible-teaching church is the extended family God had in mind to care for those who are alone, wounded, destitute, and weak in body or mind."

"You are so right! I suppose I am hoping . . ." but she didn't finish her thought.

"I should tell you more about Terry's progress, which is nothing short of astounding. When we looked at Terry's comprehension as he watched us sign or watched us speak and compared it to his reading comprehension? We discovered that *reading* his strongest suit! It is also the communication method improving the quickest."

"He reads?"

"Yes, indeed. Of course, he doesn't read as proficiently as we'd like *yet*. That said, we've found that he has an absolutely voracious appetite for reading. To that end, we've given him books, and he devours them. He's currently reading at a fifth-grade level, but I see that improving rapidly.

"We've also given him paper and a no-frills electric typewriter. He is actually quite taken with the machine, both for what it can do and how it works. Knowing he reads print better than he reads sign language, we can ask him more detailed questions by typing them out ahead of time or on the spot. Conversely, Terry is learning to respond more fully to our questions by typing his responses."

"But how in the world did he learn to read?"

"Good question. According to the school records we've obtained, Terry was continually bullied and misunderstood by his teachers, often treated like he was retarded and incapable of learning. His grades tell us he could read very little at that time.

"Going out on a limb here, my perception is that he learned to read primarily through closed captions on TV. His mother had to have purchased the TeleCaption adaptor we found on Terry's TV back when captioning first started. Consequently, Terry learned a great many things from watching the television programs that provided captioning. By the way, did you know that when I asked Terry to pack what he needed most, he packed an old dictionary?"

"Really? Does he know how to use it?"

"Indeed, he does! If Terry doesn't understand a word, he immediately looks it up. Reading and comprehension aside for a moment, Terry's *speech* is both primitive and inarticulate, the product of never having heard speech. Sadly, unless we can provide him with some measure of hearing, we won't see much improvement on that front. Without him actually hearing how words sound and learning how to imitate those sounds, it will take our speech therapists years to undo Terry's ingrained garbled speech patterns and replace them with more accurate ones.

"Deaf children who haven't yet learned inaccurate speech patterns fare better than Terry will in that regard. This is why I hope we can provide him with some level of hearing."

"What can be done for him?"

"Won't know until we test him—hopefully soon. We can test his sensorineural and bone conduction levels at the same time. I have hope Terry will qualify for cochlear implantation, given that you found he pressed his hands, face, and head against the larger organ pipes in order to hear them. Implantation technology has come a long way since its introduction, and an implant may be Terry's only route toward better speech."

"When can you test him?"

"Perhaps as early as Friday. I have introduced him to our audiologist. Dr. Gibson will visit Terry multiple times to build their acquaintance. When Terry is ready, Dr. Gibson and I will walk Terry over to our clinic, and Dr. Gibson will test both his level of sensorineural hearing and bone conduction."

Hawke heard her sigh a happy sigh.

"Overall, Richard? Things are going well for Terry, and I am grateful to the Lord for bringing him to us."

NOT EVERYTHING WAS turning up roses for Terry. Grace's Friday evening report was not as reassuring as previous ones.

"I have some less than positive news to share, I'm afraid,"

"What's that?"

"We've discovered that Terry suffers from severe, debilitating tinnitus."

"Uh, I recall you telling me what tinnitus is, but would you give me the rundown again?"

"Sure. Basically, tinnitus is noise in the patient's head, unheard by anyone other than the patient. People who suffer from tinnitus describe their noise as ringing, buzzing, tinkling, tinging, jangling, sawing, and so forth. It can be regular, that is continuous, or irregular, that is, periodic. Sadly, while the causes of tinnitus may be structural ear problems, age-related hearing loss, a number of diseases, or neurological damage—perhaps even possess a psychosomatic basis—we don't really understand the *why* or *how* part.

"In Terry's case, stress seems to bring on an attack, as you witnessed when you surprised him that day in his basement living space. However, Terry's tinnitus is so severe, it can reduce him to hurting himself in an attempt to make it stop."

"This tinnitus thing? That's why he started beating his head against the wall?"

"Yes, it is, which is why we are monitoring his stress level. As soon as we can confidently transport him without upsetting his stable state of mind, we will arrange for a neurologist to examine him. We are searching for the right one now. In all likelihood, the many beatings Terry suffered at his father's hands left him with residual brain damage, and could be what causes Terry's tinnitus."

"I will continue to pray for Terry, Grace."

"Thank you. I'm praying for him too."

"And his arm?"

"Much improved. Infection is under control, and his doctor has removed the stitches."

"Grace, when will we be able to interview Terry and ask him questions about the deaths of Mary Alice Waite and Esther Grunbaum? In particular, we need to understand the bloodletting rituals."

"I understand, but Terry is in an emotionally fragile state at present. I will let you know when I deem him able to bear your questions."

Saturday, November 11

HAWKE'S SATURDAY EVENING call found Grace rejoicing. "I have wonderful news, Richard. The test results indicate that Terry is an excellent candidate for cochlear implant!"

"That *is* good news. Any word on the neurologist front?"

"Not yet, but to add more difficulty to the logistics of transporting Terry, we'll need to take him to a bigger city where the neurologist has access to a relatively new diagnostic tool, a computed tomography or CT scanning machine. We'll be gone two or three days."

Hawke expelled a long breath. "That's a lot to digest, a lot for you to man-age. What with your regular clinic duties, you must be stretched to the max."

Far too harried to see me.

"I suppose you're right. Because I committed to overseeing Terry's care and to visiting him several times each day, I had to rearrange my calendar. Linda has rescheduled my family therapy sessions and moved a short list of regular patients to evening or weekend appointments. It also meant shifting my dinner last week with Dr. Bill. Dinner with Dr. Bill . . . and you?"

On his end, Hawke was momentarily taken aback. "Wow. I totally forgot about that dinner. Been a bit distracted."

"Says you! How does this coming Monday evening work for you? Terry is scheduled with our sign language tutor the entire afternoon, and I have no evening appointments that day. That means I can leave early to come home and cook. And breathe."

"Maybe you should rest instead of cook. I could take you out?"

"Thank you, but I find cooking restful. Besides, I promised Dr. Bill that he would meet you that evening."

Great.

"Okay, but could you keep tomorrow afternoon open for just us? I could meet you for church, take you to lunch afterward?"

"Unfortunately, I have longstanding plans with my lady's kinship group Sunday." She sounded as disappointed as he felt. "Will you be able to make dinner with me and Dr. Bill Monday, say, seven o'clock?"

Hawke sighed to himself. "Sure. I'll be there."

Along with the mysterious Dr. Bill who is, apparently, quite anxious to size me up.

CHAPTER 23

THEY HAVE MY SON *stitched up tighter than a Thanksgiving turkey, locked inside the hospital's so-called "secure ward,"* he fumed. *Can't get anywhere near him.*

Yet.

Marek decided to ditch his present job and find something closer to his son. He easily snagged a night job at the hospital. Apparently they had trouble keeping reliable help for laborious, mindless tasks such as sweeping and mopping floors, hauling out the trash, and rolling bins of soiled linens and such down to the laundry.

First thing he did was to cozy up to the young man he worked with. The kid had been at the hospital for a couple of years, was a trove of information, and loved to hear himself talk. Didn't mind answering questions, either, if it meant he could show off his "insider" info . . . like where to sneak a smoke during work hours, how to snitch food from the kitchen, what parts of the hospital's security could be gotten around versus what couldn't, and when the guards took breaks and changed shifts.

Things were progressing nicely when, the third morning after his shift ended, he went out to the parking lot to drive back to his room. Instead, he found Trixie's car being hooked up to a tow truck while two police officers stood by, their eyes surveilling the lot.

Just like that, his ride was gone. And since the bus didn't run late at night when he had to report for work, he had no way to get from his room to his job! He cursed under his breath and went back inside to think through his next steps.

Gotta abandon my digs, find another place to stay. Something really close. And warm.

Suddenly, Marek had an audacious idea. He took the freight elevator down to the hospital's basement and explored the area where the facility's steam power plant resided.

It's nice and warm down here, hospital has restrooms on every floor, and I can get coffee and food from the cafeteria. Easy enough to steal blankets and a pillow from the laundry room. Just gotta tuck myself into some hidden corner to sleep during the day and show up for my shift on time each night.

He was searching out a place to sleep when an unwelcome thought intruded. *If the police know Trixie's car was stolen, they likely know it was stolen by her killer. And since it was parked in the hospital parking lot, how long will it be before that snoopy detective and his partner come sniffing around?*

Can't have that.

He worried his thumbnail against his teeth. *What I need are some distractions. Bloody little come-hither "somethings" to pull Detective Hawke and Partner Pig's attention elsewhere and keep it there . . . while I work out the best way to get at my son.*

HAWKE CLOCKED OUT at 5:00. He drove home, showered, dressed, fed Ontario, and was at Grace's door by 6:56 p.m. *Right on the nose.* When she answered the bell, he was struck anew by her loveliness . . . and by his visceral response.

Her usually smooth and upswept hair hung down in waves upon her shoulders. Each lustrous curl glowed against the candle-lit room behind her, and her green-gold eyes gleamed. Oh, how he wanted her, wanted to bury himself in her sweetness and warmth! And wanted everyone else in the world to stay far away from them.

Selfish, he thought. *That's what I am. I want her all to myself.*

"Hello, Richard."

"*Grace.*" Without thought he took a strand of her hair and rubbed its silkiness between his fingers.

"You're beautiful, you know," he whispered.

She breathed deeply and smiled.

They were wrapped up in the moment.

Together.

Until a voice inside queried, "Are you going to leave the man out in the cold, Gracie?"

"Oh! No, indeed. Please come in, Richard." Closing the door behind him, she made introductions.

"Richard, this is William Upton, my guardian, dear friend, and business partner; Dr. Bill, this is Detective Sergeant Richard Hawke."

So this is Grace's Dr. Bill. And if Hawke read Grace right, this meeting was nothing short of crucial to her.

All right then. I'll do my best.

"A pleasure to meet you, sir," Hawke said, extending his hand.

They exchanged the handshake, each appraising the other. The older man was tall and still handsome for his age, although thin and slightly stooped. Dr. Upton frowned just slightly as he returned Hawke's greeting, no doubt studying the handiwork of the same tire iron that killed Steve.

"Glad you could join us, Detective Hawke." He stole a second look at Hawke's face before averting his eyes.

Hawke was accustomed to first reactions to his appearance, to the scar that couldn't be missed. He didn't miss Dr. Bill's implied note of possessiveness either. Glad you could join *us?* He opted for safer ground immediately.

"Thank you. And Hawke is fine, or Rick."

"Rick then, although Grace calls you Richard?"

Shrugging, Hawke responded, "She's the only one."

"Oh. Yes, I see." More than one meaning conveyed.

Good grief.

He was relieved when Grace called them to the table. Over dinner they relaxed although Hawke found it hard to escape the notion that his words, manners, and character were being closely inspected, his worth evaluated.

For her part, Grace steered the conversation masterfully, turned it onto broad avenues in order to keep dinner conversation pleasant and light. Both she and Dr. Upton were surprised and pleased to find Hawke a history buff, partial to World War II. Dr. Upton warmed to the topic.

"I served in the Pacific myself, a Navy physician on destroyer duty, later on Guam, and after that, the Philippines," he related. "Not much specialization was needed other than an iron stomach and limitless energy. I saw more death than I ever care to again, let me tell you. Did you serve?"

"Yes, sir. Four years in the Corps, two of them in 'Nam. My brother and I joined together. He stayed on, career Marine, but as soon as I rotated out, I entered the police academy."

"Any further education, Rick?"

"I took night classes and earned a BA in criminal justice."

"I see. What school was that?"

"Just a state college extension program." *Nothing fancy*, he growled to himself.

"And now you're a detective sergeant in—what did you tell me, Gracie? Homicide?" Bill pursed his lips. "Tell me, Rick: Isn't police work, particularly homicide, something of a morbid profession?"

Hawke considered the question before answering. "Perhaps no more so than being a doctor. People die. While you and Grace work to prevent death and improve lives, I investigate suspicious and unwarranted deaths, and sometimes, God willing, my partner and I provide answers and justice for the families of the deceased and for our community."

Bill said nothing in response, but he studied Hawke.

Nothing quite like being the bug under a magnifying glass.

While serving dessert, Grace put in, "As a matter of fact it was through my *Morning Line* interview that Richard and I met. He was investigating the death of the church organist."

"Oh? Has anything come of that?"

"Her death will be ruled an accident . . . eventually. At present, my team and I are focused on two recent murders. You may have read about them."

"Stabbings, weren't they?"

"Yes."

"Will you solve those cases, do you think?"

"We have positively identified our suspect and hope to apprehend him shortly." Hawke shrugged. "I can't comment further."

"Of course. Official business and all."

Hawke nodded. Grace then insisted on cleaning up—leaving the two men alone in the living room.

And here it comes.

For the next quarter of an hour, Dr. Upton probed Hawke's family, age, career expectations, and personal life. Through it, Hawke remained studiously open and deferential. Upton may have thought himself subtle—and an untrained ear may have believed he was merely making conversation—but Hawke, a master at dislodging vital details, subtly or otherwise, allowed himself to be quizzed. He stood the man's interrogation with unruffled nonchalance.

The one topic Bill never broached was Hawke's faith.

Interesting. If I were a father figure checking out the man courting my daughter, his relationship with Christ would be the first concern on my list.

It was a relief when Grace finally joined them.

She offered coffee; afterward, she seated herself at the opposite end of the sofa . . . well away from Hawke. He sighed inwardly. Obviously, spending any actual quality time with Grace tonight was out of the question.

Then Bill changed the subject. "So, Gracie, how was the convention this year? Willard seemed to think it worthwhile. Any recent breakthroughs and new technologies to consider?"

"I sat in on some especially good lectures. For his part, Willard met an audiologist he thinks we should consider bringing on. However, after giving it some thought, I'm not in favor of expanding that side of the clinic at this time. We don't have the only audiologists in the city, but we *are* the only ENT group that offers family therapy for the hearing impaired. It's my opinion that we should grow that leg of our practice. It is what makes our clinic unique and will grow our patient list."

Willard. Hawke wasn't sure what "bringing on" another audiologist entailed, but since Willard suggested it, Hawke wasn't in favor of it either.

"Willard's usually pretty forward thinking, but I agree with you, Grace. Anyway, enough about business. He said the two of you had dinner with the Gundersons. How are they?"

"They're fine."

"It was nice of them to invite the two of you to their home."

Grace wasn't looking at Hawke. "I suppose."

"Willard also said they've invited you up over Christmas to ski. Will you be going?"

"I really haven't thought about it, Bill. More coffee, Richard?"

"No. I've had enough, thanks."

Grace flushed uncomfortably, and Hawke chastised himself.

You were doing so well. Had to blow it during the last inning, didn't you?

At 9:30, Hawke excused himself. It hadn't been much of an enjoyable evening, plus the fatigue of the last couple weeks seemed to be weighing on him. He thanked Grace, conveying a longing in his look that she couldn't possibly mistake. Perhaps one moment at the door?

"I'll see Detective Hawke out," Dr. Bill stated. When Grace meekly acquiesced, Hawke turned from her in disgust.

"You're all right, Rick. I'm glad to have met you." Bill said at the door. Offering his hand he added, "Hope to see you again."

Hawke returned his handshake. Resisted the impulse to add, "I'll bet," and retreated to his car. He hadn't felt so patronized since his rookie days.

As his car churned through slush toward his apartment, Hawke reviewed the evening. Apparently, in Grace's eyes, he'd vaulted some invisible hurdle this evening and been received by Grace's father figure—albeit with grudging courtesy. But what had been a sweet, budding relationship with Grace last week, now felt unexpectedly loaded with complication.

And how did that Willard guy fit in—other than high up in Bill Upton's estimation, especially compared to "You're all right, Rick. I'm glad to have met you," and "Hope to see you again."

Just not any time soon, right?

Sinking into a black humor, Hawke found himself speculating, wondering how serious his relationship with Grace actually was. And whether it was going anywhere at all.

Sinking deeper, he thought, *If I'm being honest, I'm clearly too messed up for her. Grace deserves more. Definitely deserves a whole, unbroken man.*

CHAPTER 24

TUESDAY, NOVEMBER 14

HAWKE PASSED A lousy night. He tossed, turned, and got up multiple times for one reason or another, but whatever position he lay in, his thoughts refused to shut down and let him rest. Near 4:00 a.m., Hawke gave up the fight. Ontario, who usually slept on the far corner of his bed, warbled a protest when the blinding overhead bedroom lights came on.

Ten minutes later Hawke was out the door, headed for the gym. After a punishing workout, he showered, dressed, and headed for a diner where the coffee was hot, bottomless, and stout enough to grow hair on a man's back. He guzzled five cups trying to get himself moving, ate a breakfast that sank like lead in his stomach, and waited to leave for work until long after the waitress had cleared his dishes, hoping beyond hope his heart might find the peace of mind he sought and craved.

Finally, right there in his back corner booth, he folded his hands together and prayed. "Lord, I'm struggling here. I thought . . . I really thought . . ."

What had he thought?

That Grace Warner was the woman he'd dreamed of meeting all his life? That she embodied everything he could want in a best friend, a life partner, a godly wife? That just because they were both believers, it somehow meant God had brought them together for a purpose?

Or was it more probable that he wasn't the right man for a woman like her? That he could never—by any stretch of the imagination—be the right man for a woman like her?

"Okay, I get it," he whispered. "I'm not prime marriage material; I'm not even a run-of-the mill candidate as a husband. I'm damaged goods, whereas this *Willard* dude is a rising star in Grace's field and is likely her clinic's next partner—not to mention, cultured, good looking, runs in the right circles, *and skis.*

"Me, I'm a working stiff. I will never live up to Dr. Bill's expectations and have no desire to strap two boards to my feet and head down a snow-crusted mountain, dodging trees at fifty miles an hour. I can think of better ways to die, thank you very much."

He bowed his head on his hands. "I get it. I'm not good enough for Grace." Sighing, he added, "I can give her up if you tell me to, Lord. I can. For you. Just . . . please help me let her go."

He sat up. Unclenched his hands. Nodded to himself. "Yeah. Okay. It'll be okay . . . because it will be right for *her*."

But when Hawke left the diner, that unsettled feeling was still with him, so he drove. He had no destination in mind, just aimless wandering up and down city streets while he attempted to find that elusive place of peace, "I need to have myself together before I arrive at work."

What he found was that his car wanted to cruise by Grace's apartment.

"Nope," he muttered, turning his car toward work. "Not going to torture myself."

THE CLOCK ON Homicide Division's wall read 9:30 when he strode off the elevator. His team of three jumped to their feet *en masse*.

He hadn't stepped into the aisle leading to his cubicle before they swarmed him, talking at once.

"Where have you been?" Dov demanded, worry creasing his forehead. "You've never been late to work before. Never. Not once!"

Browning interrupted with, "Man, Hawke! Thought certain we'd have to roll out Hostage Rescue or SWAT the way Mayer's been wringing his hands. Maybe get a call from the state bulls, saying they'd found you in a snowbank."

Percival added, "Hey, Hawke? I think I have a lead. A good one."

Hawke stared at the man. "What'd you say?"

"I think he said we have a lead," Browning supplied.

"*I* have a lead, Browning. *You* did diddlysquat."

Browning shifted from foot to foot. "Yeah, whatever."

Hawke scowled. "My desk. Now. Quit blocking the aisle!"

To Dov he shot, "And what is up with you? You'd think I'd vanished off the face of the earth the way you're acting."

"Nearly four years. You've never *once* been late in nearly four years! Thought you'd wrecked your car or something."

"Well, mark it on your calendar. Stick a gold star on it: I was late—God forbid it happens again."

He shoved past Percival to reach his desk. Sat. Folded his arms. "Okay. I'm here. Not lying on a frozen, blood-soaked road. So spill it."

Percival practically vibrated with excitement. "Sure, sure. Remember you asked us to check with dispatch and review every 911 call and officer response for the past several weeks?" Percival pointed to the two pins on

Hawke's map marking the Claremont and Vincent Delano's shop. "You said any 911 calls and officer responses that fall inside this neighborhood."

"And?"

"And I did." He sniffed at Browning. "*I* did. So get this: On Friday night, October 20, officers responded to a 911 call at the home of Gary and Eloise Armistead, 20265 Glenwood Avenue." He pointed to the map. "That's right about here. Old, upscale neighborhood, a mile from the Claremont."

Hawke stood and squinted at the map.

"The Armisteads hosted a catered party for friends that evening. Party went off without a hitch, but the caterer, one Wanda Farley, who left by the back door close to midnight, thought someone tried to attack her on her way to her car. Her ride was parked in the alley behind the Armistead's house to save space out front for the guests."

"What did the responding officers find?"

"Not a blessed thing. Ms. Farley said she swung her purse at the attacker and connected with him. She also screamed her lungs out, and the guy—she was convinced it was a man—must have run away. By the time Mr. Armistead and his driver got to her, there was nothing to see. They called the police anyway, because Ms. Farley insisted."

"I'm still waiting for the lead, Percy."

Percival grinned; Hawke had never called him by his nickname. "We called the Armisteads and asked for a list of guests and a list of all the services they hired for the party that evening. In addition to the caterers, they hired a florist, a bartender, and two security guards. Wanna guess what security firm they used?"

Hawke sat down hard. "Same as the Claremont?"

"Give the man a cigar!" Percival chortled.

"You've called them? Gotten the names of the two guards?"

"Yup. Galen Truett and Stan Wallace."

Dov shook his head. "You've been sitting on this all morning?"

Percival ducked his head. "Just waiting for the boss to get in."

Hawke snorted. "Well, the boss is 'in,' and I want these men picked up ASAP. Mayer, call the security firm back and find out if they're working and if so, where. Browning and Percival, I want background checks on both men. Each of you take one."

Percival dashed toward his cubicle. "You got it, Hawke."

"Ditto," Browning threw over his shoulder.

DOV GOT ON his phone. "This is Detective Mayer, City Homicide Division. Did you speak to Detective Percival earlier this morning regarding two of your employees, Galen Truett and Stan Wallace?"

"Yeah, that was me."

"Good. We need to know where they are at present, sir. Urgent police matter."

"Sure; happy to help. Galen is one of our regular employees. He's actually on the clock right now."

"I need that address."

"Okay, but he doesn't get off until two o'clock, and we don't like our guards distracted while working."

"You misunderstand me. We are heading to his job site to pick him up. *Now*. Make arrangements to relieve him."

"I suppose I could do that—"

"It wasn't a request."

"Uh, understood." The man rattled off the address.

"And the second guard, Stan Wallace?"

"Stan is more of a part-time employee, and he's not working today. Here's the address we have on file. It's a boarding house, one of those daily, weekly, or monthly residences." He read it off and Dov copied it down.

"You have a phone number for that place?"

"We do, but it's for a common phone in the boarding house hallway."

"Actually, that works for me." Dov wrote down the boarding house phone number, thanked the man, hung up, and dialed. It rang and rang. He hung up and called it again.

On the sixth ring, a woman picked up. "Make it quick. I'm up to my elbows in bread dough."

"Detective Mayer, City Homicide Division. I'm looking for Stan Wallace. I understand he rents from you?"

"Not no more. Moved out, coupla weeks ago. Wasn't here all that long. Maybe two weeks?"

"No forwarding address?"

The woman laughed in his ear. "Like we ask for that!"

Dov hung up and jogged to Hawke's cubicle. "Galen Truett is on the job, but Stan Wallace is in the wind."

"That stands to reason," said Percival, right behind him, loud with excitement. "I tried to pull background on Wallace, but the social security number his work gave us belongs to some guy who died decades ago."

Browning, puffing and out of breath behind him, added, "But Truett checks out. He's squeaky clean."

Hawke's mouth curved into a not-so-nice smile. "Well, isn't that all kinds of interesting. Say, Percy? What was Aneta Gretzky's maiden name again?"

"Walas. Aneta Walas—wait! *Walas* is the name on the old social security number I pulled. *Stanislav Walas*. Now I get you, Hawke: Marek Gretzky stole Stanislav Walas's identity and changed his name to Stan Wallace!"

Hawke's less-nice-by-the-moment smile widened. "I'll bet you five bucks, Percy, that if you dig into Aneta Walas' family tree, you'll find this same Stanislav Walas was either Aneta's father or her paternal grandfather."

He stood up to address his team, but across the division floor, the other homicide detectives paused what they were doing to listen in. "Gentlemen, Mayer and I have met our killer, face to face—Marek Gretzky, aka Stan Wallace. Get copies of Stan Wallace's photo ID from the security company, write up Marek Gretzky's physical description and alias, and update our BOLO. Flag it 'Urgent' and 'Armed and Presumed Dangerous.'"

"On it!" Percival shouted, halfway to his desk, as Dov and Browning rushed to theirs.

The approving, unified gaze of the entire floor was fixed on Hawke. Even McCormick, arms folded across his chest, stood in his doorway watching. He caught Hawke's eye and nodded his approbation.

Hawke sat down, acknowledging to himself that the hardest part of this case was still ahead. For the second time this day, he folded his hands and bowed his head. "Lord, we need to find this madman and catch him before he kills again. Please help us."

CHAPTER 25

HE WAS DEEP in sleep he desperately needed when the persistent ringing of his phone finally roused him. He groaned when he saw the time: 2:59 a.m.

"Rick? Dov."

"This had better be good."

"Dispatch called, and we've got another body. Definitely our case. An attendant at Sparkle Laundry, a 24-hour laundromat, Saunders and Alvera. Vic is a woman about 45; same M.O. as Vincent Delano and Trixie Lawson. And Rick, get this? We have a witness who saw a man wearing a green coat."

"Be there in twenty."

He used his car's siren to clear a path through the few cars on the road, pushing the speed limit all the way. When he arrived, he found four squad cars, the ME's van, a news crew, and a large group of spectators obscuring the laundromat. He rolled his ride up onto the sidewalk and elbowed his way to the cordon where the officers let him through.

He entered the laundromat, and Dov waved him over to the body still sprawled by an open dryer, but out of sight of the front entrance. She lay on her back, arms at her side, a plethora of stab wounds pockmarking her chest. It was the blood deliberately spattered across her face that marked the case as theirs.

"You said you have a witness?"

"Over there."

An aged wino sat alone on a bench, corralled by a uniformed beat cop. The rheumy black eyes in his grizzled face darted fearfully back and forth as Hawke approached and towered over him.

"Looks like you got yourself involved in a bad scene, old timer." Hawke caught a whiff of the guy and backed off a step.

"Ain't done nuthin' wrong. No way, no sir!" He twisted his fingers together and refused to meet Hawke's eyes.

"But you saw the man who stabbed that woman, didn't you?"

The old guy shook his head vehemently.

Hawke withdrew a stick of gum from his pocket. "I only ask because, if you *did* see him . . ." He took his time unwrapping the gum and putting it in his mouth. Time enough for his words to sink in, "Why, if you saw *him*, he likely saw you, too."

Horror dawned on the old man's face. He shot his eyes toward the dead woman being loaded in the ME's van, then jerked his head around to Hawke.

"I jus' come here at night, b'fore nine o'clock, an' Dottie? She lets me get my bones warm if I don't pester her none." He was starting to shake.

"Dottie?"

"Yeah, that's her is dead. I sweeps th' floors an' dumps th' trash an' most nights she give me a cup of coffee. I allus come 'round jest b'fore nine o'clock when she lock th' front door. See, after nine, she only let customers in if'n she knows 'em or if'n they looks righteous t' her. But, las' night, I sees this man come outta here before I git here. Got him a real nice green coat—you know, with all them pockets and buttons and snaps and such?"

He licked his lips. "I'm awful thirsty."

"Later. What else did you see?"

"Well, after he comes out an' when I push on th' door, it's locked, an' that ain't right. Dottie don't lock up b'fore I git there, no way. Well, I knocks, but she don't come, so I goes to th' back door, too. She still don't answer, so I goes on my way."

"But you came back?"

"Too cold t'night, don'tcha know. 'Bout t' freeze t' death, so I comes back and knock again, but still no Dottie. Then I knows certain somethin's real wrong, so I peeks through th' winders all 'cross th' front and . . ." he swallowed hard, "an' at th' last winder, that's when I sees th' curly top of her head on th' floor, peekin' out from th' row of dryers . . . and lotsa blood."

"Did you call the police right away or did you wait? And where did you find a phone?"

"Called th' police straight off. Gots a pay phone on th' corner. Din't have a quarter, but th' zero gets me th' operator, y'know, and she puts me on with th' police. I tol' them eve'thing I tol' you, and I says, 'I'll bet you that man in th' green coat done for her!'"

"What made you think he killed her? He could have been just any other customer."

"Well, he weren't carryin' no laundry when he come out, were he? Nope. No, sir."

Hawke smiled and nodded. "What did this man look like, besides the coat? Age, hair color, height?"

"Not a young feller, fo' shore. Fifty maybe? But I don't see his face an' hair good 'counta he got th' hood on his coat up."

"Would you recognize him if you saw him again?"

He shrugged. "Dunno."

"And what is your name?"

The man shook his head resolutely.

"No name, huh? Well, look, if we need to talk to you again, where do you live?"

"Live?" The old guy laughed without mirth. "Out there." He waved his hand at the street.

"I see."

Hawke addressed himself to the uniformed cop standing by.

"Deliver this guy to Homicide Division for us? I don't want him out on the street even if we have to book him for vagrancy." He fished a ten from his wallet. "And get him and yourself something warm and filling to eat, while you're at it?"

Leaving the old man with the cop, Hawke and Dov walked toward their respective cars, both obscured by the press of onlookers. At the police cordon, Sharon Richmond and a news team confronted them.

Hawke sighed. He was not in the mood. His body was still short on sleep, his temper shorter still.

Microphone in hand, a camera fixed on her and rolling, Sharon went coolly into her spiel, while blocking his path. "Sharon Richmond, *Morning Line News*, on the scene of another bloody knife slaying. Behind me is Detective Sergeant Richard Hawke, the officer in charge of the ongoing investigations into the brutal murders of Vincent Delano and Trixie Lawson."

She pivoted on her heel. "Detective Hawke, when can the citizens of this city expect this blood bath to end? Do you foresee the imminent arrest of this murderer?" Her tough tone was calculated to provoke a newsworthy response from him.

Instead he chuckled, and asked a question of his own. "Miss Richmond, doesn't your show go on the air a couple hours from now?" He cocked his head. "What's that? Goodness. I think I hear makeup calling for you—and you wouldn't want to be late for makeup, would you?"

Her cheeks went white under his mocking grin, all neatly recorded by her cameraman. Before she could frame a retort, Hawke yanked Dov though the crowd, leaving her stiff and wordless before the camera lens.

"Insufferable woman. Listen, have Percival take the old guy's statement and try to pry a name out of him? Then run a sixpack by him. See if he can I.D. Marek Gretzky."

SHARON RICHMOND'S ICY stare followed Hawke as his car backed off the sidewalk and into the street. She was determined to make the city's serial killer her path to a coveted evening news anchor position on her network.

Not a lot could stop Sharon once she'd set her cap on an objective; she'd figure out an angle to recoup today's loss too.

But for the moment, with Hawke's glib parting shot searing her pride, her ambition took a side step to include a personal resolve: *I will discredit Richard Hawke in the process.*

Oh, yes. I will destroy him.

BRADLEY DENNISON, *Morning Line's* local news announcer, found himself benched when Sharon Richmond yanked him unceremoniously from the Monday morning news slot. Sharon's version of the city news, however, took a turn away from the norm. Instead of covering all the top local stories, she announced the city's third knifing murder and provided what amounted to an editorial.

Dennison grimaced, even as he admitted Sharon certainly knew how to capture an audience's attention: "By pandering to the basest of their natures," he muttered.

"WE'RE LIVE IN FIVE, four, three . . ." The rest of the count was silent.

When the count reached zero, Sharon spoke into the camera. "This morning, while most of the city is focused on impending snow storms, stalled public transportation, whether or not the sanitation workers will strike, and not to mention," here she smiled with winning savvy, "who will play in the year-end bowl games," she took a deep breath and sobered her expression, "another victim of this city's serial killer lies in the city morgue. Details of the death of one Dottie Pyzell, the city's *third* knifing victim, can be gleaned from your local newspapers."

The camera zeroed in, and she spoke as though unburdening herself to her closest friends and confidants.

"I will, however, tell you that *Morning Line*, your very own local news source, was on the scene immediately following the discovery of Ms. Pyzell's body in what is now *a series of three* bloody and bizarre knifings. In charge of the investigations is one Detective Sergeant Richard Hawke, whose reputation for tough police work is legend."

Homicide's BOLO came up in a window beside Sharon's sober face, and included both the prison photo of Marek Gretzky and the image of a Sears winter coat, hunter green, size 44. The camera zoomed in first on the prison photo.

"The bulletin issued by Detective Hawke's team tells us that the suspect-at-large is this man, one Marek Gretzky, fifty-four years of age, recently released from prison."

The window then zoomed in on the coat. "Gretzky is said to be wearing a green coat identical to this one. The bulletin also lists the suspect as being both armed and dangerous."

She turned slightly to her right, and the camera followed her. "Given the seriousness of the situation, I confess that *Morning Line* has questions. You see, at the crime scene in the earliest hours of this morning, and while attempting to gather a statement from Detective Hawke, our news team was puzzled by the detective's lack of candor and what can only be termed an inappropriate display of levity.

"I asked Detective Hawke when city citizens could expect some answers, the very question on every city resident's lips. As you can see, however, his response consisted of a light and frivolous comeback."

A cleverly edited version of Sharon's confrontation with Hawke, *without audio*, played as she spoke. Her taunting verbal challenge was lost on her audience. As she intended, they saw only her sober expression while, over the video, they listened to her commentary. In contrast to Richmond's professionalism, Hawke's silent but joking manner came across loud and clear.

"In view of the urgency of the situation, this journalist wonders how much of Detective Hawke's fabled ability is being exerted to put an end to the danger this killer presents."

Shaking her head gently with faux disappointment, Sharon went in for the clincher. "Frankly, Detective Hawke's humor with regard to these killings makes one question if his attitude is a reflection of the city's police force as a whole. One must wonder whether we can expect a timely resolution to this string of vicious murders . . . or if our police force even possesses the requisite concern for the city's citizenry.

"Frankly, if the very detective charged with leading the apprehension of this monstrous killer does not take the safety of our citizens seriously, I would caution all city residents to exercise their own abundance of caution. Obviously, no one else will."

The rest of the show was anti-climactic as far as Sharon was concerned. Flushed with success, she brushed off Bradley's complaints. Already stung into anger he followed and cornered her in her office.

"Quite the slam against our city's finest, Sharon, throwing the mayor under the bus at the same time—not to mention you turning the format of this program into a tabloid." Dennison's bronzed forehead darkened as he spat his words. "On the bright side, I'm certain our viewers enjoyed waking up to your repugnant sensationalism. I mean, who doesn't like a side of blood and salacious gossip with their corn flakes? No doubt our ratings will reflect your 'tasteful' commentary."

"Why, thank you, Bradley. Yes, I'm certain our ratings will rise as a consequence of my creative approach." She held the door. "Now get out."

He sniped over his shoulder, "Because the managers always appreciate *unsolicited* innovation."

The studio managers had been supportive of her in the past. After all, her personality had saved *Morning Line* three years ago from its long, boring ratings decline. She was confident management would applaud her newest modification.

She breathed a little threat at Bradley's back. "Perhaps I'll 'innovate' *your* position, Bradley, *dear*. Permanently."

HE CURSED LONG and loud. *Since that police bulletin came out, I see my face staring back at me wherever I turn. My face and a picture of my coat straight out of the Sears catalog!*

Good thing he didn't need the coat during work hours. He hung it in the hospital locker assigned to him. But if he needed to leave the hospital during the day?

I need to do something about it. Now.

At the end of his shift, he filched a can of black spray paint from one of the hospital's facility supply cabinets, and stuffed it down the back of his pants to keep it warm. Into the brittle morning cold he went, with the coat stuffed under his arm, to a nearby park. He picked a secluded space between the trees, opened wide the coat and spread it across the boughs of an ever-green, outside up. Shivering and working as quickly as he could, before the paint can got too cold, he gave his coat a light spray from a couple feet away.

The result was a sort of camouflage look. As soon as the paint on the fabric dried enough not to smear, Marek pulled it back on. He walked through the park for an hour to rid the coat of the distinctive odor of spray paint.

The result wouldn't last nor would the coat escape a discriminating eye, but he hoped it would keep him from getting pinched until he swapped it out. Too bad. He'd grown fond of Vincent Delano's hunter-green winter coat.

I'll pick up a new one from my next "distraction" and ditch the old, he told himself, *or maybe leave the old coat with my victim's body to thumb my nose at you, Hawke.* He snickered. *Man, that Sharon Richmond sure loves ragging on you, Detective.*

At the thought of the journalist, his snicker became a scowl. *Sharon Richmond. That woman calls herself a 'journalist' and has the nerve to taunt me? Hmm. And should I let her insults go unanswered?*

Oh, I think not.

"OUR HOMELESS GUY picked Marek Gretzky's photo out of a six pack of men in the same age group. We also got his signed statement," Browning reported.

"Do we have his name yet?"

"Nope. Refuses to give it. No prints in the system, either."

"Okay. Have a uniform run him back to the laundromat. Oh . . . and give him this before you kick him loose." Hawke handed Browning a heavy-duty leaf bag.

"What's in the bag?"

"Just a few things I figure he could use."

He'd dug out a sleeping bag, some warm socks, a lined sweatshirt the old guy would probably swim in, and added a few toiletries and foodstuffs to the bag.

"Huh."

"Doesn't hurt to be kind."

Browning eyed him speculatively, but took the bag without further comment.

On his office wall Hawke had tacked up the same blown-up photo of Marek Gretzky used in the BOLO. He'd taken to staring at it periodically, memorizing his features.

"I'm going to know you better than you know yourself before this is all over, Marek, and I do mean over," he promised the picture. Hawke imagined he detected a coldly vacant look in Marek's eyes, even though he was smiling easily.

"Don't think I won't find you," Hawke whispered. "I promise you I will . . . and you can take that to the bank."

GRACE WAS STILL smoldering over Bill's uncharacteristic and asinine behavior. She had intended to introduce Richard and Dr. Bill to each other over a congenial dinner, but Monday evening hadn't gone as she'd hoped, not in any sense of the word. Richard had left distant and . . . hurt? And never in her wildest imaginings had she believed Dr. Bill capable of being a snob.

Yes, a *snob*.

He had astonished her! All that nonsense implying she and Willard were an acknowledged couple just because they had dinner together with the Gundersons and were invited up to ski after Christmas.

Bill had left her apartment without comment and, over the past two days, had avoided allusions to the dinner party. Grace, for her part, had ignored him altogether.

It was evident to Linda, and probably others at the clinic, that her relationship with Bill was strained. As for Willard Drake? Grace had, without reason, snubbed him cold, two days in a row.

I wonder: Does he feel guilty for treating Richard like he came from the other side of the tracks?

Or does he feel guilty for treating me like an incompetent juvenile? He's probably scouring his conscience, wondering what he's done to offend me.

But all Grace could think about was Richard. She hoped they could discuss the uncomfortable evening. Talk it over. Sort it out. Certainly, he was mature enough in his faith to forgive Bill's incivility.

Wasn't he?

I need to apologize for Bill's interrogation and assure Richard that I had no part in it. He will understand. He won't hold it against me.

Or would he?

Richard hadn't called Tuesday as usual, nor had he yet called this evening.

She told herself he was distracted by two more murders and the mounting pressure at work, and tried to assure herself nothing had changed between them—rationalizations that did nothing to alleviate her increasing concern.

A hundred times she resolved to phone him herself—something she'd been taught was "forward" and unacceptable in a woman.

"Good heavens; it's 1989. Just call him!"

The truth was, she couldn't bring herself to face his open rejection, if that's what his silence implied. But what if another day passed without him calling? Would it . . . could it mean he'd lost interest in her?

Lost interest?

How could a man, a *godly* man 'lose interest' when he had shared some of the deepest aspects of his faith with her, had worshipped beside her, had prayed with her?

Or I've been a naive fool. Friends tried to warn me. Said I could easily be another in a long line of women Richard Hawke has toyed with.

Grace felt an unfamiliar stab of pain behind her ribs. It left her breathless, her heart throbbing.

She was surprised when that dear, soft Voice whispered a question. *Which friends warned you, Grace? Your Christian friends, or the gossips from your school days?*

"Not my Christian friends, Lord, but . . ."

Then are you being fair to Richard to believe their slander? He was honest with you about his past . . . before he came to me.

Slowly she hearkened to the Lord's mild rebuke, and turned toward him to settle her heart.

MAREK TOOK THE bus and got off in the area he'd selected, several miles from the hospital and nowhere near his last "distraction." He would choose his next victim based solely on his needs: male, large in size, moderately prosperous, no wedding ring on his hand, and wearing a thick winter parka—any color but green. Furthermore, the man needed to be alone and *on foot.*

He found his victim at a corner drugstore when he overheard the man talking on the pay phone near the lunch counter.

"Hello. I'd like to make a dinner reservation, 6:00 p.m. Table for one."

Ah! Perhaps the perfect mark. Let's find out, shall we?

Marek shadowed the man to his detached brownstone walkup. Once he had the man's address, he wandered into a nearby Christmas village and browsed through the various village shops and vendors, sampling cookies, caramel corn, and cider. He returned to the man's brownstone and was waiting for him when he exited his home. He followed the man to the restaurant where he'd made dinner reservations.

Marek, to pass the time, ate his dinner at a cheap café down the road. He returned to the restaurant afterward and followed his mark home to his apartment as twilight was settling into night.

Marek moved quietly and put a modest distance between himself and the mark until the man started up the steps to his door. He quickened to a run and closed the distance between them as the man, sensing danger, fumbled for his keys. He hit the man from behind just after the key turned in the lock, shoving them both through the open doorway. A swift kick to the man's head made certain he was out. Marek closed and locked the door and checked the apartment for other dwellers.

Satisfied they were alone in the brownstone, Marek stripped the man of his coat and valuables. He was certain the man had money squirrelled away in his home, and he'd been right. A little slice here, a little slice there, and—*ta-da!*—the man was magically eager to give up his stash. Marek then took his time, extracting every ounce of pleasure possible from his prisoner's tearful pleas and cries of pain.

When playtime was over, Marek staged the body *just so* and went about his other business. He counted the cash the man had confessed to hiding in his pantry and folded it into his hip pocket. Grabbed a grocery sack and filled it with food too. Finally, he selected his new coat—not the more formal grey overcoat the man had worn to dinner, but the navy blue parka he'd worn earlier that day. He left the black-splotched green coat hanging on the hall tree for Detective Hawke and Partner Pig to find and caught the last bus of the evening back to the hospital.

CHAPTER 26

FRIDAY, NOVEMBER 17

SHARON RICHMOND'S coverage of the third murder rocketed city-wide concern to a breathless fever pitch. It was no wonder then, when Chief McCormick held a press conference Friday, noon, to announce a *fourth victim*, one Thomas Buttry, the media about lost its collective mind.

Feeding off of Richmond's fearmongering, every paper and magazine in the city posted banner headlines and "citizen warnings" across their front pages while television and radio newscasters provided hourly "updates" that amounted to nothing more than repeated details and baseless speculation.

The coverage had several immediate effects. Neighborhoods in and around the expanded "kill zone" saw an increase in the sale of mace, whistles, and dead bolts. Gun shops saw an uptick in handgun and ammo sales.

Harder to deal with were the neighborhood watch groups determined to patrol and protect the public. Hawke had seen it before when a particularly violent crime such as rape rose in volume. Many of the public, understandably, looked with favor on the vigilante-like patrols. Officers on the streets, however, walked a thin, difficult line when it came to bands of well-meaning citizens roaming the streets by night. The uniformed officers didn't know of which to be more leery: criminals or the public safety watchdogs.

Of course, *Morning Line's* anchor, Sharon Richmond—who seemed to have swallowed the bulk of the program—ran the most explicit and up-to-the-moment coverage of the fourth victim's death, with an emphasis on "explicit." She seemed bent on being the acknowledged authority with regard to the murders. Somehow, she managed to dredge up and proclaim every crime scene detail along with the specifics of Homicide's investigation into Marek Gretzky and his activities.

It was exactly the sort of coverage to inspire a sensible criminal to leave town or hole up, change his routine, and shift his methods . . . completely undoing the investigative progress.

"Thanks a lot, Richmond," Hawke muttered.

"The lady has a source," Dov observed, "and we just might have a leak."

Hawke turned inward. *Do we? Is someone in the department leaking information to Sharon Richmond?*

For good measure, Sharon could be counted on to insert the occasional jab aimed at Hawke. Hawke figured his name was becoming as well-known as Marek Gretzky's and he didn't know whether to laugh or fume. He did know it had been a mistake to antagonize Sharon Richmond. In response, she was doing her best to make his life an ongoing torment.

Homicide's tip line, staffed by all available on-duty and willing off-duty homicide detectives, was inundated with calls. Hawke and his team, with so many of the calls originating with eccentrics or "loons," were hard-pressed to distinguish the nonsense from actual tips. Those answering the calls logged everything from "I confess! I killed those people. I also killed John F. Kennedy in my previous life" to the eleven individuals who claimed to be Marek Gretzky himself.

Regardless of how ludicrous or unlikely a tip might seem, every report or confession had to be screened and uniformed officers dispatched to pick up possible suspects and bring them to Homicide Division for questioning.

A few of the crazies saved the police the trip and turned up on their own.

"I never dreamed so many people were obsessed with knives," Dov muttered. "Would you look at this?" He kicked a box on the floor next to his desk filled with a variety of knives in all shapes and sizes.

"Where'd that come from?"

"Some lady brought it in. Apparently, her boy's been collecting them for years. Keeps the box under his bed."

"Did we pick him up?"

"No need; he carried the box in for her. I tell you, Rick, people are nuts. And those who really aren't nuts? I get the feeling some of them want you to *think* they are—which totally messes with my head. Take, for example, the guy with the box of knives?" Dov gestured over his shoulder. "That's him, leaning against the wall."

Hawke gaped. "You mean the guy with purple hair and purple velvet bellbottoms?"

"Yup. Oh yeah; I forgot. He goes by the name—get this—*Purple Haze*."

"No way."

"Look; here's our most up-to-date printout of the calls that have come in and here's a list of suspects currently lined up for questioning. This is yet a further list of those suspects yet to be picked up, *and*," he handed the stack to Hawke with a flourish, "you'll find my Christmas wish list. On top."

"Been a good boy?" Hawke started perusing the transcripts of calls received.

"Yessir. I'd like my Mercedes in red, please, sir."

"Only have blue ones in stock."

"Shoot. Ain't that my luck?" Dov pushed himself away from his desk with a sigh. "Gotta go. A hot prospect is waiting in Interview 1 for me to extract his confession."

Hawke nodded and wandered back to his cubicle to sift through the reports in his hand.

RICHARD DID NOT call Wednesday evening nor did he call Thursday. By Friday morning, Grace had placed her relationship with Richard firmly in the Lord's hands and walked away from her prayer time in peace. She also went to work that morning and spoke candidly to Bill about his behavior at her dinner.

She was sharp and pointed. Bill only nodded.

I wasn't emotional; I didn't overreact. Everything I said, needed to be said, she told herself.

Determined to move on with her life, she plunged deeper into her work. She studied her calendar and made plans to ensure she'd be too busy and too preoccupied to dwell on what might have been.

Her support group already took up Tuesday evenings, and she decided to join a Friday evening single women's Bible study, starting the week after Thanksgiving.

The Tuesday support group is growing. Getting a little crowded. I'll ask about adding another meeting on Thursdays, she thought.

That left Monday and Wednesday evenings to fill.

Last year, she'd given a series of lectures titled *The Traumatic Effects of Acquired Hearing Impairment: Patient and Family*. City View Hospital was a teaching hospital whose medical school was on the opposite side of the hospital from the Physician's Annex. A mid-sized lecture hall within the hospital's medical school afforded her a location to present the lectures, and was easy for her to access. The medical school, more or less a mirror building to the Physician's Annex, also connected to the hospital by a similar sky bridge.

The prominent location and two dozen locally televised PSAs had garnered her an audience of interning physicians, other interested medical staff, and the public at large. She enjoyed presenting the lectures. She incorporated her own experience of losing her hearing in her adolescence and relished the lively discussions that followed.

The lectures had been well received, and the hospital's medical school had been after her to repeat the series. She called, accepted the invitation, and added the recurring item to her Wednesday evening schedule. The series would begin the week following Thanksgiving.

Generally, she finished up a lecture or a session with her family therapy group around 8:30. The drive home took another 30 minutes and rounded out her day.

Since it was Friday evening and the next single women's Bible study was a week away, Grace stayed late at work. She attacked the endless mountain of paperwork on her desk. By seven o'clock, she'd made a sizable dent in it.

On her way home, she stopped and ate dinner at a cozy "mom and pop" diner near her apartment where they didn't mind her dawdling over her meal. Alone. Just killing time.

I need to fill my Monday evenings too. Perhaps I'll ask a different girlfriend from Bible study to meet me for dinner each Monday, she thought.

When she arrived home, she showered and went straight to bed.

She thought she was more than ready to nod off—*should* have been tired enough to sleep. She just couldn't stop wondering why Richard had stopped calling.

CHAPTER 27

MONDAY, NOVEMBER 20

HAWKE HAD CONCENTRATED the bulk of his time and energy over the weekend sustaining the search for Marek Gretzky. He and his team pulled double shifts, and he worked every available detective until their eyes glazed over from lack of sleep. Everything he did centered on one and only one goal: Find Gretzky.

But it just wasn't "happening" to quote McCormick.

The long hours made it easier not to think about Grace, easier not to call her to explain his actions. But the long nights made it impossible for him not to ache for her.

Now, first crack out of the box Monday morning, the chief wanted an update.

"Bottom line, our BOLO hasn't generated any helpful responses, the tip line hasn't yielded any actionable intel, and we haven't turned up Marek Gretzky's workplace or where he's living. That's not to say something won't pop any day now. Our people are motivated and working as hard as they can, Sir."

Chief McCormick had grown solemn and preoccupied as the case wore on. New lines engraved around his eyes bespoke his worry.

"How long do you think I can justify the expenditure for all these off-duty personnel for the tip line, Hawke? My budget is already in hot water, there's still another month to go in this year, and money is nearly gone. I have requested emergency funding, but who knows whether we'll get approval or not?"

Chief McCormick's questions didn't ring with his usual cynicism, Hawke realized. The man was being bluntly honest. Hawke didn't answer right away.

"Have you seen this?" McCormick pushed a folded paper to Hawke. The headlines weren't relevant to the case. But when McCormick flipped the paper over, the headline below the fold blared,

City Residents Wonder: Who's Next?

"The press is increasingly hostile to us, don't you think, Hawke?" it was a statement requiring a response.

"It would seem they're taking their cue from *Morning Line*."

"I thought so, too." McCormick looked at him coldly. "Now I want to know why Sharon Richmond is carrying on a personal vendetta against you."

Hawke shrugged. "I may have ticked her off last week; nothing that I would consider offensive enough to blast me directly or indirectly. It's my opinion that she may have, uh, received a personality transplant from Cruella de Vil?"

"And you're Andrew Carnegie in a tux? What you consider inoffensive has been known to cause brain bleeds. I declare, Hawke, sometimes I believe you're more trouble than you're worth. If I didn't know we'll get crucified if we don't get this guy pretty soon I'd be forced to pull you off this case. As it is, you're our best option." He clenched his teeth and dismissed him with, "You're responsible, Hawke. *Make it happen*."

Like I didn't know that, Chief.

"SHARON," MAY INQUIRED brightly, "Did you enjoy your flowers?"

Intent on previewing some video footage, Sharon didn't respond at first. When she did, she asked with only half her attention, "What flowers?"

"A florist delivery guy was here yesterday after you'd left for the day. Roses, I think he said. I sent him over to your apartment."

"I never got them."

"Oh dear. I hope the gentleman who sent them isn't upset that they didn't arrive?"

While she found it hard to believe her demanding employer had a hot relationship going on, May Miller was kindhearted enough to wish Sharon had more to her life than just *Morning Line*.

"Frankly," Sharon replied, dismissing the interruption, "I've no idea who would have ordered them."

Nor do I care, her tone implied.

May let the subject drop.

A KNOCK SOUNDED on her office door before it opened and Dr. Bill stuck his head inside. "Grace, may I come in?"

"Oh. Hi, Bill." She forced a pleasant tone.

Even after she'd gotten her hurt feelings off her chest, things weren't right between the two of them, and they both knew it. Would they ever be again?

Bill closed her office door. "May I sit down?"

"You don't have to ask, Bill." Grace avoided eye contact.

"Would you sit with me? Please? I have something to say, to tell you."

Grace admitted to herself, *We need to get this resolved.* As she made her way to the sofa and sat beside him, she was faintly shocked to discover that her heart toward Bill was cold and hard. And yet she thought she'd dealt with Bill's hurtful behavior!

They faced each other, and Bill said, "Thanksgiving is this Thursday, Grace. I know we usually spend it together, but . . . this year I'm going to take a little break from our tradition."

Grace watched him suspiciously; Thanksgiving was the last thing on her mind.

"I'm getting up there, you know; seventy-two last March."

He smiled fondly at her but she sat in stony, frozen silence. "Haven't been to any of my old stomping grounds in many a year, so I've decided to take advantage of the holiday weekend and take a little trip."

"What? Where?"

He smiled at her again. "Jesse and I are going to Hawaii to see the Pearl Harbor Memorial. We leave tomorrow."

"Jesse? Our *patient*, Jesse?" She frowned. "Isn't this trip rather sudden?"

Bill nodded. "His daughter is a travel agent. One of her first-class bookings canceled at the last minute, so Jess and I are getting quite the deal on our tickets."

"Fine." Her response was rigid.

"Don't you want to know why I decided to go, Gracie?"

She fiddled with her watchband. "I can only assume it's what you prefer."

"Do you think I want to be away from the only person in this world I love and call my family?"

Grace's eyes misted over. She averted them and kept silent.

"You know, Grace, when God, fate, or whatever you choose to call it, handed me a daughter to finish raising, I was flummoxed. Astounded. At a total loss! And yet I was more thankful for the privilege of raising you than any other blessing I'd ever received. I'd been given a family, and with it, a new lease on life.

"I'm not saying I haven't made my share of mistakes over the years, but I tried to do a good job, to be everything your dad would have been for you. He was a good, kind man, and this I know: He would be proud, very proud of the woman you've become and proud of what you've achieved."

"You . . . you achieved it with me, Bill. I could never have done it alone." Grace dropped her head in shame, letting the tears fall.

"Now, now, honey, I'm not trying to toot my own horn. What I'm trying to say is that you're not a young girl anymore. You don't need a father figure hanging over your shoulder, deciding what is best for you. You know your own mind . . . and heart. And I know that I blew it. I meddled in your affairs like the father of a 16 year old, not the father of a grown woman . . . you know when."

He softly touched her shoulder. "Your Detective Hawke showed incredible restraint that evening. He should have spit in my eye, and I would have deserved it. Instead, he exhibited only deference. For that, he has my respect."

"He's not my Detective Hawke." Grace choked on the words.

He gently tugged her chin up and peered at her with concern. "It's been a week! You haven't seen him since?"

"No."

"He hasn't called?"

She shook her head abjectly. "Oh Bill, I'm so inept with men, I mean the ones I actually like. No, Richard hasn't called, and I don't think he will. I think he's done with me."

Bill pondered her words for a long moment. "Then will you let this old fool interfere once more? It's the last time, I promise. Jess and I will have a wonderful holiday touring Hawaii. You," he squeezed Grace's hand, "you should invite Detective Hawke—Richard—to be your guest for Thanksgiving dinner, just the two of you. He said his folks live upstate. You could make this dinner very special."

"And if he declines my invitation?"

He studied her. "Well, I didn't take the man for a fool, but I could be wrong."

GRACE KNELT BY her bed late that night and prayed. "Lord, I don't know what you would have me do. I am grateful for you restoring my relationship with Dr. Bill, but despite what he suggested, I'm not . . . comfortable asking Richard to a one-on-one Thanksgiving dinner. It doesn't seem proper for me to act in a manner that suggests I am pursuing him."

She sighed. "But I will do whatever you ask of me. Please, would you speak to me while I am sleeping?"

CHAPTER 28

"YOU HAVE A VISITOR, Hawke." The officer winked then withdrew his head from Hawke's cubicle and spoke to the visitor. "Here you are, miss."

Hawke shuffled through the clutter on his desk trying to put to rights the stacks of reports he'd been going through. When he looked up, Grace, a slight smile on her lips, stood in the aisle just outside his cubicle.

He must have held his breath, because when he let it out his heart was loud in his ears.

"Hello, Richard."

"Hey, Grace. I, uh, can I help you?" A bit unsteady, he got up to clear off the chair beside his desk.

He could smell the faint, warm scent of her perfume as she sat. He turned his desk chair so that they were facing each other. Had to restrain himself from taking her hand. They were silent for a long, uncomfortable minute.

"You look tired," she stated.

"I've been swamped with this case. Kind of goes with the territory."

She nodded and looked him full in the face. "I understand. The clinic is busier than ever. Even my surgery time is up."

The half-hearted laugh that burbled from her throat told him she was nervous.

"Anyway, Dr. Bill happened to mention yesterday that he's going on vacation, leaving tomorrow, and I," she cleared her throat, "remembered you don't have family in town, so I was wondering if you'd care to . . . have Thanksgiving dinner with me? I'll be cooking."

Hawke felt his resolve slipping precariously; if he ever stepped foot in her apartment again, he'd never want to leave. And immediately, his mind posted the list of all the ways he wasn't the right man for her. Rather bluntly he blurted out, "Sorry. I've already accepted an invitation."

"Yes, of course. I mean, Thanksgiving being just two days away, everyone already has plans. Well, then." She stood briskly to her feet. "They say it never hurts to ask. Perhaps some other time."

She looked right through him as she spoke, and he knew without a doubt there would never be "some other time." This was it.

Their finale.

He cursed himself inwardly. "I appreciate the invitation, Grace, but—"

His lame response was cut short as his partner stopped in the aisle and peered into Hawke's cubicle.

DOV AFFECTED A suitably apologetic expression. "Sorry; didn't realize you had a visitor."

Sure, I didn't. The two of you were drowning, so I ran over here to toss you a lifeline.

He grinned at Grace. "Hey, Dr. Warner. Nice to see you."

She stared at her hands. He glanced from her to Hawke. "What's up?"

Neither of them answered, and his partner gave him a look that would have frosted Florida in July.

Guess you'd rather drown.

Dov began backing up. "I'll just come back later. Again, nice to see you, Dr. Warner."

"Actually, I was just leaving, Detective Mayer. Would you care to walk me out?"

He glanced toward Hawke who remained stonily silent.

"Sure."

What else could he say? He guided her out through the maze of desks and cubicles to the elevator and pressed the down button. While they waited for the car to arrive, Dov mentioned casually, "Have any plans for Thanksgiving, Doctor?"

"None whatsoever." Her words were clipped; she looked away to blink back tears.

"That's great! My wife Lisa and I would love to have you. How does 2:00 p.m. work for you?"

"I didn't mean—I wasn't fishing for an invite!"

"No you weren't. I asked *you*, remember?"

"You're very kind. Detective, but I don't feel that—"

"Hey, it's Dov, remember? And look, frankly? I have to insist. Fact is, Lisa threatened my life if I didn't invite a guest this year to help eat my mother's dinner. See, Mom lives alone now, and she looks forward all year to fixing a fabulous Thanksgiving dinner. But there's only the three of us to eat it, right? Lisa and I gain five pounds each just sitting down to the table. And all day long she smiles and says, 'Eat! Eat!' at about the same rate she demands, 'When are you going to give me grandchildren?' Know what I mean?"

Grace smiled in spite of herself.

"So, actually, you're doing me a huge favor, 'cause otherwise my life will come to an end Thursday the moment Mom leaves—and you'd be to blame, right? So, two o'clock, okay?"

The elevator arrived, and he stood over the threshold, preventing the doors from closing. He pulled a business card from his shirt pocket and jotted on it.

"Here you go. Directions to our place. I suggest you leave fifteen minutes earlier than you'd think, because everybody gets lost when I give directions." He grinned triumphantly and handed her the scribbled card. "See you Thursday."

Laughing, Grace accepted the card and saw the writing did indeed need deciphering.

"All right, and please tell your wife—Lisa is it?—that I'm looking forward to meeting her."

"You bet. See you then."

Dov stepped away from the elevator and waved as the doors closed. He chortled under his breath all the way back to his desk.

Lisa is gonna be tickled pink.

Thanksgiving dinner was either going to be a huge success, or come Monday he was going to be looking for a new partner . . . because Hawke was supposed to show up to dinner at 2:20, with dinner actually scheduled for 2:30.

Well, somebody had to do something, I mean, seeing as how Rick is totally off his rocker.

Yeah, Lisa would definitely approve.

CHAPTER 29

THURSDAY, NOVEMBER 23, THANKSGIVING

LISA MAYER PLACED the chrysanthemum arrangement on the table and stood back to evaluate its effect. Her table was laid in brownstone crockery over a daffodil yellow linen cloth on which the golds, russets and oranges of the mums bloomed as though they had grown there. From the kitchen she heard the clank of yet another pot as Dov's mother constructed the meal.

Dov's mother, Ruth, was a truly excellent cook, Lisa admitted, something she would never be. But then again, Ruth wouldn't know one end of the advertising game from the other, and she, Lisa, was going far in that business. In particular, this last promotion and its eleven percent pay increase was going to give her and her husband the ability to buy a house, a home in a decent neighborhood where their kids could grow up fairly removed from crime and pollution.

Ruth would appreciate the "kids" part. Lisa reached inside a desk drawer in the dining room and pulled out some realtor brochures. She'd even considered asking Dov if they could move Ruth closer to where they bought so they could be there for her in the years ahead when she needed them. In turn, Ruth would likely want to babysit when Lisa went back to work. Knowing Ruth, she'd have a fit if Lisa tried to hire a nanny or use a daycare. Family and home were everything in Ruth's world, whereas Lisa hadn't had either until she'd met Dov.

Two weeks late, but I won't say a word to anyone until I'm sure, she promised herself again. But she'd made an appointment with her doctor and another to start looking for a house. *The* house. A real home.

"Lisa, dear, come and taste. Does the dressing need more sage or onion? I need another opinion."

No you don't, Lisa thought fondly. *You have never under-seasoned anything in your life, certainly not in the nine years I've been married to your son. In your heart, cooking is communal and love. And for you? I would sample the moon.*

She tasted the dressing, made thoughtful, considering faces, and agreed with Ruth's "I think a bit more thyme, don't you? A pinch more sage?"

"How's the table, dear?" Ruth asked after she'd made the adjustments.

"Come see." She took her mother-in-law's plump arm and led her to the dining room.

"Ah, beautiful! You have a way with color that makes a joy, right here." She touched her breast. "When do your friends arrive, Lisa, dear?"

Ruth never called her anything other than "Lisa, dear," and Lisa would love her mother-in-law forever.

"Dr. Warner is due at 2:00 p.m. Rick will be here around 2:20, just before we sit down to eat."

"A doctor—and a woman at that! Wonderful! But is it not strange that they come at different times?" Ruth looked puzzled.

"Maybe Dov told one of them wrong." Which he had. Intentionally.

Lisa bent and fussed with a napkin to hide her face. *This had better work, or sparks will fly—and not the kind of sparks Dov and I are hoping to kindle*, she thought as she reconsidered the little scam she and Dov were running to bring Rick and his friend back together.

Dov believed Rick and Grace were made for each other. Then again, Dov's concern over his partner's state of mind fluctuated.

"He went through a terrible time after his former partner died," Dov had told her. "His 'faith,' as he calls it, has made a difference—I can't deny that—but he's alone too much and drives himself too hard. He needs to find a woman who will love him back into wholeness."

Like you loved me, Lisa thought, understanding completely.

Ruth's thoughts had gone elsewhere. "Someday," she murmured dreamily, "someday there will be little faces around this table."

Perhaps sooner than you think.

"Yes, someday, Mama—from your lips to God's ears."

Ruth smiled fondly at her daughter-in-law, who had, quite literally, taken the words from Ruth's own mouth.

Then she said timidly. "Lisa, I tell you a thing no one knows. Not even Leshem."

Lisa winced at Dov's first name, the one he detested, but she listened politely.

"Leshem was not the only son I bore."

Amazed, Lisa stopped fussing with the napkins and stared.

"See, no one still alive knows except me. And now you."

"What happened, Mama?"

"Your Leshem was my first baby; he was fine and healthy! But later on, the doctor found out I didn't have what they called the Rh thing in my blood, and the doctor said my next baby could have problems. Oy! What problems, I thought? I was pregnant again when Leshem was eighteen months old. We were so happy to have babies . . ."

She sighed. "But the little boy was born too soon. He was tiny and all blue. They said . . . they said my body rejected him."

Lisa put her arm around Ruth, sensing a pain much deeper than the loss.

"Your body may have rejected him, Mama, but that is not the same as *you* rejecting him. You cannot force your body to do what it cannot do, can you? But I know this: That baby boy would have been as greatly loved as you love Dov."

"Yes, he was loved and so wanted. But we didn't try for more babies after that. The doctor said it would probably happen again, but we couldn't allow another child to suffer like that. Such a shame for us to not have more children, Samuel and I, but we bore it. At least we had a son! And we told each other we would have grandchildren someday to comfort us."

"You will, Ruth. I promise." Lisa wiped away a tear and hugged her mother-in-law.

"*Tush*, darling girl," Ruth said. "The children will come—in God's time."

She sighed dramatically. "I only hope it is before I am too old."

Lisa choked down a laugh—Ruth was all of fifty-four.

Dov, fresh from a shower, walked in on them.

"This is cozy." He glanced out their window to the street below. "Hey, there's Dr. Warner's car. Listen, Mama, please don't say anything about Rick coming to dinner. Please. It's, ah, like a surprise."

"A surprise? Well!" She was delighted.

The bell rang, and Lisa hurried to answer it. A lot of snow was falling already, and the forecast was for several inches by nightfall. The woman standing on the porch was lovely, with snow glittering like stars in her dark, upswept hair. Lisa smiled as she brought her in.

"Dr. Warner, I'm Lisa Mayer. We are *so* glad you've come to spend Thanksgiving with us. May I take your coat?"

"Dr. Warner!" Dov shook her hand and impulsively gave her a hug. "This is my sweetheart, Lisa, and my mama, Ruth Mayer."

"A doctor, my goodness," Ruth beamed. "And so pretty!"

Blushing, Grace replied, "Please just call me Grace, all of you. Thank you for welcoming me into your home. It's very nice to be here."

"Grace is a lovely name! A perfect name for you. Come by the fire, dear, and melt the snow. Soon we'll all sit down together to a fine meal, just as soon as—"

"Oh, yes, Mama's a wonderful cook, Grace," Lisa interrupted, "and her strudel is to die for. We're having it for dessert."

"Of course, how forgetful of me," Ruth put her hand over her mouth.

Grace was confused. "Beg your pardon?"

"Coffee, Grace?" Dov turned to his mother. "Mama, would you mind getting Grace a cup?" To Grace he asked, "What do you think of Lisa's table?"

"Absolutely stunning. With these colors you can forget it's trying hard to be winter outside."

Having arrived on safe conversational ground, twenty minutes passed quickly until the doorbell rang again.

Lisa shot Dov a hopeful glance and let Hawke in. This time Mama came to the rescue.

"Detective Hawke! I'm so glad you come to dinner today! Come in, come in. We have a surprise for you."

Grace Warner, her face flaming, stood up when she heard Hawke's name, and Dov refused to meet her accusing look. Oblivious, Ruth led Hawke over to Grace. Lisa let her breath out slowly as Hawke had the presence of mind to be pleasantly amused rather than rude. He greeted everyone in turn before saying hello to Grace.

"Hello, Grace. Good to see you."

"Richard."

Externally they behaved naturally, sat together and drank coffee until dinner. And a superb meal it was: roast turkey, dressing on the side, assorted pickled vegetables, braided breads, cranberry sauce, creamed peas and potatoes, and Waldorf salad. But the conversation would have died a painful, strained death had not Dov turned it to their case.

"Grace, how is Terry getting along?"

She lit up. "You would not believe the changes in him. He's blooming like a flower in the sun. All the secure ward nurses and orderlies have been wonderful, as have the clinic staff working with him. He's becoming much more adept at sign language, and is learning how pleasant it is to have friends around him."

She laughed. "For example, I've asked our clinic staff and the secure ward's staff to play games with Terry whenever they can spare a few minutes. Games are entertaining, but they are also a means of normalizing person-to-person socialization. Turns out, Terry's mother played card and board games with Terry, and he has sorely missed doing so. Now he's genuinely pleased to see staff members when they arrive carrying a new game."

Rick cleared his throat. "Will he see the neurologist any time soon?"

"Yes. We finally have an appointment for Terry to see one of the best in the state next month."

"And the wounds on his arm?"

"Almost healed." She hesitated, then added, "At this point, I can speak to Terry about most anything. For example, he told me about his mother's fears that someday someone might find them, and he's related some of the strange behaviors his mother expected of him in order to keep the two of them hidden. She apparently never said who this 'someone' was; Terry came to think of the 'someone' as a sort of boogeyman, not knowing that 'someone' was his father.

"Now, because we've told him his father is alive, Terry's only reticence is whenever we allude to the man. We know as a child Terry suffered terribly at his father's hands; it may take years before he can talk about that abuse."

Ruth, eyes wide, asked no questions, so Dov provided her with the barest of contexts. "Mama, the young man Dr. Warner speaks of is deaf. He was raised in strange circumstances, and Dr. Warner is working with him. He was very afraid when we found him. I'm glad he's doing so well."

"As am I," Rick murmured.

Lisa stood. "Shall I clear the table now? No, Mama. You cooked; let me clear the table, all right?"

Grace stood. "And I will help."

"Well, then! I shall serve dessert," Ruth responded.

THE WOMEN'S DEPARTURE to the kitchen left Dov to spend an uncomfortable quarter hour alone with Hawke while the three women cleaned up.

"Interesting, the way you set this up," Hawke remarked, stretching out his legs from the easy chair he occupied. His eyes were heavily ringed with fatigue, but he was more like himself today.

"Glad you think so, Rick. Having a nice time?"

"I generally like to plan my own nice times, but sure. It's all right. So when did you and Grace work this out?"

"Uh, Grace had no part in it, Rick. She didn't know you'd be here anymore than you knew she would be. When I heard she didn't have an invitation for Thanksgiving, well, I naturally assumed inviting her was the right thing to do. I mean, Lisa would've thought it pretty poor of me not to, you know."

Hawke cut in with semisweet sarcasm. "Don't put this on Lisa, Dov, although we both know she's every bit as sneaky as you are."

"No hard feelings?"

"Nah." Then his grin took on a nasty quirk. "Just know that I'll be sure to return the favor, Dov. You can count on it."

"Great," he muttered.

"What?"

"Nothing. Not a thing."

GRACE FELT LIKE every bite of food was lying dormant in her stomach, just waiting for an opportunity to come back up. Although outwardly pleasant, Richard had been as chagrined as she was throughout dinner. Nevertheless, she knew he was angry.

Well she was angry, too. She'd played along, made nice, and would thank the Mayers for a wonderful meal, but she'd already decided, when it was over, she and Richard were going to talk.

And I am going to have my say.

Around five o'clock, Grace expressed her thanks and made her good-byes. Ruth fetched her coat.

"Such a lovely couple you make, dear," she beamed, completely unaware of the undercurrents.

"Thank you," was all Grace could manage. She drove to a restaurant, drank more coffee for an hour, used the phone book from the restaurant's pay phone, and found her way to the address under Richard's name. It was a graying apartment building; his was on the second floor facing the river.

She knocked.

HAWKE HADN'T BEEN expecting Grace or anyone else; he was wearing gym shorts, and a towel hung around his neck. And the second he opened the door, Ontario attempted to run out between his legs. He barely caught the cat in time to prevent his escape.

"Grace!" He followed her eyes to his perspiring chest. "Trying to work off some of Ruth's strudel. Sit-ups."

"This will only take a few minutes. I have something to say to you."

She swept by him and into the living room without waiting to be invited. The room was sterile and mildly cluttered; his revolver hung in its shoulder harness from the back of a chair.

"Uh, would you like to sit down?" Hawke didn't know why he felt embarrassed. It had been disconcerting to see her again today, of course, but he'd made a good decision a week or so back.

And I always stick by my decisions.

He'd been friendly all afternoon, too. Well, not friendly, more like casual. Polite?

But now, catching sight of the set of her chin, he realized he knew her well enough not to relish what was coming.

I should have had that talk with her instead of just disappearing from her life.

"Richard." She didn't sound unreasonable. "I'm not going to cry 'foul' about us. I'm not a child; I can handle my feelings. But I did come here to set the record straight: I had no idea you were going to be at the Mayers' today. If I'd known, I would never have accepted Dov's invitation. You've made it clear by default that we won't be seeing each other anymore, and I don't pursue men who aren't interested in me—I don't need to.

"That said, and for whatever your reasons, you insulted me and insulted my intelligence by not having the courage and decency to end it, end *us*. All you had to say was, 'Grace, I'm not interested in you anymore.' As a man who professes to be a follower of Christ, what you chose *not* to say was cowardly and cruel. Yes, *cruel*."

Sparks flashed in her eyes. "To top it off, today you treated me like a complete stranger. Well, Richard Hawke, I am no coward. At least I have the moral integrity to tell you to your face that I'm sorry we're not seeing each other anymore. I can also say I'll get over it. All I really want at this point is to know *why*. Why did you break it off?"

"Grace, I apologize."

"You apologize?" Her voice rose, shaking.

"Yes. I did some serious thinking, and you're right: I didn't tell you because I wasn't brave enough to face you. I was afraid I would go back on my decision because . . . because I *wanted* to be with you."

"I'm here now. Tell me your reasons." She lifted the slender point of her chin toward him.

He—stupidly—attempted to lighten up the mood. "Hey, don't lead with your chin, Gracie."

"Don't tell me what to do, and don't you presume to call me Gracie." Her tone was icy.

"Uh, right. Sorry." Feeling more and more like a complete jerk, Hawke launched into his explanation, but even as he spoke, his "reasoned decision" didn't feel or sit right.

"You, Grace, are a magnificent woman. You're smart, educated, and beautiful. But what am I? I'm not highly educated like you; I'm blue collar all the way. I'll never make the kind of money that would give you the life to which you're accustomed.

"Then there's my profession, and both you and Dr. Bill are right: My job is dangerous. This—" he pointed to his scar, "this or something worse will happen again."

Grace waited for him to continue, but Hawke had run out of dumb excuses. Or had he?

"And, uh, I don't . . . ski."

She frowned. "What?"

"I don't *ski*. And stuff like that."

"I hate skiing."

He frowned. "You do?"

"Yes; I dislike being cold, and I hate sliding down a mountain with my heart in my throat. What I need to know is, are you a believer? A follower of Christ?"

He sensed a trap and momentarily hesitated. "You know I am."

"Okay, then did you pray about it? Pray about us?"

"Yes, I did."

"And what was God's answer?"

"His answer? I . . . I prayed. Then I made my decision."

"I see. *You* made *your* decision." A long moment passed, eye to eye, before Grace dropped her gaze. All the anger went out of her, leaving her calm. Or was it deflated?

Broken?

"Thank you, Richard. I understand now." She said it with a trace of sympathy that momentarily irritated Hawke. Ontario rubbed up against her, and she scratched his head absently, adding, "You know, you and Bill are a lot alike."

"What? Not even!"

"Oh, yes; in fact, you are, although, hopefully, Bill has seen the error of his ways since I confronted him. But before this week, you were both apparently just fine with telling me—*this magnificent, smart, educated woman*—how I should feel. Deciding whom I should love. Treating me like a fifteen-year-old orphan, emotionally unable to make my own choices."

Her anger sparked again and she glared at him. "You have a list a reasons we're not meant for each other, but did you ever think to ask *me* if your so-called reasons mattered?"

She stood and moved toward the door. "I loved you, Richard. I was beginning to hope the Lord had a future for us, but now I can see why we aren't suited, why it wouldn't work."

"I—"

"*No*. You once told me, 'I choose to trust God for his best for me,' but that was a lie. The truth is? *I* trust God. *You do not*."

Hawke didn't think it was possible to feel more like a worm than he did when she finished. He rubbed his hand over his face and followed her to the door, scooping up Ontario before he made another break for it.

"Look, Grace, I'm sorry. I—"

"Not as sorry as I am, Detective Hawke."

She swept out his door and did not look back.

CHAPTER 30

SHARON RICHMOND'S solemn eyes stared into the camera. "City police have not released the identity of the serial killer's latest victim pending notification of next of kin. What we know at present is that the victim is a thirty-nine-year-old female whose manner of death is consistent with four previous *and unsolved* murders in less than a month.

"We again caution city residents to take appropriate precautions while we wait, impatiently, for the city's detectives to *do their jobs*, and apprehend this monster, *Marek Gretzky*."

Hawke and Dov stood in front of the division's television not far from Homicide's communal coffee urn. Hawke's eyes narrowed as Richmond ended her rant. *Her name was Jerusha Washington, mother of two*, he thought, *and I'm glad your "source," whomever it is, didn't pass you that info. Her children deserve more respect than your salacious reporting.*

Beside him, Dov held and studied a calendar on which he'd jotted the names of Gretzky's victims on the date of their deaths.

"Gretzky killed his first two victims about a week apart, then nothing for nine days. These last three, though? Only days apart."

Although finding Grace at the Mayer's Thanksgiving dinner had dismayed Hawke and angered him against his partner, he had not been able to hold onto that anger for long. Sunday, his pastor had taught on forgiveness and had emphasized how even little roots of offense could alter and eventually ruin close relationships.

I don't want to ruin my relationship with Dov, Hawke realized. *Lord, I need your help here.*

After church, Hawke had gone home and prayed through to forgiveness. Although he felt relief afterward, the relief exposed what remained in his heart: grief. Not grief concerning Dov, though. No, the regret he felt was from Grace's visit, the pain he'd caused her, and her definitive goodbye.

"I loved you, Richard. I was beginning to hope the Lord had a future for us, but now I can see why we aren't suited, why it wouldn't work . . . I trust God. You do not."

And he couldn't escape the sense that he'd made a terrible, unredeemable mistake.

But Lord, I prayed about my relationship with Grace! I thought . . . I thought I was making the right decision.

But had he made the right choice? Or had he merely sought the Lord's approval of his own conclusion, rather than asking for and waiting on the Lord to speak his will concerning Grace?

"Hawke? Did you hear me? With only days between these last three murders, it's like Gretzky is . . ." Dov paused, considering how to phrase his thought.

"I think the word you're looking for is 'escalating.' Big surprise: Our serial killer is escalating."

"Actually, I was teasing out another idea. That is, until you jumped in."

"Oh? Do tell."

Lord, was it a horrible mistake?

"Haven't worked it out yet. It's right on the tip of my tongue though, you know? Almost but not quite there?"

Short on sleep and uncomfortable with where his conscience was taking him, Hawke's temper flared. "Well, since it's 'right on the tip of your tongue,' let me know when you find it. In the meantime, get back to work."

Miffed, Dov stomped back to his cubicle without responding.

"SHARON, I'D LIKE to see you for a few minutes, if you don't mind." The way Saul Beech, head of City Studios, Station WASY, said it, albeit with a smile, Sharon knew something was up.

"Sure, Saul. Give me a minute? Just need to tidy up a few loose ends."

"That'll be fine."

Aggrieved, Sharon wondered, *Now what?* She threw her assistant some hasty notes to type up, gave her appearance the 'once over,' and marched into Saul's suite of offices. She was surprised that the two deputy station heads were on hand when she walked in, but it confirmed her suspicion that she wasn't there for kudos. She greeted them with faint nods.

"Sit down please, Sharon. Coffee?"

"No, thanks. I'd just as soon get to the point."

"The point, then." Saul swiveled his chair toward her and surveyed her with his heavy-lidded eyes. "For the record, Sharon, Wally, Sid, and I are in agreement when we say you're a fine *Morning Line* anchor, an asset to the show. You handle current issues brilliantly and guest personalities with real finesse. Since you've been *Morning Line's* anchorwoman, the program's ratings have recaptured their former status. We've all been proud of the show."

"Thank you." Sharon's ego received the stroke. *Maybe this isn't going to be bad.*

"Until recently."

Uh-oh.

"You know, I took a little time off last month. I thought I could leave the show and be reasonably certain that it would chug along without throwing a rod through the engine while I was away. Imagine my surprise, when I returned and found that, for whatever reasons, you'd misplaced your professional objectivity and, I might add, your respect for us as the decision-making body of not only this show, but this station." He pursed his thick lips. "I believe you wished to say something, Sid?"

Apparently, Sid had more than a few words ready to go. "Yes, indeed. Sharon, for the past six weeks, you've been steadily eroding the format of our morning show. *Morning Line* is supposed to produce the kind of news, celebrity profiles, and trendy bits that people enjoy waking up to. It makes them glad to draw the drapes, put the coffee on, get ready for, and head off to work.

"You also know we've been open to innovative and fresh ideas, but we've always reviewed them first, then given our approval—if warranted. You must realize that it was never our intention for you to turn *Morning Line* into a daytime version of 60 minutes or 20/20!"

He ended rather hot and Saul interposed himself to cool the situation.

"Thank you, Sid. Your comments are right on the money. Back to you, Sharon. Your anchorwoman status gives you a lot of editorial leeway, more than in most places, I might add." He shifted his bulk to a more comfortable position. "Yet you have also used your 'celebrity' status to make unapproved changes to other employee positions—and some of your co-workers are decidedly unhappy with you."

"Bradley, I suppose?" Sharon kept a sharp rein on her tongue, but inside, she was seething.

"Among others. You can't yank people out of their jobs, jerk them around, and expect them not to complain, Sharon, on top of which you exceeded your authority."

She was silent for a moment and the three men bided their time.

If they wanted me out, she reasoned, *they would have said so already.*

What they were waiting for was the "correct response." Give them that, and she'd be off the hook.

Her crumbling hopes staged one last sortie, and she spoke, knowing she was gambling.

"Would you mind giving me your opinion of my coverage of the city's serial killer, Saul?"

Saul sniffed. "Sure. Here it is: Let the big boys handle the blood and gore, Sharon. That's not what we hired you for."

She stiffened in outrage. "Let the big boys? I'll have you know—"

Saul raised a commanding finger and cut her off. "Don't you *dare* get your back up at me, missy. Let's have a very clear understanding—right here, right now—of your role at this station. I'm your boss; I pay your salary. You will follow format, you will stay within the established lines provided for artistic license, and you will *steer clear* of the serial killer case from this moment forward. Not a word from your mouth about it on my airwaves. Not one."

He frowned. "Just so you know? I have friends, very influential friends at City Hall, who have called to complain about you. They're not happy that you're undercutting the police department and especially the detective in charge of the serial killer investigation.

"And you had better believe that when my friends aren't happy, I'm not happy. According to them, this Hawke fellow is the best detective in the state, *and he's running his butt into the ground to catch this loony-tune!*"

Saul's voice had been steadily rising until it was a roar. "*Nobody wants or needs your uninformed input muddying already murky waters and terrorizing the city by sowing seeds of mistrust!*"

He wagged his finger, and his eyes narrowed. "Do you understand me?"

Sharon nodded, her neck so tight she could barely move it.

Saul sat back. Breathed. "Good. Then let's get *Morning Line* back on track. You have a bright future ahead, Sharon. Don't push it."

She rose and retreated as gracefully as possible. Telling May nothing more than that she was going home for the day, she took her Nissan 300ZX from the parking garage and headed for her preferred shopping center.

A few furious hours and several thousand dollars later, she had calmed enough to return to her apartment. Next to her on the seat were bags holding two expensive outfits, a new coat, and a pair of designer shoes—all from excusive shops. A gold bracelet sparkled on her wrist, a treat she'd denied herself until today.

Some women binge on chocolate or wine, she told herself. *I have better taste than that.*

AN HOUR AFTER the testy end to their last conversation, Dov confronted Hawke as he poured himself another cup of the sludge marinating in the division's coffee urn. "I have it now."

Hawke sighed. "Okay, let's hear it."

"I put myself in Marek's shoes, tried to set myself in his head. Started to wonder *why* the guy was escalating."

Hawke shrugged. "Isn't it usually the killer's need for more of the thrill he gets from killing? When killing the third and fourth time doesn't give him quite the same high as his first and second victims gave him, he begins to kill more often. Frustrated that the kill is no longer doing it for him, he devolves into a frenzy and loses control. Makes mistakes. Falls apart. Hopefully, the killings are running *him* now, not the other way 'round, because that means Gretzky will be making mistakes soon."

"But what if . . . what if . . ."

"For heaven's sake, spit it out, Mayer!"

"Just . . . just follow me." Dov strode to Hawke's cubicle and pointed at the city map on Hawke's wall. "Look. Esther Grunbaum, Vincent Delano, Trixie Lawson, and the attempt on Wanda Farley. Nice, tight oval. Even though Grunbaum's death wasn't murder, we included her in our workup because we believed the location of her death, combined with the two murder locations, would help us identify the neighborhood where Gretzky lived and worked, and *it did*. Checking 911 calls in that circled area led us to Wanda Farley, and that led us to identifying Gretzky's alias."

"Go on."

"But when we add Dottie Pyzell, Thomas Buttry, and Jerusha Washington, they are, literally, all over the map." Dov picked up three blue pushpins and swapped them out for the red pins marking the three cases.

"Tells us Gretzky doesn't live or work where he used to," Hawke sniffed. "We've forced him to move."

"Well, at first glance, it also doesn't tell us where he likely lives and works now. What I mean is, look at these three pins. Each is a couple miles from the other. However," Dov selected a piece of chalk and drew lines on the map to connect the pins, "if you connect the pins, what do you get?"

"A triangle," Hawke muttered, staring at the city map. "A very large triangle."

"Yeah, *intentionally* large. See, Gretzky might think he's pulling us away from his base of operations, deliberately misleading us, but—"

"But by doing so, he's actually putting himself in the center of the triangle?"

"Yes, but like you said, it's a pretty big triangle. We need to figure out where, in approximately the center of this zone, he lives. How do we do that?"

"Put your finger in the center, close as you can estimate, Dov."

As Dov did so, Hawke grabbed up a scribing compass and fitted one end with a stick of chalk. "Okay, move your finger." Hawke adjusted the compass's unit of measurement down to an inch and placed the pointed end of one compass leg where Dov's finger had been, scribed a chalk circle around the pointed leg, then removed the compass.

He and Dov leaned in together to study the circle. Dov's breath hissed as he saw the largest facility within the circle.

"That's City View Hospital, Hawke! Marek knows where Terry is, and he's going after him. We should warn Grace that Marek is making a play for Terry. The secure ward may need reinforcements."

Hawke reached for his phone, dialed her office number, and reached her voicemail. "Grace, I need you to call me ASAP." He hung up and called her receptionist, Linda.

"Upton-Warner Clinic, Linda speaking."

"Linda, Detective Hawke here. I need to speak to Dr. Warner, urgently."

He waited several seconds before she said, "I am sorry, Detective. Dr. Warner is not available to take your calls. Goodbye."

Stunned, Hawke murmured, "She hung up on me."

"Why would she do that?" Dov demanded.

"I . . . we . . . Grace and I may have had a disagreement."

"And now she's not taking your calls? What kind of 'disagreement' would do that?"

Worry thundered in Hawke's chest. "The kind where I sort of broke it off with her . . . a week ago," he muttered.

Dov stared at him, dumbfounded. "You did what?"

"I had . . . reasons."

"You had reasons. Really? You know something, Richard Hawke? You're an idiot."

Hawke didn't disagree. "I can't wait around. Need to see the chief."

"No, you hold up a sec. Did you even pray about it? Pray about her? You and her? Like, you and her *together*?"

Dov's questions galled Hawke, and he raised his voice, "Hey, aren't you the agnostic Jew in our partnership, the scoffing skeptic?" Even louder, he demanded, "Why should *you* care if I pray or don't pray?"

Dov shouted back, "I care because I care about *you*, you pigheaded, mule-brained idiot! And for the record? Grace is one in a thousand—no, one in ten thousand! She is perfect for you, you—"

"Yeah, yeah. I heard you: pigheaded, mule-brained idiot."

Across the division floor, cautious eyes lifted above cubicle walls. Just far enough to watch. A few heads nodded their agreement with Dov. Others shook their heads side to side to register disapproval in Hawke's direction.

"Get back to work, you lazy busybodies!" Hawke bellowed.

Spying eyes disappeared faster than sugar-free cookies at a Weight Watchers meeting.

Hawke calmed. Slowly exhaled. "You're right, Dov. Right about every-thing. But I've ruined my chance with her."

He moved away. "You call Grace—she'll take your call. Tell her that Marek Gretzky may be in or near the hospital, scoping it out, trying to get at Terry. I need to see the chief and arrange extra security for Terry."

HAWKE WAS SO deeply asleep that when he awakened abruptly around 3:00 a.m., he didn't immediately know where he was. *Oh yeah. I'm home. Home in bed.*

He laid there, willing his body back to sleep, but from the moment he awakened, his mind had fastened on the case that now consumed all his time and concentration. When sleep stubbornly refused to return, he hauled himself up and stumbled to the kitchen to make coffee.

Based on the triangulation of the last three murders, Hawke's team agreed: Somehow, Marek Gretzky had sussed out where his son was stashed, and he was intent on getting to him. They also agreed that Gretzky was playing the game well. He was staying ahead of the police by dint of intelligence and wit and evading them at every turn. With Terry as his endpoint.

Hawke desperately needed a break from the case. His body needed rest, yet every time he looked at a calendar it issued a silent rebuke, and the pressure piled up in his head.

How do I stop Marek Gretzky, Lord? How do we catch him? And how do we keep Terry safe from this madman's grasp?

Idly, he doodled on a magazine left on the kitchen table while the coffee brewed. The table was strewn with reading material. Reading was how he spent most of his meals at home. He scribbled on, absently, until he looked down.

Gracie. He'd traced each letter over until the word stood out, bold and dark.

"*Don't you presume to call me Gracie.*"

Ouch.

Acknowledging that it was ill-advised, he allowed his imagination to conjure an image of Grace, her damp, sweet smelling hair curling down on her shoulders, the gold flecks of her eyes sparkling.

Her eyes. Green and warm amber. They glimmer like sun dappled stones bathed in deep creek water.

He shivered, and a great longing gripped him. How he craved her nearness! For many minutes he wrestled in the grasp of his longing, until reason reasserted itself.

He was more than bone weary, his fatigue more than this case, more than the pressure he was under. He usually thrived on challenge. Instead, the career for which he'd worked so long now felt like nothing more than a heavy grind. Likewise, Hawke didn't need a shrink to tell him that waking out of a sound sleep in the middle of the night was one of the classic symptoms of depression.

"I need . . . something more in my life. Lord."

Unbidden, a passage in Matthew came to him, the very words of Jesus:

Do not store up for yourselves treasures on earth,
where moths and vermin destroy,
and where thieves break in and steal.
But store up for yourselves treasures in heaven,
where moths and vermin do not destroy,
and where thieves do not break in and steal.
For where your treasure is, there your heart will be also.

The voice echoing in his heart, whispered, *Where is your heart, Richard Hawke?*

Taken aback, he blinked. *Good question.*

He poured himself a mug of black brew and sat down to truthfully and subjectively analyze his life anew.

Funny, me having to sort through my desires when I've always known what I wanted and have gone right after it.

He rubbed his eyes, hard. *Lord, what I truly want is you and your will for my life—so why am I experiencing the clichéd midlife crisis?*

He might have laughed aloud if he didn't hurt so deeply and feel too much alone. Down at his feet Ontario stretched, extended both front paws and proceeded to 'happy scratch' his leg. Exasperated, Hawke shook him off, and Ontario stalked away, tail in the air.

Who am I fooling? Cats don't cut it.

His ponderings again turned to Grace, and every thought of her was tinged with painful regret. Just what did he feel for her, since she was the only woman on his mind—other than feeling confused and off-balance?

Certainly he'd never had the feelings he had for Grace with another woman; she was unique in all his experience, though she was neither coy nor beguiling. Maybe that was a big part of her attraction: She lacked the guile and brass of more "sophisticated" women.

I love her, he conceded at last. *I esteem her, desire her, and want the comfort of her companionship.*

Were he and Grace, in spite of all his reasonings, suited to each other? Like two pieces cut from one, was she his match? He wondered if he "fit" her in the same way.

What about the list I made? Our vast differences and the dangers of my profession?

He'd explained his reasoning to her but what was her response? She felt sorry for him.

Was his shortsightedness the cause of her pity?

The pain dug deeper. He wasn't merely off-balance anymore; he was listing, shipping water over the side, his hull about to heel over.

Goodbye, Titanic.

Lord, please help me!

He opened his drapes and stared out into the city's night. In another hour he might begin to notice the dark fading towards gray. His lips compressed into a hard line.

Grace was too invested in her relationship with Christ not to expect the same commitment from him. Furthermore, anything less than an offer of marriage from him would be pointless—and not just "marriage" but *holy matrimony*, where vows pledged actually meant "till death do us part," not "till I don't feel the same about you as I used to."

If I'm being honest with myself, I'd be disappointed if she wanted anything less.

Dov and Lisa had a good marriage, even when, on occasion, they fought like cats and dogs. Dov was a good cop, too.

But not as good as you, whispered a snarky voice. He answered back, *But would he be a better detective if he was as miserable as you are?*

He examined the Mayers further. Sure, they had their differences. Dov wanted children right away. Lisa wanted to wait.

"My mother says she wants to be a Jewish grandmother, and I'd like to help her out," Dov once threw at Lisa in front of Hawke.

"Then she should have been a good Jewish mother and had a lot more little Jewish babies!" Lisa had hurled back. "Tell her not to die young and she'll get her wish, but I'd like to get a few things lined up first, like a house in a decent neighborhood with decent schools. Is that all right?"

They always made up afterward. Yup, they had a good relationship.

Hawke suddenly paled. Children?

Grace will want children.

It dawned on him that while he'd been working and clawing his way to a sergeant's rank in Homicide relatively early in his career, the age at which he'd be a Little League dad had been inexorably ticking upward too. His mind, before he gave it permission, calculated that if he married this year and had a child next year, he'd be close to forty-six or forty-seven when the kid first went to bat.

A sense of loss quickened in him. Suddenly anxious, Hawke rubbed at the scar's tight line across his nose.

"I *am* experiencing a midlife crisis!" He spoke aloud, tasting the impact of the words.

Wearily he poured himself another cup of coffee and thought of his folks, his brothers, their wives and children, and all their subtle or not-so-subtle hints. Were they trying to convey the message that time was irreclaimable, that time could deceive and rob you, that you really can't have it all?

With Thanksgiving over, Christmas was looming.

Soon I'll be receiving the predictable invitations calling for "Uncle Rick" to come home for the holidays. They ask, but I don't roll with childbirth, teething, mortgages, and college funds, so I always make up reasons and send my excuses.

"What did I just say?" He ran back the tape of his internal conversation and found the line that had stung him.

I always make up reasons and send my excuses.

"That . . . that's exactly what I did to Grace. I made a list of reasons and excuses." He didn't much like this realization.

Brows bunched together, he experimentally summoned a Christmas "back home" with Grace by his side. It wasn't hard. He envisioned his mother's pleased expression and his brothers' kids clamoring for Aunt Grace and Uncle Rick to "Watch me! Watch me!"

It was a bittersweet scene, a life he wasn't convinced he was brave enough to embark on.

What! I'm afraid?

Yes, you are . . . but should you allow fear to stop you?

Grace had lived most of her life with fears and inhibitions. Had she stayed there? No. She had pushed herself forward anyway. And she was willing to risk it all every single day. Like she said, she was no coward.

Profoundly convicted, Hawke slouched into the living room and lowered himself into a chair in the dark. Truth slapped him upside the head and humbled him.

In all its niceties, disguised as professionalism, duty, and loyalty, *he was afraid.*

No, he was unequivocally terrified.

But the fear of being alone had, at long last, become greater than his fear of falling, then *failing*, at love—and dear God, *Grace knew!*

She was spot on.

And here he sat, wondering and weighing whether he was more afraid of living the rest of his pitiful existence without Grace than he was of what a commitment to her would extract from him.

Pathetic!

Oh yeah, hardened criminals shake in their boots when they face me, Detective Sergeant Richard Hawke. Why, one glance at my iron jaw and they trip all over themselves to implicate their accomplices and cut a deal. Give me the scent and I'm on the trail. Merciless and implacable, I always get my man. Yup. I'm a real tough guy.

Lord God, I am so screwed up. Please help me.

Alone, in the dark, tears trickled down his cheeks, slipped through his fingers, and dropped onto the carpet.

CHAPTER 31

AS SHE DID EACH day that she worked, Sharon Richmond climbed out of bed at 3:45 a.m. and stretched for five minutes. After stretching, she showered and washed her hair.

Her routine after showering was to dry her hair and dress in stylish casual clothes, pick up the garment bag she'd packed the night before containing her on-camera outfit, and take the elevator down to her car in her apartment building's parking garage. During her twenty-minute drive, she would drink an OJ and mentally run over the outline of the day's show. She knew the route to the studio like the back of her hand, and would arrive at the stage entrance no later than 5:30 a.m. Once in her dressing room, her stylist would do her hair and makeup.

Sharon held to the same rigid schedule five days a week, forty-eight weeks a year. To her upwardly scheming mind, anything short of perfection was unacceptable. She permitted absolutely nothing to interfere with her performance and appearance on the job. She even strictly curtailed her social life, so that the occasional late night over the weekend would not throw off the high standards she demanded of herself.

Sharon also tolerated nothing less than excellence in her staff and personal relationships. Her husband discovered early on in their marriage that he would always rank below her career in Sharon's priorities. He'd been gone for two years now. Sharon didn't miss him or their defunct marriage, but she did prize the expensive penthouse apartment he'd left her.

Her view from the balcony atop The Wood Chimes' fifteenth floor was matchless.

FAR BELOW, IN the basement garage of The Wood Chimes, security guard Roland LaRusso made the twenty-first round of his shift. He walked four rounds an hour, starting at 11:00 p.m., took half an hour for lunch at 4:00 a.m., and skipped one round after eating while he logged a few winks.

Marek knew the guard's schedule just like he knew Sharon Richmond's schedule. Between 5:05 and 5:10 each morning, her flashy 1988 Nissan 300ZX would emerge from the underground garage and shoot away in the direction of the studio.

He sniggered softly. *Not this morning.*

It had required only a little ingenuity to uncover Sharon's address. Last week, dressed in a clean hospital orderly's uniform, he'd posed as a florist's delivery boy. Carrying a long white box stuffed with newspaper, he'd arrived at *Morning Line's* television station after Sharon had left for the day.

"The gentleman who ordered these roses said if they didn't get to that Morning Line lady in good shape, he'd complain to my boss." His affectation of nervous worry was quite good—good enough to fool Sharon's assistant, May Miller.

"Here's her address. Deliver the flowers to the guard in the lobby. He'll get them to her." The address was for an elite apartment complex with a fancy name, The Wood Chimes.

Several evenings later, dressed in khakis closely resembling the uniform of The Wood Chimes' security guards, he'd stood vigil outside the parking garage, waiting for a way in. For a high security building, it had been ridiculously easy for Gretzky to conceal himself in the shadows near the garage entrance and slip inside on the heels of a late-arriving resident.

Once inside the garage, he'd reconnoitered the place, learned the guard's schedule, and quietly made his way to an expensive RV parked in the garage along an end wall.

I won't be bothered. No one's crazy enough to take a rig like this out in winter weather.

He'd jimmied the RV's side door and climbed inside. The setup was perfect for him. He kept track of the guard throughout his shift that night, noted Richmond's early departure time, and left through a side door before the morning guard change.

Now he was back, ready to complete his plan. The RV's battery had enough juice in it to warm the pricy tin can, and he found microwavable food in the cupboards. Warm and fed, he set the RV owner's fancy clock radio alarm, turned the volume down low, and went to sleep until soft music woke him early the next morning. Tamping down his excitement, he readied himself.

At 4:45, LaRusso strolled by. *Right on time.*

Marek stepped out behind him, took him down, dragged him behind the RV, and relieved him of his keycard. Marek entered the elevator, inserted the keycard, and pressed the button for the penthouse, the only apartment on the fifteenth floor.

Convenient, that, Marek giggled.

He stepped out onto the penthouse level at precisely 4:52. Plenty of time to intercept Sharon on her way out her apartment door. He carried only a lightweight gym bag: It held everything he needed.

ALEX BELLAMY, the day-shift garage guard, a much younger man than LaRusso, arrived to relieve LaRusso at 8:00 a.m. *Odd.* The night guard wasn't waiting, champing at the bit like he usually was.

"Hey, LaRusso! Yo! Where are you, man?"

Bell made a quick circuit of the garage. Nothing. He checked the guard shack. He found LaRusso's lunch box, but not the guard's flashlight.

He got on the phone. "Hey, Boss? I'm here, on shift, but LaRusso ain't. Nope. Walked the perimeter. No sign of him. What do you want me to do?"

Bell frowned. "What do you mean, 'do my job.' I *am* doing my job. I'm here, aint I? Just wanted you to know I didn't see LaRusso."

He sighed. "Look, I'm no snitch. Just kinda worried 'cuz he left his lunch box. That's not like him. Yeah, yeah. I'm on it."

INCREDULOUS AT HIS luck this morning, Bradley Dennison hastened to assume the anchor slot for *Morning Line*. While he checked his hair, he chortled over Richmond's unexplained tardiness.

Our shining star, Sharon Richmond, always such a nag about punctuality, is late! Oh, man! Am I gonna love watching her eat crow, he gloated.

What was odd was that no one had a clue where she might be, and she wasn't answering her phone. Dennison snickered under his breath. He was probably one of the few at the station who knew about Richmond's reprimand yesterday. It was quite the gratifying tidbit, and he was holding it close, watching for the prime opportunity to let it "slip."

He rechecked the program schedule, briefed the woman filling his regular news slot, and sallied forth to do his level best to unseat Sharon. Permanently.

One good program, he coached himself, *and I could be on my way.*

MAY WAS MORE than a little concerned. For the seventh time she dialed Sharon's apartment. For the seventh time, no one answered. May had seen how enraged her boss was yesterday when she'd left. But to not come into work, to not even call? That was *not* Sharon Richmond's style.

Loyalty warred against May's sense of self-preservation until, contrary to her better judgment, she decided to contact The Wood Chimes' management. She was dialing the complex's office number when a messenger sped by her door, and the image of a florist bearing a white box of roses flashed across her mind.

Sharon said she didn't receive the flowers. She denied knowing who they could have been from, and demonstrated little interest in them.

May sighed. Sharon's personal life was an enigma to her. She vacillated again and chewed her lip. *I suppose it's possible for Sharon to have misplaced her common sense,* she temporized.

Without dialing the last digit, she hung up.

"I HAVE LATE ROUNDS, two patients I will discharge tomorrow, followed by an appointment to see Terry. After that, my family therapy group," Grace told Bill from his office doorway. "Care to have a very late dinner with me?"

"Thank you for the invitation, but I can't this evening. I promised Jess I'd play chess with him right after work. We're ordering in Chinese."

"But you just returned from Hawaii with him Sunday evening!"

"I know, but what can I say? The man needs a lesson in gracious losing. Listen, I won't stay long at Jesse's. Want me to drop you off a fortune cookie on my way home?" His expression was innocent but his eyes twinkled.

She smiled. "I'd love to come home to some hot egg drop soup."

"I'll do better than just soup."

"Thank you, Bill; it will be nice to come home to something yummy. Say hello to Jess for me? And don't stay at his place too late. You know how the roads ice up as soon as it turns dark."

"I used to tell you to be careful and not stay out late, Gracie." The rift was healed enough to offer a small inside joke.

Cocking one eyebrow she responded airily, "Ah, yes. The balance of power has shifted."

"Hmph."

Grace cleaned up her desk, locked up, said goodnight to Linda, and headed for the hospital.

HE WATCHED HER as she crossed the sky bridge into the hospital, observed the refined, confident manner in which she carried herself. Oh, that will change soon enough.

He smiled a knowing, secret smile behind his mask as a simple janitor. Just as he'd learned the night guard's schedule at Sharon Richmond's apartment, he had watched the doctor closely enough to learn her schedule. It varied from day to day, but a few things were as regular as clockwork.

It's Tuesday. She will visit my son inside that blasted secure ward, then attend her "family therapy" group meeting where she dishes out her lying hogwash.

This is your last "family therapy" session, dear doctor. I'll be waiting for you where you least expect me.

Phone books were useful that way.

An hour later, he hotwired a car in the hospital parking lot, drove to her address, pulled into a slot marked "Visitors," and climbed the four ice-slicked steps from the townhouse complex's rear parking lot to her unit's back porch. His movements were confident, telegraphing to anyone watching that he belonged there.

The upper part of the door had a window composed of a grid of multiple small panes. Without so much as a glance down the back side of the connecting units, he lifted his coat-padded elbow and smashed it through the pane closest to the deadbolt. He reached through the now empty frame and turned the lock. Quick and easy.

He closed the door behind him, switched on the light beside the door, and found himself in her kitchen. He located a broom and dustpan and swept up the shards of broken glass with meticulous care. The pieces clinked against each other as he dumped them into the nearly empty waste can. Next, he removed a small sheet of clear plastic from under his coat and taped it into the empty frame, then dropped the curtain over his work.

He wanted nothing to alert her when she came home. No draft or debris. Nothing out of the ordinary.

Don't want to ruin the surprise, do I?

He could hardly wait to see her alarm shift to fear, then abject terror. Next came the bargaining part where he teased and cajoled his victims— giving them options, offering promises in exchange for information . . . or favors. In the end, though, he always brought them to full submission and, ultimately, resignation.

Restrain yourself, old boy. Remember—don't rush it. Just quick, light cuts that sting a bit at first. Hold off on the deeper ones that really hurt and bleed. Much more fun to take your time. But don't forget: You must make her tell you the best way to get into the secure ward. She will only tell you while she still has hope, before she knows you never tell the truth, and before she's too weak to answer.

For an hour he relaxed in her living room, watching her television with the volume all the way down and the lights off so he wouldn't miss her key in the kitchen door.

He cocked his head. *What's that?* He'd heard the crunch of tires on frozen slush and the slam of a car door. Someone had parked out front on the curb. Could she have chosen to park out front rather than climb the icy back steps?

No worries, my lovely.

He switched off the set and crept into the kitchen where he stood just inside the swinging doors. His initial plan had been to hide in her bedroom, but this was better. If she went straight to her bedroom from the front door, he'd have both exits blocked off. All he need do is follow her into the bedroom. And if by chance she came to the kitchen first, well, the gleaming linoleum was white and clean, the perfect, pristine backdrop . . .

The key turned in the lock, the door swung open, and he felt the chill draft that accompanied it. Soft living room lights winked on, followed by steps across the carpeting approaching the kitchen.

With one twist of his wrist, the blade *snicked* open, a barely perceptible sound that made his blood race. He was ready, his mouth open, smiling with anticipation.

The kitchen doors swung inward, and he lunged forward to wrap his arms about her neck. Instead, he encountered a tall older man balancing three white take-out cartons.

Marek jerked back, momentarily disconcerted.

BILL REACTED THE only way he could—by thrusting the food cartons at the intruder. His attacker swung his arm at the cartons, sweeping them aside. They hit the floor and burst on impact, spewing their contents.

Bill retreated through the swinging doors and raced with jerky steps for the front entrance. He had seen the gleam of the knife, had glanced in the intruder's face. In an instant, Bill knew he faced certain death.

Terrible fear for Grace coursed through him. He fumbled the front door open and made it into the cold, onto the porch. He tripped down the steps and strode toward his car, shouting, "Help! Help me!"

Sudden pain washed over his panic—unanticipated and gripping pain that clamped off his cries for help as easily as shutting off a water tap. He marveled at his sudden inability to draw a breath. When a spasm of agony rocketed down his left arm, he understood.

Oh, no! No, not now! He slumped to his knees on the sidewalk, then sprawled face down on the frigid cement.

Gracie!

Darkness slowly smothered him.

SHAKING OFF HIS shock, Marek turned to follow the old man, but he put his foot into what smelled like spilled Chinese takeout. He slid on the linoleum and struck his knee on the corner of the doorway to the living room. By the time he got to his feet to massage his aching knee, the old man was hollering for help.

It's too late to stop him. Too risky, he decided. If anyone heard the old man, they would open their doors and see him.

I'll find the woman later, he promised himself. *No one will interfere a second time.* Pocketing his knife and stepping around the strewn food, he fled down the steps toward the parking lot.

A gust from the open front door blew through the house and hit the kitchen door. He heard it slam shut behind him.

GRACE SPENT A FEW minutes visiting with her two patients before filling out discharge papers. Her first patient, a young man of thirteen who'd undergone tympanoplasty to repair a burst eardrum caused by untreated infection, flirted shamelessly with her. He lit up in grateful adoration when she returned his playful banter.

The other patient, Bobby Lao, age three, was sleeping soundly. Grace had lobbied his parents to allow her to remove Bobby's chronically infected tonsils due to the boy's ongoing cycle of infection and his allergic reaction to most antibiotics. His mother welcomed Grace's company. She was several years younger than Grace, vibrant and talkative, full of her active life.

Grace tried to picture herself as the mother of an active toddler, tried to place herself in the other woman's shoes, but she couldn't see herself there, couldn't put it together. With a halfhearted smile, she left the woman bending over her little boy, stroking his head.

After rounds, Grace played a game of Scrabble with Terry, whose vocabulary and sign language skills were growing exponentially. She then spent the next hour with her family therapy group. Not surprising her, attendance was light and the normal time of chatting and answering questions afterward shorter than usual. Coming into the city on a freezing winter night was not a pleasant prospect.

Grace drove home through sparse traffic, her tires crunching through frozen streets. She looked forward to a hot bath and the dinner Dr. Bill would have left her. She parked in her assigned spot and climbed to the back door. She reached for the handle, but before she put her key to the lock, she was surprised when the handle turned and the door opened.

"What in the world . . ."

Cautiously, she switched on the light . . . and stared in amazement at the fried rice and vegetables strewn across her linoleum.

"Oh, no! Have I been . . . robbed?"

That's when she realized the stiff breeze hitting her was coming from her front door. Her *wide-open* front door. She tiptoed around the mess, strode across the living room, and was about to shut and lock the front door when she caught a glimpse of Bill's prostrate form lying on the sidewalk where he'd fallen.

"Bill!" Her shriek resounded in the cold night.

Within seconds she was kneeling by him, assessing his condition. Between sobs, her training acted for her. His face was gray and clammy, and his pulse, only intermittent, faded to nothing under her fingers. She immediately began CPR and screamed for help between breaths.

Two neighbors came to her aid at last, one returning immediately to his house to summon an ambulance. She continued CPR. Finally, Bill's color seemed to improve and she heard sirens drawing near. Paramedics pried her away so they could take over.

She was faint and lightheaded when they put Bill in the ambulance. At her request, one of her neighbors closed up her house. She climbed into the ambulance and sat near Bill's feet, watching the paramedics, clutching Bill's pipe in her hand. It must have fallen out of his shirt pocket and been near him on the sidewalk. All she knew was she found it in her grasp and she clung to it as if having it could force Bill to be all right. She shook with cold and fear.

Lord Jesus, please save my daddy Bill! Please!

Two hours later the cardiac specialist they'd called briefed her.

"Dr. Warner? Zack Morton. Your father, is he?" The surgeon wasn't much older than she was.

"My guardian. Just tell me, please."

"Right. He was in pretty rough shape when he came in, as I'm sure you already knew. We've determined that, in addition to the hypothermia, he did have a major cardiac event. Mr. Upton is how old?"

Grace gulped. "Dr. Upton. He's seventy-two."

"He's a physician too?"

"Yes. Upton-Warner Clinic."

"Ah! Over at City View." Nodding, he went on. "The next few days will tell us how it's going to go. We are monitoring him closely and supporting him as best we can. How is his general health? Any problems before this? High blood pressure or diabetes?"

"None of those. He's been in great health, works full time and has never had any heart complaints."

"Good to hear. However, we're going to keep him in the ICU until we run tests to determine the extent of damage his heart has sustained, and what treatment we can provide."

She understood only too well. Dr. Bill was in critical condition. They might not be able to help him. Realistically it could go either way.

He might die.

She turned away, numb. *Oh Bill! My daddy Bill! I am so sorry we fought.*

Someone from the unit's nurse's station brought her a cup of coffee. Grace sipped it gratefully. Around 11:00 p.m. they allowed her in to see him, to touch his hand and speak words of love into his ear. Then she was told to go home.

"Could you call me a taxi?" Grace asked the nurse who'd been so kind and solicitous.

"Wouldn't you rather I call a friend?" the solicitous nurse asked. "You should have someone with you. You really should," she insisted.

"Frankly, I would rather stay."

"You should rest then," the nurse encouraged her. "He may need you tomorrow."

"I suppose I could call someone," but she could think of no one she wanted with her. Her responses were sluggish and distracted, and she was so weary. Why couldn't she just slide into nothingness? Her throat ached with unshed tears.

She diagnosed herself offhandedly. *Shock.*

She stood at the phone bank in the corridor fully intending to call Jess Galt. The man was Bill's friend. He would want to know, want to help. Instead, she wondered vaguely if Richard were alone tonight, if he would care enough to come, even because it was just the decent, Christian sort of thing to do. What she knew he would do for any . . . friend.

Except they weren't even that now.

With reckless abandon, she inserted the coins and dialed. She'd bully him into coming if she had to, because, regardless of the consequences, she *needed* him. Wanted him! Surely he would come?

The phone rang several times, clunked noisily as the receiver fell to the floor and was retrieved.

The voice that spoke was groggy. "Hawke here."

"Richard? It's Grace. I . . . I need you, Richard."

"Grace?" He was more alert now.

"I'm at West View Med. Dr. Bill is . . . he's had a heart attack. Richard . . . Bill is the only family I have!"

She swallowed. The tightness in her throat was agony.

"Do you want me to come, Grace?" She heard his feet hit the floor, him fumbling with his clothes.

Do you want me to come? Her heart jumped into her throat.

"Never mind," he interjected. "I'm coming whether you want me to or not."

"Oh, Richard! Are you?"

"On my way. Be there quick as I can. Hold tight to Jesus, Babe."

Babe?

She hung up the phone and clutched her aching throat.

❧

IT TOOK HAWKE thirty minutes to make the run from his apartment to West View Med. Thirty long minutes before his rushing, get-out-of-my-way stride brought him to her side.

Relief in the form of tears slid down her face, and even before he reached her, he held out his arms to her. As he wrapped her up in his embrace, her restraint gave way. He held her close and tight while she wept. When she was reduced to shuddering sobs, he guided her to a sofa, sat down, and pulled her close to him.

"Lord Jesus, please help Grace; please comfort her!" he murmured over and over.

The Lord must have been listening to his prayers, because a soft glow rose on her otherwise wan face, and the stress lines across her forehead relaxed. Not long after, her even breathing told him she had slipped into an exhausted sleep.

"You rest now, Babe. It's going to be all right."

He remained awake through the long hours of the night, watching over her, once gently stroking the sweet curve of her cheek.

Praying . . .

And listening.

CHAPTER 32

THE EARLY MORNING bustle of the hospital disturbed her, and she awakened and recalled the past night in a rush. She was still snuggled tightly against his chest.

Hawke grimaced at her through bleary eyes. "How's Sleeping Beauty?"

"Better, I think. Thank you." The grip on her throat had eased, but she still felt like she'd been half-strangled.

"Coffee?"

"Oh, yes!"

"Why don't we check on Dr. Bill first?"

She obtained permission to enter the ICU and stand by Bill's bed. His complexion was pale, even in the early light. She picked up his hand, checked his pulse, and examined his fingernails. Then she read the entries on his chart. His chest rose in rhythmic accord with the respirator. She kissed him and whispered in his ear, but he gave no response. Quietly she quitted the room.

Hawke, his cheeks darkened by overnight stubble, cracked a yawn. "C'mon. Let's wash our faces and get that coffee." He yawned again.

After they washed up, they caught an elevator to the basement cafeteria. On the way down, he took her hand.

Grace blinked against the hope that rushed into her heart.

"I'm glad you called me, Grace." Hawke's tired eyes creased into a smile.

"I'm grateful you came, Richard."

They stood looking at each other, appraising the other's meaning. Then the door slid open and they stepped out. Together.

Something has changed, Grace realized in wonder.

THAT SAME DAWN, Bradley Dennison again subbed for Sharon on *Morning Line*. He mentally encouraged her, *No rush. Stay away as long as you like, Sweetheart.*

When the show finished airing, Saul Beech was heard shouting in the studio, but not at *him*; he was filling anchor slot just fine. Nevertheless, the studio heads were fit to be tied over Sharon's unscheduled absence.

For the first time, Bradley wondered if something might be wrong. *Where are you, Sharon? What are you up to?*

"STAR OR NO STAR," May Miller muttered in agitation, "things can turn on a dime in this business, and it isn't just Sharon's job hanging by a thread."

She again dialed the offices at The Wood Chimes. This time she stayed on the line.

TOWARD THE END of breakfast Hawke said, "I need to report in, see what's on my plate this morning. Are you going to stay or should I drop you home?"

She shook her head slowly. "I can't leave."

"I thought as much. All right, how about I swing by your place sometime this morning, pick up whatever you need, and bring it to you before noon. This evening, I can take you to get some dinner, then check you into that hotel across the street where you can stay close to Bill. How's that sound?"

Too good to be true, her heart throbbed.

She replied, "That sounds like a good plan, only I am scheduled to give a lecture tonight—in a conference room over in the medical school wing. I can reschedule my other appointments today, but this lecture has been extensively publicized."

"Do you think it wise not to cancel? Will you have adequate time to prepare?"

"Since I have given these lectures before, I believe I can manage. That said, I would hate to miss having dinner with you."

"I feel the same. What time will you finish your lecture?"

Was there an answering yearning in his reply?

"Around 8:15, perhaps 8:30."

"Can you hold off the hungries until then?"

Not trusting herself to speak she nodded.

Hawke matter-of-factly said, "Okay. Jot down what you need me to fetch from your place, Gracie, and lend me your key. I'll check in at work, run over to your place, and be back here before noon."

She wrote out where he could find her overnight bag and what clean clothes and toiletries she required.

Scanning the list, he chuckled softly. "Gonna feel pretty comfortable in your home after rummaging through your dresser."

Not sure how to take him, Grace stared back evenly. *I am in deep now, Richard Hawke. So if this is just a pseudo-chivalrous joke on your part, know this: You'll break my heart.*

He had to have seen her thoughts flit across her face, because he sobered.

"You are not a passing fling to me, Grace, nor will I give up on us this time. You have my word. I'll bring your things before noon and catch up to you this evening as soon as I finish work."

Her heart quickened. *You have my word?*

He added, "If I happen to get to your lecture early, perhaps I can sit in on it? Would that be allowed? If so, which floor?"

"Seventh, and yes; it's open to the public. I think you'll find it . . . educational."

She rose from the table, needing to gather her wits about herself.

Call the office. Have Linda tell the clinic staff about Bill. Ask her to shunt my patients in immediate need over to Willard and reschedule the rest. We'll have to curtail Bill's schedule for the next few weeks too.

Hawke stood, too, and interrupted her thoughts. "Good to know your lecture is open to the public. I'll try to make it. And Grace?"

"Yes?"

"Let's talk at dinner tonight . . . about us."

Heart pounding, she answered low, "I would like that."

"See you then." He smiled, reached out, and hugged her tight. "The Lord watch over you and keep you safe this day, Gracie."

RUDY BARRISTER, general manager of The Wood Chimes, stopped at the entrance to Sharon Richmond's penthouse apartment. Wagoner, a seasoned security specialist, accompanied him. Rudy fingered the master pass key in his hand.

The usually reticent and discreet-to-a-fault GM would never have deigned to enter a tenant's residence under normal circumstances. He believed, quite firmly, in a policy of privacy and noninterference when it came to the comings and goings of his tenants.

He would have stuck to his guns, too, except the parking garage's day guard, Alex (his wife's bothersome cousin), had reported to the day manager that the garage night guard, LaRusso, had not been present when Alex arrived on the job yesterday morning.

What the kid didn't know was that LaRusso had not shown up for work last night either, forcing Rudy to pull in Wagoner, on overtime. It was Wagoner who had found LaRusso, bound, gagged, and seriously concussed behind an RV parked in the garage. Rudy had called an ambulance and had LaRusso removed to a hospital forthwith.

Rudy felt his face heat. He was angry because ample *security* made this facility profitable, angry because he paid through the nose *for the best*. He was angry because when residents felt the stirrings of insecurity, they began to lose confidence, he lost tenants, and word got around—oh, yes, it did!

Fortunately, and somewhat puzzling, no assaults or robberies had accompanied the "LaRusso incident" as he called it, so Rudy had not notified the police. By contract, the "incident" entitled LaRusso to generous compensation and medical care. The guard could accept the compensation package, but—again by contract—only if he abided by the terms of the compensation, said terms that forbade him to file a police report or speak of the incident to anyone.

Rudy had, however, called in extra security to inspect every vehicle in The Wood Chimes' garage and to walk all fifteen floors of the building seeking indications of theft or vandalism. In addition, this morning Rudy had personally phoned or visited every tenant he could reach, just to "check in" and, in the course of the conversation, gently inquire if they were satisfied with the facility's security.

If he or his security had found evidence of a crime, Rudy would then have notified the police, but not until then. No, Rudy was determined to handle any unpleasantness "in house." The only fly in the ointment had been his wife's loudmouth cousin, Alex, who also insisted that Miss Richmond's pricey Nissan sports car had not moved so much as an inch the last forty-eight hours.

Rudy had discounted Alex's observation with, "The streets are awash in slush and ice. No doubt, Miss Richmond arranged for a car and driver rather than subject her vehicle to salt damage." And so, because he'd fielded no complaints and LaRusso was recovering, he'd started to breathe easy—right up until the call came from Sharon Richmond's assistant insisting upon a wellness check.

Now, standing at her door, Rudy had a bad, a *very* bad feeling. And why did it have to be *her*, that pretentious, belittling harridan? Although Rudy had rung the bell repeatedly, if she *did* happen to be inside her apartment not wishing to be disturbed, he would never hear the end of it.

Rudy exhaled, inserted the master key, and let the door swing inward.

A smell that Rudy could not identify but that made his stomach twist, halted him on the threshold. Wagoner's eyes went wide. He gulped and swallowed. Finally, Rudy jerked his chin, ordering Wagoner to go first. Four steps and a turn to the right brought them to Sharon Richmond's living room.

A body lay on its back, arms to its sides, and it took a moment for Rudy and Wagoner's minds to register what their eyes were seeing. Nothing recognizable remained of the body's face. Congealing blood, more than the carpets could possibly soak up, puddled around the head like spoiled pudding, and where her striking features had once been . . .

Rudy felt the blood in his head drain to his feet.

Wagoner tried to catch him before he fainted.

Didn't quite manage it.

DOV WATCHED dispassionately as the crime scene techs photographed the apartment and collected evidence samples. He kept his eyes averted from the body. He'd already been to the bathroom once, hacking up his breakfast. So had a couple of the responding officers.

Hawke had gone green too when they arrived. Then he'd hardened himself like he usually did. Even now, Dov could feel his partner's icy detachment. He glanced sideways at Hawke. He was as grim and gray as death himself . . . but also strangely distracted.

"Dov, I want you to take point on the investigation. Get Percival and Browning here. Have them take over until the crime techs and ME finish while you interview Sharon's coworkers, particularly her assistant. See what you can piece together. I'll meet the three of you back at the division in, say, two or three hours."

"And you?"

"I have an errand to run."

"Okay, but just an offhand observation? I'd say Marek Gretzky didn't much care for Richmond's sensational reporting."

"Have to agree, Dov."

Hawke's next words took on an whimsical note. "You know, I just realized that if it hadn't been for Sharon Richmond interviewing Grace on *Morning Line* the morning Mary Alice Waite's body was found, I might never have met her."

"Met who? Sharon Richmond?"

"No, Grace."

"Oh." Tentatively, Dov inquired, "Have you seen or talked to Grace since your, ah, breakup?"

"Yeah." He looked up and smiled a weary smile. "Her Dr. Bill had a heart attack yesterday. I kept Grace company at the hospital through the night, so I'm running on zero sleep."

He stared off into space. "I never dreamed she would call me if she needed help."

Dov skewered Hawke with a look. "In an emergency she called *you?*"

"Incredible, right? I know I really screwed things up, but maybe now . . ." He drifted off again to Dov's somewhat amused concern.

"You know, Rick, if we manage to catch this guy pretty soon, you could take some time off. Get rested up. You're looking pretty sorry."

"Time off? Yeah. I suppose I have some vacation accumulated."

"Some? If you took it all at once, they'd call it a sabbatical."

"A vacation sounds good," and he drifted away again, muttering under his breath, "Yeah. With Grace. Maybe a long honeymoon, if she'll have me."

Dov hid his delight. "I should get Percy and Browning here ASAP, then hotfoot it over to the station, huh?"

Dov had to wait for Hawke to respond. When he did, he muttered a distracted, "Uh, right. See you back at the ranch."

Hawke turned on his heel and sort of wandered out.

Dov followed behind, shaking his head.

IT WAS NEARLY 11:00 a.m. when Dov reached Richmond's station and asked for Richmond's assistant, May Miller.

"What can I do for you, Detective?" The short Asian woman had a magnificent, high-wattage smile, even white teeth set against the contrast of warm maroon skin.

Crud. She doesn't know yet.

"Uh, Miss Miller, you called the management of The Wood Chimes this morning, requesting a wellness check on Sharon Richmond. Is that correct?"

Her smile vanished. "That's right. Sharon didn't come into work yesterday or this morning. I'm concerned."

"Understandable." Dov drew a breath. "Miss Miller, the manager of The Wood Chimes, acting on your request, did open Miss Richmond's apartment this morning. I'm sorry to be the one to tell you, but they discovered that Miss Richmond was deceased. It's believed she was killed quite early Tuesday morning."

"K-killed?" May took a shaky step backwards.

Dov gestured her to a chair.

"Why don't you sit down. Better? Look, I'm sorry to be the one to give you the news. It appears that Miss Richmond was the victim of the knifer we've been looking for . . . the one she's been reporting on."

"She was murdered? By that serial killer?"

"We believe so."

"Oh, n-no . . . " May shuddered and a sob caught her words.

"Listen, Miss Miller, I know you're shocked and grieved, but I need to ask you a few questions so we can find this guy. Maybe what I could do is go visit the station manager . . . Mr. Beech, is it? And come back in a few minutes when you've had a chance to collect yourself?"

Agreeing silently, May led him into the hall. From there she pointed towards Saul's suite of offices. Tears were now coursing down her smooth cheeks, attracting the attention of passing studio personnel.

Dov thanked her and was cleared by Saul Beech's receptionist into the inner sanctum.

"What's going on?" Saul Beech stood in front of his desk, obviously a man who faced trouble straight on.

"Mr. Beech, I have some rather distressing news."

"Tell me." His large florid face tightened up for the blow.

"The management of The Wood Chimes called 911 this morning to report that they had discovered Sharon Richmond's death."

Saul walked around his desk and sat heavily, expression vacant.

"Mr. Beech?"

"A minute. Just . . . give me a minute."

"Yes, sir." Dov stepped back and gave him a minute. Gave him two.

"Detective . . . what'd you say your name was?"

"Mayer."

"Detective Mayer, was it . . . do you think Sharon might have . . . "

"Committed suicide?"

He nodded, relieved yet flinching at the quick response.

"No, sir, she did not kill herself." *No way in Hades*, Dov said to himself.

"No? Then what?"

"That is, primarily, why I'm here, Mr. Beech. Sharon was reporting rather regularly on a series of homicides, the city's serial murderer."

"The maniac knife guy? What? Are you saying she was . . . stabbed and cut up, like the others?"

Dov inclined his head and thought for a moment he was going to lose the beefy exec.

"Mr. Beech, you assumed it was suicide when I first mentioned Miss Richmond's death. Why?"

Saul turned his heavy-lidded eyes to Dov. "Sharon was doing those reports without authorization. The other studio heads and I had a meeting with Sharon Monday after her show to curtail what we considered inappropriate format for *Morning Line*. It wasn't a pleasant exchange. Sharon got more than a little hot under the collar, and I had to . . . yank her back into line. So, when she didn't come to work yesterday and today and you said she was dead . . . well, you can understand my concern."

Dov surveyed the man with interest.

"You're saying Sharon wasn't authorized to air those reports?"

"It was more than that. See, I was out of town for several weeks when it began. My associates, the other studio heads, are—were—to be truthful, a little afraid of Sharon. She has—*had*—a very forceful personality. Anyway, her reporting got way out of hand; it was sensationalistic, possibly libelous. I pulled her off the killer's story—no ifs ands or buts about it."

"Libelous?" Dov kept his voice vaguely disinterested.

"Maybe I shouldn't say this to you, but Sharon really had it in for that cop, Detective Hawke? Never missed an opportunity to ding him. You know the guy?"

Dov leveled a cold gaze on Beech. "Actually, Richard Hawke is my partner and the finest detective I know. And I have to agree that Richmond's unwarranted speculations libeled him, sullied his reputation. As a result of her coverage, Hawke has lost the confidence of the mayor and police commissioner."

Beech scowled. "Like I said, she was not authorized to run with that story. Fact is, I have a close friend, lost his wife at the Claremont last month. He says his wife wasn't killed by this nut job, that she had a heart attack that evening. My friend's got nothing but good to say about the guy Sharon kept running down. Far as I'm concerned, the man's only fault was running into Sharon's buzzsaw—and him flipping the script on her. And I'd have to say Sharon didn't take public embarrassment well. Rather, she was known to hold grudges."

"I see."

Dov spent a few more minutes chatting up the man and sharing a few insights into the case, before he wended his way back to May Miller. Along the way, he encountered stares, some tearful, others serious or merely curious.

The word was out.

May jumped when he reappeared.

"Doing better now?" he asked.

She nodded. "A little shaky and on edge."

"Is it okay to ask you a few questions then?"

She nodded again.

"Right. Uh, Miss Miller, it's pretty obvious to us that Sharon's attacker was the very person she'd dwelled on at length in *Morning Line's* news. Do you have any idea why she was so fixated on this particular case?"

May paused and considered.

"Sharon was talented—extremely so. She knew it, of course, and she had the raw ambition to match. I got the impression that she felt the story could be a stepping stone."

"To a more prestigious job?"

"Yes. She wanted a primetime news anchor slot."

"Did you enjoy working with Sharon?"

"It was all right. She wasn't easy to work for, but she was fair."

"What about the others on the show?"

"Well, Sharon wasn't one to mince words if she didn't like the way something was handled. But before she was hired, the show was dying, so Saul gave her a lot of latitude in producing it."

"Is that how her serial killer coverage got out of hand?"

"I think so. Anyway, no one could deter Sharon once she had the bit in her teeth."

"Except Saul Beech."

"Yes. When he returned from his trip, he put his foot down, and Sharon took it hard. She was furious when she left the studio Monday, mid-morning."

"That's what I picked up from Mr. Beech. One more question: Can you think of any unusual occurrence in the past few weeks? For example, Miss Richmond wasn't listed in the phone book, so we'd like to figure out how the killer knew where she lived."

May paled before Dov's eyes. "I may have told him."

"Excuse me?"

"A florist's delivery man. Last week. He came in after Sharon left for the day, and I told him—" she choked on her words. "I told him she lived at The Wood Chimes, that he could leave the flowers—roses, he said—at the office. But Sharon? When I asked her a couple days later how she liked the flowers, she said she'd never received them."

Yeah, that would do it, Dov thought.

CONCERNED FOR GRACE and her needs, but worrying over the scene he'd left at Richmond's apartment and the added weight her sensational murder would pile on top of him, Hawke muttered to himself, "What a time for that woman to go and get herself killed."

He unlocked and opened Grace's front door. The scent of cooked food, not unpleasant, greeted him, but he was mission-focused. Bypassing the swinging doors leading to her kitchen, he turned down the hall, and walked straight to Grace's bedroom. He found her overnight case, gathered the items she needed, and packed them into the case. He was in and out in five minutes, locking the door behind him. The drive to West View Med cut another half hour out of his day, but nothing on this planet could move him to let Grace down.

He found her in the ICU, standing by Bill's bed. He knocked softly on the glass. When she turned, she lit up . . . and his heart did backflips.

He grinned back. Softly, under his breath, he added, "You, my boy, have a terminal case."

Grace blinked. Burst into laughter he couldn't hear through the glass.

"Well, crud. She reads lips."

"Yes, I do," she mouthed, holding her middle with both arms.

He nodded, laughing with her, then held up her overnight case.

"I'm sorry I can't stay, even long enough for a coffee break," he told her when she came out to get the case. "We've had another murder."

"Marek Gretzky?"

"I have no doubts, but, in addition, it's . . ."

She waited for him to finish.

"It's something of a celebrity murder this time. I'm going to be strapped for a while."

"I suppose that horrible newswoman will blame you again?"

Hawke blanched. "Uhh . . ."

"What is it? What did I say?"

Hawke exhaled. "The latest victim? The celebrity? It's Sharon Richmond."

"Oh, no! Oh . . . goodness. I don't know how to feel about this. It's terrible, of course, but . . . oh dear. At least she won't be haranguing you on-air anymore?"

"Sorry, Grace, but it actually isn't good news for me. Sure, *Sharon* won't be beating me up on her program, but now the rest of the media will do it for her, rebroadcasting every sensational clip they can lay their hands on. That aside, I'm still planning to take you to a late dinner this evening, but I probably won't make it to your lecture."

"I understand. I have patient emergencies. I get it."

He saw that she did and was relieved. "Thank you."

"Of course. And thank you again for fetching clean clothes for me. Changing into clothes I haven't slept in will refresh me."

"And Bill?"

Her smile was wan but hopeful. "He's doing better than Dr. Morton expected. He thinks Bill may wake up soon."

"Thank you, Jesus!" Hawke said fervently.

CHAPTER 33

DOV RETURNED TO Homicide, weary and hungry. Hawke jumped on him the moment he stepped off the elevator.

"Can I grab a bite to eat first? Didn't even have time for breakfast."

"You can eat after you debrief me."

Dov sighed, and Hawke pumped him for every detail.

"When I finished talking to this Saul Beech guy, I found out he's friends with Arthur Grunbaum. Get this, Art has been telling Beech that you're the best detective in the state."

Hawke's phone rang; he ignored it.

"Are you serious?"

"Serious as a wrecking ball—as in the wrecking ball that landed on Sharon Richmond Monday after *Morning Line* wrapped up. Beech chewed her out. Ordered her to stop reporting on the murders."

Hawke's phone rang a second time. He didn't pick it up.

"That won't stop the rest of the local media. If anything, they'll rally behind Sharon and come down on me harder than she did. And if McCormick gets another call from the mayor's office? He's all but said he'll pull me from the case."

McCormick stepped out of his office, phone receiver in hand, and yelled across the floor. "Hawke! I know you're over there. Pick up your blasted phone!

Hawke jerked the receiver off the ringing base.

Under his breath he mouthed, "Speak of the devil . . ." Then, "Yes, Chief?"

Hawke listened and sobered. His mouth dropped in disbelief. A minute later, he sat up straight, the makings of a grin pulling at his mouth.

"Yes, sir. You bet I am. Yes, sir. Thank you, Chief."

He replaced the receiver slowly, weeks of tension draining from his body. He grinned weakly. "That was Chief McCormick."

"No kidding. And?"

"Saul Beech just finished calling both the police commissioner and the mayor. Read a formal apology to them for any and all statements made by his station's employees critical of the city police department in general and me personally. Then he asked that any contemplated action unfavorable to my career be dismissed. McCormick said the man offered to make a public apology on his station—and get this? The mayor took him up on his offer."

"Wow. So . . ."

"So the mayor is happy, the commish is happy, the chief is happy, and I'm grateful to get the three of them off my back."

"Yup. Sure takes the heat off us."

Hawke turned his gaze on Dov. Fixed him with a look, his expression reflective, then serious.

Dov froze like a deer in oncoming headlights. Did not move a muscle.

"Dov."

Dov coughed nervously. "Yeah?"

"Thank you."

He shrugged. "Hey, what for?"

"You know what for. You pulled Beech's string today."

"Did I?" He fidgeted uncomfortably. "I can't remember—my memory is fogged by hunger pangs."

"Really?"

"Yeah, really. No breakfast, no lunch. I'm starving. Feel . . . faint . . ."

"Good grief. Stop with the theatrics and I'll order you a pizza."

"Extra-large. Sausage *and* pepperoni."

"What? You want *pork* on your pizza?"

"Nonobservant Jew, remember? Sausage *and* pepperoni."

"Done."

HOURS LATER, DOV polished off the last two slices of an extra-large pizza, and let out a satisfied burp. He tossed the box in Hawke's trash.

"Not what I'd planned for breakfast, lunch, and dinner, but it did the trick. Can we please go home now?"

Hawke, hunched over piles of case notes, brooded. "We know Marek is after his son. I'm just grateful Grace had the wherewithal to suggest stashing Terry in the hospital's secure ward. Marek may be lurking around that hospital, but he'll never make it past the security there. What we need is a plan to lure Marek in and trap him."

"Look, the only plan I'm interested in at the moment is the one that takes me home to my loving wife, a hot shower, and a good night's sleep. Do you see what time it is, Rick? It's going on 6:30."

Dov picked a very unkosher bit of sausage out of his teeth. "By the way, just a reminder that *you* have been up all night. Have you taken a gander in a mirror? You look like death warmed over. I just want to get home at a decent time for a change. You? You *really* need to sleep."

"Yeah, all right, Dov. You go on home."

Hawke's phone rang. He grabbed it up. "Detective Hawke."

Dov didn't hear the caller's response, but when Hawke replied, "Hey, Grace. What's up? How's Bill?" he was suddenly less interested in clocking out.

"RICHARD, THEY EXTUBATED Bill a few hours ago, and he has been trying to wake up since then. He keeps mumbling something, either to me or to himself. What concerns me is how agitated he becomes when I talk to him. When I attempt to calm him, he gets more agitated. Dr. Morton doesn't understand either."

"Can you make out what he's mumbling?"

"Something that sounds like 'kitchen.'"

"Whose kitchen?"

"Maybe mine? He was supposed to drop off Chinese for my dinner. That's why he was at my house, but . . . oh!"

"But what?"

"I always come in the back door after parking my car, and I just remembered that before I found Bill on the sidewalk out front, I found Chinese food strewn all over the kitchen floor. I nearly stepped in the middle of it but managed to avoid it. I forgot about the mess and somehow assumed Bill was on his way in, not out, when he suffered his heart attack."

A small, sharp memory picked at the back of Hawke's mind.

What was it? A scent? A smell?

"Could he have put the boxes in your kitchen and was on his way out the door when his heart attack happened?"

"Well, yes, he had to have taken the food into the house, right? How else would it have gotten there? That said, most heart attack victims don't get very far before they collapse. Perhaps Bill started having chest pain, dropped the food, and tried to reach his car."

As if she were reasoning with herself, she added, "But why didn't he use my house phone to call an ambulance instead? He knows better!"

"And you say he's agitated?"

"And keeps muttering 'kitchen,' over and over."

A cold hand snaked up Hawke's spine. Ran its fingers down its length.

"Whatever you do, Grace, don't go home—I'm serious." He glanced up and Dov nodded. "Dov and I are headed to your place now. Do *not* go home for any reason, got it?"

"Y-you're scaring me, Richard."

"I don't mean to scare you—I mean you to be *safe*. What time will you leave for your lecture?"

"I'm actually leaving now. I'm supposed to arrive early to set up. Don't worry about me. I'm expecting a good-sized audience, and if I finish before you get to the hospital, I'll wait for you with Terry in the secure ward."

"I like that idea; after your lecture, get to the secure ward and stay put. I'll come up to get you when I arrive. See you in a few hours."

Hawke slammed the receiver onto its base. "Let's go, Dov; follow me in your car."

IT WAS AFTER seven o'clock when Hawke pulled up to Grace's dark house and parked behind Bill's car. He still had Grace's key ring and had her house key ready when Dov joined him on the porch. They entered Grace's house together. Hawke switched on the lights in the living room, then pushed open the kitchen doors and hit the light switch on the wall.

And there it was, that scent he'd noticed earlier: Chinese takeout. Dried rice and congealing sauce were flung across the floor along with burst white cartons glued to the floor in the middle of the mess.

"Cleanup on aisle five, Rick."

"Yup. I'll handle it."

"Still need me to stick around?"

Hawke frowned. "No. You go on home."

Because I have this feeling that something's not quite right. Lord?

"Great. See you tomorrow." Dov backed out of the kitchen.

Hawke heard the front door close while he was searching for a broom and dustpan to clean up with. *Most heart attack victims don't get very far before they fall*, he thought idly while sweeping up sticky debris. *So, how did Bill make it outside, almost to the curb?*

Lord, if I'm missing it, please show me?

He grabbed the waste can out from under the sink. When he emptied the dustpan into the can, he heard the faint clink of glass.

Grace must have broken something.

He had most of the mess in the can in a few minutes, then he dampened handfuls of paper towels to wash the tacky linoleum. Not a great job, but good enough for the moment.

"Ouch!" Snatching up his hand, Hawke plucked a thin shard of glass from his finger and examined the cut. Not deep, just messy. He ran his finger under the faucet and absentmindedly stared at the inch-long piece of glass while the water washed the blood down the drain.

This is flat glass. Not from a dish or a water glass.

Lord, I am beat.

Huh. Flat glass. Could be window glass?

Wrapping a folded paper towel around his finger, he glanced around the kitchen, then lifted the corner of the back door curtain, revealing a neatly taped square of plastic.

Ah. She broke this windowpane.

He'd fix it for her. Tomorrow, after work.

Actually, an entry door with window glass is an invitation for burglary. What Grace needs here is a solid door without windows . . .

A few bits of dried rice stared up at him, right at the threshold and onto the door's kickplate. Pulse quickening, he unlatched and opened the door and spotted a frozen blob of sweet and sour sauce inside a snowy footprint on her porch.

"I nearly stepped in the middle of it but managed to avoid it."

His stomach lurched as he put the pieces together.

Marek Gretzky.

This is his footprint.

He's after Grace.

Like he targeted Sharon Richmond.

He slammed and locked her doors, raced to his car, slid in, and grabbed his radio. Simultaneously he started the engine and backed into the street. He stuffed the gear into drive and floored it. His car leapt forward.

"Dispatch, this is Detective Richard Hawke, Homicide, badge number 97212. Patch me through to Detective Mayer. Also, I want SWAT and all available back up at City View Hospital and Medical School ASAP. Serial murder suspect Marek Gretzky on premises. Treat as armed and extremely dangerous. Over."

"We copy, Detective Hawke. Detective Mayer standing by."

"Dov, did you hear?"

"Yeah, Hawke. I'm rolling, and Percival and Browning will meet us there—with bells on!" Excitement bubbled in Dov's voice.

"Listen, Dov." Hawke's hands were clammy. He took a deep breath. "He's after Grace."

"What? Run that again."

"After you left her place, I found a broken window pane in her back door and a glob of food on the porch inside a *man's* footprint! He was there, Dov. Marek was in Grace's house!"

Sirens wailing, he plowed through a red light, downshifted and barely made the next corner on four wheels.

"Marek broke in and was waiting for her, but I think Bill Upton showed up first, and they surprised each other. Bill probably threw the cartons of food at Marek and got away through the front door, only to have a heart attack out on the sidewalk." Hawke was flowing with perspiration as vivid images of Sharon Richmond's butchered face flooded his thoughts.

His car accelerated up the on-ramp to the expressway and rocketed forward as he stomped down hard. "Right now Grace should be in the medical school wing at City View giving a lecture—a lecture that gets out minutes from now. If everyone leaves before she's packed up, she's going to be alone!"

Dov heard Hawke's voice crack and falter. He chewed his bottom lip and said the first thing that came to him. "Have you prayed, Rick? And what about that Tanakh portion you have pinned at your desk?"

Peace swept into Hawke's heart. "Right. You're right! I'm praying now. Thank you for the reminders, Dov."

Lord, thank you for my friend and partner. Thank you for using him to remind me: "*Many are the plans in a person's heart, but it is the* LORD'*s purpose that prevails.*"

"I trust you, Lord. Your purpose *will* prevail this night."

He called dispatch again. "Listen, call City View Hospital and speak to their security officer in charge. Tell him the same thing I relayed to SWAT and all available officers. The suspected serial knife killer is on their premises. Treat as armed and extremely dangerous. But I also need you to have them send an armed response to the seventh-floor auditorium in the medical school where Dr. Grace Warner is giving a lecture. She is the target. Repeat: Dr. Warner is the target."

"We copy, Detective Hawke."

"Next, I need you to call Dr. Warner's office and leave voicemail. Here's the message I want you to leave."

The odds of Grace picking up her messages before she encountered Gretzky were practically nil, but he had to try.

Hawke spoke as concisely as he could. "Grace, you are in danger. Marek Gretzky was in your house and will likely be waiting for you after your lecture ends. Call security and insist on an armed escort to the secure ward. You'll be safe there."

He swallowed. "If . . . if you find yourself alone in the medical school, lock yourself in an office or a classroom. I'm coming. So is half the police force. Hold tight. Hold on to Jesus. I love you."

He exhaled. "That's it. Do you have all of it?"

"10-4, Detective Hawke. Will request armed response from City View Hospital security to Dr. Warner's location, seventh-floor medical school auditorium, and will relay to your message to voicemail at the number you provided."

"Thank you."

The dispatcher's usually controlled voice cracked. "We're praying for you here, Hawke. Dispatch out."

CHAPTER 34

HER AUDIENCE LAUGHED heartily, including Grace. *Finally*. It had taken a while to thaw them out. Being that this was the first lecture in this iteration of her series, she was new to the majority of the attendees. However, Grace had discovered that relating some of the more comic moments of her own life as well as her practice helped her to connect to her listeners.

Still chuckling she added, "I should mention the time I had to remove a sprouted pinto bean from a little girl's ear. She told her mother that a neighbor child had promised that if she put a bean in her ear, it would come out her mouth.

"The mother took her straight to the doctor, but the child's pediatrician couldn't see the bean. The mother then decided her daughter had gotten it out herself or had made the whole thing up—right up until the day the bean began to sprout. That sprout was half an inch long when I retrieved the bean from her ear!"

There was more laughter. A bit more ease.

"I'm glad," Grace was still smiling but sounding more serious, "that you can laugh with me, because for those who are not medical students—students who are required to attend, by the way," which led to more laughter, "it's likely you are here because something less than humorous has happened recently, either to you, personally, or to someone you love.

"Unfortunately, hearing loss isn't a visible handicap or one that other people can easily understand and sympathize with. Thus, you may be just beginning to understand how isolating and lonely hearing loss can be."

She paused to ensure she had their attention. "Only those who have experienced the isolation of no longer hearing the simple conversations around you can truly sympathize. Only those who have experienced hearing loss know how useless or stupid others may presume you are, and treat you accordingly."

Grace switched on an overhead projector and laid a transparency on it. Her outline was projected against a screen at the front of the auditorium. As she continued, she moved the pertinent part of the outline into view. She knew that a portion of the forty or more individuals in the room were laughing only because everyone else laughed. The pain on that woman's face for instance, gave her away. She was unable to follow Grace as she lectured, but the outline, a tactic Grace always used, would help.

"In no order of importance, let me list the most commonly occurring difficulties of adapting to hearing loss.

"Most of your medical and technical support will not feel your agony and frustration. Not understanding, some providers may imply that if you *just tried harder*, you could hear better."

She glanced up. "Medical students? Don't let this be you."

Several students shifted uncomfortably.

"You may begin to feel that *you* are at fault for your hearing loss.

"Others will presume to advise you to live less productive and satisfying lives; in their way they will urge you to accept being less than you were— less than you know you are.

"Because a hearing loss isn't a visibly broken, bruised, or bleeding body part, you may wonder if you are taking up the doctor's valuable time. Sadly, some hearing specialist physicians actually feel that way too. *Find a new doctor.*

"And, finally, hearing loss often results in communication breakdowns, emotional fatigue, defeatist thinking, and eventual surrender."

Reaching up to her left ear she extracted the aid from inside the canal and held it up. A surprised ripple ran through the group. Grace extracted the second aid from her other ear, slid them into her sweater pocket, and smoothed her hair. The strands felt so different lying on her shoulders rather than covering her ears. She visualized Richard, that warm, dreamy expression on his face, rubbing a strand of her hair between his fingers.

"You're beautiful, you know . . ."

She cleared her throat and refocused. "I am a physician, an Ear, Nose, Throat specialist. I am also a practicing psychiatrist, providing family therapy to those with hearing loss and their loved ones.

"Whether you are a medical student, I am one of you. Or if you are someone experiencing hearing loss, I am one of you. For those with hearing loss, I feel just as uncomfortable and alienated as any of you without my hearing aids. Nevertheless, I have made it my practice during these lectures to go without them to demonstrate that hearing loss is that and *only* that. It is not loss of mental capacity; it is not loss of value.

"I have learned to compensate in many ways, and so can you or your future patients. I can read lips. You can also—yes, even you doctors. I work a normal, demanding job. You can too. I have a social life, and I've made the adjustments necessary to live a happy, independent life. All of you can also, if you *choose* to and if you work to acquire the coping skills I've mentioned."

Grace felt her audience's hope rise. This moment was worth it all to her, worth the years of study, work, and unceasing commitment. "Thank you. I hope you enjoyed this introductory lecture and will return to attend the rest of my series."

The applause was generous, the question and answer period lively. Grace had a volunteer write the questions on transparencies as they were asked and put them on the screen where all could see them. Answers and suggestions followed.

At 8:15 when she dismissed, a few people loitered to talk to her. This part was especially fun and rewarding, and Grace had a policy never to rush anyone away. As the room cleared, she spent a few minutes packing up her briefcase and filing the transparencies into the box before giving her thoughts over to Richard and their late dinner date.

Oh, Richard! What will this night decide?

She glanced around. All was in order. She switched off the auditorium lights and stepped into the lighted hallway. Down two levels and around the corner from the elevator bank, the sky bridge to the hospital waited for her.

HE DIDN'T WAIT until she finished and the auditorium cleared out. While she spoke and her audience was occupied, he went down two floors to close and lock the wide double doors to the fifth-floor sky bridge connecting the medical wing to the hospital. The doors were only to be closed and locked in the event of fire and only security guards had keys, but, *voila!*

He snickered. He'd picked up so many useful tidbits (including keys) merely by watching and listening . . . . *and by slicing a guard or two to incentivize them and hiding their bodies afterward—but who's counting?*

With the doors locked, anyone wanting to cross from the medical wing to the hospital would be forced to take the elevator or the stairs down to the ground floor and cross there. And as soon as the doctor's audience was gone, he would shut down the elevators too. He had the elevator keys, also, giving him complete control of the two cars.

The woman doctor keeping him from his son would not be able to escape the medical wing by crossing the sky bridge, nor would she be able to take the elevator down to the school's ground floor and cross to the hospital there.

Oh, she could run, but he'd hear her—which would make for excellent hunting, even more exciting because the school's empty halls and stairwells were superb sound amplifiers.

Before he ended her, she'd tell him exactly what he wanted. Yes, just as the guards he'd tortured and killed earlier this evening had given him what he needed to close the sky bridge and shut down the elevators, *she* would provide him with access to the secure ward.

GRACE HEFTED THE box of course materials in her left arm and grasped the handle to her briefcase in her right. The load was awkward, but she could manage. Halfway down the hall she remembered her hearing aids were still in her pocket. She wouldn't have forgotten to put them in if she hadn't been so preoccupied with thoughts of Richard.

"Let's talk at dinner tonight . . . about us," he'd said.

Richard. She smiled. He hadn't been able to make it to the lecture because of Sharon Richmond's murder. She didn't mind. She would visit with Terry and wait in the secure ward for Richard to pick her up for dinner.

Sharon Richmond.

She shuddered. The ambitious woman who'd slandered Richard repeatedly was dead. The city's networks this evening were probably in a frenzy over the details surrounding the death of one of their own, a fellow journalist fallen prey to the same merciless serial killer she'd reported on in graphic detail.

Grace picked up her pace, arrived at the elevator bank, and pressed the call button. The car eventually arrived and opened. She stepped inside, rested the heavy box on the railing, and pressed the down button.

Oh, right. Still need to put in my aids.

Dropping her briefcase in the elevator, she fished in her pocket for her aids. She had them in her hand when the car stopped on the fifth floor and the doors opened.

He stood in the elevator doorway, a gleaming knife in his hand.

His eyes were flat. Empty.

Marek Gretzky.

She shrieked, grasped the box with both hands, and ran at him, shoving the box into his chest and throwing him off balance. Grace kept pushing the box until Gretzky tripped and fell backward. Something crunched underfoot as she stumbled out of the elevator, but escape was all she cared about.

Run! Run to the sky bridge!

The pounding of her heart thundered in her chest, and her breath choked and whistled in her throat. At the main corridor, she rounded the corner to her right and raced toward the main junction where the sky bridge crossed over to the safety of the hospital.

"No!"

The wide doors were shut. She slammed her body into them, once, twice, three times, but they refused to open. But they were never to be locked!

Grace checked behind her and choked on a sob. Gretzky was only yards away, stalking forward with long, deliberate steps, his mouth spread in a wide, mad grin.

Grace fled the sky bridge junction in the only direction available to her: down a side hallway. She spotted a glowing green exit sign and ran toward it. When she yanked on the door she glanced behind her. He was coming!

She stepped out onto the dark landing, horrified to realize that the steps were metal, the stairwell encased in concrete walls.

It's one big echo chamber in here. I won't be able to hear him, but every step I take will shout my location.

My aids. Put them in. Quick. Her fingers sought their comforting shapes in her pocket—

No! I dropped them in the elevator!

A sob swelled in her breast. "Oh God! Please help me!"

She peered through the glass in the door, saw his advancing shadow on the wall. Leaning over the railing she stared down the stairwell five flights to ground level—where her every step would be broadcast in echoing fullness to her assailant, while his threatening footfalls would be chilly silence to her.

If I can make him think I went down the stairs, he might follow. In the meantime, there has to be an unlocked room nearby where I can hide!

She had but seconds to make up her mind. She pushed open the door, pulled off a shoe, and left it stuck between the door and the doorframe. The other shoe she dropped close by then ran toward the hallway intersection, her stockinged feet skidding around the corner.

The first door she tried was locked, as was the second. Keeping one eye on the hall behind her, she jiggled several more knobs. Every door down the hallway was locked.

It occurred to her that her only escape route was, after all, a fire exit.

I have to get to the other exit on the opposite side of the building.

She glanced behind her, and he walked out of the shadows, not more than twenty feet away.

Grace bolted, turned left at the next junction, and raced down yet another hallway, frantic.

"Help me!"

A young man locking an office door heard her and looked up. He gaped quizzically. Grace recognized him as a hospital intern.

"Thank God!" she gasped, then, "Oh no! Quick—follow me!"

Grace pointed toward Gretzky and shouted, "Run!" as she sprinted toward the corner of the building. The intern, not understanding what was happening, lifted his hand to Gretzky as he approached.

"Hey, what are you—"

His words ended in a squeal of pain as Gretzky leapt forward and his knife whipped through the air, across the intern's abdomen.

Grace whirled about at the intern's painful cry. Watched him collapse to his knees, then fall forward. Down the long length of the hall, Grace and Gretzky faced each other, the intern's body sprawled on the floor in a growing pool of glistening blood.

Gretzky was excited and primed, waiting for her to make her move.

Lord, please help me get myself together. I must think! Think! Find the other fire exit. Try each floor's door on the way down. Get out of the stairwell and run across the floor to the opposite fire exit. Get out at the bottom. Run to the hospital.

Grace shuddered. *What if all the stairwell doors on the way down and even at the bottom are locked? I'll be trapped!*

Gretzky tipped his head. Frowned a little. Seemed confused.

"Sara?"

Grace backed up a step. She couldn't read his lips well from this far away. What was he saying?

"Sara, is that you?"

Is he saying Sara?

She took another cautious step back.

"Sara, please don't run away from me. Please don't make me angry."

Grace read about half his words. Enough for fear to jitter its way through her body, leaving her weak.

He's delusional.

"You're so beautiful, Sara," he called. "So lovely . . ." He ended on a puzzled, whimsical note. "I don't want to hurt you again. I . . . I love you. I have been waiting so long for you."

Grace backed yet another step.

He reached out a hand. "Please. Please come to me."

Grace bolted, rounded the turn, and sprinted down the hallway. She knew, without hearing a thing, that Gretzky was behind her. Gaining on her.

She could hear nothing, yet a tingling whine in her head made itself known. Grew louder. Sent sharp pain through her skull.

"Tinnitus. Stress," she mumbled, spying the next junction ahead. "Not real. Stop it!"

Grace felt the temptation to give in. Give up. She yearned to stop, slide down the wall to the floor, squeeze her eyes closed, and shut out the terror. Longed to open them again in her own bed, knowing she'd had a nightmare—that it was all just a bad dream!

Immediately she felt that sweet Voice stir down deep in her spirit. *You cannot check out, Grace Warner. Get your wits about you and keep moving. I will help you.*

Grace sucked in a breath. "Yes, Lord."

The seed of an idea broke ground. *If only there were a way for me to even the odds! Like Audrey Hepburn in* Wait Until Dark. *Her character was blind, terrorized and pursued in her own home by a seeing murderer.*

Hepburn's character had cut the lights to level the playing field.

"But I'm deaf. Not blind," she sobbed.

A fire alarm mounted on the wall straight ahead of her caught her eye. Grace stared at it.

Even the odds?

In a blink, the seed blossomed and bore fruit.

She narrowed her eyes and whispered to Gretzky, "If *I can't hear you*, why should you get to hear *me?*"

She plowed into the alarm and yanked the handle down. All she heard of the warbling alarm was a low note fading in and out, yet it gave her hope. Down the hall to her left, she saw the glowing green exit sign she sought, and raced for it. Threw open the door to the stairwell. As she moved from the landing to the stairs, she could feel the pulsing of the claxon in the air around her.

"We're on even terms now, *creep.*" Her jaw set, one hand on the railing, she ran down the stairs as quickly as her shaky legs could carry her. She would run to the bottom, praying the ground-floor exit was unlocked, then run across to the hospital and take refuge in the fifth-floor secure ward.

Where Richard would meet her.

HE FELT CONFUSED. Perplexed. *Sara . . . .why was she running away? Hadn't he been waiting for her? For . . . years?*

A nagging memory pricked him but never quite made it through. Then the sirens went off, and he turned toward the sky bridge.

Fire alarm. Won't they need to evacuate the hospital? If they do, won't they also evacuate my son? And if they do evacuate him, this will be easier than I thought.

He still wanted the woman, even though he wasn't entirely convinced she was Sara.

She can't use the elevators; the only option she has are the stairwells. Yes, she is on her way down, but I know where she's headed. I can beat her there. Two birds with one stone.

He jogged back to the sky bridge, unlocked the doors, and walked through, closing them behind him. In his custodial uniform, he was just another hospital employee.

The hospital's fifth floor was a picture of organized pandemonium—nurses and orderlies shouting, patient beds being pushed into the elevators. He entered a men's restroom not far from the secure ward to escape the turmoil. He studied himself in the mirror, sponged a fine spray of blood from his shirt, then cracked the door and held it with his toe, his eye on the entrance to the secure ward.

And waited.

SNOW WAS DRIFTING to the ground when Grace exited the stairwell onto the medical school's ground floor. Her stockings were torn and she was shivering with cold, but she didn't slow. She ran straight into the breezeway connecting the school to the hospital. But when she pushed through the doors into the hospital ER and urgent care area and tried to reach the elevators, she ran into chaos.

"Ma'am, we are preparing to evacuate the hospital," a guard shouted at her. "All elevators are reserved for patient evacuation only."

Grace didn't bother arguing with him; if the hospital were to evacuate, the secure ward would evacuate also, and Marek Gretzky would go after Terry.

Terry! I must warn him.

She ran to the nearest hospital fire exit, yanked open the door, and started climbing.

HAWKE'S VEHICLE SKIDDED to a halt, sirens dying, joining firetrucks and ambulances already overflowing the parking lot. Unchecked alarms rang in the night as Hawke ran to a knot of firemen readying to enter the darkened school. His eyes traveled upward.

Gracie!

The alarms were her cry for help.

"Chief. Detective Sergeant Hawke, Homicide Division. Call your men off. There's no fire."

The chief and his adjutant stared at him.

"What do you mean, Detective?"

Dov appeared at his side, grasped his arm, and pointed at Percival and Browning.

"SWAT's not here yet, but we're ready to go, Rick."

Hawke turned back to the chief. "Chief, what I mean is there's no fire; the serial knifer is in there and the fire alarm is a call for help. Get your men clear of here and call off the evacuation. Tell hospital security to have patients and staff shelter in place and bar the doors."

The chief hesitated for only seconds before he barked orders.

Hawke did a quick head count. Him, his team, and four uniforms. It would have to be enough.

"Dov, take Percival up the hospital elevator to the fifth floor and position yourself there." His finger pointed at the sky bridge. "Guard that bridge from both directions. Nobody crosses it."

"You got it, Hawke." They rushed off.

"Browning? You four officers? You're with me."

They reached the medical school's front doors and he bellowed at some firemen, "Break this in!"

Two axe-wielding firemen fractured the glass entrance doors. Hawke, Browning, and the officers clambered through the empty door frames. Hawke pushed the call buttons on the elevators. Nothing happened.

"Think he's got the cars propped open up top?" Browning asked.

"That or something like. We'll have to climb."

He signaled the uniformed officers. "We're going up to smoke out our suspect. Guard the elevators and both fire exits—two of you go around the building and set your positions on the exit there, you other two, position yourselves here.

"Listen, we know our suspect is armed with a knife, but that doesn't mean he isn't carrying a firearm, so be on your guard. I don't care what uniform he's wearing, any *man* tries to exit this building? You take him down. Can you do that?"

One of the uniformed officers asked, "This the serial knifer?"

Hawke nodded.

"Oh, yeah. We've got this."

Hawke crossed to the stairwell. "Browning, with me." He started climbing. Browning followed.

TEN MINUTES LATER, Grace cracked open the fifth-floor fire exit and peeked through. Her nerves were strung to the breaking point. At some point during her climb, the fire alarm had cut off abruptly, the evacuation canceled. She had expected to see Terry and the other secure ward patients being herded downstairs. Instead, the halls were eerily empty.

Terry's ward was several yards away. She noticed a hospital guard peering through the ward's reinforced window glass, scanning for danger up and down the hall. Grace stepped out of the exit cautiously, and stuck her head around the corner. She saw no one in that direction. In fact, every post on the floor was abandoned, every door on the floor closed.

They're in lockdown, she realized. *Richard! He must be here, and he knows I pulled the alarm.*

Angled across from the secure ward were restrooms. She watched their doors for a full minute before waving at the guard behind the glass to get his attention.

His eyes widened. He motioned to her, so she sprinted toward him.

Halfway to the guard, out of the corner of her eye, she saw the men's room door fly open; a figure rushed toward her. *Gretzky!* She sought to angle away from his grasping hands, but they twined themselves around her waist and into her hair and jerked her off her feet. Immediately he began to drag her in the direction of the sky bridge.

She kicked and screamed. The pain as he wrenched her head and neck by her hair was awful, yet he only gathered his grasp more tightly and began running towards the breezeway, half dragging, half carrying her. His lips were moving but she couldn't hear him. Grace struggled uselessly.

The light changed. Forcing her eyes open, Grace saw they were crossing the sky bridge. Her neck hurt terribly, yet Gretzky pulled her onward, and her heart sank.

Lord? I wanted to save Terry. I thought I was doing the right thing.

Gretzky came to a stop. He wrapped his arm around Grace's neck and yanked her to her feet. She managed to get her feet under her and relieve some of the strain on her neck.

Then she understood why Gretzky had stopped. At the end of the sky bridge inside the doors to the medical school she spied Richard. He stood alone, his weapon drawn.

He shouted something.

Gretzky shouted a response and, still facing Richard, began dragging Grace back toward the hospital. He stopped again and whirled toward the hospital side of the bridge.

Detectives Mayer and Percival, their weapons drawn but angled down, blocked the hospital end of the bridge.

That was when Marek Gretzky pulled his knife, lifted it where it could be seen, and flicked it open. He laid it under Grace's jaw and, *soft as a caress*, drew it across her skin.

She scarcely felt it bite, yet the warm flow down her neck told her she was cut.

BROWNING HAD FALLEN farther and farther behind on the climb up to the fifth floor until Hawke figured the overweight detective had been forced to sit down and catch his breath. Hawke couldn't allow himself such luxury. Not with Grace's life on the line.

When he found the sky bridge doors closed, he crept up to them. Since the doors had no windows, he had no idea what he'd find on the other side. Slowly, quietly, he tested one handle. When it turned under his hand, he eased the door open enough to slip his head through.

What he saw halfway across the bridge almost put him on his knees.

Grace!

Gretzky had his fingers twined through Grace's beautiful hair and her neck twisted in an unnatural angle. Her face was etched in agony.

"Let her go, Gretzky."

"She's mine! Mine! I've waited years to find her again!"

Hawke worked to control his breathing. *Lord? What is he ranting about?* Then it came to him.

"Do you mean Sara? You've been waiting to find Sara?"

Gretzky's mouth opened. He seemed confused. "Sara?"

"Sara died, Marek. Remember?"

Gretzky blinked repeatedly as though dust had blown in his eyes. He squeezed Grace's neck until she moaned.

"Wait—you're hurting her! Marek, you're *hurting Sara.* Is that what you want to do? Hurt her? Hurt her *again?*"

"No . . . I don't want to hurt her . . . I want her to love me—*to obey me!*"

The man's confusion grew, but a noise behind him caught his attention and he whirled.

Dov and Percival stood at the other end of the bridge. They lowered their weapons so they weren't pointed at Grace.

Suddenly Grace sagged in Gretzky's grip. And behind Hawke, near enough to deafen him, a weapon roared.

Gretzky's head snapped back. In slow motion, he tilted and fell backwards, carrying Grace with him.

"Grace!" Hawke sprinted forward and worked to free Grace's hair from Gretzky's grip. "Someone get a doctor! Gracie, can you hear me?"

Dov knelt beside Hawke and rolled the lifeless body of Marek Gretzky off of Grace. A single hole above his right eye oozed red fluid. His eyes were open, more human in death than in life.

Hawke cradled Grace in his arms. She was unconscious, but he found a pulse on her bruised and bleeding neck. He quickly pulled a handkerchief from his pocket and pressed it flat on the shallow cut, then looked around, trying to understand what had happened.

Browning, standing a couple feet away, bent over and clasped his knees. He shuddered and spewed the contents of his stomach.

Percival patted him on the back. "You're okay, man. You're okay." He handed his partner a handkerchief. "Well done, Browning."

"Never . . . never shot anyone before." He glanced at Hawke with shame in his eyes. "I'm sorry I stalled out on the stairs, Boss. Got here late. I'll . . . I'll lose the weight. I promise. Won't let you down again."

Hawke exhaled. Struggled to convey his gratitude. "You came through, Browning. I . . . *we* need our team to be the best we can be. I'll help you get in shape."

"Thanks, Boss."

At that moment, Grace's eyes fluttered open and filled with fear.

Hawke bent toward her and said softly, "Grace, I have you! You're okay, I have you. Gretzky is gone."

She didn't immediately respond, and her eyes fastened on his mouth.

"Grace, if you can't hear me, can you read my lips? Gretzky is gone and you're safe! And listen—if you'll have me, my heart is yours. Forever. I won't leave. Not ever again."

Her lids drooped closed but, very faintly, the corners of her mouth curved up.

She'd 'heard' enough.

POSTSCRIPT

HAWKE, DOV, GRACE, and Terry Gretzky met in a small Upton-Warner conference room. The two detectives watched Grace and Terry converse. They watched, because very little of the conversation between the doctor and her patient was audible to them. Grace and Terry's hands signed at rapid-fire speed. Terry's eyes danced with pleasure; Grace's smile was joyous. Hawke also watched the flash of the diamond engagement ring on her left hand as she signed, and he smiled too.

He and Dov were in the conference room to, at last, interview Terry Gretzky. The young man was leaving the secure ward today, moving to a group home where he would continue to learn, grow, mature, and eventually live a productive life on his own.

The bill for Terry's stay in the hospital's secure ward had been staggering, but thanks to an agreement Art Grunbaum made with the hospital, the bill was expunged. In return, City View Hospital would gain a spanking-new pediatric wing—The Esther Grunbaum Children's Care Center—and as part of the deal, the hospital zeroed out Terry's bill. In a side "deal," Art and a few of his buddies, including Saul Beech, chipped in to pay for Terry's upcoming cochlear implant surgery.

Yes, life was looking up for this remarkable man, this survivor, and Hawke was glad.

Grace turned to him. Still signing for Terry's sake, she said aloud, "All right, Detective Hawke. You may ask your questions."

He and Dov had formulated a list of the questions they most needed answers to in order to understand Terry's actions and close out the investigations into the deaths of Mary Alice Waite and Esther Grunbaum. Hawke opened one of two file folders and withdrew a typed sheet. He began with the most basic of questions while Dov took notes.

Terry's responses confirmed much of what they'd assumed about his early life in Brockport. Hawke and Dov also verified the strict rules his mother imposed on Terry after his mother moved them to the city, rules intended to protect him from his abusive and homicidal father should he ever leave prison.

As Terry became more comfortable with Hawke leading the interview, they reached the questions about the two cases no one could answer except Terry.

Hawke gentled his expression. "Terry, the day Mary Alice Waite died, why were you hiding in the choir loft?"

Terry frowned. His hands twitched, but he did not respond. Grace gained his attention, saying, "Terry, you are not in trouble. The police just need to close out their investigations. Please answer."

Terry, with his eyes fixed on the table, signed, "Music. I wanted the music."

Grace signed and spoke aloud for the detectives' sake, "You are deaf. How can you hear the organ?"

Terry replied, "I feel it in my hands and in my head."

"By touching the pipes? By leaning against them? Putting your face and head on them?"

"Yes."

"Bone conduction," Grace murmured. "The way a cochlear implant works."

Hawke asked and Grace signed, "Terry, did you push Mary Alice Waite down the stairs?"

"Nooo!" Terry shouted the word, as much as his tight, underdeveloped vocal cords allowed him to, and his answer was understandable, even in its guttural state.

"Thank you," Hawke replied, jotting a note. "When she fell, was it because she was scared? Because you startled her?"

Terry began to tremble. "Didn't mean to," he signed three times. "Sorry! Sorry! Sad."

Hawke caught his attention, looked directly at him, and spoke slowly. "We understand. It was an accident. We do not blame you."

Terry wiped his eyes, settled a little, and Hawke continued.

"When Mary Alice fell down the stairs, you cut yourself."

Terry's head immediately fell toward his chest and his breathing became labored.

"He's scared," Dov offered. "Ashamed, too, I think."

Grace touched Terry's arm. "It's all right," she signed. "We just want to understand."

"Had to," Terry signed and Graced translated for the detectives.

"But it must have hurt a lot," Hawke said. "Can you tell us why you had to?"

They beat around the question for a quarter of an hour before Grace cajoled the response Hawke was looking for.

"My fault. Killed her. Only blood can pay."

There it was. Finally.

"But you didn't mean to hurt her," Grace signed.

Terry shook his head. "Killed her. Must pay with blood."

It was the moment Hawke had been waiting for.

He said quietly, "Grace, ask Terry if he's still talking about Mary Alice."

Grace was surprised, but she asked him, "Are you talking about Mary Alice? Did you kill Mary Alice?"

Terry shook his head and opened and closed his thumb and the first two fingers of his hand three times: "*No. No. No.* I said no."

"Ask him this: Are you talking about Sara?"

Grace's mouth dropped open. "Sara Curry?"

"Yes."

She recovered and signed to Terry, "Did you kill Sara Curry?"

"Yes," Terry signed back, weeping, his head bowed in terrible grief and shame.

"Who said you killed Sara?" Hawke demanded.

Grace signed, and Terry looked at Hawke. "My father, I think," he signed.

Slowly and deliberately, Hawke said, "*He lied to you.*"

Grace's eyes went wide, but not as wide as Terry's.

"Your father killed Sara, Terry, not you. Your father was depraved, a sociopath whose evil knew no boundaries."

Grace said softly, "I'll have to explain those terms, depraved and sociopath, Richard. I don't think Terry knows them."

"Take as long as you need. Terry deserves the truth as much as we do."

The back and forth between Grace and Terry took a while and was of great interest to Hawke to watch.

"Richard, Terry says he doesn't believe you. He wants you to explain how you know he didn't kill Sara."

"You're the shrink who specialized in psychopathy, Grace. You can spot a sociopath at twenty paces. Terry was ten years old when Sara was savagely stabbed twenty-three times. Did Terry *then* and does he *now* have the mental and emotional capacity or inclination for that level of brutality?"

"Not on your life," she declared. "He carried a knife for personal protection when we met him, but he's functionally phobic when it comes to committing or even witnessing violence."

"Which agrees with what his therapist said back then. And remember when I asked you to explain gaslighting? That terminology fits Marek

Gretzky's profile to a 't.' Marek was all about *control*. It's how I know *he* killed Sara."

Hawke shifted. He folded his hands on the tabletop in front of him. "I want to run this down for all of us, starting with Sara's death. See, I believe Marek wanted Sara, was just as obsessed with her as her uncle was, and repeatedly tried to seduce her. When she rebuffed him, he became even more determined to have his way with her—or, if she refused him again, *kill* her, so no one else could have her.

"Of course, Terry knew nothing of his father's obsession until Marek took Terry with him that day . . . the day he killed Sara."

"Wait! Why . . . why would Marek take Terry . . . that day?"

"Plain and simple? Leverage. Marek knew Sara was fond of Terry. Narcissist that he was, Marek would have had no qualms about threatening to hurt Terry if Sara didn't give him what he wanted. It was all about control, right?"

Grace swallowed. "But . . ."

"I know: unspeakably ghastly. But I'm thinking it didn't quite work out how Marek planned. I'm convinced that, when Sara still refused Marek, *she fought him*. That's when Marek stabbed Sara again and again . . . and forced Terry to watch."

Grace stuttered, "He-he made Terry watch?"

Hawke studied his hands. "Knowing how Terry felt about Sara, I'm going to assume he would have done his best to defend her. Just remember he was only ten years old, and Marek beat him regularly. Still, Marek probably restrained Terry at the outset, tied him up so he, Marek, would have his hands free to abuse Terry as a means to threaten and control Sara. Only Terry can tell you the actual details . . . and the rest of what happened."

Grace's voice shook. "The rest? There's more?"

Hawke nodded. "Once Sara was dead, Marek began to browbeat Terry to 'convince' him that *he* was, by way of his 'defects,' *responsible* for Sara's death."

He took a deep breath. "I also believe Marek threatened to kill Terry's mother if Terry ever spoke of Sara's death to a living soul. It would explain why, when the female counsellor interviewed Terry, she reported that Terry appeared 'deeply conflicted' about something."

Hawke paused before adding, "Finally, Marek forced Terry to 'pay' for Sara's death through the blood ritual."

Grace held up her hands. "Stop. Please stop . . . I . . ." She shook her head. "I don't think I can agree with you. If Merek made Terry cut himself, wouldn't he still have the scars?"

"Have you looked?"

Grace stared at Richard. "I dressed the wounds on his arm. I didn't see any old scarring on him."

"You didn't see them because you weren't looking for them . . . and because they were obscured." He added, "It's taken me all this time to unpack the entirety of this heinous and outrageous crime, but I have the last piece of the puzzle right here."

Hawke opened the second folder. "This is a copy of Terry's medical record from the hospital where he was treated after the police rescued him and his mother from Marek. It took a while for the hospital to search its archives and locate this twenty-one-year-old paper record."

He cleared his throat. "The record begins with the ER intake form and the list of injuries Terry suffered during that horrible night: Serious head and neck trauma. Bruises and hematomas over most of his body. Suspected broken ribs. And multiple cuts on his body, *including two on his left forearm*, still healing."

Hawke looked up. "Ask Terry to show you his arm, Grace."

The room was quiet as Grace made a careful examination of Terry's forearm. When she finished, she pulled down his sleeve, gently patted his shoulder, and signed "thank you."

Her eyes were damp when she looked at Hawke and said. "He cut himself over the old scars."

"That's what I figured, and . . . I'm sorry to add more to this sad tale. Fast forward to the night Marek took Terry and his mother prisoner in the domestic violence shelter. We know that Marek physically, verbally, and emotionally abused both Terry and his mother for seven hours. The big question is *why*. Why did he take them captive? He wasn't a suspect, was off the hook because of Sara's uncle's suicide."

Grace's face creased in concentration. "But Aneta had left Marek and taken Terry into hiding. With Terry no longer under Marek's thumb, was he afraid Terry would tell the police the truth?"

Hawke sighed. "I think that's it in a nutshell. It's my belief that, during the seven-hour standoff, Marek tortured *Terry's mother* and threatened to kill her until Terry, already traumatized by Sara's death, capitulated. Terry's love for his mother was the leverage by which Marek utterly broke Terry. Marek convinced Terry that he was not merely *responsible* for Sara's death but *factually* guilty of killing Sara as well. Marek planted his false narratives in Terry's mind and forced him to confess his guilt again and again, *ad nauseam.*

"He even made the kid acknowledge in front of his mother that he, Terry, had performed the blood ritual over Sara's body to atone for her death.

Marek's endgame? Use Terry's confession as insurance should the police take another look at Sara's death."

"That and Marek was certifiably whacko and *had* to feel in control," Dov added softly.

"Yes, and because Terry had already sustained serious head trauma, injuries to his brain that kept him in and out of consciousness for a month, his subconscious hid much of that night from him. All he has believed since then is that he did, indeed, murder Sara Curry."

Grace put her face in her hands and sobbed, "That poor child! He had to have been so traumatized, so confused!"

Terry, uncertain what was happening, pulled in on himself.

Hawke nodded. "In my entire life, I have never seen this level of evil. It's a wonder Terry survived the physical and psychological horror his father put him through."

He looked away. "Of course, those seven hours were the last straw for Aneta Gretzky. It's why, until her dying day, she strove to protect Terry the only way she knew how: Hide. Become invisible."

Hawke pointed his chin at Terry. "Tell him what I said, please. All of it."

That conversation took some time.

Afterward, they were quiet for a while until Grace said in a thoughtful voice, "Terry has alluded to hearing voices, one that warns him to be careful, the other that insists he should cut himself."

Hawke asked, "Is it a longshot to assume that one of those voices, the voice cautioning him to be careful, started as his mother's? Or that the other voice was Marek's, verbally and physically beating his false version of Sara's death into Terry's head?"

Grace slowly nodded. "I cannot disagree, but Terry has believed himself guilty of Sara's death for more than two decades."

Hawke answered, "You will have to help him accept the truth, that the only person responsible for Sara's murder was Marek himself. His mode of killing Vincent Delano, Trixie Lawson, Dottie Pyzell, Thomas Buttry, Jerusha Washington, and Sharon Richmond makes that *fact* quite clear."

Then Hawke sighed. "You have a lot of work ahead of you, Grace. Helping Terry sort his true memories from the false narrative Marek shoved down Terry's throat will be neither easy nor quick, but I figure you're up for the job."

"And I am more than willing."

"Good. I have just one more question for Terry." He faced the man. "Terry, would you please explain why, when you cut yourself, you dribbled your blood on Mary Alice and Esther Grunbaum's faces?"

Terry sat still for a while. Grace, Hawke, and Dov watched and waited.

At long last, Terry signed to Grace, "The voice said the blood was for payment."

"There's one of those voices," Dov whispered.

"For payment?" Hawke asked. "Can you ask Terry to explain further?"

"Terry says the voice called it a word he can't say or spell."

"Is the word 'atonement'?" Hawke asked.

Grace side-eyed him before she spelled out the word and slowly spoke it aloud several times with Terry watching her lips.

"Yes," Terry signed back, growing excited as he read Grace's lips. "That's the word the voice said. I have never seen it spelled out."

Hawke didn't generally carry a briefcase, but he did today. He opened it and pulled a thick book with a red padded cover from the briefcase, set it on the table, opened it to a random page, and turned it so Terry could see it. Grace and Dov leaned over to look too.

What they saw was a children's Bible with colorful comic-book-type illustrations. Terry touched one illustration's "bubble" and, with his finger under each word, started reading silently.

He looked up. "I like this book," he signed.

Hawke smiled softly, turned the book to 1 John, chapter 2, and slid it over to Terry. He pointed to the first and second verses, which he'd highlighted in a soft yellow.

Terry studied the verses and the picture beside the verses. He pointed to the picture of Jesus on the cross and signed, "Why did they do that to him? No one ever told me."

"He let them do it so he could make atonement for us with his blood—to pay for our sins. My sins and your sins."

Grace signed Hawke's words for Terry.

Terry gawked. "For me?"

"Yes, for you. I cannot pay for my sins, Terry, and you cannot pay for yours. Only one person's blood was *good enough* to pay for all of our sins. That person is Jesus, come to earth as God's Son in human form."

Grace signed quickly, trying to keep up with Hawke. Terry stared at her hands, fascinated.

Hawke took a breath, then continued. "Terry, Jesus freely chose to die on that cross, like in the picture, in order to *atone* for our sins. Jesus is God's atonement for the sins of the entire world."

Hawke got Terry's attention, and waited until he was watching Hawke's mouth. Hawke slowly recited from memory,

"My dear children,
. . . we have an advocate with the Father

—Jesus Christ, the Righteous One.
He is the atoning sacrifice
for our sins, and not only for ours,
but also for the sins of the whole world."

Hawke paused, then added, "Grace, tell Terry that the voice in his head telling him to cut himself was his father's voice, and his father was a liar."

As Terry watched Grace's hands, he again gaped.

"Tell Terry his father lied about everything he ever told him. He lied when he said Terry killed Sara. He lied when he told Terry he had to pay for Sara's death. He especially lied about blood atonement, since only Jesus can make atonement for our sins. Tell Terry that he should not believe anything his father ever said to him. Not one thing."

Grace signed and signed; she and Terry spoke for several minutes.

"One last point as we close out our interview," Hawke said. "Please tell Terry that this Bible is his, a gift from me. I even had his name embossed on the cover."

After Grace told Terry about his name being on the cover, Terry closed the Bible and studied the gold letters on its cover. His fingers gently traced the lettering, then he smiled at Hawke.

"Thank you," he signed.

"You're welcome," Hawke signed back . . . and Terry grinned.

With that, Hawke and his partner stood. They shook Terry's hand and took the elevator down to the parking garage.

Dov had been silent through the most of the interview. Until now.

"Rick, what you told Terry, is that what you believe? That Jesus is the atonement—like how the blood of the Passover lamb atoned for the sins of Israel?"

"That's it, exactly. Jesus was called 'The Lamb who takes away the sins of the world' for a reason, Dov. He is the true Passover lamb. Let's talk about him sometime soon when I can show you these things in your own Scriptures. Jesus is your Messiah too, you know."

Dov scoffed half-heartedly. "I dunno about that, Rick."

Hawke grinned. "Oh? Think maybe you should pray about it?"

THE END

ABOUT THE AUTHOR

VIKKI KESTELL'S passion for people and their stories is evident in her readers' affection for her characters and unusual plotlines. Two often-repeated sentiments are, "I feel like I know these people," and, "I'm right there, in the book, experiencing what the characters experience."

Vikki holds a PhD in organizational learning and instructional technologies. She left a career of twenty-plus years in government, academia, and corporate life to pursue writing full time. "Writing is the best job ever," she admits, "and the most demanding."

Vikki and her husband, Conrad Smith, make their home in Albuquerque, New Mexico.

To keep abreast of new book releases, sign up for Vikki's newsletter on her website, **http://www.vikkikestell.com**, find her on Facebook at **http://www.facebook.com/Vikki.Kestell**, or follow her on BookBub, **https://www.bookbub.com/authors/vikki-kestell**.

Faith-Filled Fiction™

www.faith-filledfiction.com | www.vikkikestell.com